The Best of
The Hardy Boys®

CLASSIC COLLECTION

Volume 1

❖

The Tower Treasure

The Secret of the Old Mill

The Haunted Fort

❖

By Franklin W. Dixon

❖❖❖
Grosset & Dunlap • New York

THE TOWER TREASURE copyright © 1987, 1959, 1955, 1927
by Simon & Schuster, Inc. THE SECRET OF THE OLD MILL
copyright © 1990, 1962, 1955, 1927 by Simon & Schuster, Inc.
THE HAUNTED FORT copyright © 1993, 1965 by Simon &
Schuster, Inc. All rights reserved. THE BEST OF THE HARDY
BOYS CLASSIC COLLECTION Volume 1 published in 2004 by
Grosset & Dunlap, a division of Penguin Young Readers Group,
345 Hudson Street, New York, New York 10014. THE HARDY
BOYS® is a registered trademark of Simon & Schuster, Inc.
GROSSET & DUNLAP is a trademark of Penguin Group (USA)
Inc. Printed in the U.S.A.

ISBN 0-448-43627-2   10 9 8 7 6 5 4 3 2 1

The Hardy Boys Mystery Stories®

THE TOWER
TREASURE

BY

FRANKLIN W. DIXON

GROSSET & DUNLAP
Publishers • New York
A member of The Putnam & Grosset Group

CONTENTS

CHAPTER I

The Speed Demon

FRANK and Joe Hardy clutched the grips of their motorcycles and stared in horror at the oncoming car. It was careening from side to side on the narrow road.

"He'll hit us! We'd better climb this hillside—and fast!" Frank exclaimed, as the boys brought their motorcycles to a screeching halt and leaped off.

"On the double!" Joe cried out as they started up the steep embankment.

To their amazement, the reckless driver suddenly pulled his car hard to the right and turned into a side road on two wheels. The boys expected the car to turn over, but it held the dusty ground and sped off out of sight.

"Wow!" said Joe. "Let's get away from here before the crazy guy comes back. That's a dead-end road, you know."

The boys scrambled back onto their motorcycles and gunned them a bit to get past the intersecting road in a hurry. They rode in silence for a while, gazing at the scene ahead.

On their right an embankment of tumbled rocks and boulders sloped steeply to the water below. From the opposite side rose a jagged cliff. The little-traveled road was winding, and just wide enough for two cars to pass.

"Boy, I'd hate to fall off the edge of this road," Frank remarked. "It's a hundred-foot drop."

"That's right," Joe agreed. "We'd sure be smashed to bits before we ever got to the bottom." Then he smiled. "Watch your step, Frank, or Dad's papers won't get delivered."

Frank reached into his jacket pocket to be sure several important legal papers which he was to deliver for Mr. Hardy were still there. Relieved to find them, Frank chuckled and said, "After the help we gave Dad on his latest case, he ought to set up the firm of Hardy and Sons."

"Why not?" Joe replied with a broad grin. "Isn't he one of the most famous private detectives in the country? And aren't we bright too?" Then, becoming serious, he added, "I wish we could solve a mystery on our own, though."

Frank and Joe, students at Bayport High, were combining business with pleasure this Saturday morning by doing the errand for their father.

Even though one boy was dark and the other

fair, there was a marked resemblance between the two brothers. Eighteen-year-old Frank was tall and dark. Joe, a year younger, was blond with blue eyes. They were the only children of Fenton and Laura Hardy. The family lived in Bayport, a small but thriving city of fifty thousand inhabitants, located on Barmet Bay, three miles inland from the Atlantic Ocean.

The two motorcycles whipped along the narrow road that skirted the bay and led to Willowville, the brothers' destination. The boys took the next curve neatly and started up a long, steep slope. Here the road was a mere ribbon and badly in need of repair.

"Once we get to the top of the hill it won't be so rough," Frank remarked, as they jounced over the uneven surface. "Better road from there into Willowville."

Just then, above the sharp put-put of their own motors, the two boys heard the roar of a car approaching from their rear at great speed. They took a moment to glance back.

"Looks like that same guy we saw before!" Joe burst out. "Good night!"

At once the Hardys stopped and pulled as close to the edge as they dared. Frank and Joe hopped off and stood poised to leap out of danger again if necessary.

The car hurtled toward them like a shot. Just when it seemed as if it could not miss them, the driver swung the wheel about viciously and the sedan sped past.

"Whew! That was close!" Frank gasped.

The car had been traveling at such high speed that the boys had been unable to get the license number or a glimpse of the driver's features. But they had noted that he was hatless and had a shock of red hair.

"If I ever meet him again," Joe muttered, "I'll —I'll—" The boy was too excited to finish the threat.

Frank relaxed. "He must be practicing for some kind of race," he remarked, as the dark-blue sedan disappeared from sight around the curve ahead.

The boys resumed their journey. By the time

they rounded the curve, and could see Willowville in a valley along the bay beneath them, there was no trace of the rash motorist.

"He's probably halfway across the state by this time," Joe remarked.

"Unless he's in jail or over a cliff," Frank added.

The boys reached Willowville and Frank delivered the legal papers to a lawyer while Joe guarded the motorcycles. When his brother returned, Joe suggested, "How about taking the other road back to Bayport? I don't crave going over that bumpy stretch again."

"Suits me. We can stop off at Chet's."

Chet Morton, who was a school chum of the Hardy boys, lived on a farm about a mile out of Bayport. The pride of Chet's life was a bright yellow jalopy which he had named Queen. He worked on it daily to "soup up" the engine.

Frank and Joe retraced their trip for a few miles, then turned onto a country road which led to the main highway on which the Morton farm was situated. As they neared Chet's home, Frank suddenly brought his motorcycle to a stop and peered down into a clump of bushes in a deep ditch at the side of the road.

"Joe! That crazy driver or somebody else had a crack-up!"

Among the tall bushes was an overturned blue sedan. The car was a total wreck, and lay wheels upward, a mass of tangled junk.

"We'd better see if there's anyone underneath," Joe cried out.

The boys made their way down the culvert, their hearts pounding. What would they find?

A close look into the sedan and in the immediate vicinity proved that there was no victim around.

"Maybe this happened some time ago," said Joe, "and—"

Frank stepped forward and laid his hand on the exposed engine. "Joe, it's still warm," he said. "The accident occurred a short while ago. Now

I'm sure this is the red-haired driver's car."

"But what about him?" Joe asked. "Is he alive? Did somebody rescue him, or what happened?"

Frank shrugged. "One thing I *can* tell you. Either he or somebody else removed the license plates to avoid identification."

The brothers were completely puzzled by the whole affair. Since their assistance was not needed at the spot, they climbed out of the culvert and back onto their motorcycles. Before long they were in sight of the Mortons' home, a rambling old farmhouse with an apple orchard at the rear. When they drove up the lane they saw Chet at the barnyard gate.

"Hi, fella!" Joe called.

Chet hurried down the lane to meet them. He was a plump boy who loved to eat and was rarely without an apple or a pocket of cookies. His round, freckled face usually wore a smile. But today the Hardys sensed something was wrong. As they brought their motorcycles to a stop, they noticed that their chum's cheery expression was missing.

"What's the matter?" Frank asked.

"I'm in trouble," Chet replied. "You're just in time to help me. Did you meet a fellow driving the Queen?"

Frank and Joe looked at each other blankly.

"Your car? No, we haven't seen it," said Joe. "What's happened?"

"It's been stolen!"

"Stolen!"

"Yes. I just came out to the garage to get the Queen and she was gone," Chet answered mournfully.

"Wasn't the car locked?"

"That's the strange part of it. She was locked, although the garage door was open. I can't see how anyone got away with it."

"A professional job," Frank commented. "Auto thieves always carry scores of keys with them. Chet, have you any idea when this happened?"

"Not more than fifteen minutes ago, because that's when I came home with the car."

"We're wasting time!" Joe cried out. "Let's chase that thief!"

"But I don't know which way he went," Chet protested.

"We didn't meet him, so he must have gone in the other direction," Frank reasoned.

"Climb on behind me, Chet," Joe urged. "The Queen can't go as fast as our motorcycles. We'll catch her in no time!"

"And there was only a little gas in my car, anyway," Chet said excitedly as he swung himself onto Joe's motorcycle. "Maybe it has stalled by this time."

In a few moments the boys were tearing down the road in pursuit of the automobile thief!

CHAPTER II

The Holdup

CHET MORTON'S jalopy was such a brilliant yellow that the boys were confident it would not be difficult to pick up the trail of the auto thief.

"The Queen's pretty well known around Bayport," Frank remarked. "We should meet someone who saw it."

"Seems strange to me," said Joe, "that a thief would take a car like that. Auto thieves usually take cars of a standard make and color. They're easier to get rid of."

"It's possible," Frank suggested, "that the thief didn't steal the car to sell it. Maybe, for some reason, he was making a fast getaway and he'll abandon it."

"Look!" Chet exclaimed, pointing to a truck garden where several men were hoeing cabbage plants. "Maybe they saw the Queen."

"I'll ask them," Frank offered, and brought his motorcycle to a stop.

He scrambled over the fence and jumped across the rows of small plants until he reached the first farm hand.

"Did you see a yellow jalopy go by here within the past hour?" Frank asked him.

The lanky old farmer leaned on his hoe and put a hand to one ear. "Eh?" he shouted.

"Did you see a fellow pass along here in a bright yellow car?" Frank repeated in a louder tone.

The farmer called to his companions. As they ambled over, the old man removed a plug of tobacco from the pocket of his overalls and took a hearty chew.

"Lad here wants to know if we saw a jalopy come by," he said slowly.

The other three farm hands, all rather elderly men, did not answer at once. Instead, they laid down their hoes and the plug of tobacco was duly passed around the group.

Frank grit his teeth. "Please hurry up and answer. The car was stolen. We're trying to find the thief!"

"That so?" said one of the men. "A hot rod, eh?"

"Yes. A bright yellow one," Frank replied.

Another of the workers removed his hat and mopped his brow. "Seems to me," he drawled, "I did see a car come by here a while ago."

"A yellow car?"

"No—'twarn't yeller, come to think of it. I guess,

anyhow, it was a delivery truck, if I remember rightly."

Frank strove to conceal his impatience. "Please, did any of you—?"

"Was it a brand-new car, real shiny?" asked the fourth member of the group.

"No, it was an old car, but it was painted bright yellow," Frank explained.

"My nephew had one of them things," the farmer remarked. "Never thought they was safe, myself."

"I don't agree with you," still another man spoke up. "All boys like cars and you might as well let 'em have one they can work on themselves."

"You're all wrong!" the deaf man interrupted. "Let the boys work on the farm truck. That way they won't get into mischief!" He gave a cackling sort of laugh. "Well, son, I guess we ain't been much help to you. Hope you find the critter that stole your hot rod."

"Thanks," said Frank, and joined the other boys. "No luck. Let's go!"

As they approached Bayport, the trio saw a girl walking along the road ahead of them. When the cyclists drew nearer, Frank's face lighted up, for he had recognized Callie Shaw, who was in his class at Bayport High. Frank often dated Callie and liked her better than any girl he knew.

The boys brought their motorcycles to a stop

beside pretty, brown-eyed Callie. Under one arm she was carrying a slightly battered package. She looked vexed.

"Hi, Callie! What's the matter?" Frank asked. "You look as if your last friend had gone off in a moon rocket."

Callie gave a mischievous smile. "How could I think that with you three friends showing up? Or are you about to take off?" Then her smile faded and she held out the damaged package. "Look at that!" she exclaimed. "It's your fault, Chet Morton!"

The stout boy gulped. "M-my fault? How do you figure that?"

"Well, dear old Mrs. Wills down the road is ill, so I baked her a cake."

"Lucky Mrs. Wills," Joe broke in. "Callie, I'm feeling terribly ill."

Callie ignored him. "That man in the car came along here so fast that I jumped to the side of the road and dropped my package. I'm afraid my cake is ruined!"

"What man?" Joe asked.

"The one Chet lent his car to."

"Callie, that's the man we're looking for!" Frank exclaimed. "Chet didn't lend him the car. He stole it!"

"Oh!" said Callie, shocked. "Chet, that's a shame."

"Was he heading for Bayport?" Joe asked.

"Yes, and at the speed he was making the poor Queen travel, you'll never catch him."

Chet groaned. "I just remembered that the gas gauge wasn't working. I guess the car had more gas in it than I thought. No telling where that guy may take my Queen."

"We'd better go to police headquarters," Frank suggested. "Callie, will you describe this man?"

"All I saw," she answered, "was a blur, but the man did have red hair."

"Red hair!" Frank fairly shouted. "Joe, do you think he could be the same man we saw? The one who wrecked his own car?"

Joe wagged his head. "Miracles do happen. Maybe he wasn't hurt very much and walked to Chet's house."

"And helped himself to my car!" Chet added.

Frank snapped his fingers. "Say! Maybe the wrecked car *didn't* belong to that fellow—"

"You mean he'd stolen it, too!" Joe interrupted.

"Yes—which would make him even more desperate to get away."

"Whatever are you boys talking about?" Callie asked.

"I'll phone you tonight and tell you," Frank promised. "Got to dash now."

The boys waved good-by to Callie and hurried into town. They went at once to Chief Ezra Collig, head of the Bayport police force. He was a tall, husky man, well known to Fenton Hardy and his two sons. The chief had often turned to the private detective for help in solving particularly difficult cases.

When the boys went into his office they found the police chief talking with three excited men. One of these was Ike Harrity, the old ticket seller at the city ferryboat office. Another was Policeman Con Riley. The third was Oscar Smuff, a short, stout man. He was invariably seen wearing a checkered suit and a soft felt hat. He called himself a private detective and was working hard to earn a place on the Bayport police force.

"Smuff's playing up to Collig again," Joe whispered, chuckling, as the boys waited for the chief to speak to them.

Ike Harrity was frankly frightened. He was a timid man, who had perched on a high stool behind the ticket window at the ferryboat office day in and day out for a good many years.

"I was just countin' up the mornin's receipts," he was saying in a high-pitched, excited voice, "when in comes this fellow and sticks a revolver in front of my nose."

"Just a minute," interrupted Chief Collig, turning to the newcomers. "What can I do for you boys?"

"I came to report a theft," Chet spoke up. "My hot rod has been stolen."

"Why, it was one of those crazy hot rods this

fellow drove!" Ike Harrity cried out. "A yellow one!"

"Ha!" exclaimed Oscar Smuff. "A clue!" He immediately pulled a pencil and notebook from his pocket.

"My Queen!" shouted Chet.

Chief Collig rapped on his desk for quiet and asked, "What's a queen got to do with all this?"

Chet explained, then the chief related Harrity's story for him.

"A man drove up to the ferryboat office and tried to hold up Mr. Harrity. But a passenger came into the office and the fellow ran away."

As the officer paused, Frank gave Chief Collig a brief account of the wrecked blue sedan near the Morton farm.

"I'll send some men out there right now." The chief pressed a buzzer and quickly relayed his orders.

"It certainly looks," Joe commented, "as if the man who stole Chet's car and the fellow who tried to hold up the ferryboat office are the same person!"

"Did you notice the color of the man's hair?" Frank asked Mr. Harrity.

Smuff interrupted. "What's that got to do with it?"

"It may have a great deal to do with it," Frank replied. "What was the color of his hair, Mr. Harrity?"

"Dark brown and short cropped."

Frank and Joe looked at each other, perplexed. "You're sure it wasn't red?" Joe asked.

Chief Collig sat forward in his chair. "What are you driving at, boys? Have you some information about this man?"

"We were told," said Joe, "that the guy who stole Chet's car had red hair. A friend of ours saw him."

"Then he must have turned the jalopy over to someone else," Chief Collig concluded.

At this moment a short, nervous little man was ushered into the room. He was the passenger who had gone into the ferryboat office at the time of the attempted holdup. Chief Collig had sent for him.

The newcomer introduced himself as Henry J. Brown of New York. He told of entering the office and seeing a man run away from the ticket window with a revolver in his hand.

"What color was his hair?" Frank asked eagerly. "Did you notice?"

"I can't say I did," the man replied. "My eyes were focused on that gun. Say, wait a minute! He had red hair. You couldn't miss it! I noticed it after he jumped into the car."

Oscar Smuff looked bewildered. "You say he had red hair." The detective turned to Mr. Harrity. "And you say he had dark hair. Somethin' wrong somewhere!" He shook his head in puzzlement.

The others were puzzled too. Frank asked Mr. Brown to tell once more just when he had noticed the red hair.

"After the fellow leaned down in the car and popped his head up again," the New Yorker replied.

Frank and Joe exchanged glances. Was it possible the red hair was a wig and the thief had put it on just before Mr. Brown had noticed him? The boys kept still—they didn't want any interference from Smuff in tracking down this clue.

Harrity and Brown began to argue over the color of the thief's hair. Finally Chief Collig had to rap once more for order. "I'll send out an alarm for both this holdup man and for Chet's car. I guess that's all that can be done now."

Undaunted by their failure to catch the thief, the Hardy boys left police headquarters with Chet Morton. They were determined to pursue the case.

"We'll talk with Dad tonight, Chet," Frank promised. "Maybe he'll give us some leads."

"I sure hope so, fellows," their friend replied as they climbed onto the motorcycles.

The same thought was running through Frank's and Joe's minds: maybe this mystery would turn out to be their first case!

CHAPTER III

The Threat

"YOU'RE getting to be pretty good on that motor-cycle, Frank," Joe said as the boys rode into the Hardy garage. "I'm not even scared to ride alongside you any more!"

"*You're* not scared!" Frank pretended to take Joe seriously. "What about me—riding with a daredevil like you?"

"Well," Joe countered, "let's just admit that we're both pretty good!"

"It sure was swell of Dad to let us have them," Joe continued.

"Yes," Frank agreed. "And if we're going to be detectives, we'll get a lot of use out of them."

The boys started toward the house, passing the old-fashioned barn on the property. Its first floor had been converted into a gymnasium which was used after school and on week ends by Frank and Joe and their friends.

The Hardy home, on the corner of High and Elm streets, was an old stone house set in a large, tree-shaded lawn. Right now, crocuses and miniature narcissi were sticking their heads through the light-green grass.

"Hello, Mother!" said Frank, as he pushed open the kitchen door.

Mrs. Hardy, a petite, pretty woman, looked up from the table on which she was stuffing a large roasting chicken and smiled.

Her sons kissed her affectionately and Joe asked, "Dad upstairs?"

"Yes, dear. He's in his study."

The study was Fenton Hardy's workshop. Adjoining it was a fine library which contained not only books but files of disguises, records of criminal cases, and translations of thousands of codes.

Walking into the study, Frank and Joe greeted their father. "We're reporting errand accomplished," Frank announced.

"Fine!" Mr. Hardy replied. Then he gave his sons a searching glance. "I'd say your trip netted you more than just my errand."

Frank and Joe had learned early in their boyhood that it was impossible to keep any secrets from their astute father. They assumed that this ability was one reason why he had been such a successful detective on the New York City police force before setting up a private practice in Bayport.

"We ran into some real excitement," Frank said, and told his father the whole story of Chet's missing jalopy, the wrecked car which they suspected had been a stolen one also, and the attempted holdup at the ferryboat office.

"Chet's counting on us to find his car," Joe added.

Frank grinned. "That is, unless the police find it first."

Mr. Hardy was silent for several seconds. Then he said, "Do you want a little advice? You know I never give it unless I'm asked for it." He chuckled.

"We'll need a lot of help," Joe answered.

Mr. Hardy said that to him the most interesting angle to the case was the fact that the suspect apparently used one or more wigs as a disguise. "He may have bought at least one of them in Bayport. I suggest that you boys make the rounds of all shops selling wigs and see what you can find out."

The boys glanced at the clock on their father's large desk, then Frank said, "We'll have time to do a little sleuthing before closing time. Let's go!"

The two boys made a dash for the door, then both stopped short. They did not have the slightest idea where they were going! Sheepishly Joe asked, "Dad, do you know which stores sell wigs?"

With a twinkle in his eyes, Mr. Hardy arose from the desk, walked into the library, and opened a file drawer labeled "W through Z." A moment later he pulled out a thick folder marked WIGS:

Manufacturers, distributors, and retail shops of the world.

"Why, Dad, I didn't know you had all this information—" Joe began.

His father merely smiled. He thumbed through the heavy sheaf of papers, and pulled one out.

"Bayport," he read. "Well, three of these places can be eliminated at once. They sell only women's hair pieces. Now let's see. Frank, get a paper and pencil. First there's Schwartz's Masquerade and Costume Shop. It's at 79 Renshaw Avenue. Then there's Flint's at Market and Pine, and one more: Ruben Brothers. That's on Main Street just this side of the railroad."

"Schwartz's is closest," Frank spoke up. "Let's try him first, Joe."

Hopefully the boys dashed out to their motorcycles and hurried downtown. As they entered Schwartz's shop, a short, plump, smiling man came toward them.

"Well, you just got under the wire fellows," he said, looking up at a large old-fashioned clock on the wall. "I was going to close up promptly tonight because a big shipment came in today and I never have time except after business hours to unpack and list my merchandise."

"Our errand won't take long," said Frank. "We're sons of Fenton Hardy, the detective. We'd like to know whether or not you recently sold a red wig to a man."

Mr. Schwartz shook his head. "I haven't sold a red wig in months, or even rented one. Everybody seems to want blond or brown or black lately. But you understand, I don't usually sell wigs at all. I rent 'em."

"I understand," said Frank. "We're just trying to find out about a man who uses a red wig as a disguise. We thought he might have bought or rented it here and that you would know his name."

Mr. Schwartz leaned across the counter. "This man you speak of—he sounds like a character. It's just possible he may come in to get a wig from me. If he does, I'll be glad to let you know."

The boys thanked the shopkeeper and were about to leave when Mr. Schwartz called, "Hold on a minute!"

The Hardys hoped that the dealer had suddenly remembered something important. This was not the case, however. With a grin the man asked the boys if they would like to help him open some cartons which had arrived and to try on the costumes.

"Those folks at the factory don't always get the sizes marked right," he said. "Would you be able to stay a few minutes and help me? I'll be glad to pay you."

"Oh, we don't want any money," Joe spoke up. "To tell you the truth, I'd like to see your costumes."

Mr. Schwartz locked the front door of his shop,

then led the boys into a rear room. It was so filled with costumes of all kinds and paraphernalia for theatrical work, plus piles of cartons, that Frank and Joe wondered how the man could ever find anything.

"Here is today's shipment," Mr. Schwartz said, pointing to six cartons standing not far from the rear entrance to his shop.

Together he and the boys slit open the boxes and one by one lifted out a king's robe, a queen's tiara, and a Little Bopeep costume. Suddenly Mr. Schwartz said:

"Here's a skeleton marked size thirty-eight. Would one of you boys mind trying it on?"

Frank picked up the costume, unzipped the back, and stepped into the skeleton outfit. It was tremendous on him and the ribs sagged ludicrously.

"Guess a fat man modeled for this," he remarked, holding the garment out to its full width.

At that moment there was a loud rap on the front door of the store. Mr. Schwartz made no move to answer it. "I'm closed," he said. "Let him rap."

Suddenly Frank had an idea. The thief who used wigs might be the late customer, coming on purpose at this hour to avoid meeting other people. Without a word to the others, he dashed through the doorway into the store and toward the front entrance.

He could vaguely see someone waiting to be admitted. But the stranger gave one look at the leaping, out-of-shape skeleton and disappeared in a flash. At the same moment Frank tripped and fell headlong.

Mr. Schwartz and Joe, hearing the crash, rushed out to see what had happened. Frank, hopelessly tangled in the skeleton attire, was helped to his feet. When he told the others why he had made his unsuccessful dash to the front door, they conceded he might have a point.

"But you sure scared him away in that outfit," Joe said, laughing. "He won't be back!"

The boys stayed for over half an hour helping Mr. Schwartz, then said good-by and went home.

"Monday we'll tackle those other two wig shops," said Frank.

The following morning the Hardy family attended church, then after dinner Frank and Joe told their parents they were going to ride out to see Chet Morton. "We've been invited to stay to supper," Frank added. "But we promise not to get home late."

The Hardys picked up Callie Shaw, who also had been invited. Gaily she perched on the seat behind Frank.

"Hold on, Callie," Joe teased. "Frank's a wild cyclist!"

The young people were greeted at the door of the Morton farmhouse by Chet's younger sister

Iola, dark-haired and pretty. Joe Hardy thought she was quite the nicest girl in Bayport High and dated her regularly.

As dusk came on, the five young people gathered in the Mortons' kitchen to prepare supper. Chet, who loved to eat, was in charge, and doled out various jobs to the others. When he finished, Joe remarked, "And what are you going to do, big boy?"

The stout youth grinned. "I'm the official taster."

A howl went up from the others. "No workee, no eatee," said Iola flatly.

Chet grinned. "Oh, well, if you insist, I'll make a little side dish for all of us. How about Welsh rabbit?"

"You're elected!" the others chorused, and Chet set to work.

The farmhouse kitchen was large and contained a group of windows in one corner. Here stood a large table, where the young people decided to eat. They had just sat down when the telephone rang. Chet got up and walked out in the hall to answer it. Within a minute he re-entered the kitchen, his eyes bulging.

"What's the matter?" Iola asked quickly.

"I— I've been th-threatened!" Chet replied.

"Threatened!" the others cried out. "How?"

Chet was so frightened he could hardly speak, but he managed to make the others understand that a man had just said on the telephone, "You'll never get your jalopy back. And if you don't lay off trying to find me or your car, you're going to get hurt!"

"Whew!" cried Joe. "This is getting serious!"

Callie and Iola had clutched their throats and were staring wild-eyed at Chet. Frank, about to speak, happened to glance out the window toward the barn. For an instant he thought his eyes were playing tricks on him. But no! They were not. A figure was sneaking from the barn and down the lane toward the highway.

"Fellows!" he cried suddenly. "Follow me!"

CHAPTER IV

Red Versus Yellow

BY THE time the Hardy boys and Chet had raced from the Mortons' kitchen, the prowler was not in sight. Thinking he had run across one of the fields, the three pursuers scattered in various directions to search. Joe struck out straight ahead and pressed his ear to the ground to listen for receding footsteps. He could hear none. Presently the three boys met once more to discuss their failure to catch up to the man, and to question why he had been there.

"Do you think he was a thief?" Joe asked Chet. "What would he steal?"

"Search me," the stout boy replied. "Let's take a look."

"I believe he was carrying something, but I couldn't see what it was," Frank revealed.

The barn door had not been closed yet for the night and the boys walked in. Chet turned on the lights and the searchers gazed around.

"Look!" Frank cried suddenly.

He pointed to the floor below the telephone extension in the barn. There lay a man's gray wig.

"The intruder's!" Joe exclaimed.

"It sure looks so," Frank agreed. "And something must have scared him. In his hurry to get away he must have dropped this."

Frank picked up the wig and examined it carefully for a clue. "No identifying mark in it. Say, I have an idea," he burst out. "That man phoned you from here, Chet."

"You mean he's the one who threatened me?"

"Yes. If you know how, you can call your own telephone number from an extension."

"That's right."

Chet was wagging his head. "You mean that guy bothered to come all the way here to use this phone to threaten me? Why?"

Both Hardys said they felt the man had not come specifically for that reason. There was another more important one. "We must figure it out. Chet, you ought to be able to answer that better than anybody else. What is there, or was there, in this barn to interest such a person?"

The stout boy scratched his head and let his eyes wander around the building. "It wouldn't be any of the livestock," he said slowly. "And it couldn't be hay or feed." Suddenly Chet snapped his fingers. "Maybe I have the answer. Wait a minute, fellows."

On the floor lay a man's wig

He disappeared from the barn and made a bee-line for the garage. Chet hurried inside but was back in a few seconds.

"I have it!" he shouted. "That guy came here to get the spare tire for the jalopy."

"The one you had is gone?" Frank asked.

Chet nodded. He suggested that perhaps the man was not too far away. He might be on some side road changing the tire. "Let's find out," he urged.

Although the Hardys felt that it would be a use-less search, they agreed to go along. They got on their motorcycles, with Chet riding behind Joe. The boys went up one road and down another, covering the territory very thoroughly. They saw no parked car.

"Not even any evidence that a driver pulled off the road and stayed to change a tire," Frank re-marked. "No footprints, no tool marks, no treads."

"That guy must have had somebody around to pick him up," Chet concluded with a sigh.

"Cheer up, Chet," Frank said, as they walked back to the house. "That spare tire may turn out to be a clue in this case."

When the boys entered the kitchen again, they were met with anxious inquiries from Callie and Iola.

"What in the world were you doing—dashing

out of here without a word?" Callie asked in a shaking voice.

"Yes, what's going on? You had us frightened silly," Iola joined in. "First Chet gets a threatening phone call, and then suddenly all three of you run out of the house like madmen!"

"Calm down, girls," Frank said soothingly. "I saw a prowler, and we were looking for him, but all we found was this!" He tossed the gray wig onto a chair in the hall.

Suddenly there was a loud wail from Chet. "My Welsh rabbit! It's been standing so long it will be ruined!"

Iola began to giggle. "Oh, you men!" she said. "Do you suppose Callie and I would let all that good cheese go to waste? We kept that Welsh rabbit at just the right temperature and it isn't spoiled at all."

Chet looked relieved, as he and the others took their places at the table. Although there was a great deal of bantering during the meal, the conversation in the main revolved around Chet's missing jalopy and the thief who evidently wore hair disguises to suit his fancy.

Frank and Joe asked Chet if they might take along the gray wig and examine it more thoroughly. There might be some kind of mark on it to indicate either the maker or the owner. Chet readily agreed.

But when supper was over, Callie said to Frank with a teasing gleam in her eyes, "Why don't you hot-shot sleuths examine that wig now? I'd like to watch your super-duper methods."

"Just for that, I will," said Frank.

He went to get the wig from the hall chair, and then laid it on the kitchen table. From his pocket he took a small magnifying glass and carefully examined every inch of the lining of the wig.

"Nothing here," he said presently.

The hair was thoroughly examined and parted strand by strand to see if there were any identifying designations on the hair piece. Frank could discover nothing.

"I'm afraid this isn't going to help us much," he said in disgust. "But I'll show it to the different wig men in town."

As he finished speaking the telephone rang and Iola went to answer it. Chet turned white and looked nervous. Was the caller the man who had threatened him? And what did he want?

Presently Iola returned to the kitchen, a worried frown on her face. "It's a man for you, Chet. He wouldn't give his name."

Trembling visibly, Chet walked slowly to the telephone. The others followed and listened.

"Ye-yes, I'm Chet Morton. N-no, I haven't got my car back."

There was a long silence, as the person on the other end of the line spoke rapidly.

"B-but I haven't any money," Chet said finally. "I— Well, okay, I'll let you know."

Chet hung up and wobbled to a nearby chair. The others bombarded him with questions.

The stout boy took a deep breath, then said, "I can get my jalopy back. But the man wants a lot of money for the information as to where it is."

"Oh, I'm glad you're going to get your car back!" Callie exclaimed.

"But I haven't got any money," Chet groaned.

"Who's the man?" Frank demanded.

There was another long pause before Chet answered. Then, looking at the waiting group before him, he announced simply, "Smuff. Oscar Smuff!"

His listeners gasped in astonishment. This was the last thing they expected to hear. The detective was selling information as to where Chet would find his missing jalopy!

"Why, that cheap so-and-so!" Joe cried out angrily.

Chet explained that Smuff had said he was not in business for his health. He had to make a living and any information which he dug up as a detective should be properly paid for.

Frank shrugged. "I suppose Smuff has a point there. How much does he want for the information, Chet?"

"His fee is twenty-five dollars!"

"What!" the others cried out.

After a long consultation it was decided that

the young people would pool their resources. Whatever sum they could collect toward the twenty-five dollars would be offered to Oscar Smuff to lead them to Chet's car.

"But make it very plain," Frank admonished, "that if it's not your jalopy Smuff leads us to, you won't pay him one nickel."

Chet put in a call to Smuff's home. As expected, the detective grumbled at the offer of ten dollars but finally accepted it. He said he would pick up the boys in half an hour and take them to the spot.

About this time Mr. and Mrs. Morton returned home. Chet and Iola's father was a good-looking, jolly man with his son's same general build and coloring. He was in the real-estate business in Bayport and ran the farm as a hobby.

Mrs. Morton was an older edition of her daughter Iola and just as witty and lighthearted. But when she learned what had transpired and that her son had been threatened, she was worried.

"You boys must be very careful," Mrs. Morton advised. "From what I hear about Smuff, this red-haired thief could easily put one over on him. So watch your step!"

Chet promised that they would.

"Good luck!" Callie called out, as Smuff beeped his horn outside the door. "And don't be too late. I want to hear the news before I have to go home."

Red Versus Yellow

Frank, Joe, and Chet found Smuff ent. communicative about where they were going. seemed to enjoy the role he was playing.

"I knew I'd be the one to break this case," he boasted.

Joe could not resist the temptation of asking Smuff if he was going to lead them to the thief as well as to the car. The detective flushed in embarrassment and admitted that he did not have full details yet on this part of the mystery.

"But it won't be long before I capture that fellow," he assured the boys. They managed to keep their faces straight and only hoped that they were not now on a wild-goose chase.

Twenty minutes later Smuff pulled into the town of Ducksworth and drove straight to a used-car lot. Stopping, he announced, "Well, here we are. Get ready to fork over that money, Chet."

Smuff nodded to the attendant in charge, then led the boys down a long aisle past row after row of cars to where several jalopies were lined up against a rear fence. Turning left, the detective finally paused before a bright red car.

"Here you are!" said Smuff grandly, extending his right hand toward Chet. "My money, please."

The stout boy as well as the Hardys stared at the jalopy. There was no question but that it was the same make and model as Chet's.

"The thief thought he could disguise it by painting it red," Smuff explained.

"Is that your guess?" Frank asked quietly.

Oscar Smuff frowned. "How else could you figure it?" he asked.

"Then there'll be yellow paint under the red," Frank went **on**. "Let's take a look to make sure."

It was evident that Smuff did not like this procedure. "So you doubt me, eh?" he asked in an unpleasant tone.

"Anybody can get fooled," Frank told him. "Well, Chet, let's operate on this car."

The detective stood by sullenly as Frank pulled out a penknife and began to scrape the red paint off part of the fender.

CHAPTER V

The Hunt Is Intensified

"Hey!" Oscar Smuff shouted. "You be careful with that penknife! The man who owns this place don't want you ruinin' his cars!"

Frank Hardy looked up at the detective. "I've watched my father scrape off flecks of paint many times. The way he does it, you wouldn't know anybody had made a mark."

Smuff grunted. "But you're not your father. Easy there!"

As cautiously as possible Frank picked off flecks of the red paint in a spot where it would hardly be noticeable. Taking a flashlight from his pocket, he trained it on the spot.

Joe, leaning over his brother's shoulder, said, "There was light-blue paint under this red, not yellow."

"Right," Frank agreed, eying Smuff intently.

The detective reddened. "You fellows trying to

tell me this isn't Chet's jalopy?" he demanded. "Well, I'm telling you it is, and I'm right!"

"Oh, we haven't said you're wrong," Joe spoke up quickly. Secretly he was hoping that this was Chet's car, but reason told him it was not.

"We'll try another place," Frank said, straightening up, and walking around to a fender on the opposite side.

Here, too, the test indicated that the car had been painted light blue before the red coat had been put over it.

"Well, maybe the thief put blue on and then red," said Smuff stubbornly.

Frank grinned. "We'll go a little deeper. If the owner of this establishment objects, we'll pay for having the fenders painted."

But though Frank went down through several layers of paint, he could not find any sign of yellow.

All this time Chet had been walking round and round the car, looking intently at it inside and out. Even before Frank announced that he was sure this was not the missing jalopy, Chet was convinced of it himself.

"The Queen had a long, thin dent in the right rear fender," he said. "And that seat cushion by the door had a little split in it. I don't think the thief would have bothered to fix them up."

Chet showed his keen disappointment, but he was glad that the Hardys had come along to help him prove the truth. But Smuff was not giving up the money so easily.

"You haven't proved a thing," he said. "The man who runs this place admitted that maybe this is a stolen car. The fellow who sold it to him said he lived on a farm outside Bayport."

The Hardys and Chet were taken aback for a moment by this information. But in a moment Frank said, "Let's go talk to the owner. We'll find out more about the person who brought this car in."

The man who ran the used-car lot was very cooperative. He readily answered all questions the Hardys put to him. The bill of sale revealed that the former owner of the red jalopy was Melvin Schuster of Bayport.

"Why, we know him!" Frank spoke up. "He goes to Bayport High—at least, he did. He and his family moved far away. That's probably why he sold his car."

"But Mr. Smuff said you suspected the car was stolen," Joe put in.

The used-car lot owner smiled. "I'm afraid maybe Mr. Smuff put that idea in my head. I did say that the person seemed in an awful hurry to get rid of the car and sold it very cheap. Sometimes when that happens, we dealers are a little afraid to take the responsibility of buying a car, in case it is stolen property. But at the time Mr. Schuster came in, I thought everything was on the level and bought his jalopy."

Frank said that he was sure everything was all right, and after the dealer described Melvin Schuster, there was no question but that he was the owner.

Smuff was completely crestfallen. Without a word he started for his own car and the boys followed. The detective did not talk on the way back to the Morton farm, and the boys, feeling rather sorry for him, spoke of matters other than the car incident.

As the Hardys and Chet walked into the Morton home, the two girls rushed forward. "Did you find it?" Iola asked eagerly.

Chet sighed. "Another one of Smuff's bluffs," he said disgustedly. He handed back the money which his friends had given to help pay the detective.

Frank and Joe said good-by, went for their motorcycles, and took Callie home. Then they returned to their own house, showered, and went to bed.

As soon as school was over the next day, they took the gray wig and visited Schwartz's shop. The owner assured them that the hair piece had not come from his store.

"It's a very cheap one," the man said rather disdainfully.

Frank and Joe visited Flint's and Ruben Brothers' shops as well. Neither place had sold the gray wig. Furthermore, neither of them had had a customer in many weeks who had wanted a red wig, or who was in the habit of using wigs or toupees of various colors.

"Today's sleuthing was a complete washout," Joe reported that night to his father.

The famous detective smiled. "Don't be discouraged," he said. "I can tell you that one bit of success makes up for a hundred false trails."

As the boys were undressing for bed later, Frank reminded his brother that the following day was a school holiday. "That'll give us hours and hours to work on the case," he said enthusiastically.

"What do you suggest we do?" Joe asked.

Frank shrugged. Several ideas were brought up by the brothers, but one which Joe proposed was given preference. They would get hold of a large group of their friends. On the theory that the thief could not have driven a long distance away because of the police alarm, the boys would make an extensive search in the surrounding area for Chet's jalopy.

"We'll hunt in every possible hiding place," he stated.

Early the next morning Frank hurried to the telephone and put in one call after another to "the gang." These included, besides Chet Morton, Allen Hooper, nicknamed Biff because of his fondness for a distant relative who was a boxer named Biff; Jerry Gilroy, Phil Cohen, and Tony Prito. All were students at Bayport High and prominent in various sports.

The five boys were eager to co-operate. They agreed to assemble at the Hardy home at nine o'clock. In the meantime, Frank and Joe would lay out a plan of action.

As soon as breakfast was over the Hardys told their father what they had in mind and asked if he had any suggestions on how they might go about their search.

"Take a map," he said, "with our house as a radius and cut pie-shaped sections. I suggest that two boys work together."

By nine o'clock his sons had mapped out the search in detail. The first recruit to arrive was Tony Prito, a lively boy with a good sense of humor. He was followed in a moment by Phil Cohen, a quiet, intelligent boy.

"Put us to work," said Tony. "I brought one of my father's trucks that he isn't going to use to-day." Tony's father was in the contracting business. "I can cover a lot of miles in it."

Frank suggested that Tony and Phil work together. He showed them the map, with Bayport as the center of a great circle, cut into four equal sections.

"Suppose you take from nine o'clock to twelve on this dial we've marked. Mother has agreed to stay at home all day and act as clearing house for our reports. Call in every hour."

"Will do," Tony promised. "Come on, Phil. Let's get going!"

The two boys were just starting off when Biff and Jerry arrived at the Hardy home on motorcycles. Biff, blond and long-legged, had an ambling gait, with which he could cover a tremendous amount of territory in a short time. Jerry, an excellent fielder on Bayport High's baseball team, was of medium height, wiry, and strong.

Biff and Jerry were assigned to the section on the map designated six to nine o'clock. They were given further instructions on sleuthing, then started off on their quest.

"Where's Chet?" Mr. Hardy asked his sons. "Wasn't he going to help in the search?"

"He probably overslept. Chet's been known to do that," Frank said with a grin.

"He also might have taken time for a double breakfast," Joe suggested.

Mrs. Hardy, who had stepped to the front porch, called, "Here he comes now. Isn't that Mr. Morton's car?"

"Yes, it is," Frank replied.

Chet's father let him off in front of the Hardy home and the stout boy hurried to the porch. "Good morning, Mrs. Hardy. Good morning, Mr. Hardy. Hi, chums!" he said cheerily. "Sorry to be late. My dad had a lot of phoning to do before he left. I was afraid if I'd tried to walk here, I wouldn't have arrived until tomorrow."

At this point Mr. Hardy spoke up. "As I said before, I think you boys should work in twos. There are only three of you to take care of half the territory." The detective suddenly grinned boyishly. "How about me teaming up with one of you?"

Frank and Joe looked at their dad in delight. "You mean it?" Frank cried out. "I'll choose you as my partner right now."

"I have a further suggestion," the detective said. "It's not going to take you fellows more than three hours to cover the area you've laid out. And there's an additional section I think you might look into."

"What's that?" Joe inquired.

"Willow Grove. That's a park area, but there's also a lot of tangled woodland to one side of it. Good place to hide a stolen car."

Mr. Hardy suggested that the boys meet for a picnic lunch at Willow Grove and later do some sleuthing in the vicinity. "That is, provided you haven't found Chet's jalopy by that time."

Mrs. Hardy spoke up. "I'll fix a nice lunch for all of you," she offered.

"That sure would be swell," Chet said hastily. "You make grand picnic lunches, Mrs. Hardy."

Frank and Joe liked the plan, and it was decided that the boys would have the picnic whether or not they had found the jalopy by one o'clock. Mrs. Hardy said she would relay the news to the other boys when they phoned in.

Chet and Joe set off on the Hardy boys' motor-cycles, taking the twelve-to-three segment on the map. Then Mr. Hardy and Frank drove off for the three-to-six area.

Hour after hour went by, with the searchers constantly on the alert. Every garage, public and private, every little-used road, every patch of woods was thoroughly investigated. There was no sign of Chet's missing yellow jalopy. Finally at one o'clock Frank and his father returned to the Hardy home. A few moments later Joe and Chet returned and a huge picnic lunch was stowed aboard the two motorcycles.

When the three boys reached the picnic area they were required to park their motorcycles out-side the fence. They unstrapped the lunch baskets and carried them down to the lake front. The other boys were already there.

"Too bad we can't go swimming," Tony re-marked, "but this water's pretty cold."

Quickly they unpacked the food and assembled around one of the park picnic tables.

"Um! Yum! Chicken sandwiches!" Chet cried gleefully.

During the meal the boys exchanged reports on their morning's sleuthing. All had tried hard but failed to find any trace of the missing car.

"Our work hasn't ended," Frank reminded the others. "But I'm so stuffed I'm going to rest a while before I start out again."

All the other boys but Joe Hardy felt the same way and lay down on the grass for a nap. Joe, eager to find out whether or not the woods to their right held the secret of the missing car, plunged off alone through the underbrush.

He searched for twenty minutes without finding a clue to any automobile. He was on the point of returning and waiting for the other boys when he saw a small clearing ahead of him. It appeared to be part of an abandoned roadway.

Excitedly Joe pushed on through the dense undergrowth. It was in a low-lying part of the grove and the ground was wet. At one point it was quite muddy, and it was here that Joe saw something that aroused his curiosity.

"A tire! Then maybe an automobile has been in here," he muttered to himself, although there were no tire marks in the immediate vicinity. "No footprints, either. I guess someone tossed this tire here."

Remembering his father's admonitions on the value of developing one's powers of observation, Joe went closer and examined the tire.

"That tread," he thought excitedly, "looks familiar."

He gazed at it until he was sure, then dashed back to the other boys.

"I've found a clue!" he cried out. "Come on, everybody!"

CHAPTER VI

The Robbery

JOE HARDY quickly led the way into the swampy area as the other boys trooped along, everyone talking at once. When they reached the spot, Chet examined the tire and exclaimed:

"There's no mistake about it! This is one of the tires! When the thief put on the new one, he threw this away."

"Perhaps the Queen is still around," suggested Frank quickly. "The thief may have picked this road as a good place to hide your jalopy until he could make a getaway."

"It would be an ideal place," Chet agreed. "People coming to Willow Grove have to park at the gate, so nobody would come in here. But this old road comes in from the main highway. Let's take a look, fellows."

A scrutinizing search was begun along the abandoned road in the direction of the highway. A moment later Frank and Chet, in the lead, cried out simultaneously.

"Here's a bypath! And here are tire marks!" Frank exclaimed. To one side was a narrow roadway, almost overgrown with weeds and low bushes. It led from the abandoned road into the depths of the woods.

Without hesitation Frank and Chet plunged into it. Presently the roadway widened out, then wound about a heavy clump of trees. It came to an end in a wide clearing.

In the clearing stood Chet Morton's lost jalopy!

"My Queen!" he yelled in delight. "Her own license plates!"

His shout was heard by the rest of the boys, who came on a run. Chet's joy was boundless. He examined the car with minute care, while his chums crowded around. At last he straightened up with a smile of satisfaction.

"She hasn't been damaged a bit. All ready to run. The thief just hid the old bus in here and made a getaway. Come on, fellows, climb aboard. Free ride to the highway!"

Before leaving, the Hardys examined footprints left by the thief. "He wore sneakers," Frank observed.

Suddenly Chet swung open the door and looked on the floor. "You mean he wore *my* sneakers. They're gone."

"And carried his own shoes," Joe observed. "Very clever. Well, that washes out one clue. Can't trace the man by his shoe prints."

"Let's go!" Chet urged.

He jumped into the car and in a few seconds the engine roared. There was barely sufficient room in the clearing to permit him to turn the jalopy about. When he swung around and headed up the bypath, the boys gave a cheer and hastened to clamber aboard.

Lurching and swaying, the car reached the abandoned road and from there made the run to the main highway. The boys transferred to Tony's truck and the motorcycles, and formed a parade into Bayport, with Frank and Joe in the lead. It was their intention to ride up to police headquarters and announce their success to Chief Collig.

"And I hope Smuff will be around," Chet gloated.

As the grinning riders came down Main Street, however, they noticed that no one paid any attention to them, and there seemed to be an unusual air of mystery in the town. People were standing in little groups, gesticulating and talking earnestly.

Presently the Hardys saw Oscar Smuff striding along with a portentous frown. Joe called out to him. "What's going on, detective? You notice we found Chet's car."

"I've got something more important than stolen cars to worry— Hey, what's that?" Detective Smuff stared blankly, as the full import of the discovery filtered his consciousness.

The boys waited for Smuff's praise, but he did not give it. Instead, he said, "I got a big mystery to solve. The Tower Mansion has been robbed!"

"Good night!" the Hardys chorused.

Tower Mansion was one of the show places of Bayport. Few people in the city had ever been permitted to enter the place and the admiration which the palatial building excited was solely by reason of its exterior appearance. But the first thing a newcomer to Bayport usually asked was, "Who owns that house with the towers over on the hill?"

It was an immense, rambling stone structure overlooking the bay, and could be seen for miles, silhouetted against the sky line like an ancient feudal castle. The resemblance to a castle was heightened by the fact that from each of the far ends of the mansion arose a high tower.

One of these had been built when the mansion was erected by Major Applegate, an eccentric, retired old Army man who had made a fortune by lucky real-estate deals. Years ago there had been many parties and dances in the mansion.

But the Applegate family had become scattered until at last there remained in the old home only Hurd Applegate and his sister Adelia. They lived in the vast, lonely mansion at the present time.

Hurd Applegate was a man about sixty, tall, and stooped. His life seemed to be devoted now to the collection of rare stamps. But a few years before he had built a new tower on the mansion, a duplicate of the original one.

His sister Adelia was a maiden lady of uncertain years. Well-dressed women in Bayport were amused by her clothes. She dressed in clashing colors and unbecoming styles. Hurd and Adelia Applegate were reputed to be enormously wealthy, although they lived simply, kept only a few servants, and never had visitors.

"Tell us about the theft," Joe begged Smuff.

But the detective waved his hand airily. "You'll have to find out yourselves," he retorted as he hurried off.

Frank and Joe called good-by to their friends and headed for home. As they arrived, the boys saw Hurd Applegate just leaving the house. The man tapped the steps with his cane as he came down them. When he heard the boys' motorcycles he gave them a piercing glance.

"Good day!" he growled in a grudging manner and went on his way.

"He must have been asking Dad to take the case," Frank said to his brother, as they pulled into the garage.

The boys rushed into the house, eager to find out more about the robbery. In the front hallway they met their father.

"We heard the Tower Mansion has been robbed," said Joe.

Mr. Hardy nodded. "Yes. Mr. Applegate was just here to tell me about it. He wants me to handle the case."

"How much was taken?"

Mr. Hardy smiled. "Well, I don't suppose it will do any harm to tell you. The safe in the Applegate library was opened. The loss will be about forty thousand dollars, all in securities and jewels."

"Whew!" exclaimed Frank. "What a haul! When did it happen?"

"Either last night or this morning. Mr. Applegate did not get up until after ten o'clock this morning and did not go into the library until nearly noon. It was then that he discovered the theft."

"How was the safe opened?"

"By using the combination. It was opened either by someone who knew the set of numbers or else by a very clever thief who could detect the noise of the tumblers. I'm going up to the house in a few minutes. Mr. Applegate is to call for me."

"I'd like to go along," Joe said eagerly.

"So would I," Frank declared.

Mr. Hardy looked at his sons and smiled. "Well, if you want to be detectives, I suppose it is about as good a chance as any to watch a crime investigation from the inside. If Mr. Applegate doesn't object, you may come with me."

A few minutes later a foreign-make, chauffeur-driven car drew up before the Hardy home. Mr.

Applegate was seated in the rear, his chin resting on his cane. The three Hardys went outside. When the detective mentioned the boys' request, the man merely grunted assent and moved over. Frank and Joe stepped in after their father. The car headed toward Tower Mansion.

"I don't really need a detective in this case!" Hurd Applegate snapped. "Don't need one at all. It's as clear as the nose on your face. I *know* who took the stuff. But I can't prove it."

"Whom do you suspect?" Fenton Hardy asked.

"Only one man in the world could have taken the jewels and securities. Robinson!"

"Robinson?"

"Yes. Henry Robinson—the caretaker. He's the man."

The Hardy boys looked at each other in consternation. Henry Robinson, the caretaker of the Tower Mansion, was the father of one of their closest chums! Perry Robinson, nicknamed "Slim," was the son of the accused man!

That his father should be blamed for the robbery seemed absurd to the Hardy boys. They had met Mr. Robinson upon several occasions and he had appeared to be a good-natured, easygoing man with high principles.

"I don't believe he's guilty," Frank whispered.

"Neither do I," returned his brother.

"What makes you suspect Robinson?" Mr. Hardy asked Hurd Applegate.

"He's the only person besides my sister and me who ever saw that safe opened and closed. He could have learned the combination if he'd kept his eyes and ears open, which I'm sure he did."

"Is that your only reason for suspecting him?"

"No. This morning he paid off a nine-hundred-dollar note at the bank. And I know for a fact he didn't have more than one hundred dollars to his name a few days ago. Now where did he raise nine hundred dollars so suddenly?"

"Perhaps he has a good explanation," Mr. Hardy suggested.

"Oh, he'll have an explanation all right!" sniffed Mr. Applegate. "But it will have to be a mighty good one to satisfy me."

The automobile was now speeding up the wide driveway that led to Tower Mansion and within a few minutes stopped at the front entrance. Mr. Hardy and the two boys accompanied the eccentric man into the house.

"Nothing has been disturbed in the library since the discovery of the theft," he said, leading the way there.

Mr. Hardy examined the open safe, then took a special magnifying glass from his pocket. With minute care he inspected the dial of the combination lock. Next he walked to each window and the door to examine them for fingerprints. He asked Mr. Applegate to hold his fingers up to a strong light and got a clear view of the whorls and lines on the inside of the tips. At last he shook his head.

"A smooth job," he observed. "The thief must have worn gloves. All the fingerprints in the room, Mr. Applegate, seem to be yours."

"No use looking for fingerprints or any other evidence!" Mr. Applegate barked impatiently. "It was Robinson, I tell you."

"Perhaps it would be a good idea for me to ask him a few questions," Mr. Hardy advised.

Mr. Applegate rang for one of the servants and instructed him to tell the caretaker to come to the library at once. Mr. Hardy glanced at the boys and suggested they wait in the hallway.

"It might prove less embarrassing to Mr. Robinson that way," he said in a low voice.

Frank and Joe readily withdrew. In the hall they met Mr. Robinson and his son Perry. The man was calm, but pale, and at the doorway he patted Slim on the shoulder.

"Don't worry," he said. "Everything will be all right." With that he entered the library.

Slim turned to his two friends. "It's got to be!" he cried out. "My dad is innocent!"

CHAPTER VII

The Arrest

FRANK and Joe were determined to help their chum prove his father's innocence. They shared his conviction that Mr. Robinson was not guilty.

"Of course he's innocent," Frank agreed. "He'll be able to clear himself all right, Slim."

"But things look pretty black right now," the boy said. He was white-faced and shaken. "Unless Mr. Hardy can catch the real thief, I'm afraid Dad will be blamed for the robbery."

"Everybody knows your father is honest," said Joe consolingly. "He has been a faithful employee —even Mr. Applegate will have to admit that."

"Which won't help him much if he can't clear himself of the charge. And Dad admits that he did know the combination of the safe, although of course he'd never use it."

"He knew it?" repeated Joe, surprised.

"Dad learned the combination accidentally. It was so simple one couldn't forget it. This was how it happened. One day when he was cleaning the library fireplace, he found a piece of paper with numbers on it. He studied them and decided they were the safe combination. Dad laid the paper on the desk. The window was open and he figured the breeze must have blown the paper to the floor."

"Does Mr. Applegate know that?"

"Not yet. But Dad is going to tell him now. He realizes it will look bad for him, but he's going to give Mr. Applegate the truth."

From the library came the hum of voices. The harsh tones of Hurd Applegate occasionally rose above the murmur of conversation and finally the boys heard Mr. Robinson's voice rise sharply.

"I *didn't* do it! I tell you I *didn't* take that money!"

"Then where did you get the nine hundred you paid on that note?" demanded Mr. Applegate.

Silence.

"Where did you get it?"

"I'm not at liberty to tell you or anyone else."

"Why not?"

"I got the money honestly—that's all I can say about it."

"Oh, ho!" exclaimed Mr. Applegate. "You got the money honestly, yet you can't tell me where it came from! A pretty story! If you got the money honestly you shouldn't be ashamed to tell where it came from."

"I'm not ashamed. I can only say again, I'm not at liberty to talk about it."

"Mighty funny thing that you should get nine hundred dollars so quickly. You were pretty hard up last week, weren't you? Had to ask for an advance on your month's wages."

"That is true."

"And then the day of this robbery you suddenly have nine hundred dollars that you can't explain."

Mr. Hardy's calm voice broke in. "Of course I don't like to pry into your private affairs, Mr. Robinson," he said, "but it would be best if you would clear up this matter of the money."

"I know it looks bad," replied the caretaker doggedly. "But I've made a promise I can't break."

"And you admit being familiar with the combination of the safe, too!" broke in Mr. Applegate. "I didn't know that before. Why didn't you tell me?"

"I didn't consider it important."

"And yet you come and tell me now!"

"I have nothing to conceal. If I had taken the securities and jewels I wouldn't be telling you that I knew the combination."

"Yes," agreed Mr. Hardy, "that's a point in your favor, Mr. Robinson."

"Is it?" asked Mr. Applegate. "Robinson's just clever enough to think up a trick like that. He'd figure that by appearing to be honest, I'd believe he is honest and couldn't have committed this robbery. Very clever. But not clever enough. There's plenty of evidence right this minute to convict him, and I'm not going to delay any further."

In a moment Mr. Applegate's voice continued, "Police station? Hello . . . Police station? . . . This is Applegate speaking—Applegate—Hurd Applegate. . . . Well, we've found our man in that robbery. . . . Yes, Robinson. . . . You thought so, eh?—So did I, but I wasn't sure. . . . He has practically convicted himself by his own story. . . . Yes, I want him arrested. . . . You'll be up right away? . . . Fine. . . . Good-by."

"You're not going to have me arrested, Mr. Applegate?" the caretaker cried out in alarm.

"Why not? You're the thief!"

"It might have been better to wait a while," Mr. Hardy interposed. "At least until there was more evidence."

"What more evidence do we want, Mr. Hardy," the owner of Tower Mansion sneered. "If Robinson wants to return the jewels and securities I'll have the charge withdrawn—but that's all."

"I can't return them! I didn't take them!" Mr. Robinson defended himself.

"You'll have plenty of time to think," Mr. Applegate declared. "You'll be in the penitentiary a long time—a long time."

In the hallway the boys listened in growing excitement and dismay. The case had taken an abrupt and tragic turn. Slim looked as though he might collapse under the strain.

"My dad's innocent," the boy muttered over and over again, clenching his fists. "I *know* he is. They can't arrest him. He never stole anything in his life!"

Frank patted his friend on the shoulder. "Brace up, pal," he advised. "It looks discouraging just now, but I'm sure your father will be able to clear himself."

"I— I'll have to tell Mother," stammered Slim. "This will break her heart. And my sisters—"

Frank and Joe followed the boy down the hallway and along a corridor that led to the east wing of the mansion. There, in a neat but sparsely furnished apartment, they found Mrs. Robinson, a gentle, kind-faced woman, who was lame. She was seated in a chair by the window, anxiously waiting. Her two daughters, Paula and Tessie, twelve-year-old twins, were at her side, and all looked up in expectation as the boys came in.

"What news, son?" Mrs. Robinson asked bravely, after she had greeted the Hardys.

"Bad, Mother."

"They're not—they're not—arresting him?" cried Paula, springing forward.

Perry nodded wordlessly.

"But they can't!" Tessie protested. "Dad *couldn't* do anything like that! It's wrong—"

Frank, looking at Mrs. Robinson, saw her suddenly slump over in a faint. He sprang forward and caught the woman in his arms as she was about to fall to the floor.

"Mother!" cried Slim in terror, as Frank laid Mrs. Robinson on a couch, then he said quickly to his sister, "Paula, bring the smelling salts and her special medicine."

Perry explained that at times undue excitement caused an "attack." "I shouldn't have told her about Dad," the boy chided himself.

"She'd have to know it sooner or later," Joe said kindly.

In a moment Paula returned with the bottle of smelling salts and medicine. The inhalant brought her mother back to consciousness, and Paula then gave Mrs. Robinson the medicine. In a few moments the woman completely revived and apologized for having worried everyone.

"I admit it was a dreadful shock to think my husband has been arrested," she said, "but surely something can be done to prove his innocence."

Instantly Frank and Joe assured her they would do everything they could to find the real thief, because they too felt that Mr. Robinson was not guilty.

The next morning, as the brothers were dressing in their room at home, Frank remarked, "There's a great deal about this case that hasn't come to the surface yet. It's just possible that the man who stole Chet Morton's car may have had something to do with the theft."

Joe agreed. "He was a criminal—that much is certain. He stole an automobile and he tried to hold up the ticket office, so why not another robbery?"

"Right, Joe. I just realized that we never inspected Chet's car for any clues to the thief, so let's do it."

The stout boy did not bring his jalopy to school that day, so the Hardys had to submerge their curiosity until classes and baseball practice were over. Then, when Mrs. Morton picked up Chet and Iola, Frank and Joe went home with them.

"I'll look under the seats," Joe offered.

"And I'll search the trunk compartment." Frank walked to the back of the car and raised the cover. He began rooting under rags, papers, and discarded schoolbooks. Presently he gave a cry of victory.

"Here it is! The best evidence in the world!"

Joe and Chet rushed to his side as he held up a man's red wig.

Frank said excitedly, "Maybe there's a clue in this hair piece!"

An examination failed to reveal any, but Frank said he would like to show the wig to his father. He covered it with a handkerchief and put it carefully in an inner pocket. Chet drove the Hardys home.

They assumed that their father was in his study on the second floor, and rushed up there and into the room without ceremony.

"Dad, we've found a clue!" Joe cried. Then he stepped back, embarrassed, as he realized there was someone else in the room.

"Sorry!" said Frank. The boys would have retreated, but Mr. Hardy's visitor turned around and they saw that he was Perry Robinson.

"It's only me," said Slim. "Don't go."

"Hi, Slim!"

"Perry has been trying to shed a little more light on the Tower robbery," explained Mr. Hardy. "But what is this clue you're talking about?"

"It might concern the robbery," replied Frank. "It's about the red-haired man." He took the wig from his pocket and told where he had found it.

Mr. Hardy's interest was kindled at once. "This seems to link up a pretty good chain of evidence. The man who passed you on the shore road wrecked the car he was driving, then stole Chet's, and afterward tried to hold up the ticket office. When he failed there, he tried another and more successful robbery at the Tower."

"Do you really think the wig might help us solve the Tower robbery?" asked Perry, taking hope.

"Possibly."

"I was just telling your father," Slim went on, "that I saw a strange man lurking around the grounds of the mansion two days before the robbery. I didn't think anything of it at the time, and in the shock of Dad's arrest I forgot about it."

"Did you get a good look at him? Could you describe him?" Frank asked.

"I'm afraid I can't. It was in the evening. I was sitting by a window, studying, and happened to look up. I saw this fellow moving about among the trees. Later, I heard one of the dogs barking in another part of the grounds. Shortly afterward, I saw someone running across the lawn. I thought he was just a tramp."

"Did he wear a hat or a cap?"

"As near as I can remember, it was a cap. His clothes were dark."

"And you couldn't see his face?"

"No."

"Well, it's not much to go on," said Mr. Hardy, "but it might be linked up with Frank and Joe's idea that the man who stole the jalopy may still have been hanging around Bayport." The detective thought deeply for a few moments. "I'll bring all these facts to Mr. Applegate's attention, and I'm also going to have a talk with the police authorities. I feel they haven't enough evidence to warrant holding your father, Perry."

"Do you think you can have him released?" the boy asked eagerly.

"I'm sure of it. In fact, I believe Mr. Applegate

is beginning to realize now that he made a mistake."

"It will be wonderful if we can have Dad back with us again," said Perry. "Of course things won't be the same for him. He'll be under a cloud of suspicion as long as this mystery isn't cleared up. I suppose Mr. Applegate won't employ him or anyone else."

"All the more reason why we should get busy and clear up the affair," Frank said quickly, and Joe added, "Slim, we'll do all we can to help your father."

CHAPTER VIII

An Important Discovery

WHEN the Hardy boys were on their way home from school the next afternoon they noticed that a crowd had collected in the vestibule of the post office and were staring at the bulletin board.

"Wonder what's up now?" said Joe, pushing his way forward through the crowd with the agility of an eel. Frank was not slow in following.

On the board was a large poster. The ink on it was scarcely dry. At the top, in enormous black letters, it read:

$1000 REWARD

Underneath, in slightly smaller type, was the following:

The above reward will be paid for information leading to the arrest of the person or persons who broke into Tower Mansion and stole jewels and securities from a safe in the library.

The reward was being offered by Hurd Applegate.

"Why, that must mean the charge against Mr. Robinson has been dropped!" exclaimed Joe.

"It looks like it. Let's see if we can find Slim."

All about them people were commenting on the size of the reward, and there were many expressions of envy for the person who would be fortunate enough to solve the mystery.

"A thousand dollars!" said Frank, as the brothers made their way out of the post office. "That's a lot of money, Joe."

"I'll say it is."

"And there's no reason why we haven't as good a chance of earning it as anyone else."

"I suppose Dad and the police are barred from the reward, for it's their duty to find the thief if they can. But if we track him down we can get the money. It'll be a good sum to add to our college fund."

"Let's go! Say, there's Slim now."

Perry Robinson was coming down the street toward them. He looked much happier than he had the previous evening, and when he saw the Hardy boys his face lighted up.

"Dad is free," he told them. "Thanks to your father, the charge has been dropped."

"I'm sure glad to hear that!" exclaimed Joe. "I see a reward is being offered."

"Your father convinced Mr. Applegate that it

must have been an outside job. And the work of a professional thief. Chief Collig admitted there wasn't much evidence against Dad, so they let him go. It's a great relief. My mother and sisters were almost crazy with worry."

"No wonder," commented Frank. "What's your father going to do now?"

"I don't know," Slim admitted. "Of course, we've had to move from the Tower Mansion estate. Mr. Applegate said that even though the charge had been dropped, he wasn't altogether convinced in his own mind that Dad hadn't had something to do with the theft. So he dismissed him."

"That's tough luck. But your dad will be able to get another job somewhere," Frank said consolingly.

"I'm not so sure about that. People aren't likely to employ a man who's been suspected of stealing. Dad tried two or three places this afternoon, but he was turned down."

The Hardys were silent. They felt very sorry for the Robinsons and were determined to do what they could to help them.

"We've rented a small house just outside the city," Slim went on. "It's cheap and the neighborhood is kind of bad, but we'll have to get along."

Frank and Joe admired Slim. There was no false pride about him. He faced the facts as they came, and made the best of them. "But if Dad doesn't get a job, it will mean that I'll have to go to work full time."

"Why, Slim—you'd have to quit school!" Joe cried out.

"I can't help that. I wouldn't want to, for you know I was trying for a scholarship. But—"

The brothers realized how much it would mean to their chum if he had to leave school. Perry Robinson was an ambitious boy and one of the top ten in his class. He had always wanted to continue his studies and go on to a university, and his teachers had predicted a brilliant career for him as an engineer. Now it seemed that all his ambitions for a high school diploma and a college education would have to be given up because of this misfortune.

Frank put an arm around Slim's shoulders. "Chin up," he said with a warm smile. "Joe and I are going to plug away at this affair until we get to the bottom of it!"

"It's mighty good of you fellows," Slim said gratefully. "I won't forget it in a hurry." He tried to smile, but it was evident that the boy was deeply worried. When he walked away it was not with the light, carefree step which the Hardys associated with him.

"What's the first move, Frank?" Joe asked.

"We'd better get a full description of those jewels. Perhaps the thief tried to pawn them. Let's try all the pawnshops and see what we can find out."

"Good idea, even if the police have already done it." Frank grinned. Then he sobered. "Do you think Applegate will give us a list?"

"We won't have to ask him. Dad should have that information."

"Let's find out right now."

When the boys returned home, they found their father waiting for them. "I have news for you," he said. "Your theory about the wrecked auto being stolen has been confirmed. Collig phoned just now and told me the true ownership had been traced by the engine number. Car belongs to a man over in Thornton."

"Good. That's one more strike against the thief," Joe declared.

But a moment later the boys met with disappointment when they asked their father for a list of the stolen jewels.

"I'm willing to give you all the information I have," said Fenton Hardy, "but I'm afraid it won't be of much use. Furthermore, I'll bet I can tell just what you're going to do."

"What?"

"Make the rounds of the pawnshops to see if any of the jewels have been turned in."

The Hardy boys looked at each other in amazement. "I might have guessed," said Frank.

Their father smiled. "Not an hour after I was called in on the case I had a full description of all those jewels in every pawnshop in the city. More than that, the description has been sent to jewelry firms and pawnshops in other cities near here, and also the New York police. Here's a duplicate list if you want it, but you'll just be wasting time calling at the shops. All the dealers are on the lookout for the jewels."

Mechanically, Frank took the list. "And I thought it was such a bright idea!"

"It *is* a bright idea. But it has been used before. Most jewel robberies are solved in just this manner—by tracing the thief when he tries to get rid of the gems."

"Well," said Joe gloomily, "I guess *that* plan is all shot to pieces. Come on, Frank. We'll think of something else."

"Out for the reward?" asked Mr. Hardy, chuckling.

"Yes. And we'll get it, too!"

"I hope you do. But you can't ask me to help you any more than I've done. It's my case, too, remember. So from now on, you boys and I are rivals!"

"It's a go!"

"More power to you!" Mr. Hardy smiled and returned to his desk.

He had a sheaf of reports from shops and agencies in various parts of the state, through which he had been trying to trace the stolen jewels and securities, but in every case the report was the same. There had been no lead to the gems or the bonds taken from Tower Mansion.

When the boys left their father's study they went outside and sat on the back-porch steps.

"What shall we do now?" asked Joe.

"I don't know. Dad sure took the wind out of our sails that time, didn't he?"

"I'll say he did. But it was just as well. He saved us a lot of trouble."

"Yes, we might have been going around in circles," Frank conceded.

Joe wagged his head. "It looks as if Dad has the inside track on the case—in the city, anyway."

"What have you got in mind?" Joe asked.

"To concentrate on the country. We started out to find the thief because he stole Chet's car. Let's start all over again from that point."

"Meaning?"

"Mr. Red Wig may have come back to the woods expecting to use Chet's car again, and—"

"Frank, you're a genius! You figure the guy may have left a clue by accident."

"Exactly."

Fired with enthusiasm once more, the brothers called to Mrs. Hardy where they were going, then set off on their motorcycles. After parking them at the picnic site, the brothers once more set off for the isolated spot where the jalopy had been hidden.

Everything looked the same as it had before, but Frank and Joe examined the ground carefully for

Frank and Joe examined the circular marks

new footprints. They found none, but Joe pointed out six-inch circular marks at regular intervals.

"They're just the size of a man's stride," he remarked, "and I didn't notice them before."

"I didn't either," said Frank. "Do you suppose that thief tied pads onto his shoes to keep him from making footprints?"

"Let's see where they lead."

The boys followed the circular marks through the thicket. They had not gone far when their eyes lighted up with excitement.

"Another clue!" Joe yelled. "And this time a swell one!"

CHAPTER IX

Rival Detectives

"MAYBE," Frank said with a grin, "Dad will take us into his camp when he sees these!"

"*Just* a minute," Joe spoke up. "I thought we were rivals now, and you and I have to solve this mystery alone to earn the reward."

Frank held up a man's battered felt hat and an old jacket. "If these belong to that thief, I think we've earned the money already!"

He felt through the pockets of the jacket, but they were empty. "No clue here," he said.

"This hat has a label, though—New York City store," said Joe.

"And the coat, too," Frank added. "Same shop. Well, one thing is sure. If they do belong to the thief, he never meant to leave them. The labels are a dead giveaway."

"He must have been frightened off," Joe concluded. "Maybe when he found that Chet's jalopy was gone, he felt he'd better scram, and forgot the coat and hat."

"What I'd like to know," Frank said, "is whether some hairs from that red wig may be in the hat."

Joe grinned. "Bright boy." He carried the hat to a spot where the sunlight filtered down through the trees and looked intently at the inside, even turning down the band. "Yowee! Success!" he yelled.

Frank gazed at two short strands of red hair. They looked exactly like those in the wig which the boys had found.

Joe sighed. "I guess we'll *have* to tell Dad about this. He has the wig."

"Right."

Frank and Joe hurried home, clutching their precious clues firmly. Mr. Hardy was still in his study when his sons returned. The detective looked up, frankly surprised to see them home so soon. There was the suspicion of a twinkle in his eyes.

"What! More clues!" he exclaimed. "You're really on the job."

"You bet we have more clues!" cried Frank eagerly. He told the boys' story and laid the hat and jacket on a table. "We're turning these over to you."

"But I thought you two were working on this case as my rivals."

"To tell the truth," said Frank, "we don't know what to do with the clue we've found. It leads to New York City."

Mr. Hardy leaned forward in his desk chair as Frank pointed out the labels and the two strands of red hair.

"And besides," Frank went on, "I guess the only way to prove that the thief owns these clothes is by comparing the hairs in the hat with the red wig. And Joe and I don't have the wig."

With a grin the detective went to his files and brought it out. "Chief Collig left this here."

The strands of hair were compared and matched perfectly!

"You boys have certainly made fine progress," Mr. Hardy praised his sons. He smiled. "And since you have, I'll let you in on a little secret. Chief Collig asked me to see what I could figure out of the wig. He says there's no maker's name on it."

"And there isn't?" Joe asked.

His father's eyes twinkled once more. "I guess Collig's assistants weren't very thorough. At any rate, I discovered there's an inner lining and on that is the maker's name. He's in New York City and I was just thinking about flying there to talk to him. Now you boys have given me a double incentive for going."

Frank and Joe beamed with pleasure, then suddenly their faces clouded.

"What's the matter?" Mr. Hardy asked them.

Joe answered. "It looks as if you're going to solve the case all alone."

"Nothing of the sort," the detective replied. "The person who bought the wig may not have given his name. The hat may have been purchased a long time ago, and it isn't likely that the clerk who sold it will remember who bought it. The same with the jacket."

Frank and Joe brightened. "Then the case is far from solved," Frank said.

"All these are good leads, however," Mr. Hardy said. "There is always the chance that the store may not be far from where the suspect lives. Though it's a slim chance, we can't afford to overlook anything. I'll take these articles to the city and see what I can do. It may mean everything and it may mean nothing. Don't be disappointed if I come back empty-handed. And don't be surprised if I come back with some valuable information."

Mr. Hardy tossed the wig, coat, and hat into a bag that was standing open near his desk. The detective was accustomed to being called away suddenly on strange errands, and he was always prepared to leave at a moment's notice.

"Not much use starting now," he said, glancing at his watch. "But I'll go to the city first thing in the morning. In the meantime, you boys keep your eyes and ears open for more clues. The case isn't over yet by any means."

Mr. Hardy picked up some papers on his desk, as a hint that the interview was over, and the boys left the study. They were in a state of high excitement when they went to bed that night and could not get to sleep.

"That thief must be pretty smart," murmured Joe, after they had talked long into the night.

"The smarter crooks are, the harder they fall," Frank replied. "If this fellow has any kind of a record, it won't take long for Dad to run him down. I've heard Dad say that there is no such thing as a clever crook. If he was really clever, he wouldn't be a crook at all."

"Yes, I guess there's something in that, too. But it shows that we're not up against any amateur. This fellow is a slippery customer."

"He'll have to be mighty slippery from now on. Once Dad has a few clues to work on he never lets up till he gets his man."

"And don't forget *us*," said Joe, yawning. With that the boys fell asleep.

When they went down to breakfast the following morning Frank and Joe learned that their father had left for New York on an early-morning plane. Their mother remarked, "I'll be so relieved when he gets back. So often these missions turn out to be dangerous."

She went on to say that her husband had promised to phone her if he wasn't going to be back by suppertime. Suddenly she added with a tantalizing smile, "Your father said he might have a surprise for you if he remains in New York."

Mrs. Hardy refused to divulge another word. The boys went to school, but all through the morning could scarcely keep their minds on studies. They kept wondering how Fenton Hardy was faring on his quest in New York and what the surprise was.

Slim Robinson was at school that day, but after classes he confided to the Hardys that he was leaving for good.

"It's no use," he said. "Dad can't keep me in school any longer and it's up to me to pitch in and help the family. I'm to start work tomorrow at a supermarket."

"And you wanted to go to college!" exclaimed Frank. "It's a shame!"

"Can't be helped," replied Perry with a grimace. "I consider myself lucky to have stayed in school this long. I'll have to give up all those college plans and settle down in the business world. There's one good thing about it—I'll have a chance to learn supermarket work from the ground up. I'm starting in the receiving department." He smiled. "Perhaps in about fifty years I'll be head of the firm!"

"You'll make good at whatever you tackle," Joe assured him. "But I'm sorry you won't be able to go through college as you planned. Don't give up hope yet, Slim. One never knows what may happen. Perhaps the thief who *did* rob Tower Mansion will be found."

Frank and Joe wanted to tell Slim about the clues they had discovered the previous day, but the same thought came into their minds—that it would be unfair to raise any false hopes. So they said good-by and wished him good luck. Perry tried hard to be cheerful, but his smile was very faint as he turned away from them and walked down the street.

"I sure feel sorry for him," said Frank, as he and Joe started for home. "He was such a hard worker in school and counted so much on going to college."

"We've just *got* to clear up the Tower robbery, that's all there is to it!" declared his brother.

As they neared the Hardy home, the boys' steps quickened. Would they find that their father had returned with the information on the identity of the thief? Or was he still in New York? And were they about to share another of his secrets?

CHAPTER X

A Sleuthing Trip

FRANK and Joe's first stop was the Hardy garage. Looking in, they saw that only Mrs. Hardy's car was there. Their father had taken his sedan to the airport and not brought it back.

"Dad's not home!" Joe cried excitedly. "Now we'll hear what the surprise is." Dashing into the kitchen, he called, "Mother!"

"I'm upstairs, dear," Mrs. Hardy called back.

The boys rushed up the front stairway two steps at a time. Their mother met them at the door of their bedroom. Smiling broadly, she pointed to a packed suitcase on Frank's bed. The boys looked puzzled.

Next, from her dress pocket, Mrs. Hardy brought out two plane tickets and some dollar bills. She handed a ticket and half the money to each of her sons, saying, "Your father wants you to meet him in New York to help him on the case."

Frank and Joe were speechless for a moment,

then they grabbed their mother in a bear hug. "This is super!" Joe exclaimed. "What a surprise!"

Frank looked affectionately at his mother. "You sure were busy today—getting our plane tickets and money. I wish you were going too."

Mrs. Hardy laughed. "When I go to New York for a week end I want to have fun with you boys, not trot around to police stations and thieves' hide-outs!" she teased. "I'll go some other time. Well, let's hurry downstairs. There's a snack ready for you. Then I'll drive my detective sons to the airport."

In less than two hours the boys were on the plane to New York City. Upon landing there, they were met by Mr. Hardy. He took them to his hotel, where he had engaged an adjoining room for them. It was not until the doors were closed that he brought up the subject of the mystery.

"The case has taken an interesting turn, and may involve considerable research. That's why I thought you might help me."

"Tell us what has happened so far," Frank requested eagerly.

Mr. Hardy said that immediately upon arriving in the city he had gone to the office of the company which had manufactured the red wig. After sending in his card to the manager he had been admitted readily.

"That's because the name of Fenton Hardy is

known from the Atlantic to the Pacific!'' Joe interjected proudly.

The detective gave his son a wink and went on
with the story. " 'Some of our customers in trouble, Mr. Hardy?' the manager asked me when I
laid the red wig on his desk.

" 'Not yet,' I said. 'But one of them may be if I
can trace the purchaser of this wig.'

"The manager picked it up. He inspected it
carefully and frowned. 'We sell mainly to an exclusive theatrical trade. I hope none of the actors
has done anything wrong.'

" 'Can you tell me who bought this one?' I asked.

" 'We make wigs only to order,' the manager
said. He pressed a button at the side of his desk. A
boy came and departed with a written message. 'It
may be difficult. This wig is not a new one. In fact,
I would say it was fashioned about two years ago.'

" 'A long time. But still—' I encouraged him,"
the detective went on. "In a few minutes a bespectacled elderly man shuffled into the office in
response to the manager's summons.

" 'Kauffman, here,' the manager said, 'is our
expert. What he doesn't know about wigs isn't
worth knowing.' Then, turning to the old man, he
handed him the red wig. 'Remember it, Kauffman?'

"The old man looked at it doubtfully. Then he
gazed at the ceiling. 'Red wig—red wig—' he muttered.

" 'About two years old, isn't it?' the manager prompted.

" 'Not quite. Year'n a half, I'd say. Looks like a comedy-character type. Wait'll I think. There ain't been so many of our customers playin' that kind of a part inside a year and a half. Let's see. Let's see.' The old man paced up and down the office, muttering names under his breath. Suddenly he stopped, snapping his fingers.

" 'I have it,' he said. 'It must have been Morley who bought that wig. That's who it was! Harold Morley. He's playin' in Shakespearean repertoire with Hamlin's company. Very fussy about his wigs. Has to have 'em just so. I remember he bought this one, because he came in here about a month ago and ordered another like it.'

" 'Why would he do that?' I asked him.

"Kauffman shrugged his shoulders. 'Ain't none of my business. Lots of actors keep a double set of wigs. Morley's playin' down at the Crescent Theater right now. Call him up.'

" 'I'll go and see him,' I told the men. And that's just what we'll do, Frank and Joe, after a bite of supper."

"You don't think this actor is the thief, do you?" Frank asked in amazement. "How could he have gone back and forth to Bayport so quickly? And isn't he playing here in town every night?"

Mr. Hardy admitted that he too was puzzled. He was certain Morley was not the man who had worn the wig on the day the jalopy was stolen, for the Shakespearean company had been playing a three weeks' run in New York. It was improbable, in any case, that the actor was a thief.

The three Hardys arrived at Mr. Morley's dressing room half an hour before curtain time. Mr. Hardy presented his card to a suspicious doorman at the Crescent, but he and his sons were finally admitted backstage and shown down a brilliantly lighted corridor to the dressing room of Harold Morley. It was a snug place, with pictures on the walls, a potted plant in the window overlooking the alleyway, and a rug on the floor.

Seated before a mirror with electric lights at either side was a stout little man, almost totally bald. He was diligently rubbing creamy stage make-up on his face. He did not turn around, but eyed his visitors in the mirror, casually telling them to sit down. Mr. Hardy took the only chair. The boys squatted on the floor.

"Often heard of you, Mr. Hardy," the actor said in a surprisingly deep voice that had a comical effect in contrast to his diminutive appearance. "Glad to meet you. What kind of call is this? Social —or professional?"

"Professional."

Morley continued rubbing the make-up on his jowls. "Out with it," he said briefly.

"Ever see this wig before?" Mr. Hardy asked

him, laying the hair piece on the make-up table.

Morley turned from the mirror, and an expression of delight crossed his plump countenance. "Well, I'll say I've seen it before!" he declared. "Old Kauffman—the best wigmaker in the country —made this for me about a year and a half ago. Where did you get it? I sure didn't think I'd ever see this red wig again."

"Why?"

"Stolen from me. Some low-down sneak got in here and cleaned out my dressing room one night during the performance. Nerviest thing I ever heard of. Came right in here while I was doing my stuff out front, grabbed my watch and money and a diamond ring I had lying by the mirror, took this wig and a couple of others that were around, and beat it. Nobody saw him come or go. Must have got in by that window."

Morley talked in short, rapid sentences, and there was no mistaking his sincerity.

"All the wigs were red," he stated. "I didn't worry so much about the other wigs, because they were for old plays, but this one was being used right along. Kauffman made it specially for me. I had to get him to make another. But say—where did you find it?"

"Oh, my sons located it during some detective work we're on. The crook left this behind. I was trying to trace him by it."

Morley did not inquire further. "That's all the help I can give you," he said. "The police never did learn who cleaned out my dressing room."

"Too bad. Well, I'll probably get him some other way. Give me a list and description of the articles he took from you. Probably I can trace him through that."

"Glad to," said Morley. He reached into a drawer and drew out a sheet of paper which he handed to the detective. "That's the same list I gave the police when I reported the robbery. Number of the watch, and everything. I didn't bother to mention the wigs. Figured they wouldn't be in any condition to wear if I did get them back."

Mr. Hardy folded the list and put it in his pocket. Morley glanced at his watch, lying face up beside the mirror, and gave an exclamation. "Suffering Sebastopol! Curtain in five minutes and I'm not half made up yet. Excuse me, folks, but I've got to get on my horse. In this business 'I'll be ready in a minute' doesn't go."

He seized a stick of grease paint and feverishly resumed the task of altering his appearance to that of the character he was portraying at that evening's performance. Mr. Hardy and his sons left. They made their way out to the street.

"Not much luck there," Frank commented.

"Except through Mr. Morley's stolen jewelry," his father reminded him. "If that's located in a pawnshop, it may lead to the thief. Well, boys, would you like to go into the theater via the front entrance and see the show?"

"Yes, Dad," the brothers replied, and Joe added, "Tomorrow we'll try to find out the name and address of the thief through his coat and hat?"

"Right," the detective said.

The Hardys enjoyed the performance of *The Merchant of Venice* with Mr. Morley as Launcelot Gobbo, and laughed hilariously at his comedy and gestures.

The next morning the detective and his sons visited the store from which the thief's jacket and hat had been purchased. They were told that the styles were three years out of date and there was no way to tell who had bought them.

"The articles," the head of the men's suit department suggested, "may have been picked up more recently at a secondhand clothing store." The Hardys thanked him and left.

"All this trip for nothing." Joe gave a sigh.

His father laid a hand on the boy's shoulder. "A good detective," he said, "never sighs with discouragement nor becomes impatient. It took years of persistence to solve some famous cases."

He suggested that their next effort be devoted to doing some research in the city's police files. Since Mr. Hardy had formerly been a member of the New York City detective force, he was permitted to search the records at any time.

Frank and Joe accompanied him to headquarters and the work began. First came a run-down on any known New York criminals who used disguises. Of these men, the Hardys took the reports on the ones who were thin and of medium height.

Next came a check by telephone on the whereabouts of these people. All could be accounted for as working some distance from Bayport at the time of the thefts, with one exception.

"I'll bet he's our man!" Frank exclaimed. "But where is he now?"

CHAPTER XI

Anxious Waiting

THE suspect, the Hardys learned, was out of prison on parole. His name was John Jackley, but he was known as Red Jackley because when caught before going to prison he had been wearing a red wig.

"He lives right here in New York, and maybe he's back home by this time," Joe spoke up. "Let's go see him."

"Just a minute," Mr. Hardy said, holding up his hand. "I don't like to leave Mother alone so long. Besides, in this type of sleuthing three detectives together are too noticeable to a crook. This Jackley may or may not be our man. But if he is, he's probably dangerous. I want you boys to take the evening plane home. I'll phone the house the minute the thief is in custody."

"All right, Dad," his sons chorused, though secretly disappointed that they had to leave.

When they reached home, Frank and Joe learned that their mother had been working on the case from a completely different angle. Hers was the humanitarian side.

"I went to call on the Robinsons to try to bolster their spirits," she said. "I told them about your trip to New York and that seemed to cheer them a lot. Monday I'm going to bake a ham and a cake for you to take to them. Mrs. Robinson isn't well and can do little in the kitchen."

"That's swell of you!" Frank said admiringly. "I'll go."

Joe told them he had a tennis match to play. "I'll do the next errand," he promised.

Monday, during a change of classes, Frank met Callie Shaw in the corridor. "Hi!" she said. "What great problem is on Detective Hardy's mind? You look as if you'd lost your best criminal!"

Frank grimaced. "Maybe I have," he said.

He told Callie that he had phoned home at noon confidently expecting to hear that his father had reported the arrest of the real thief of the Applegate money and the exoneration of Mr. Robinson. "But there was no word, Callie, and I'm worried Dad may be in danger."

"I don't blame you," she said. "What do you think has happened?"

"Well, you never can tell when you're dealing with criminals."

"Now, Frank, you're not trying to tell me your

father would let himself get trapped?" Callie said.

"No, I don't think he would, Callie. Maybe Dad hasn't returned because he still hasn't found the man he was looking for."

"Well, I certainly hope that thief is caught," said Callie. "But, Frank, nobody really believes Mr. Robinson did it!"

"Nobody but Hurd Applegate and the men who employ people. Until they find the man who *did* take the stuff, Mr. Robinson is out of a job."

"I'm going over to see the Robinsons soon. Where are they living?"

Frank gave Callie the address. Her eyes widened. "Why, that's in one of the poorest sections of the city! Frank, I had no idea the Robinsons' plight was that bad!"

"It is—and it'll be a lot worse unless Mr. Robinson gets work pretty soon. Slim's earnings aren't enough to take care of the whole family. Say, Callie, how about going over to the Robinsons' with me after school? Mother's sending a ham and a cake."

"I'd love to," Callie agreed. The two parted at the door of the algebra teacher's classroom.

As soon as the last bell had rung, Frank and Callie left the building together. First they stopped at the Shaw house to leave the girl's books.

"I think I'll take some fruit to the Robinsons," Callie said, and quickly filled a bag with oranges, bananas, and grapes.

When the couple reached the Hardy home, Frank asked his mother if any messages had come. "No, not yet," she answered.

Frank said nothing to her about being concerned over his father, as he tucked the ham under one arm and picked up the cakebox. But after he and Callie reached the street, he again confided his concern to Callie.

"It does seem strange you haven't heard anything," she admitted. "But don't forget the old saying, 'No news is good news,' so don't worry."

"I'll take your advice," Frank agreed. "No use wearing a sour look around the Robinsons."

"Or when you're with me, either," Callie said, tossing her head teasingly.

Frank hailed an approaching bus bound for the section of the city in which the Robinsons lived. He and Callie climbed aboard. It was a long ride and the streets became less attractive as they neared the outskirts of Bayport.

"It's a shame, that's what it is!" declared Callie abruptly. "The Robinsons were always accustomed to having everything so nice! And now they have to live here! Oh, I hope your father catches the man who committed that robbery—and soon!"

Her eyes flashed and for a moment she looked so fierce that Frank laughed.

"I suppose you'd like to be the judge and jury at his trial, eh?"

"I'd give him a hundred years in jail!" Callie declared.

When they came to the street where the Robinsons had moved they found that it was an even poorer thoroughfare than they had expected. There were small houses badly in need of paint and repairs. Shabbily dressed children were playing in the roadway.

At the far end of the street stood a small cottage that somehow contrived to look homelike in spite of the surroundings. The picket fence had been repaired and the yard had been cleaned up.

"This is where they live," said Frank.

Callie smiled. "It's the neatest place on the whole street."

Paula and Tessie answered their knock. The twins' faces lighted up with pleasure when they saw who the callers were.

"Frank and Callie!" they exclaimed. "Come in."

The callers were greeted with kindly dignity by Mrs. Robinson. She looked pale and thin but had the same self-possession she had always shown at Tower Mansion.

"We can't stay long," Callie explained. "But Frank and I just thought we'd run out to see how you all are. And we brought something for you."

The fruit, ham, and cake were presented. As the twins ohed and ahed over the food, Mrs. Robinson's eyes filled with tears. "You are dear people," she said. "Frank, tell your mother I can't thank her enough."

Frank grinned as Mrs. Robinson went on, "Callie, we shall enjoy this fruit very much. Many thanks."

Paula said, "It's a wonderful gift. Say, did you know Perry got a better job the second day he was at the supermarket?"

"No. That's swell," Frank replied. "It didn't take the manager long to find out how smart Slim is, eh?"

The twins giggled, but Mrs. Robinson said dolefully, "I wish my husband could find a job. Since no one around here will employ him, he is thinking of going to another city to get work."

"And leave you here?"

"I suppose so. We don't know what to do."

"It's so unfair!" Paula flared up. "My father didn't have a thing to do with that miserable robbery, and yet he has to suffer for it just the same!"

Mrs. Robinson said to Frank hesitantly, "Has Mr. Hardy discovered anything—yet?"

"I don't know," Frank admitted. "We haven't heard from him. He's been in New York following up some clues. But so far there's been no word."

"We hardly dare hope that he'll be able to clear Mr. Robinson," the woman said sorrowfully. "The whole case is so mysterious."

"I've stopped thinking of it," Tessie declared. "If the mystery is cleared up, okay. If it isn't—we won't starve, at any rate, and my father knows *we* believe in him."

"Yes, I suppose it doesn't do much good to keep talking about it," agreed Mrs. Robinson. "We've gone over the whole matter so thoroughly that there is nothing more to say."

So, by tacit consent, the subject was changed and for the rest of their stay Frank and Callie chatted of doings at school. Mrs. Robinson and the girls invited them to remain for supper, but Callie insisted that she must go. As they were leaving, Mrs. Robinson drew Frank to one side.

"Promise me one thing," she said. "Let me know as soon as your father returns—that is, if he has any news."

"I'll do that, Mrs. Robinson," Frank agreed. "I know what this suspense must be like for you and the twins."

"It's terrible. But as long as Fenton Hardy—and his sons—are working on the case, I'm sure it will be straightened out."

Callie and Frank were unusually silent all the way home. They had been profoundly affected by the change that the Tower Mansion mystery had caused in the lives of the Robinsons. Callie lived but a few blocks from the Hardy home, and Frank accompanied her to the door.

"See you tomorrow," he said.

"Yes, Frank. And I hope you'll hear good news from your father."

The boy quickened his steps and ran eagerly into the Hardy house. Joe met him.

"Any phone call?"

Joe shook his head. "Mother's pretty worried that something has happened to Dad."

CHAPTER XII

A Disturbing Absence

ANOTHER whole day went by. When still no word had come from Mr. Hardy, his wife phoned the New York hotel. She was told that the detective had checked out the day before.

Discouraged and nervous about the new mystery of their father's disappearance, Frank and Joe found it almost impossible to concentrate on their studies.

Then, the following morning when Mrs. Hardy came to awaken them, she wore a broad smile. "Your father is home!" she said excitedly. "He's all right but has had a bad time. He's asleep now and will tell you everything after school."

The boys were wild with impatience to learn the outcome of his trip, but they were obliged to curb their curiosity.

"Dad must be mighty tired," Joe remarked, as Mrs. Hardy went downstairs to start breakfast. "I wonder where he came from."

"Probably he was up all night. When he's working on a case, he forgets about sleep. Do you think he found out anything?"

"Hope so, Frank. I wish he'd wake up and tell us. I hate to go back to school without knowing."

But Mr. Hardy had not awakened by the time the boys set out for school, although they lingered until they were in danger of being late. As soon as classes were over, they shattered all records in their race home.

Fenton Hardy was in the living room, and as they rushed in panting, he grinned broadly. He looked refreshed after his long sleep and it was evident that his trip had not been entirely without success, for his manner was cheerful.

"Hello, boys! Sorry I worried you and Mother."

"What luck, Dad?" asked Frank.

"Good and bad. Here's the story: I went to the house where Red Jackley was boarding. Although he seemed to be an exemplary parolee, I decided to watch him a while and try to make friends."

"How could you do that?"

"By taking a room in the same house and pretending to be a fellow criminal."

"Wow!" Joe cried. "And then?"

"Jackley himself spoiled everything. He got mixed up in a jewel robbery and cleared out of the city. Luckily, I heard him packing, and I trailed him. The police were watching for him and he couldn't get out of town by plane or bus. He outwitted the police by jumping a freight on the railroad."

"And you still followed?"

"I lost him two or three times, but fortunately I managed to pick up his trail again. He got out of the city and into upper New York State. Then his luck failed him. A railroad detective recognized Jackley and the chase was on. Up to that time I had been content with just keeping behind him. I had still hoped to pose as a fellow fugitive and win his confidence. But when the pursuit started in earnest, I had to join the officers."

"And they caught Jackley?"

"Not without great difficulty. Jackley, by the way, was once a railroad man. Strangely enough, he worked not many miles from here. He managed to steal a railroad handcar and got away from us. But he didn't last long, for the handcar jumped the tracks on a curve and Jackley was badly smashed up."

"Killed?" Frank asked quickly.

"No. But he's in a hospital right now and the doctors say he hasn't much of a chance."

"He's under arrest?"

"Oh, yes. He's being held for the jewel thefts and also for the theft from the actor's dressing room. But he probably won't live to answer either charge."

"Didn't you find out anything that would connect him with the Tower robbery?"

"Not a thing."

The boys were disappointed, and their expressions showed it. If Red Jackley died without confessing, the secret of the Tower robbery would die with him. Mr. Robinson might never be cleared. He might be doomed to spend the rest of his life under a cloud, suspected of being a thief.

"Have you talked to Jackley?" Frank asked.

"I didn't have a chance—he wasn't conscious."

"Then you may never be able to get a confession from him."

Fenton Hardy shrugged. "I *may* be able to. If Jackley regains consciousness and knows he's going to die, he may admit everything. I intend to see him in the hospital and ask him about the Tower robbery."

"Is he far away?"

"Albany. I explained my mission to the doctor in charge and he promised to telephone me as soon as it was possible for Jackley to see anyone."

"You say he used to work near here?" Joe asked.

"He was once employed by the railroad, and he knows all the country around here well. Then he became mixed up in some thefts from freight cars, and after he got out of jail, turned professional criminal. I suppose he came back here because he is so familiar with this area."

"I promised to call Mrs. Robinson," Frank spoke up. "Okay to tell her about Jackley?"

"Yes, it may cheer her up. But ask her not to tell anyone."

Frank dialed the number and relayed part of his father's story. The accused man's wife was overwhelmed and relieved by the news, but promised not to divulge the information. Just as Frank finished the call, the doorbell rang. Frank ushered in the private detective Oscar Smuff.

"Your pa home?" he asked.

"Yes. Come in." Frank led the way into the living room.

Smuff, although he considered himself a topnotch sleuth, stood in awe of Fenton Hardy. He cleared his throat nervously.

"Good afternoon, Oscar," said Mr. Hardy pleasantly. "Won't you sit down?"

Detective Smuff eased himself into an armchair, then glanced inquiringly at the two boys. At once Mr. Hardy said, "Unless your business is *very* private, I'd like to have my sons stay."

"Well, I reckon that'll be all right," Smuff conceded. "I hear you're working on this Applegate case."

"Perhaps I am."

"You've been out of town several days," Smuff remarked cannily, "so I deduced you must be workin' on it."

"Very clever of you, Detective Smuff," Mr. Hardy said, smiling at his visitor.

Smuff squirmed uneasily in his chair. "I'm workin' on this case too—I'd like to get that thousand-dollar reward, but I'd share it with you. I was just wonderin' if you'd found any clues."

Mr. Hardy's smile faded. He said, with annoyance, "If I went away, it is my own business. And if I'm working on the Tower robbery, that also is my business. You'll have to find your own clues, Oscar."

"Well, now, don't get on your high horse, Mr. Hardy," the visitor remonstrated. "I'm just anxious to get this affair cleared up and I thought we might work together. I heard you were with the officers what chased this here notorious criminal Red Jackley."

Mr. Hardy gave a perceptible start. He had no idea that news of the capture of Jackley had reached Bayport, much less that his own participation in the chase had become known. The local police must have received the information and somehow Smuff had heard the news.

"What of it?" Mr. Hardy asked in a casual way.

"Did Jackley have anything to do with the Tower case?"

"How should I know?"

"Wasn't that what you were workin' on?"

"As I've told you, that's my affair."

Detective Smuff looked sad. "I guess you just don't want to co-operate with me, Mr. Hardy. I was thinkin' of goin' over to the hospital where this man Jackley is and questionin' him about the case."

Mr. Hardy's lips narrowed into a straight line. "You can't do that, Oscar. He isn't conscious. The doctor won't let you see him."

"I'm goin' to try. Jackley'll come to some time and I want to be on hand. There's a plane at six o'clock, and I aim to leave my house about five-thirty and catch it." He thumped his chest in admiration. "Detectives don't have to show up for a plane till the last minute, eh, Mr. Hardy? Well, I'll have a talk with Jackley tonight. And I may let you know what he says."

"Have it your own way," said Mr. Hardy. "But if you take my advice you'll not visit the hospital. You'll just spoil everything. Jackley will talk when the times comes."

"So there is somethin' in it!" Smuff said triumphantly. "Well, I'm goin' over there and get a confession!" With that he arose, stumped out of the room, and left the house.

CHAPTER XIII

Teamwork

AFTER Smuff left the house, Mr. Hardy sat back with a gesture of despair. "That man," he said, "handles an investigation so clumsily that Red Jackley will close up like a clam if Smuff manages to question him."

At that moment the telephone rang. The boys listened excitedly as Mr. Hardy answered. "Hello. . . . Oh, yes, doctor. . . . Is that so? . . . Jackley will probably live only until morning? . . . I can see him. . . . Fine. . . . Thank you. Good-by."

The detective put back the receiver and turned to the boys. "I'll take that six-o'clock plane to Albany. But if Smuff goes too, it may ruin everything. The Albany police and I must question Jackley first."

"When's the next commercial flight after six?" Joe asked.

"Seven o'clock."

"Then," said Frank, "Smuff can take that one and question Jackley later. Come on, Joe. Let's see what we can do to help Dad!"

"Don't you boys do anything rash," their father warned.

"We won't."

Frank led the way outdoors and started walking down the street.

"What's on your mind?" Joe asked as they reached the corner.

"We must figure out how to keep Detective Smuff in Bayport until seven o'clock."

"But how?"

"I don't know yet, but we'll find a way. We can't have him bursting into that hospital room and spoiling the chance of Dad's getting a confession. Smuff might ruin things so the case will never be solved."

"You're right."

The brothers walked along the street in silence. They realized that the situation was urgent. But though they racked their brains trying to think of a way to prevent Detective Smuff from catching the six-o'clock plane, it seemed hopeless.

"Let's round up our gang," Joe suggested finally. "Perhaps they'll have some ideas."

The Hardys found their friends on the tennis courts of Bayport High.

"Hi, fellows!" called Chet Morton when he saw

Frank and Joe approaching. "You're too late for a game. Where've you been?"

"We had something important to do," Frank replied. "Say, we need your help."

"What's the matter?" asked Tony Prito.

"Oscar Smuff is trying to win that thousand-dollar reward and get himself on the Bayport police force by interfering in one of Dad's cases," Frank explained. "We can't tell you much more than that. But the main thing is, we want to keep him from catching the six-o'clock plane. We—er— don't want him to go until seven."

"What do you want us to do?" Bill Hooper asked.

"Help us figure out how to keep Smuff in Bayport until seven o'clock."

"Without having Chief Collig lock us up?" Jerry Gilroy put in. "Are you serious about this, Frank?"

"Absolutely. If Smuff gets to a certain place before Dad can, the case will be ruined. And I don't mind telling you that it has something to do with Slim Robinson."

Chet Morton whistled. "Oh, ho! I catch on. The Tower business. If that's it, we'll make sure the six-o'clock plane leaves here without that nutty detective." Chet had a special dislike for Smuff, because the man had once reported him for swimming in the bay after hours.

"So our problem," said Phil solemnly, "is to

keep Smuff here and keep out of trouble ourselves."

"Right."

"Well," Jerry Gilroy said, "let's put our heads together, fellows, and work out a plan."

A dozen ideas were put forth, each wilder than the one before. Biff Hooper, with a wide grin, went so far as to propose kidnaping Smuff, binding him hand and foot, and setting him adrift in the bay in an open boat.

"We could rescue him later," he said. The proposal was so ridiculous that the others howled with laughter.

Phil Cohen suggested setting the detective's watch back an hour. That plan, as Frank observed, was a good one except for the minor difficulty of laying hands on the watch.

"We might send him a warning not to take a plane before seven o'clock," Tony Prito said, "and sign it with a skull and crossbones."

"That's a keen idea!" Chet cried enthusiastically. "Let's do it!"

"Wait a minute, fellows," Frank spoke up. "If Smuff ever found out who wrote it, we'd be up to our necks in trouble. We could all be arrested!"

"I know!" Joe cried suddenly, snapping his fingers. "Why didn't I think of it before? And it's so simple, too."

"Well, tell us!" Frank urged.

Joe explained that every once in a while he and Frank went down to Rocco's fruit store to act as clerks while the owner went home to supper. He stayed open evenings until nine.

"Rocco's is only a block from Smuff's house. Smuff knows Frank and I go there, so he wouldn't be surprised to see us in the neighborhood. I suggest that the bunch of us meet casually down near the store and one boy after another stop Smuff to talk. Maybe we can even get him into the shop. You know Smuff loves to eat."

"You can't hate him for that," Chet spoke up. "I'll be glad to invite him in and buy him an apple for his trip."

"A fifteen-minute delay for Smuff is all we need," Frank said.

"I think it's a swell idea," Biff spoke up. "And I'm sure Mr. Rocco will co-operate."

"Who's going to persuade him?" Phil asked.

"That's Frank and Joe's department," Jerry replied.

Rocco was a hard-working man who had come from Italy only a few years ago. He was a simple, genial person and had great admiration for the Hardy boys.

The whole group made their way toward the fruit store, but only the Hardys went inside. The others spread out to watch for Smuff, who was expected to leave his house soon. Each boy went over his part in the plan.

When Frank and Joe walked into the fruit store, they found the dark-eyed Rocco sorting oranges. *"Buona sera,"* he said. "Good evening. How you like my fix the place?"

"Looks swell," Frank answered. "New bins. Better lights." Then he added, "How does your neighbor Smuff like it?"

Rocco threw up his hands in a gesture of disgust. "Oh, that man! He make me mad. He say I charge too much. He tell me I ought to go back to old country."

"Don't pay any attention to him," Joe advised. "Say, Mr. Rocco," he went on, "you look tired. Why don't you go home for an hour or so and let Frank and me take over here?"

"You think I look tired? That worry my wife. Then Rosa say I must close up early." Rocco sighed. "You very kind boys. I do what you say. Come back six-thirty."

As Rocco removed his apron, he said, "I fix trash in yard to burn. You do that?"

"Glad to."

Rocco showed them a wire incinerator in the yard, then left the store. Five minutes later there was a whistle from the street. A signal from Jerry! Frank and Joe went to the front door to watch. Smuff was just backing his car out of the driveway. As prearranged, Phil hurried over and stopped him.

The detective and the boy apparently got into

an argument, but it did not last long enough to satisfy Frank and Joe. The conversation took less than two minutes, then Smuff backed around into the street.

"Hey, Frank," said Joe, "I have an idea. Go light that trash. Make it a roaring fire!"

Without further explanation he dashed into the street, but Frank figured out what was in his brother's mind. He dashed through the store and into the yard. Quickly he lighted the papers in the incinerator in several places. The rubbish blazed lustily.

Joe was intently watching the scene down the street. Smuff was now being "interviewed" by Biff, and Chet came forward to urge Smuff to take some fruit with him on his trip. The detective hesitated, then shook his head and started off in his car.

Only five of the necessary fifteen-minute delay had elapsed! Joe hesitated no longer. Running down the street, he held up one hand for the oncoming car to stop.

"Come quick, Smuff!" he called out. "There's a fire back of Rocco's!"

"Well, you put it out. I'm in a hurry!" the detective told the boy tartly.

"You mean you'd let all of Bayport burn down just because you're in a hurry?" Joe pretended to scoff.

Smuff winced, but still did not move. Joe said,

"Where's the fire?" Smuff cried out

starting back to the store, "Well, Frank and I will have to take care of it alone."

This brought the detective to action. He realized he might be missing a chance to become a hero! In a flash he drove his car down the street and parked in front of the fruit store.

"Where's the fire?" Smuff cried out, nearly bumping into Frank who was dashing from the front door of Rocco's.

"The fire—is—back there—in the yard." Frank pretended to pant. "You go look and see if we ought to turn in an alarm."

Smuff dashed inside the store and hurried to the yard. By this time the Hardys' friends had gathered in Rocco's fruit store. They asked excitedly what was going on.

"Frank! Joe!" yelled Smuff from the rear of the store. "Where's Rocco? Where's a pail? Where's some water?"

CHAPTER XIV

The Confession

"Rocco's not around," Joe replied to Smuff. "There's water in the sink—in the back. Shall I call the fire department?"

"No, I can manage this," Smuff declared. "But where's a pail?"

Frank dashed into the back room and found a pail under the sink. He filled it with water and handed the pail to Smuff, who hurried to the yard. He doused the incinerator flames which hissed and crackled, then died.

"Some people have no sense," Smuff commented. "The idea of anyone starting a fire, then going off and leaving it! I'll bet that was Rocco's work! As for you boys—you had to call me. Didn't have the savvy to put out a simple fire."

"Good thing you were around," Frank observed, suppressing a smile.

"I'll say it was," Smuff agreed. "And Chief Collig is sure goin' to hear about this."

"Oh, please don't tell him about us," Joe spoke up, half closing his eyes so Smuff could not see the twinkle in them.

"I didn't mean that. Oscar Smuff is no squealer. I mean Collig is goin' to hear what *I* did." The detective chuckled. "One more notch in my gun, as the cowboys say."

Suddenly Smuff sobered and looked at his wrist watch. "Oh, no!" he cried out. "Ten minutes to six! I can't make my plane!"

"That's a shame," Frank said consolingly. "But cheer up, Smuff, there's a seven-o'clock plane for Albany. I wish you luck in your interview."

Smuff stormed out of the fruit store and disappeared with his car. The Hardys and their friends burst into roars of laughter which did not stop until a woman customer came into the shop. All the boys but Frank and Joe left.

Rocco returned at six-thirty, pleased that so much fruit had been sold during his absence. "You better salesman than Rocco." He grinned widely.

The Hardys went home, well-satisfied with their day's work. The six-o'clock plane had left without Smuff. Their father could make his trip to the hospital without the annoying detective's interference.

Fenton Hardy did not return home until the

next afternoon. When the boys came from school they found him in high spirits.

"Solved the mystery?" Joe asked eagerly.

"Practically. First of all, Jackley is dead."

"Did he confess?"

"You're not very sympathetic toward the poor fellow, Joe. Yes, he confessed. Fortunately, Oscar Smuff didn't show up while Jackley was talking."

Frank and Joe glanced at each other and their father smiled quietly. "I have an idea," he said, "that you two sleuths know more about this Smuff business than you would care to tell. Well, anyhow, the Albany police and I had a clear field. I saw Jackley before he died and questioned him about the Tower robbery."

"Did he admit everything?"

"Jackley said he came to Bayport with the intention of robbery. He stole a car, smashed it up, and took Chet's. Then he went to rob the ticket office. When he failed in that he decided to hang around town for a few days. He hit upon Tower Mansion as his next effort. Jackley entered the library with gloves on, opened the safe, and took out the jewelry and securities."

"What did he do with the loot?"

"That's what I'm coming to. It was not until Jackley knew he was at the point of death that he did confess to the Tower affair. Then he said, 'Yes, I took the stuff—but I didn't dare try selling any of it right away, so I hid it. You can get all the stuff back easily. It's in the old tower—'

"That was all he said. Jackley lost consciousness then and never regained it."

"When did Smuff get there?" Joe asked eagerly.

"Not until after Jackley had gone into a coma," Mr. Hardy replied. "We both sat by his bed, hoping the man would awaken, but he died within an hour. Just where Jackley hid the loot in the old tower, he was never able to say."

"Does Smuff know what Jackley said?"

"No."

"If the loot's hidden in the old Applegate tower, we'll find it in no time!" Frank exclaimed.

"Tower Mansion has two towers—the old and the new," Joe reminded him.

"We'll search the old tower first."

"The story seems likely enough," Mr. Hardy remarked. "Jackley would gain nothing by lying about it on his deathbed. He probably became panicky after he committed the robbery and hid in the old tower until he was able to get away safely. No doubt he decided to hide the stuff there and take a chance on coming back for it some time after the affair had blown over."

Joe nodded. "That was why Jackley couldn't be traced through the jewels and the bonds. They were never disposed of—they've been lying in the old tower all this time!"

"I tried to get him to tell me in just what part of the tower the loot was hidden," Mr. Hardy continued, "but he died before he could say any more."

"Too bad," said Frank. "But it shouldn't be hard to find the loot, now that we have a general idea where it is. Probably Jackley didn't hide it very carefully. Since the old tower has been unoccupied for a long time, the stuff would be safe there from snoopers."

Joe jumped up from his chair. "I think we ought to get busy and go search the old tower right away. Oh, boy! Maybe we can hand old Mr. Applegate his jewels and bonds this afternoon and clear Mr. Robinson! Let's go!"

"I'll leave it to you boys to make the search," said Mr. Hardy with a smile. "Then you can have the satisfaction of turning over the stolen property to Mr. Applegate. I guess you can get along without me in this case from now on."

"We wouldn't have got very far if it hadn't been for you," Frank declared.

"And I wouldn't have got very far if it hadn't been for you, so we're even." Mr. Hardy's smile broadened. "Well, good luck to you."

As the boys started from the study, Frank said, "Thanks, Dad. I only hope the Applegates don't throw us out when we ask to be allowed to look around inside the old tower."

"Just tell them," his father advised, "that you have a pretty good clue to where the bonds and jewels are hidden and they'll let you search."

Joe grinned. "Frank, we'll have that thousand-dollar reward before the day is over!"

The brothers raced from the house, confident that they were about to solve the Tower Treasure mystery.

CHAPTER XV

The Tower Search

WHEN the Hardy boys reached Tower Mansion at four o'clock the door was opened by Hurd Applegate himself. The tall, stooped gentleman peered at them through his thick-lensed glasses. In one hand he held a sheet of stamps.

"Yes?" he said, seemingly annoyed at being disturbed.

"You remember us, don't you?" Frank asked politely. "We're Mr. Hardy's sons."

"Fenton Hardy, the detective? Oh, yes. Well, what do you want?"

"We'd like to look through the old tower, if you don't mind. We have a clue about the robbery."

"What kind of clue?"

"We have evidence that leads us to believe the jewels and bonds were hidden by the thief in the old tower."

"Oh! You have evidence, have you?" The elderly man peered at the boys closely. "It's that rascal Robinson, I'll warrant, who gave it to you. He hid the stuff, and now he's suggesting where you might find it, just to clear himself."

Frank and Joe had not considered the affair in this light, and they gazed at Mr. Applegate in consternation. At last Joe spoke up.

"Mr. Robinson has nothing to do with this," he said. "The real thief was found. He said the loot was hidden in the old tower. If you will just let us take a look around, we'll find it for you."

"Who was the real thief?"

"We'd rather not tell you, sir, until we find the stolen property, then we'll reveal the whole story."

Mr. Applegate took off his glasses and wiped them with his handkerchief. He stared at the boys suspiciously for a few moments. Then he called out:

"Adelia!"

From the dim interior of the hallway a high feminine voice answered.

"What do you want?"

"Come here a minute."

There was a rustle of skirts, and Adelia Applegate appeared. A faded blond woman of thin features, she was dressed in a fashion of fifteen years before, in which every color of the spectrum fought for supremacy.

"What's the matter?" she demanded. "I can't sit down to do a bit of sewing without you interrupting me, Hurd."

"These boys want to look through the old tower."

"What for? Up to some mischief?"

Frank and Joe feared she would not give her consent. Frank said quietly, "We're doing some work for our dad, the detective Fenton Hardy."

"They think they can find the bonds and jewels in the tower," Hurd Applegate explained.

"Oh, they do, do they?" the woman said icily. "And what would the bonds and jewels be doing in the old tower?"

"We have evidence that they were hidden there after the robbery," Frank told her.

Miss Applegate viewed the boys with obvious suspicion. "As if any thief would be silly enough to hide them right in the house he robbed!" she said in a tone of finality.

"We're just trying to help you," Joe put in courteously.

"Go ahead, then," said Miss Applegate with a sigh. "But even if you tear the old tower to pieces, you won't find anything. It's all foolishness."

Frank and Joe followed Hurd Applegate through the gloomy halls and corridors that led toward the old tower. He said he was inclined to share his sister's opinion that the boys' search would be in vain.

"We'll make a try at it, anyway, Mr. Applegate," Frank said.

"Don't ask me to help you. I've got a bad knee. Anyway, I just received some new stamps this afternoon. You interrupted me when I was sorting them. I must get back to my work."

The man reached a corridor that was heavily covered with dust. It apparently had not been in use for a long time and was bare and unfurnished. At the end was a heavy door. It was unlocked, and when Mr. Applegate opened it, the boys saw a square room. Almost in the center of it rose a flight of wooden stairs with a heavily ornamented balustrade. The stairway twisted and turned to the roof, five floors above. Opening from each floor was a room.

"There you are," Mr. Applegate announced. "Search all you want to. But you won't find anything—of that I'm certain."

With this parting remark he turned and hobbled back along the corridor, the sheet of stamps still in his gnarled hand.

The Hardy boys looked at each other. "Not very encouraging, is he?" Joe remarked.

"He doesn't deserve to get his stuff back," Frank declared flatly, then shrugged. "Let's get up into the tower and start the search."

Frank and Joe first examined the dusty stairs carefully for footprints, but none were to be seen.

"That seems queer," Frank remarked. "If Jackley was here recently you'd think his footprints would still show. Judging by this dust, there hasn't been anyone in the tower for at least a year."

"Perhaps the dust collects more quickly than we think," Joe countered. "Or the wind may get in here and blow it around."

An inspection of the first floor of the old tower revealed that there was no place where the loot could have been hidden except under the stairs. But they found nothing there.

The boys ascended to the next floor, and entered the room to the left of the stair well. It was as drab and bare as the one they had just left. Here again the dust lay thick and the murky windows were almost obscured with cobwebs. There was an atmosphere of age and decay about the entire place, as if it had been abandoned for years.

"Nothing here," said Frank after a quick glance around. "On we go."

They made their way up to the next floor. After searching this room and under the stairway, they had to admit defeat.

The floor above was a duplicate of the first and second. It was bare and cheerless, deep in dust. There was not the slightest sign of a hiding place, or any indication that another human being had been in the tower for a long time.

"Doesn't look very promising, Joe. Still, Jackley may have gone right to the top of the tower."

The search continued without success until the

boys reached the roof. Here a trap door which swung inward led to the top of the tower. Frank unlatched it and pulled on the door. It did not budge.

"I'll help you," Joe offered.

Together the brothers yanked on the stubborn trap door of the old tower. Suddenly it gave way completely, causing both boys to lose their balance. Frank fell backward down the stairway.

Joe, with a cry, toppled over the railing into space!

Frank grabbed a spindle of the balustrade and kept himself from sliding farther down the steps. He had seen Joe's plunge and expected the next moment to hear a sickening thud on the floor five stories below.

"Joe!" he murmured as he pulled himself upright. "Oh, Joe!"

To Frank's amazement, he heard no thud and now looked over the balustrade. His brother was not lying unconscious at the bottom of the tower. Instead, he was clinging to two spindles of the stairway on the floor below.

Frank, heaving a tremendous sigh of relief, ran down and helped pull Joe to the safety of the steps. Both boys sat down to catch their breaths and recover from their falls.

Finally Joe said, "Thanks. For a second I sure thought I was going to end my career as a detective right here!"

"I guess you can also thank our gym teacher for the tricks he taught you on the bars," Frank remarked. "You must have grabbed those spindles with flash-camera speed."

Presently the boys turned their eyes upward. An expression halfway between a grin and a worried frown crossed their faces.

"Mr. Applegate," Joe remarked, "isn't going to like hearing we ruined his trap door."

"No. Let's see if we can put it back in place."

The boys climbed the stairway and examined the damage. They found that the hinges had pulled away from rotted wood. A new piece would have to be put in to hold the door in place.

"Before we go downstairs," said Joe, "let's look out on the roof. We thought maybe the loot was hidden there. Remember?"

Frank and Joe climbed outside to a narrow, rail-inged walk that ran around the four sides of the square tower. There was nothing on it.

"Our only reward for all this work is a good view of Bayport," Frank remarked ruefully.

Below lay the bustling little city, and to the east was Barmet Bay, its waters sparkling in the late afternoon.

"Dad was fooled by Jackley, I guess," Frank said slowly. "There hasn't been anyone in this tower for years."

The boys gazed moodily over the city, then down at the grounds of Tower Mansion. The many roofs of the house itself were far below, and directly across from them rose the heavy bulk of the new tower.

"Do you think Jackley might have meant the *new* tower?" Joe exclaimed suddenly.

"Dad said he specified the old one."

"But he may have been mistaken. Even the new one looks old. Let's ask Mr. Applegate if we may search the new tower, too."

"It's worth trying, anyway. But I'm afraid when we tell him about the trap door, he'll say no."

The brothers went down through the opening. They lifted the door into place, latched it, and then wedged Frank's small pocket notebook into the damaged side. The door held, but Frank and Joe knew that wind or rain would easily dislodge it.

The boys hurried down the steps and through the corridor to the main part of the house.

Adelia Applegate popped her head out of a doorway. "Where's the loot?" she asked.

"We didn't find any," Frank admitted.

The woman sniffed. "I told you so! Such a waste of time!"

"We think now," Joe spoke up, "that the stolen property is probably hidden in the new tower."

"In the new tower!" Miss Applegate cried out. "Absurd! I suppose you'll want to go poking through there now."

"If it wouldn't be too much trouble."

"It *would* be too much trouble, indeed!" she

shrilled. "I shan't have boys rummaging through *my* house on a wild-goose chase like this. You'd better leave at once, and forget all this nonsense."

Her voice had attracted the attention of Hurd Applegate, who came hobbling out of his study.

"Now what's the matter?" he demanded. His sister told him and suddenly his face creased in a triumphant smile. "Aha! So you didn't find anything after all! You thought you'd clear Robinson, but you haven't done it."

"Not yet," Frank answered.

"These boys have the audacity," Miss Applegate broke in, "to want to go looking through the *new* tower."

Hurd Applegate stared at the boys. "Well, they can't do it!" he snapped. "Are you boys trying to make a fool of me?" he asked, shaking a fist at them.

Frank and Joe exchanged glances and nodded at each other. They would have to reveal their reason for thinking the loot was in the new tower.

"Mr. Applegate," Frank began, "the information about where your stolen stuff is hidden came from the man who took the jewels and the bonds. And it wasn't Mr. Robinson."

"What! You mean it was someone else? Has he been caught?"

"He was captured but he's dead now."

"Dead? What happened?" Hurd Applegate asked in excitement.

"His name was Red Jackley and he was a notorious criminal. Dad got on his trail and Jackley tried to escape on a railroad handcar. It smashed up and he was fatally injured," Frank explained.

"Where did you get your information then?" Mr. Applegate asked.

Frank told the whole story, ending with, "We thought Jackley might have made a mistake and that it's the new tower where he hid the loot."

Hurd Applegate rubbed his chin meditatively. It was evident that he was impressed by the boys' story.

"So this fellow Jackley confessed to the robbery, eh?"

"He admitted everything. He had once worked around here and knew the Bayport area well. He had been hanging around the city for several days before the robbery."

"Well," Applegate said slowly, "if he said he hid the stuff in the old tower and it's not there, it must be in the new tower, as you say."

"Will you let us search it?" Joe asked eagerly.

"Yes, and I'll help. I'm just as eager to find the jewels and bonds as you are. Come on, boys!"

Hurd Applegate led the way across the mansion toward a door which opened into the new tower. Now that the man was in a good mood, Frank decided that this was an opportune time to tell him about the trap door. He did so, offering to pay for the repair.

"Oh, that's all right," said Mr. Applegate. "I'll

have it fixed. In fact, Robinson— Oh, I forgot. I'll get a carpenter."

He said no more, but quickened his steps. Frank and Joe grinned. Old Mr. Applegate had not even reprimanded them!

The mansion owner opened the door to the new tower and stepped into a corridor. Frank and Joe, tingling with excitement, followed.

CHAPTER XVI

A Surprise

THE rooms in the new tower had been furnished when it was built. But only on rare occasions when the Applegates had visitors were the rooms occupied, the owner stated.

In the first one Frank, Joe, and Mr. Applegate found nothing, although they looked carefully in closets, bureaus, highboys, and under the large pieces of furniture. They even turned up mattresses and rugs. When they were satisfied that the loot had not been hidden there, they ascended the stairs to the room above. Again their investigation proved fruitless.

Hurd Applegate, being a quick-tempered man, fell back into his old mood. The boys' story had convinced him, but when they had searched the rooms in the tower without success, he showed his disgust.

"It's a hoax!" he snorted. "Adelia was right. I've

132

been made a fool of! And all because of Robinson!"

"I can't understand it!" Joe burst out. "Jackley said he hid the stuff in the tower."

"If that fellow did hide the jewels and bonds in one of the towers," Applegate surmised, "someone else must have come in and taken them—maybe someone working with him. Or else Robinson found the loot right after the robbery and kept it for himself."

"I'm sure Mr. Robinson wouldn't do that," Joe objected.

"Then where did he get the nine hundred dollars? Explain that. Robinson won't!"

On the way back to the main part of the mansion, Hurd Applegate elaborated on his theory. The fact that the loot had not been found seemed to convince him all over again that Robinson was involved in some way.

"Like as not he was in league with Jackley!" the man stated flatly.

Again Frank and Joe protested that the ex-caretaker did not hobnob with criminals. Nevertheless, the Hardys were puzzled, disappointed, and alarmed. Their search had only resulted in implicating Mr. Robinson more deeply in the mystery.

Back in the hallway of the main house they met Adelia Applegate, who crowed triumphantly when she saw the search party returning empty-handed. "Didn't I tell you?" she cried. "Hurd Applegate, you've let these boys make a fool of you!"

She escorted the Hardys to the front door, while her brother, shaking his head perplexedly, went back to his study.

"We sure messed things up, Frank," Joe declared, as they walked toward their motorcycles. "I feel like a dud rocket."

"Me too."

They hurried home to tell their father the disappointing news. Fenton Hardy was amazed to hear that the stolen valuables had not been located in either tower. "You're sure you went over the place thoroughly?"

"Every inch of it. There wasn't a sign of the loot. From the dust in the old tower, I'd say no one had been there for ages," Frank replied.

"Strange," the detective muttered. "I'm sure Jackley wasn't lying. He had absolutely nothing to gain by deceiving me. 'I hid it in the old tower.' Those were his very words. And what could he mean but the old tower of Tower Mansion? And why should he be so careful to say the *old* tower? Since he was familiar with Bayport, he probably knew that the mansion has two towers, the old and the new."

"Of course, it may be that we *didn't* search thoroughly enough," Joe remarked. "The loot could be hidden under the flooring or behind a movable wall panel. We didn't look there."

"That's the only solution," Mr. Hardy agreed. "I'm still not satisfied that the stolen property isn't there. I'm going to ask Applegate to permit another search of both towers. And now, I think your mother wants you to do an errand downtown."

Mrs. Hardy explained what she wanted and Frank and Joe were soon on their motorcycles again. When the boys reached the business section of Bayport they found that Jackley's confession had already become known. The local radio station had broadcast it in the afternoon news program and people everywhere were discussing it.

Detective Smuff walked along the street looking as if he would bite the head off the first person who mentioned the case to him. When he saw the Hardy boys he glowered.

"Well," he grunted, "I hear you got the stuff back."

"I wish we had," Frank said glumly.

"What!" the detective cried out, brightening at once. "You didn't get it? I thought they said on the radio that this fellow Jackley had told your father where he hid it."

"He did. But how did the news leak out?"

"Jackley's door wasn't closed all the time. One of the other patients who was walking by the room heard the confession and spilled it. So you didn't find the loot after all! Ha-ha! That's a good one! Didn't Jackley say the stuff was hidden in the old tower? What more do you need?"

"Well, it wasn't there!" Joe retorted hotly. "Jackley must have made a mistake!"

"*Jackley* made a mistake!" Smuff continued cheerfully. "It looks like the joke's on you fellows and your father!" The would-be sleuth went on down the street, chuckling to himself.

When Frank and Joe returned home they found that Mr. Hardy had been in touch with Hurd Applegate and had convinced him that a more detailed search of the towers would be advisable.

"Boys," he said, "we'll go there directly after supper. I think we'd better not wait until tomorrow."

At seven o'clock the detective and his sons presented themselves at the Tower Mansion. Hurd Applegate met them at the door.

"I'm letting you make this search," he said as he led them toward the old tower, "but I'm convinced you won't find anything. I've talked the case over with Chief Collig. He's inclined to think that Robinson is behind it all and I'm sure he is."

"But how about Jackley's confession?" Mr. Hardy asked him.

"The chief says that could be a blind. Jackley did it to protect Robinson. They were working together."

"I know it looks bad for Robinson," Mr. Hardy admitted, "but I want to give the towers another close examination. I heard Jackley make the confession and I don't believe he was lying."

"Maybe. Maybe. But I'm telling you it was a hoax."

"I'll believe that only if I don't find anything inside or outside either tower," Mr. Hardy declared, his mouth set in a grim line.

"Well, come on, let's get started," Hurd Applegate said, unlocking the door leading to the old tower.

Eagerly the four set to work. They started at the top of the old tower and worked downward. Their investigation left no possibility untouched. All the walls were tapped for hollow sounds which might indicate secret hiding places. The floors were examined closely for signs of any recent disturbance to the wood. But the missing jewels and bonds were not located. Finally the group reached the ground floor again.

"Nothing to do but go on to the new tower," Mr. Hardy commented briefly.

"I'll have to rest and eat something before I do any more," Hurd Applegate said wearily. He led the way to the dining room where sandwiches and milk had been set out. "Help yourselves," he invited. He himself took only crackers and milk when they all sat down.

After the brief stop for refreshment, the Hardys and the mansion owner turned their attention to the new tower. Again they searched carefully. Walls and partitions were tapped and floors were sounded. Every bit of furniture was minutely examined. Not an inch of space escaped the scrutiny of the detective and his helpers.

As the search drew to a close and the loot still had not been found, Mr. Hardy remarked, "It certainly looks as if the stolen property was never hidden here by Jackley. And furthermore, there's no evidence that if he did hide it here, anyone came in to take it away."

"You mean," said Frank, "it's proof that Mr. Robinson did *not* come in here?"

"Exactly."

"Maybe not," Mr. Applegate conceded. "But it still doesn't prove he wasn't in cahoots with the thief!"

"I'm not going to give up this search yet," Mr. Hardy said determinedly. "Perhaps the loot was hidden somewhere outside the old tower."

He explained that it would be difficult to examine the grounds properly at night. "With your permission, Mr. Applegate, my sons and I will return at sunrise tomorrow morning and start work again." As the owner reluctantly nodded his assent, Mr. Hardy turned to Frank and Joe and smiled. "We ought to be able to prove our point before schooltime."

The boys, who had had no time to prepare any homework, reminded their father that a note from him to the principal would be a great help. The detective smiled, and as soon as they reached home he wrote one out, then said good night.

Frank and Joe felt as if their eyes had hardly closed when they opened them again to see their father standing between their beds. "Time to get up if you want to be in on the search," he announced.

The boys blinked sleepily, then sprang out of bed. Showers awakened them fully and they dressed quickly. Mrs. Hardy was in the kitchen when they entered it and breakfast was ready. The sun was just rising over a distant hill.

"Everything hot this morning," Mrs. Hardy said. "It's chilly outside."

The menu included hot applesauce, oatmeal, poached eggs on toast, and cocoa. Breakfast was eaten almost in silence to avoid any delay, and within twenty minutes the three Hardy sleuths were on their way.

"I see you put spades in the car, Dad," Frank remarked. "I take it we're going to do some digging."

"Yes, if we don't locate the loot hidden above ground some place."

When the Hardys reached Tower Mansion they instituted their hunt without notifying the Applegates, who, they were sure, were still asleep. Everything in the vicinity of both towers was scrutinized. Boulders were overturned, the space under the summerhouse examined by flashlight, every stone in the masonry tested to see if it could be dislodged. Not a clue turned up.

"I guess we dig," Frank stated finally.

He chose a bed of perennial bushes at the foot of the old tower where there had been recent planting, and pushed one of the spades in deep with his foot. The tool hit an obstruction. Excitedly Frank shoveled away the dirt around the spot. In half a minute he gave a cry of delight.

"A chest! I've found a buried chest!"

CHAPTER XVII

An Unexpected Find

THROWING out the dirt in great spadefuls, Frank uncovered the chest completely. It was about two feet long, six inches wide, and a foot deep.

"The treasure!" Joe cried out, running up.

Mr. Hardy was at his son's heels and looked in amazement at Frank's discovery. The boy lifted the chest out of the hole and instantly began to raise the lid on which there was no lock.

Everyone held his breath. Had the Hardys really uncovered the jewels and securities stolen from the Applegates? Frank flung back the lid.

The three sleuths stared at the contents. They had never been more surprised in their lives. Finally Joe found his voice.

"Nothing but a lot of flower bulbs!"

The first shock of disappointment over, the detective and his sons burst into laughter. The contents of the chest were such a far cry from what they had expected that now the situation seemed ridiculous.

"Well, one thing is sure," said Frank. "Red Jackley never buried this chest. I wonder who did?"

"I can answer that," a voice behind them replied, and the Hardys turned to see Hurd Applegate, clad in bathrobe and slippers, walking toward them.

"Good morning, Mr. Applegate," the boys chorused, and their father added, "You see we're on the job. For a couple of moments we thought we had found your stolen property."

Hurd Applegate's face took on a stern look. "You didn't find my securities," he said, "but maybe you have found a clue to the thief. Robinson buried that chest full of bulbs. That's what he's done with Adelia's jewelry and my securities! He's buried them some place, but I'd be willing to bet anything it wasn't on the grounds here."

Frank, realizing the man was not in a good humor this morning, tried to steer the conversation away from the stolen valuables. "Mr. Applegate," he said, "why did Mr. Robinson bury these flower bulbs here?"

The owner of Tower Mansion gave a little snort. "That man's nutty about unusual flowers. He sent to Europe for these bulbs: They have to be kept in a cool, dark place for several months, so he decided to bury them. He's always doing something queer like that. Why, do you know what he tried to get me to do? Put up a greenhouse here on the property so he could raise all kinds of rare flowers."

"That sounds like a swell hobby," Joe spoke up.

"Swell nothing!" Mr. Applegate replied. "I guess you don't know how much greenhouses cost. And besides, growing rare flowers takes a lot of time. Robinson had enough to do without fiddling around with making great big daisies out of little wild ones, or turning cowslips into orchids!"

Frank whistled. "If Mr. Robinson can do that, he's a genius!"

"Genius—that's a joke!" said Mr. Applegate. "Well, go on with your digging. I want this mystery cleared up."

It was decided that Mr. Hardy, with his superior powers of observation, would scrutinize the ground near both towers. Wherever it looked as if the ground had been turned over recently, the boys would dig at the spot. The chest of flower bulbs was carefully replaced and the dirt shoveled over it.

"Here's a place where you might dig," Mr. Hardy called presently from the opposite side of the old tower. When the boys arrived with their spades, he said, "I have an idea a dog dug up this spot and probably all you'll find is a beef bone. But we don't want to miss anything."

This time Joe's spade hit the object which had been buried. As his father had prophesied, it proved to be only a bone secreted by some dog.

The three Hardys transferred their work to the new tower. All this time Hurd Applegate had been looking on in silence. From the corners of their eyes, the Hardys could catch an expression of satisfaction on the elderly man's face.

Mr. Hardy glanced at his wrist watch, then said, "Well, boys, I guess this is our last try." He indicated another spot a few feet away. "You fellows must get cleaned up and go to school."

Undaunted by their failures so far, Frank and Joe dug in with a will. In a few moments they had uncovered another small chest.

"Wow, this one is heavy!" Frank said as he lifted it from the hole.

"Then maybe—maybe it's the stolen property!" Joe exclaimed.

Even Mr. Applegate showed keen interest this time and leaned over to raise the lid himself. The box contained several sacks.

"The jewels!" Joe cried out.

"And that flat-shaped sack could contain the securities!" Frank said enthusiastically.

Mr. Applegate picked up one of the circular bags and quickly untied the string wound about the top. His face took on a look of utter disgust. "Seeds!" he fairly shouted.

Mr. Hardy had already picked up the flat sack. He looked almost as disappointed as Mr. Applegate. "Flower catalogs!" he exclaimed. "They seem to be in various foreign languages."

Frank lifted the chest from the hole

"Oh, Robinson was always sending for things from all over the world," the Tower Mansion owner remarked. "I told him to destroy them. He paid too much attention to that stuff when he might have been doing something useful. I suppose he buried the catalogs, so I wouldn't find them."

After a long breath the elderly man went on, "Well, we've reached the end of the line. You Hardys haven't proved a thing, but you've certainly torn up my house and grounds."

The three sleuths had to admit this was true but told him they were still fired by two hopes: to clear Mr. Robinson of the charge against him, and to find the stolen property. As they put their spades back into the Hardy car, Mr. Applegate invited them into the house to wash and have a bite to eat.

"I guess you boys could do with a second breakfast," he added, and the brothers thought, "Maybe at times Mr. Applegate isn't such a bad sort."

They accepted the invitation and enjoyed the meal of waffles and honey. Their father then drove them to Bayport High.

Frank and Joe had no sooner stepped from the car than they heard their names called. Turning, they saw Iola Morton and Callie Shaw coming toward them.

"Hi, boys!"

"Hi, girls!"

"Say, did you hear what happened early this morning?" Callie asked.

"No. School called off for today?" Joe asked eagerly.

"I wish it were." Callie sobered. "It's about Mr. Robinson. He's been arrested again!"

"No!" The Hardys stared at Callie, thunderstruck. "Why?" Frank demanded.

Iola took up the story, saying that she and Chet had heard the bad news on the radio that morning. They had stopped at the Robinsons' home, when their father brought them to school, to find out more about what had happened.

"It seems that Chief Collig has an idea Mr. Robinson was in league with the thief Jackley, that man your father got the confession from. So he arrested him. Poor Mrs. Robinson! She doesn't know what to do."

"And Mr. Robinson had just managed to find another job," Callie said sadly. "Oh, can't you boys do something?"

"We're working on the case as hard as we can," Frank replied, and told the girls about their sleuthing the evening before and early that morning. At that moment the school bell rang and the young people had to separate.

Frank and Joe were deeply concerned by what they had just heard. At lunch they met Jerry, Phil, Tony, and Chet Morton and told them the news.

"This is tough on Slim," Phil remarked.

"Tough on the whole family," Chet declared.

The boys discussed the situation from all angles and racked their brains for some way in which they could help the Robinsons. They concluded that only the actual discovery of the stolen jewels and bonds would clear Mr. Robinson of the suspicion which hung over him.

"That means there's only one thing to do," Frank said. "We *must* find that loot!"

After school he and Joe played baseball for the required period, then went directly home. They had no heart for further sports activities. It was a dull, gloomy day, indicative of rain and this did not raise the boys' spirits.

Frank, who was restless, finally suggested, "Let's take a walk."

"Maybe it'll help clear the cobwebs from our brains," Joe agreed.

They told their mother they would be home by suppertime, then set off. The brothers walked mile after mile, and then, as they turned back, they were drawn as if by magnets to Tower Mansion.

"This place is beginning to haunt me," said Joe, as they walked up the driveway.

Suddenly Frank caught his brother's arm. "I just had an idea. Maybe Jackley in his deathbed confession was confused and meant some other robbery he committed. Besides, at some time in every mystery the most innocent-seeming people become suspect. What proof is there that the Applegates haven't pulled a hoax? For reasons of their own they might say that the things had been stolen from their safe. Don't forget that Dad didn't find any fingerprints on it except Mr. Applegate's."

"Frank, you've got a point there. That man and his sister act so mean sometimes, I wouldn't put it past them to be trying to cheat the insurance company," said Joe.

"Exactly," his brother agreed. "For the moment, let's play it this way. We'll pretend they're suspects and do a little spying about this place."

Instantly the boys left the roadway and disappeared among the shrubbery that lined it. Making their way cautiously, they moved forward toward Tower Mansion. The place was in darkness with the exception of three lighted rooms on the first floor.

"What's your idea, Frank?" his brother whispered. "To learn something that might tell us whether or not the Applegates are implicated in the robbery?"

"Yes. Maybe we'll get a clue if we keep our eyes and ears open."

The boys walked forward in silence. They approached the mansion from the end where the old tower stood. Somewhere, not far from them, they suddenly heard footsteps on the gravel walk. In a flash the brothers dodged behind a tree. The footsteps came closer and the boys waited to see who was approaching. Was it one of the Applegates, or someone else?

Before they could find out, the person's footsteps receded and the boys emerged from their hiding place. Suddenly a glaring light was beamed directly on them.

It came from the top room of the old tower!

CHAPTER XVIII

A Startling Deduction

"Duck!" Frank ordered in a hoarse whisper, quickly dropping to the ground.

Instantly Joe threw himself face down alongside his brother.

"You think the person with the flashlight in the tower saw us?" Frank asked.

"He could have, but maybe not. We sure went down fast."

The strong flashlight was not trained on them again. It was beamed out a window of the tower in another direction, then turned off.

"Well, what say?" Joe asked. "Shall we go on up to the mansion and continue our sleuthing?"

Frank was of the opinion that if they did, they might get into trouble. Even if they had not been recognized, the person in the tower probably had spotted them.

"I'd like to find out who was in the tower," Joe

argued. "It's just possible that the Applegates don't know anything about him."

Frank laughed quietly. "Don't let your imagination run away with you," he advised.

As the boys debated about whether to leave the grounds or to go forward, the matter was suddenly taken out of their hands. From around the corner of the tower rushed a huge police dog, growling and barking. It apparently had scented the brothers and was bounding directly toward them.

Frank and Joe started to run pell-mell, but were unable to keep ahead of the dog. In a few moments he blocked their path menacingly and set up a ferocious barking.

"I guess we're caught," Frank said. "And I hope this old fellow won't take a piece out of my leg."

The two boys tried to make friends with the animal, but he would not let them budge.

"Well, what do we do now?" Joe asked in disgust as the dog continued to growl menacingly.

"Wait to be rescued," Frank replied tersely.

A moment later they saw a bobbing light coming in their direction and presently Mr. Applegate appeared. He looked at the boys in complete astonishment.

"You fellows never give up, do you?" he remarked. "What have you been doing—more digging?"

The brothers did not reply at once. They were embarrassed at having been discovered, but relieved that the man did not suspect what they had really intended to do. The owner of Tower Mansion took their lack of response to mean he was right.

"I'm just not going to have any more of my grounds ruined," he said gruffly. "I've borrowed this watchdog, Rex, and he's going to keep everybody away. If you have any reason for wanting to see me, you'd better phone first, and I'll keep Rex chained."

"Who was up in the tower with a flashlight?" Frank asked the elderly man.

"My sister. She got it into her head that maybe she was smarter than you fellows and could find the stolen stuff in the old tower, but she didn't!" Frank and Joe suppressed grins as he went on. "And then Adelia decided to flash that high-powered flashlight around the grounds, thinking we might have a lot of curious visitors because of the publicity. Apparently she picked you up."

The boys laughed. "Yes, she did," Frank admitted. "Between her and Rex, I guess you needn't worry about any prowlers."

Frank and Joe said good night to Hurd Applegate and started down the driveway. This time the dog did not follow them. He remained at the man's side until the Hardys were out of sight.

As they trudged homeward, Joe remarked, "This seems to be our day for exciting events that fizzle out like wet fireworks."

"Yes. Nothing to show for all our work."

At supper both Mr. and Mrs. Hardy laughed at the boys' story of their encounter with the dog. Then they became serious when Frank asked his father if he thought there was a chance that the Applegates might be guilty of falsely reporting a robbery.

"It's possible, of course," the detective answered. "But the Applegates are so well-to-do I can't see any point in their trying such a thing. I believe it's best for us to stick to the original idea —that someone really did take jewels and securities from the safe, and that the person was Jackley."

As the boys were going to bed that night, Frank remarked to his brother, "Tomorrow is Saturday and we have the whole day free. I vote we set ourselves the goal of solving the mystery before night."

"A big order, but I'm with you," Joe replied with a grin.

They were up early and began to discuss what course of sleuthing they should follow.

"I think we ought to start off on a completely new tack," Joe suggested.

"In which direction?" Frank asked him.

"In the direction of the railroad."

Joe went on to explain that one thing they had not done was find out about Red Jackley's habits when he had worked around Bayport. If they could talk to one or more persons who had known him, they might pick up some new clue which would lead them to the stolen property.

"Good idea, Joe," his brother agreed. "Let's take our lunch and make an all-day trip on our motorcycles."

"Fine."

Mr. Hardy had left the house very early, so his sons did not see him. When his wife heard the boys' plan, she thought it an excellent one and immediately offered to make some sandwiches for them. By the time they were ready to leave she had two small boxes packed with a hearty picnic lunch.

"Good-by and good luck!" Mrs. Hardy called as the brothers rode off.

"Thanks, Mother, for everything!" the young detectives chorused as they started off.

When Frank and Joe reached the Bayport railroad station, they questioned the stationmaster, and learned that he had been with the company only a year and had not known Red Jackley.

"Did he work on a passenger train?" the man asked.

"I don't think so," Frank replied. "I believe he was employed as a maintenance man."

"Then," said the stationmaster, "I'd advise you to go out along the highway to the railroad crossings and interview a couple of old flagmen who are still around. Both of them seem to know everybody and everything connected with the railroad for the past fifty years." He chuckled.

The boys knew of two grade crossings some miles out of town and now headed for them. At the first one they learned that the regular flagman was home ill and his substitute had never heard of Red Jackley. Frank and Joe went on.

At the next crossing they found old Mike Halley, the flagman there, busy at his job. His bright blue eyes searched their faces for a moment, then he amazed them by saying, "You're Frank and Joe Hardy, sons of the famous detective Fenton Hardy."

"You know us?" Frank asked. "I must confess I don't recall having met you before."

"And you ain't," the man responded. "But I make it a rule to memorize every face I see in the newspapers. Never know when there's goin' to be an accident and I might be called on to identify some people."

The boys gulped at this gruesome thought, then Frank asked Halley if he remembered a railroad man named Red Jackley.

"I recollect a man named Jackley, but he wasn't never called Red when I knew him. I reckon he's the same fellow, though. You mean the one that I read went to jail?"

"That's the man!"

"He out of the pen yet?" Mike Halley questioned.

"He died," Joe replied. "Our dad is working on a case that has some connection with Jackley and we're just trying to find out something about him."

"Then what you want to do," said the flagman, "is go down to the Bayport and Coast Line Railroad. That's where Jackley used to work. He was around the station at Cherryville. That ain't so far from here." He pointed in a northerly direction.

"Thanks a million," said Frank. "You've helped us a lot."

The brothers set off on their motorcycles for Cherryville. When they came to the small town, a policeman directed them to the railroad station, which was about a half mile out of town. The station stood in a depression below a new highway, and was reached by a curving road which ran parallel to the tracks for several hundred feet.

The building itself was small, square, and very much in need of paint. A few nearby frame buildings were in a bad state of disrepair. An old wooden water tank, about seventy yards from one side of the station house, sagged precariously. At the same distance on the other side rose another water tank. This one, painted red, was of metal and in much better condition.

Frank and Joe parked their motorcycles and went into the station. A man in his shirt sleeves and wearing a green visor was bustling about behind the ticket window.

"Are you the stationmaster?" Frank called to him.

The man came forward. "I'm Jake—stationmaster, and ticket seller, and baggage slinger, and express handler, and mail carrier, and janitor, and even rice thrower. You name it. I'm your man."

The boys burst into laughter, then Joe said, "If there's anybody here who can tell us what we want to know, I'm sure it's you. But first, what do you mean you're a rice thrower?"

The station agent guffawed. "Well, it don't happen often, but when a bride and groom comes down here to take a train, I just go out, grab some of the rice, and throw it along with everybody else. I reckon if that'll make 'em happy, I want to be part of the proceedin's."

Again the Hardys roared with laughter. Then Frank inquired if the man had known Red Jackley.

"I sure did," Jake replied. "Funny kind of fellow. Work like mad one minute, then loaf on the job the next. One thing about him, he never wanted nobody to give him any orders."

"Did you know that he died recently?" Frank asked.

"No, I didn't," the stationmaster answered. "I'm real sorry to hear that. Jackley wasn't a bad sort when I knew him. Just got to keepin' the wrong kind of company, I guess."

"Can you tell us any particular characteristics he had?" Frank questioned.

Jake scratched his head above his visor. Finally he said, "The thing I remember most about Jackley is that he was a regular monkey. He was nimble as could be, racin' up and down freight-car ladders."

At that moment they heard a train whistle and the man said hurriedly, "Got to leave you now, boys. Come back some other time when I ain't so busy. Got to meet this train."

The Hardys left him and Frank suggested, "Let's eat our lunch and then come back."

They found a little grove of trees beside the railroad tracks and propped their motorcycles against a large tree.

"I'm starved," said Frank, seating himself under the tree and opening his box of lunch.

"Boy, this is good!" Joe exclaimed a moment later as he bit hungrily into a thick roast beef sandwich.

"If Jackley had only stayed with the railroad company," Frank observed as he munched a deviled egg, "it would've been better for everyone."

"He sure caused a lot of trouble before he died," Joe agreed.

"And he's caused a lot more since, the way things have gone. For the Robinsons, especially."

The boys gazed reflectively down the tracks, gleaming in the sun. The rails stretched far into the distance. Only a few hundred feet from the place where they were seated, the Hardys could see both water tanks: the dilapidated, weatherbeaten wooden one, with some of the rungs missing from the ladder that led up its side, and the squat, metal tank, perched on spindly legs.

Frank took a bite of his sandwich and chewed it thoughtfully. The sight of the two water towers had given him an idea, but at first it seemed to him too absurd for consideration. He was wondering whether or not he should mention it to his brother.

Then he noticed that Joe, too, was gazing intently down the tracks at the tanks. Joe raised a cooky to his lips absently, attempted a bite, and missed the cooky altogether. Still he continued gazing fixedly in the same direction.

Finally Joe turned and looked at his brother. Both knew that they were thinking the identical thing.

"Two water towers," Frank said in a low but excited tone.

"An old one and a newer one," Joe murmured.

"And Jackley said—"

"He hid the stuff in the old tower."

"He was a railroad man."

"Why not?" Joe shouted, springing to his feet. "Why couldn't it have been this old *water* tower he meant? He used to work around here."

"After all, he didn't say the old tower of Tower Mansion. He just said 'old tower'!"

"Frank, I believe we've stumbled on a terrific clue!" Joe said jubilantly. "It would be the natural thing for Jackley to come to his former haunts after the robbery!"

"Right!" Frank agreed.

"And when he discovered that Chet's jalopy was gone, he probably thought that the police were hot on his trail, so he decided to hide the loot some place he knew—where no one else would suspect. The old water tower! This must be the place!"

CHAPTER XIX

Loot!

LUNCH, motorcycles—everything else was forgotten! With wild yells of excitement, Frank and Joe hurried down the embankment which flanked the right of way.

But as they came to a fence that separated the tracks from the grass and weeds that grew along the side, they stopped short. Someone on the highway above was sounding a car horn. Looking up, they recognized the driver.

Smuff!

"Oh, good night!" Joe cried out.

"The last person we want to see right now," Frank said in disgust.

"We'll get rid of him in a hurry," Joe determined.

The boys turned around and climbed back up the embankment. By this time Oscar Smuff had stepped from his car and was walking down to meet the boys.

"Well, I found you," he said.

"You mean you've been looking for us?" Frank asked in astonishment.

The detective grinned. With an ingratiating air he explained to the boys that he had trailed them for miles. He had seen them leave home on their motorcycles, and almost caught up with them at the Bayport station, only to lose them. But the stationmaster had revealed the Hardys' next destination, and the aspiring sleuth had hastened to talk to the flagman, Mike Halley.

"He told me I'd find you here," Smuff said, self-satisfaction evident in his tone.

"But why do you want us?" Joe demanded.

"I've come to make a proposition," Smuff announced. "I've got a swell clue about Jackley and that loot he hid, but I need somebody to help me in the search. How about it, fellows? If old Smuff lets you in on his secret, will you help him?"

Frank and Joe were astounded at this turn of events. Did the man really know something important? Or was he suddenly becoming clever and trying to trick the Hardys into divulging what they knew? One thing the brothers were sure of: they wanted nothing to do with Oscar Smuff until they had searched the old water tower.

"Thanks for the compliment," Frank said. He

grinned. "Joe and I think we're pretty good ourselves. We're glad you do."

"Then you'll work with me?" Smuff asked, his eyes lighting up in anticipation.

"I didn't say yes and I didn't say no," Frank countered. He glanced at Joe, who was standing in back of the detective. Joe shook his head vigorously. "Tell you what, Smuff," Frank went on. "When Joe and I get back to Bayport, we'll look you up. We came out here to have a picnic lunch and relax."

Smuff's face fell. But he was not giving up so easily. "When I drove up, I saw you running like mad down the bank. Do you call that relaxing?"

"Oh, when you sit around awhile eating, your legs feel kind of cramped," Joe told him. "Anyway, we have to keep in practice for the Bayport High baseball team."

Smuff looked as if he did not know whether or not he was being kidded. But finally he said, "Okay, fellows. If you'll get in touch with me the first of the week, I can promise you a big surprise. You've proved you can't win the thousand-dollar reward alone, so we may as well each get a share of it. I've already admitted I need help to solve this mystery."

He turned and slowly ambled up the embankment to his car. The boys waved good-by to the detective and waited until he was far out of sight and they were sure he would not return. Then Frank and Joe hurried down to the tracks, vaulted the fence, and ran pell-mell toward the old water tower.

"If only we *have* stumbled on the secret!" Frank said enthusiastically.

"It'll clear Mr. Robinson—"

"We will earn the reward by ourselves—"

"Best of all, Dad will be proud of us."

The old water tower reared forlornly alongside the tracks. At close quarters it seemed even more decrepit than from a distance. When the boys glanced at the ladder with its many rungs missing, they wondered if they would be able to ascend to the top on it.

"If Jackley climbed this ladder we can too," said Frank as he stopped, panting, at the bottom. "Let's go!"

He began to scramble up the rotted wood rungs. He had ascended only four of them when there came an alarming *crack!*

"Careful!" Joe cried out from below.

Frank clung to the rung above just as the one beneath him snapped under his weight. He drew himself up and cautiously put his foot on the next rung. This one was firmer and held his weight.

"Hey!" Joe called up. "Don't break all the rungs! I want to come up too!"

Frank continued to climb the ladder as his brother began the ascent. When they came to any place where a rung had broken off, the boys were obliged to haul themselves up by main force. But finally Frank reached the top and waited until Joe was just beneath him.

"There's a trap door up here leading down into the tank," Frank called.

"Well, for Pete's sake, be careful," Joe warned. "We don't want any more accidents with trap doors."

The boys climbed onto the roof of the tower, which swayed under their weight. Both fully realized their peril.

"We can't give up now!" said Frank, and scrambled over the surface of the roof until he reached the trap door. Joe followed. They unlatched and raised the door, then peered down into the recesses of the abandoned water tank. It was about seven feet in depth and twelve in diameter.

Frank lowered himself through the opening, but clung to the rim until he was sure, from feeling around with his feet, that the floor would not break through. "It's okay," he told Joe, who followed his brother inside.

Eagerly the boys peered about the dim interior. The place seemed to be partly filled with rubbish. There was a quantity of old lumber, miscellaneous bits of steel rails, battered tin pails, and crowbars, all piled in helter-skelter fashion. At first glance there was no sign of the Applegates' stolen possessions.

"The jewels and bonds must be here somewhere," Joe declared. "But if Jackley did put the stuff here, he wouldn't have left it right out in the open. It's probably hidden under some of this junk."

Frank pulled out a flashlight and swung it around. In its glow Joe began to hunt frantically, casting aside the old pails and pieces of lumber.

One entire half of the tower was searched without result. Frank turned the flashlight to the far side and noted that a number of boards had been piled up in a rather orderly crisscrossed manner.

"Joe," said Frank, "I'd say these boards hadn't been thrown here accidentally. It sure looks as if somebody had placed them deliberately to hide something underneath."

"You're right."

Like a terrier after a bone, Joe dived toward the pile. Hastily he pulled away the boards.

Revealed in the neat little hiding place lay a bag. It was an ordinary gunny sack, but as Joe dragged it out he felt sure that the search for the Applegate property had come to an end.

"This must be it!" he exulted.

"The Tower treasure!" Frank smothered a whoop of joy.

Joe carried the sack into the light beneath the trap door.

"Hurry up! Open it!" Frank urged.

With trembling fingers Joe began to untie the

cord around the sack. There were many knots, and as Joe worked at them, Frank fidgeted nervously.

"Let me try," he said impatiently.

At last, with both Hardys working on the stubborn knots, the cord was untied and the bag gaped open. Joe plunged one hand into it and withdrew an old-fashioned bracelet of precious stones.

"Jewelry!"

"How about the securities?"

Again Joe groped into the sack. His fingers encountered a bulky packet. When he pulled it out, the boys exclaimed in unison:

"The bonds!"

The bundle of papers, held together by an elastic band, proved to be the securities. The first of the documents was a negotiable bond for one thousand dollars issued by the city of Bayport.

"Mr. Applegate's property!" Frank cried out triumphantly. "Joe, do you realize what this means? We've solved the mystery!"

The brothers looked at each other almost unbelievingly, then each slapped the other on the back. "We did it! We did it!" Joe cried out jubilantly.

Frank grinned. "And without old Smuff," he said.

"Now Mr. Robinson's cleared for sure!" Joe exclaimed. "That's the best part of solving this mystery."

"You're right!"

The boys rejoiced over their discovery for another full minute, then decided to hurry back to Bayport with the precious sack.

"You go down first, Frank," said Joe. "I'll toss the sack to you and then come myself."

He picked up the bag and was about to hoist it to his shoulders when both boys heard a sound on the roof of the tower. They looked up to see an evil-looking, unshaven man peering down at them.

"Halt!" he ordered.

"Who are you?" Frank asked.

"They call me Hobo Johnny," the man replied. "This here is my quarters and anything in it belongs to me. You got no right in my room. You can't take anything away. And t'anks for finding the wad. I never thought to look around."

Joe, taken aback a moment, now said, "You may sleep here, but this is railroad property. You don't own what's in this tower. Now go on down the ladder, so we can leave."

"So you're going to fight, eh?" Hobo Johnny said in an ugly tone. "I'll see about that!"

Without warning the trap door was slammed shut and locked from the outside!

CHAPTER XX

The Escape

"LET us out of here!" Frank shouted at Hobo Johnny.

"You can't get away with this!" Joe yelled.

The man on the water tower roof gave a loud guffaw. "You think I ain't got no brains. Well, I got enough to know when I'm well off. I ain't in no hurry to collect that treasure you found in the tower. A few days from now will be all right for me to sell it."

"A few days from now?" Joe exclaimed, horrified. "By that time we'll be suffocated or die of starvation."

Frank put an arm around his impulsive brother's shoulder. In a low tone he said, "We won't do either, Joe. I don't think it's going to be too hard to get out of here. If not by the trap door, we'll hack our way out through one side of the tank."

Joe calmed down and both boys became silent. This seemed to worry Hobo Johnny, who called down, "What're you guys up to?"

No answer.

"Okay. I'm leaving you now, but I'll be back for that treasure. Don't try any funny stuff or you'll get hurt!"

The man on the roof waited a few moments for an answer. Receiving none, he shuffled across the tower to the ladder.

"I hope he doesn't break all the rungs," said Joe worriedly. "We won't be able to get down."

Again Frank patted his brother on the shoulder. "I noticed an iron pipe running from the top of this tower to the bottom," he said. "If necessary, we can slide down the pipe."

"How long do you think we should wait before trying to break out of here?" Joe asked.

Before replying, Frank pondered the situation. Not knowing anything about Hobo Johnny's habits, he wondered how far away from the tower the man would go. If not far, the boys might find him waiting below and a tough person to handle. Finally, Frank decided that since the tramp had said he would return in an hour, he must be planning to go some distance away, perhaps to get a couple of his hobo friends to come back and help him.

"I'd say that if we leave in fifteen minutes we'll be safe," was Frank's conclusion.

Every second seemed like an hour, but finally when the fifteen minutes were up, the boys lifted a plank and tried to push up the trap door. It would not budge.

"Where do we try next?" Joe questioned.

Frank was examining the seams around the trap door with the flashlight. Presently he pointed out a section where the wood looked completely dried out.

"It shouldn't be too hard to ram a hole here, Joe. Then you can boost me up, so I can reach through and turn the handle on the lock."

Joe picked up a crowbar and jabbed the sharp end between the edge of the trap door and the board next to it. There was a splintering sound. He gave the tool another tremendous push. The seam widened. Now he and Frank together wedged the end of the crowbar up through the opening.

In a few moments they had sprung the two boards far enough apart so that Frank, by standing on Joe's shoulders, could reach his arm through the opening. He found the handle which locked the trap door and turned it. Joe pushed up the door with the plank.

The boys were free!

Frank pulled himself up through the opening and hurried to the edge of the roof. He looked all around below. Hobo Johnny was not in sight; in fact, there was no one to be seen anywhere.

"Clear field ahead!" he announced.

Now the boys began to carry out their original intention of removing the stolen property from the old water tower. Frank went back to the trap door and Joe handed up the sack, then joined his brother on the roof. The older boy went down the ladder quickly and his brother tossed the treasure to him. Joe lost no time in following.

"We'd better get away from here in a hurry!" Frank advised, and both boys sprinted to their motorcycles.

"Let's divide this stuff. It'll be easier to carry," Frank suggested.

He opened the sack and handed Joe the bundle of securities, which the boy jammed into his pocket. Frank stuffed the sack containing the jewelry into his own side pocket. Then they hopped onto their motorcycles, stepped on the starters, and roared down the road toward Bayport. It was not until they were several miles from the old water tower that the Hardys relaxed. Grins spread over their faces.

"I don't know who's going to be the most surprised—Hurd or Adelia Applegate, or Chief Collig or—"

"I have another guess—Dad!" said Frank.

"I guess you're right," Joe agreed. "And the most disappointed person is going to be one Oscar Smuff!"

"What clue do you suppose he wanted us to follow?"

"It's my idea he didn't have any. He just wanted to hook on to us and then claim the glory if we found the treasure, so Collig would give him a job on the force."

"Where do you think we ought to take these valuables?" Joe asked presently.

The boys discussed this as they covered nearly a mile of ground and finally came to the conclusion that since Hurd Applegate had given their father the job of finding the stolen property, the detective should be the one to return it to the owners.

Half an hour later the brothers pulled into the Hardy driveway and soon were overwhelming their parents with the good news.

"It's wonderful! Simply wonderful!" Mrs. Hardy cried out, hugging each of her sons.

Their father's face wore a broad grin. "I'm certainly proud of you," he said, and slapped Frank and Joe on the back. "You boys shall have the honor of making the announcement to the Applegates."

"How about Chief Collig?" Frank asked. "And we'll report Hobo Johnny to him."

"And we'll invite the Robinsons to hear the announcement," Joe added.

The detective said he thought there should be a grand meeting at the Applegates' home of everyone involved with the tower mystery. He suggested that when the boys called up, they try to arrange such a meeting for that very evening.

Frank was selected to make the report to Hurd Applegate; the others could hear the elderly man exclaim in amazement. "I didn't think you'd do it!" he said over and over again.

Shouting for his sister, he relayed the message, then said, "Adelia wants me to tell you she's the most relieved woman in all of Bayport. She never did like any of this business."

The Applegates readily agreed to a meeting at their home early that evening and insisted that Mr. Robinson be there. Mr. Hardy was to see to it that Chief Collig released the man at once.

"This is going to be a lot of fun," Frank declared at supper. "Mother, I think you should come along? Will you?"

"I'd love to," Mrs. Hardy replied. "I'd like to hear what the Applegates and Mr. Robinson and Chief Collig are going to say."

"And Chet should be there too," Joe said. "After all, it was his stolen car that gave us the clue to Red Jackley." Chet was called and gave a whoop of delight. He agreed to meet the Hardy family at the Tower Mansion.

"There's one more person who ought to attend," said Frank with a twinkle in his eye. "Oscar Smuff. I'd like to watch his face, too."

"At least we should tell him that the mystery has been solved," Joe spoke up.

Frank waited until his father had phoned Chief Collig, who promised to release Mr. Robinson at once and bring him out to the Applegates' home. Then Frank called Detective Smuff. He could not resist the temptation to keep Smuff guessing a little longer, and merely invited him to join the conference for a big surprise.

At eight o'clock one car after another arrived at the Tower Mansion. When the Hardy family walked in they found all the Robinsons there. The twins rushed up to Frank and Joe and hugged them. Slim and his father shook the brothers' hands fervently and Mr. Robinson said, "How can I ever thank you?"

There were tears in his wife's eyes and her voice trembled as she added her appreciation for what the Hardy boys had done. "You'll never know what this means to us," she said.

Oscar Smuff was the last to arrive. Instantly he demanded to know what was going on. Frank and Joe had hoped to have a little fun with him, but Tessie and Paula, unable to restrain their enthusiasm, shouted, "Frank and Joe Hardy found the jewelry and the papers! They're real heroes!"

As Frank and Joe reddened in embarrassment, Detective Smuff looked at them disbelievingly. "You!" he almost screamed. "You mean the Hardy boys found the treasure?"

As all the others nodded, Slim spoke up, "This means that my father is completely exonerated."

"But how about that nine hundred dollars?" Smuff demanded suspiciously. "What's the explanation of where your father got that?"

Mr. Robinson straightened up. "I'm sorry," he said, "but I must keep my promise to remain silent about that money."

To everyone's amazement, Adelia Applegate arose and went to stand by the man's side. "*I* will tell you where Robinson got that money," she said dramatically. "At my own suggestion I loaned it to him."

"You!" her brother shouted disbelievingly.

"Yes, this was one time when I didn't ask your advice because I knew you wouldn't agree. I knew Robinson needed the money and I really forced him to borrow it, but made him promise to tell no one where he got it. Then when the robbery took place, I didn't know what to think. I was sick over the whole affair, and I'm very, very glad everything's cleared up."

Miss Applegate's announcement astounded her listeners. Robinson stood up, shook her hand, and said in a shaky voice, "Thank you, Miss Adelia."

Hurd Applegate cleared his throat, then said, "I'd like to make an announcement. Will you all please sit down?"

After everyone had taken seats in the large living room of the mansion, the owner went on, "My sister Adelia and I have been talking things over. This whole robbery business has taught us a great lesson. In the future we're not going to be so standoffish from the residents of Bayport. We're going to dedicate part of our grounds—the part with the pond—as a picnic and swimming spot for the townspeople."

"Super!" exclaimed Chet, and Mrs. Hardy said, "I know everyone will appreciate that."

"I haven't finished," Hurd Applegate went on. "I want to make a public apology to Mr. Robinson. Adelia and I are extremely sorry for all the trouble we've caused him. Robinson, if you will come back and work for us, we promise to treat you like the gentleman you are. We will increase your salary and we have decided to build that greenhouse you want. You'll have free rein to raise all the rare flowers you wish to."

There was a gasp from everyone in the room. All eyes were turned on Mr. Robinson. Slowly he arose from his chair, walked over to Mr. Applegate, and shook his hand.

"No hard feelings," he said. "I'll be happy to have my old position back, and with the new greenhouse, I'm sure I'll win a lot of blue ribbons for you and Miss Adelia."

As he returned to his chair, Mr. Applegate said, "There is just one more item of business—the reward. The thousand-dollar reward goes to Frank and Joe Hardy, who solved the mystery of the Tower treasure."

"A thousand bucks!" exclaimed Detective Smuff.

"Dollars, Mr. Smuff—dollars!" Adelia Applegate corrected him severely. "No slang, please, not in Tower Mansion."

"One thousand iron men," Smuff continued, unheeding. "One thousand round, fat, juicy smackers. For two high school boys! And a real detective like me—"

The thought was too much for him. He dropped his head in his hands and groaned aloud. Frank and Joe did not dare look at each other. They were finding it difficult to restrain their laughter.

"Yes, a thousand dollars," Hurd Applegate went on. "Five hundred to each boy."

He took the two checks from a pocket and handed one each to Frank and Joe, who accepted them with thanks. Mr. Applegate now invited his guests into the dining room for sandwiches, cake, and cold drinks.

As Frank and Joe ate, they were congratulated over and over by the others in the room. They accepted it all with a grin, but secretly, each boy had a little feeling of sadness that the case had ended. They hoped another mystery would soon come their way, and one did at THE HOUSE ON THE CLIFF.

"Later, on the way home, Mr. Hardy asked his sons, "What are you fellows going to do with all that money?"

Frank had an instant answer. "Put most of it in the bank."

And Joe added, "Frank and I for some time have wanted to build a crime lab on the second floor of our barn. Now we can do it. All right, Dad?"

The detective smiled and nodded. "An excellent idea!"

The Hardy Boys Mystery Stories®

THE SECRET

OF THE OLD

MILL

BY

FRANKLIN W. DIXON

GROSSET & DUNLAP
Publishers • New York
A member of The Putnam & Grosset Group

CONTENTS

CHAPTER I

A Narrow Escape

"WONDER what mystery Dad's working on now?" Joe Hardy asked.

His brother Frank looked eagerly down the platform of the Bayport railroad station. "It must be a very important case, the way Dad dashed off to Detroit. We'll know in a few minutes."

Joe looked at his watch impatiently. "Train's late."

Both boys were wondering, too, about a certain surprise their father had hinted might be ready for them upon his return.

Waiting with Frank and Joe for Mr. Hardy's arrival was their best friend Chet Morton. "Your dad's cases are always exciting—and dangerous," the plump, ruddy-faced boy remarked. "Do you think he'll give you a chance to help out on this one?"

"We sure hope so," Joe replied eagerly.

"Well, if I know you fellows," Chet went on, "you'll get mixed up in the mystery, somehow—and so will I, sooner or later. There goes my peaceful summer vacation!"

Frank and Joe chuckled, knowing that Chet, despite his penchant for taking things easy and avoiding unnecessary risks, would stick by them through any peril.

Dark-haired, eighteen-year-old Frank, and blond impetuous Joe, a year younger, had often assisted their detective father, Fenton Hardy, in solving baffling mysteries. There was nothing the two brothers liked more than tackling a tough case, either with their father, or by themselves.

Chet gave a huge sigh and leaned against a baggage truck as though his weight were too much for him. "I sure could use something to eat," he declared. "I should have brought along some candy or peanuts."

The Hardys exchanged winks. They frequently needled their friend about his appetite, and Joe could not resist doing so now.

"What's the matter, Chet? Didn't you have lunch? Or did you forget to eat?"

The thought of this remote possibility brought a hearty laugh from Frank. Chet threw both boys a glance of mock indignation, then grinned. "Okay, okay. I'm going inside and get some candy from the machine."

As Chet went into the station, the Hardys

looked across to the opposite platform where a northbound train roared in. The powerful diesel ground to a halt, sparks flashing from under the wheels. Passengers began to alight.

"Did you notice that there weren't any passengers waiting to board the train?" Frank remarked.

At that moment a man dashed up the stairs onto the platform toward the rear of the train. As the train started to move, the stranger made a leap for the last car.

"Guess he made it. That fellow's lucky," Joe commented as the train sped away. "*And* crazy!"

"You're telling me!" Chet exclaimed, as he rejoined the brothers. Munching on a chocolate bar, he added, "That same man stopped me in the station and asked me to change a twenty-dollar bill. There was a long line at the ticket window, so he didn't want to wait for change there. He grabbed the money I gave him and rushed out the door as if the police were after him!"

"Boy!" Joe exclaimed. "You must be really loaded with money if you could change a twenty-dollar bill."

Chet blushed and tried to look as modest as he could. "Matter of fact, I do have a good bit with me," he said proudly. "I guess the man saw it when I pulled out my wallet to be sure the money was there."

"What are you going to do with all your cash?"

Frank asked curiously. "Start a mint of your own?"

"Now, don't be funny, Frank Hardy," Chet retorted. "You must have noticed that for a long time I haven't been spending much. I've been saving like mad to buy a special scientific instrument. After your dad arrives, I'm going to pick it up."

"What kind of hobby are you latching onto this time, Chet?" Frank asked, grinning.

From past experience, Frank and Joe knew that their friend's interest in his new hobby would only last until another hobby captured his fancy.

"This is different," Chet insisted. "I'm going to the Scientific Specialties Store and buy a twin-lensed, high-powered microscope—and an illuminator to go with it."

"A microscope!" Joe exclaimed. "What are you going to do with it—hunt for the answers to school exams?"

Frank joined Joe in a loud laugh, but Chet did not seem to think there was anything funny about it.

"Just you two wait," he muttered, kicking a stone that was lying on the platform. "You don't know whether or not I'll decide to be a naturalist or even a zoologist."

"Wow!" said Joe. "I can just see a sign: *Chester Morton, Big-game Naturalist.*"

"Okay," Chet said. "Maybe even you two great detectives will need me to help you with some of your cases."

The conversation ended with Frank's saying, "Here comes Dad's train."

The express from Detroit rolled into the station. The brothers and their friend scanned the passengers alighting. To their disappointment, Mr. Hardy was not among them.

"Aren't there any other Bayport passengers?" Frank asked a conductor.

"No, sir," the trainman called out as he waved the go-ahead signal to the engineer and jumped back onto the car.

As the train pulled out, Joe said, "Dad must have been delayed at the last moment. Let's come back to the station and meet the four-o'clock train."

"That's plenty of time for you fellows to go with me and pick up my microscope," said Chet.

The boys walked to Chet's jalopy, nicknamed Queen, parked in the station lot. The Queen had been painted a brilliant yellow, and "souped up" by Chet during one of the periods when engines were his hobby. It was a familiar and amusing sight around the streets of Bayport.

"She's not fancy, but she gets around pretty quick," Chet often maintained stoutly. "I wouldn't trade her for all the fancy cars in the showrooms."

"The gas gauge reads 'Empty,'" Joe observed, as Chet backed the jalopy from the curb. "How do you figure we'll make it downtown?"

Chet was unconcerned. "Oh, the tank's really half full. I'll have to fix that gauge."

The Hardys exchanged amused glances, knowing that Chet would soon be so absorbed in his

microscope he would forget to tinker with the car.

Suddenly Chet swung the Queen around in the parking lot. The rough gravel caught in the tire treads and rattled against the rear fenders.

"Hey! What's the big rush?" Joe demanded. "We have three whole hours to get back there!"

"Who's in a hurry?" said Chet, adding proudly, "I'm not driving fast. I just wanted to find out if I changed the turning circle of the Queen by adjusting the tie rods."

"Some adjustment!" Joe grimaced. "Think we'll get to town in one piece?"

"Huh!" Chet snorted. "You don't appreciate great mechanical genius when you see it!"

In the business center of Bayport, the boys found traffic heavy. Fortunately, Chet found a parking spot across the street from the Scientific Specialties Store and swung the car neatly into the space.

"See what I mean?" he asked. "Good old Queen. And boy, I can't wait to start working with that microscope!" Chet exclaimed as the three boys got out and walked to the corner.

"All bugs beware." Joe grinned.

"You ought to be a whiz in science class next year," Frank said while they waited for the light to change.

When it flashed green, the trio started across the street. Simultaneously, a young boy on a bicycle began to ride toward them from the opposite side of the street.

The next moment a large sedan, its horn honking loudly, sped through the intersection against the red light and roared directly toward the Hardys and Chet. Instantly Frank gave Joe and Chet a tremendous push and they all leaped back to safety. To their horror, the sedan swerved and the young boy on the bicycle was directly in its path.

"Look out!" the Hardys yelled at him.

CHAPTER II

Trailing a Detective

THE BOY on the bicycle heard the Hardys' warning just in time and swerved away from the onrushing car. He skidded and ran up against the curb.

The momentum carried the boy over the handlebars. He landed in a sitting position on the pavement, looking dazed.

"That driver must be out of his head!" Joe yelled as he, Frank, and Chet dashed over to the boy.

The sedan continued its erratic path, and finally, with brakes squealing and horn blaring, slammed into the curb. It had barely missed a parked car.

By now the Hardys and Chet had reached the boy. He was still seated on the sidewalk, holding his head. "Are you all right?" Frank asked, bending down. The boy was about fourteen years old, very thin and tall for his age.

"I—I think so." A grateful look came into the boy's clear brown eyes. "Thanks for the warning, fellows! Whew! That was close!"

Frank and Joe helped him to his feet. A crowd had gathered, and the Hardys had a hard time keeping the onlookers back. Just then the driver of the sedan made his way through the throng. He was a middle-aged man, and his face was ashen and drawn.

"I'm sorry! I'm sorry! My brakes wouldn't hold. Are you fellows all right?" The driver was frantic with worry. "It happened so fast—I—I just couldn't stop!"

"In that case, you're lucky no one was hurt," Frank said calmly.

The Hardys saw a familiar uniformed figure push through the crowd toward them.

"What's going on?" he demanded. He was Officer Roberts, a member of the local police department and an old friend of the Hardys. The driver of the car started to explain, but by this time he had become so confused, his statements were incoherent.

"What happened, Frank?" Officer Roberts asked.

Frank assured him no one was hurt, and said that apparently the mishap had been entirely accidental, and the only damage was to the boy's bicycle. The front wheel spokes were bent, and some of the paint was scratched off the fender.

The car driver, somewhat calmer now, insisted upon giving the boy five dollars toward repairs.

"I'll phone for a tow truck," Joe offered, and hurried off to make the call while Officer Roberts got the traffic moving again.

After the garage truck had left with the sedan, and the crowd had dispersed, the boy with the bicycle gave a sudden gasp.

"My envelope!" he cried out. "Where is it?"

The Hardys and Chet looked around. Joe was the first to spot a large Manila envelope in the street near the curb. He stepped out and picked it up. "Is this yours?" he asked.

"Yes! I was afraid it was lost!"

As Joe handed over the heavy, sealed envelope, he noticed that it was addressed in bold printing to Mr. Victor Peters, Parker Building, and had *Confidential* marked in the lower left-hand corner.

The boy smiled as he took the envelope and mounted his bicycle. "Thanks a lot for helping me, fellows. My name is Ken Blake."

The Hardys and Chet introduced themselves and asked Ken if he lived in Bayport.

"Not really," Ken answered slowly. "I have a summer job near here."

"Oh! Where are you working?" Chet asked.

Ken paused a moment before replying. "At a place outside of town," he said finally.

Although curious about Ken's apparent evasiveness, Frank changed the subject. He had been observing the bicycle with interest. Its handlebars were a different shape from most American models. The handgrips were much higher than the center post and the whole effect was that of a deep U.

"That's a nifty bike," he said. "What kind is it?"

Ken looked pleased. "It was made in Belgium. Rides real smooth." Then he added, "I'd better get back on the job now. I have several errands to do. So long, and thanks again."

As Ken rode off, Joe murmured, "Funny he's so secretive about where he lives and works."

Frank agreed. "I wonder why."

Chet scoffed. "There you go again, making a mystery out of it."

Frank and Joe had acquired their keen observation and interest in places and people from their father, one of the most famous investigators in the United States.

Only recently, the boys had solved *The Tower Treasure* mystery. Shortly afterward, they had used all their ingenuity and courage to uncover a dangerous secret in the case of *The House on the Cliff*.

"Come on, you two," Chet urged. "Let's get my microscope before anything else happens."

They had almost reached the Scientific Specialties Store when Joe grabbed his brother's arm and pointed down the street.

"Hey!" he exclaimed. "There's Oscar Smuff. What's *he* up to?"

The other boys looked and saw a short, stout man who was wearing a loud-checkered suit and a soft felt hat. Chet guffawed. "He acts as if he were stalking big game in Africa! Where's the lion?"

"I think"—Frank chuckled—"our friend is trying to shadow someone."

"If he is," Chet said, "how could anybody *not* know Oscar Smuff was following him?"

Oscar Smuff, the Hardys knew, wanted to be a member of the Bayport Police Department. He had read many books on crime detection, but, though he tried hard, he was just not astute enough to do anything right. The boys had encountered him several times while working on their own cases. Usually Smuff's efforts at detection had proved more hindrance than help, and at times actually laughable.

"Let's see what happens," said Joe.

In a second the boys spotted the man Oscar Smuff was tailing—a tall, trim, well-dressed stranger. He carried a suitcase and strode along as though he was going some place with a firm purpose in mind.

The boys could hardly restrain their laughter

as they watched Smuff's amateurish attempts to put into action what he had read about sleuthing.

"He's about as inconspicuous as an elephant!" Chet observed.

Smuff would run a few steps ahead of the stranger, then stop at a store window and pretend to be looking at the merchandise on display. Obviously he was waiting for the man to pass him, but Smuff did not seem to care what kind of window he was looking in. Joe nudged Frank and Chet when Oscar Smuff paused before the painted-over window of a vacant store.

"Wonder what he's supposed to be looking at," Chet remarked.

Smuff hurried on, then suddenly stopped again. He took off his jacket, threw it over his arm, and put on a pair of horn-rimmed glasses.

"Get a load of his tactics now!" Joe laughed. "He's trying to change his appearance."

Frank chuckled. "Oscar's been studying about how to tail, but he needs a lot more practice."

"He probably suspects the man has contraband in his suitcase," Joe guessed, grinning.

The tall stranger suddenly turned and looked back at Smuff. The would-be detective had ducked into a doorway and was peering out like a child playing hide-and-seek. For a moment Smuff and the stranger stared at each other. The man shrugged as though puzzled about what was going on, then continued walking.

Smuff kept up his comical efforts to shadow his quarry, unaware that the boys were following him. Near the end of the block, the man turned into a small variety store and Smuff scurried in after him.

"Come on!" said Joe to Frank and Chet. "This is too good to miss."

The boys followed. Oscar Smuff was standing behind a display of large red balloons. He was so intent on his quarry that he still did not notice the Hardys and Chet.

Frank looked around the store quickly and saw the stranger at the drug counter selecting some toothpaste. The suitcase was on the floor beside him. As they watched, the man picked up the toothpaste and his bag, and went up front to the checkout counter. He took out a bill and gave it to the woman cashier.

Immediately Smuff went into action. He dashed from behind the balloons and across the front of the store. Elbowing several customers out of the way, he grasped the man by the arm and in a loud voice announced, "You're under arrest! Come with me!"

The man looked at Oscar Smuff as though he were crazy. So did the cashier. Other people quickly crowded around.

"What's the matter?" someone called out.

The Hardys and Chet hurried forward, as the man pulled his arm away from Smuff's grasp and demanded angrily, "What's the meaning of this?"

"You know very well what's the meaning of this," Smuff blustered, and grabbed the man's arm again. "Now, miss"—Smuff turned to the cashier—"let me see the bill this man just gave you."

The woman was too surprised to refuse the request and handed the bill to the amateur detective.

Smuff took the money. The Hardys stepped up and peered over his shoulder. The bill was a five-dollar one. Suddenly the expression on Smuff's face changed to confusion and concern.

"Oh—er—a five—" he stuttered.

He dropped his hold on the man's arm and stared down at the floor. "Awfully sorry," he muttered. "It's been—a—mistake."

Both the man and the cashier looked completely bewildered. The next moment Smuff whirled and dashed from the store.

The Hardys and Chet rushed after him. They were overwhelmed with curiosity as to what Smuff thought the man had done. The boys soon overtook the would-be detective.

"What's up?" Joe demanded. "Looking for somebody suspicious?"

Oscar Smuff reddened when he realized the boys had witnessed his entire performance.

"Never mind," he said sharply. "I'll bet even you smart-aleck Hardys have made mistakes. Anyhow, this is different. I'm helping the police on a very special, very confidential case."

As he made the last statement, Smuff shrugged off his look of embarrassment and assumed an air of great importance.

"Well, I can't waste precious time gabbing with *you* three." Smuff turned and rushed off down the street.

The boys watched his bustling figure as he disappeared into the crowd. "I wonder what kind of case 'Detective' Smuff *is* working on?" Frank mused.

"I do too," Joe said, as Chet finally led the way into the Scientific Specialties Store.

Mr. Reed, the shop owner, stood behind the counter. He was a plump, pleasant man with a shock of white hair that stood erect on his head.

"Have you come for your microscope, Chet?" he asked. As he spoke, the man's head bobbed up and down and his white hair waved back and forth as though blown by the wind.

"Yes, sir, Mr. Reed," Chet said enthusiastically. "My friends, Frank and Joe, are looking forward to trying out the microscope just as much as I am."

Joe smiled a little skeptically, but Frank agreed with his chum. Chet pulled out his wallet and emptied it of ten- and twenty-dollar bills. "Here you are, Mr. Reed. I've been saving for a long time so I could get the best."

"And the best this is." Mr. Reed smiled. "I'll get the microscope you want from the stockroom." The proprietor picked up the money and disappeared into the back of the store.

While they waited, Chet pointed out the various instruments on display in the showcase. The Hardys were surprised at how much Chet had learned about microscopes and their use.

After waiting five minutes, Chet grew impatient. "Wonder what's keeping Mr. Reed," he said. "I hope he has my 'scope in stock."

At that moment Mr. Reed returned. There was a look of concern on his face.

"Don't tell me you haven't got the model." Chet groaned.

Mr. Reed shook his head. When he spoke, his voice was solemn.

"It's not that, Chet," he said. "I'm afraid that one of the twenty-dollar bills you gave me is a counterfeit!"

CHAPTER III

An Unexpected Return

"*COUNTERFEIT!*" Chet burst out. "*Counterfeit! It can't be. I just drew the money out of the bank this morning.*"

The Hardys, nonplused, stared at the twenty-dollar bill Mr. Reed was holding.

"I'm sorry, Chet," Mr. Reed said sympathetically. "But just a few days ago all the storekeepers in town were notified by the police to be on the lookout for fake twenties. Otherwise, I wouldn't have checked it. I can't understand, though, why the bank didn't detect it."

Frank's mind raced. "Wait a minute!" he exclaimed. "Chet, what about the man you made change for at the station?"

"You're right, Frank!" Joe put in. "*He* must have passed Chet the phony twenty!"

"You mean he gave it to me on purpose?" Chet asked indignantly.

"It's possible," Frank said. "Of course it would be pretty hard to prove whether he did it intentionally or not."

"What did the man look like?" Joe questioned Chet. "We got only a glimpse of him running for the train. He was medium height and stocky, but did you notice anything else about him?"

Chet thought for a few seconds. Then he said, "I do remember that the man had a sharp nose. But he was wearing sunglasses and a slouch hat, so I didn't notice much else."

The Hardys tried to fix a picture of the man in their minds. Meanwhile, Chet looked gloomily at the bogus bill.

"What luck!" he complained. "Here I am cheated out of twenty dollars and the microscope."

"I'm sorry, Chet," Mr. Reed said. "I wish there was something I could do about it."

"Don't worry, Chet," said Joe. "You'll get the microscope, anyway." He turned to his brother. "How much money do you have with you?" he asked. "I have five-fifty."

Frank emptied his pockets, but all he had was three dollars in change and bills.

"We'll lend you what we have," Joe offered. "Eight-fifty."

Although Chet protested, the Hardys insisted, and Mr. Reed added, "You can take the microscope along and pay me the balance when you can."

Frank and Joe put their money on the counter, while Mr. Reed went to wrap the instrument.

"Thanks. You're real pals," Chet said gratefully.

When the store owner returned with the package, Chet said, "I'll go right down to Dad's office and borrow the balance. We'll get back here later this afternoon. Thanks very much, Mr. Reed."

The boys were about to leave when Frank had a sudden thought.

"Mr. Reed," he said, "would you let us borrow that counterfeit bill for some close study? We'll be sure to turn it over to Chief Collig."

"Swell idea," Joe said.

The proprietor, who was familiar with the Hardys' reputation as sleuths, readily assented. Frank put the bill in his pocket and the boys left the store.

They hurried back to Chet's car and drove to Mr. Morton's real-estate office several blocks away. The office was on the street level of a small building. They entered and were greeted pleasantly by Mr. Morton's efficient secretary, Miss Benson.

"Hello, boys. Enjoying your summer vacation?"

"Yes, thanks, Miss Benson," Chet said, eying

his father's empty desk. "When will Dad be back?"

"Your father's gone for the day, Chet," she replied. "He decided to go home early."

"That's funny," Chet mused. "Dad usually stays until five at least."

"We have time to drive out to the farm before we meet the train," Joe said. "Let's go."

The Morton farm was on the outskirts of Bayport. When Chet swung the car into the driveway, Joe noticed with pleasure that Iola, Chet's sister, was waving to them from the front porch. Dark-haired Iola, slim and vivacious, was Joe's favorite date.

When they told her about the counterfeit bill, she exclaimed, "What a shame!"

Joe agreed emphatically. "And we'd sure like to get a lead on the man who passed it to Chet."

"Sounds as if you Hardys are in the mood for some sleuthing," Iola said with a twinkle in her eye.

"What's this about sleuthing?" asked attractive Mrs. Morton as she came outside and joined the group.

The boys quickly explained. Then Chet asked his mother, "Is Dad around?"

Mrs. Morton smiled. "He isn't here right now, Chet. He's attending to an important job."

Chet looked disappointed until his sister giggled and said, "Dad's not too far away." Iola winked at her mother and they both began to laugh.

"Your father's important job is at his favorite fishing spot," Mrs. Morton told Chet.

"Fishing!" Chet exclaimed. "He never goes fishing during the week!"

"He did this time," said Mrs. Morton. "I guess the good weather was too much for him to resist."

A few minutes later the boys were in the jalopy and driving down a country road bordered by woods. A half mile farther, Chet stopped and turned off the Queen's engine. The sound of rushing water could be heard.

"This is the spot," Chet announced, and they started off through the woods.

The boys soon came to a clear running stream and spotted Mr. Morton seated contentedly on the bank. He was leaning against a tree, holding his rod lightly between his knees and steadying it with his hands.

Just as the boys called a greeting to him, the line began to jerk and almost immediately the rod bent till the tip was close to the water. Mr. Morton leaped to his feet and shouted, "Just a minute, fellows! I've hooked a lulu!"

Mr. Morton was an expert. He let the fish take just enough line to bury the hook properly, then he very gently braked the reel with his thumb.

So intent was Mr. Morton on his fishing, he

was not aware that his son was now rushing down the slope toward him. Suddenly Chet slipped on a moss-covered rock and fell forward. He lost his grip on the box containing the microscope and it flew toward the water. Joe, behind Chet, leaped forward and grabbed the box.

"Whew!" Chet exclaimed, regaining his balance. "Good work, Joe! Thanks a million!"

The three boys joined Mr. Morton, who was busy landing his catch, a fine, smallmouthed black bass. He held up the fish for them to admire. "Isn't it a beauty, boys?" he said.

"Terrific, Dad," Chet replied, still out of breath from his near tumble. "And I have something to show *you*."

He unwrapped the package and held out the microscope. Mr. Morton put the fish in his creel, then studied the instrument closely.

"It's a topnotch one, son," he declared. "And just the model you wanted."

"Yes, Dad. Only there's a slight problem connected with it."

"Oh—oh." Mr. Morton chuckled good-naturedly. "I should have known from the look on your face. You didn't have enough money, after all. Well, how much do you need?"

"That isn't all there is to it," Chet hastened to inform him, and told about the counterfeit bill.

Mr. Morton's face darkened. "I hope we're not in for a flood of phony bills."

Frank nodded. "Especially since these are very clever imitations."

Chet's father handed over twenty dollars in small bills.

"Thanks, Dad."

"From now on, Chet, be careful about making change for strangers," Mr. Morton cautioned.

"I will," his son promised fervently. "Getting cheated once is enough!"

Chet paid the Hardys the money they had lent him. Then he said to his father, "I sure was surprised when Mother told me you were fishing —in the middle of the week."

Mr. Morton smiled broadly. "I've been working hard the past year on the big sale of land to Elekton Controls," he said. "I thought it was time to take an afternoon off and do some thinking while the fish were nibbling."

"Is that the property in back of the plant they just finished building?" asked Frank.

"That's right." Mr. Morton pointed upstream. "You can just see the top of the main building from here."

"The property you sold has the old Turner mill on it," Joe remarked. "Quite a contrast. A company that makes top-secret control parts for space missiles in a modern building right next to an ancient, abandoned gristmill."

"I suppose they'll tear the old place down," Frank remarked.

"No, Elekton has decided to use it," Mr. Morton went on. "I suggested to them that the old mill would make an attractive gatehouse for the plant's rear entrance. After all, it's a historic place, built by the settlers when this whole area was inhabited by Indians. The company has renovated the old mill a bit, restoring the old living quarters and adding modern facilities."

"Is someone living there?" Joe asked with interest.

"I understand a couple of their employees are," Mr. Morton replied. Then he continued, "They've even repaired the wheel, so it's turning again. Hearing the rushing water and the grinding of the wheel's gear mechanism brought back memories to me."

"About the Indians, Dad?" Chet joked.

"Not quite, son." His father smiled. "But I *can* remember when the mill produced the best flour around here. Your grandmother made many a delicious loaf of bread from wheat ground in the Turner mill."

"That's for me!" Chet said.

Everyone laughed as Mr. Morton reminisced further about having seen the mill in full operation when he was a boy. Suddenly he and the Hardys noticed that Chet had fallen silent. There was a familiar, faraway look in his eyes.

Joe grinned. "Chet, you're turning some new idea over in your mind."

"That's right," Chet said excitedly. "I've been thinking that maybe I could get a summer job at Elekton."

Mr. Morton exchanged amazed glances with the Hardys at the thought of Chet's working during the summer vacation! But, with growing enthusiasm, Chet went on:

"I could earn the twenty dollars I owe you, Dad. Besides, if I am going to be a scientist, I couldn't think of a better place to work."

"Elekton's a fine company," his father said. "I wish you luck, son."

"Thanks, Dad." Chet smiled broadly. "See you later. I have to go now and pay Mr. Reed the money I owe him."

On the drive back to town, Chet told Frank and Joe that he was going to apply for a job at the Elekton plant the next day.

"We'll go along," Joe offered. "I'd like to see the plant and the old mill."

"Swell," said Chet.

When they reached the shopping area in Bayport, Chet drove directly to Mr. Reed's store. The three boys had just alighted from the parked car when Chet excitedly grabbed his friends' arms.

"There he is!" the chubby boy exclaimed. "Right down the street—the man who gave me that phony twenty!"

CHAPTER IV

The Shadowy Visitor

"THERE he goes! Across the street!" Joe said excitedly. "Let's ask him about the counterfeit bill!"

The three boys broke into a run, dodging in and out of the crowd of afternoon shoppers. The Hardys kept their eyes trained on the stocky figure of their quarry.

But their chase was halted at the corner by a red traffic light against them. The street was congested with vehicles and it was impossible for the boys to get across.

"What luck!" Joe growled impatiently.

It seemed to be the longest red light they had ever encountered. When it changed, the threesome streaked across the street—but it was too late. The stocky man was lost to sight. The Hardys raced down the next two blocks, peering in every direction, but to no avail.

Disappointed, Frank and Joe went back to Chet, who had stopped to catch his breath.

"We lost him," Joe reported tersely.

Frank's eyes narrowed. "I have a hunch that man who passed the bogus twenty-dollar bill to Chet knew it was counterfeit. That last-second dash for the train was just a gimmick to make a fast getaway. But his showing up here in Bayport a couple hours after he took the train out of town is mighty peculiar."

Joe and Chet agreed. "He probably got off in Bridgeport," Frank went on. "That's the nearest big town."

As the boys walked back toward the Scientific Specialties Store, they speculated about the source of the supply of bogus money.

"Maybe it's Bridgeport," Frank said. "That could be one of the reasons he took the train there—to get a new supply, or palm off more."

"You mean they might actually make the stuff there?" Chet asked.

Frank shrugged. "Could be," he said. "I hope no more counterfeit bills are passed in Bayport."

"There probably will be," Chet said ruefully, "if this town is full of easy marks like me."

"Let's keep a sharp lookout for that fake-money passer from now on," Joe said, "and other clues to the counterfeit ring."

"Who knows," Chet put in, "it could turn out to be your next case."

As soon as Mr. Reed had been paid, the boys drove to Bayport Police Headquarters. Chet decided to take his microscope into headquarters and show it to Chief Ezra Collig. The keen-eyed, robust officer was an old friend of Fenton Hardy and his sons. Many times the four had cooperated on cases.

"Sit down," the chief said cordially. "I can see that you boys have something special on your minds. Another mystery?"

He leaned forward expectantly in his chair.

"It's possible, Chief," replied Frank as he handed over the counterfeit bill. Quickly the Hardys explained what had happened, then voiced their suspicions of the man who had just eluded them.

"Have there been any other reports of people receiving fake bills?" Joe asked the officer.

Chief Collig nodded. "Chet's not the first to be fooled," he replied. "Since the Secret Service alerted us to watch for these twenty-dollar bills, we've had nearly a dozen complaints. But we've instructed the people involved not to talk about it."

"Why?" Chet asked curiously.

"It's part of our strategy. We hope to trap at least some of the gang by lulling them into a feeling of false security."

The boys learned that Chet's description of

the stocky stranger tallied with what the police had on file.

"He's a slippery one," the chief added. "It sounds to me as if the man wears a different outfit each time he shoves a bill."

"Shoves?" echoed Chet.

"A shover—or passer—is a professional term for people who pass counterfeit money," Chief Collig explained. He rubbed the bogus bill between his fingers. "This is a clever forgery," he said. "Let's see what it looks like under your microscope, Chet."

It took just a minute to rig and focus the microscope. Then, under Chief Collig's directions, the boys scrutinized the faults in the bill.

"Look at the serial number," the chief pointed out. "That's the large, colored group of numbers that appears on the upper right and lower left portions of the bill."

As the boys peered at the number, Chief Collig made some quick calculations on his desk pad. "Divide the serial number by six," he went on, "and in this case, the remainder is two."

When the boys looked puzzled, the chief smiled. "On the upper left portion of the note you'll see a small letter. One that is not followed by a number. That's the check letter and in this case it's B."

The boys listened as Chief Collig further explained, "If the letter B corresponds to the remainder two, after you have done the division, it means the bill is either genuine—or a careful fake. The same way with the remainder, one. The check letter would be A or G; and with the remainder three, the check letter C or I, and so on."

"Wow! Some arithmetic!" Chet remarked.

Frank looked thoughtful. "In this case, the test of the divisional check indicates the bill is genuine."

"Exactly," Chief Collig said. "And the portrait of Jackson is good. The border, sometimes called lathe or scrollwork, is excellent."

"But, Chief," said Joe, puzzled, "everything you've mentioned points toward the bill's being the real thing."

"That's right. However, you'll see through the microscope that the lines in the portrait are slightly grayish and the red and blue fibers running through the bank note have been simulated with colored ink."

In turn, the boys peered through the microscope, observing the points the chief had called to their attention.

Chief Collig snapped off the light in Chet's microscope and pulled the bill out from under the clips that were holding it in place.

He handed the fake bill to Frank and at the same time gave him a genuine one from his wallet. "Now feel the difference in the paper quality," he directed.

Frank did so and could tell immediately that the forged bill was much rougher and thicker than the genuine one.

Just then the chief's telephone rang. He answered it, speaking quickly. When he hung up, Chief Collig said, "I must go out on a call, boys. Thanks for bringing in this bill. If you come across any others like it, or clues that might help the police, let me know. In the meantime, I'll relay your description of the suspect to the Secret Service, and also turn this bill over to them."

Chief Collig arose from his desk, and the boys walked out of the building with him. On the way, Joe said, "I wonder if Oscar Smuff has heard of the counterfeiting racket, and is—er—working on it."

"I wouldn't be surprised." The chief sighed. "That fellow will never give up."

The boys did not mention their encounter with Smuff earlier in the afternoon, but they were fairly certain that Oscar Smuff had trailed the man because he was a stranger in town and had been carrying a suitcase. The aspiring detective undoubtedly had jumped to the conclusion that the suitcase was filled with counterfeit money.

When the chief had gone, Joe glanced at his

watch. "If we're going to meet Dad's train, we'd better get started."

The three boys climbed into the jalopy and drove off. They arrived at the station just as the four-o'clock train was coming to a halt.

A moment later they spotted Mr. Hardy alighting from the rear car. "Dad!" cried Frank and Joe, and dashed to greet him, followed by Chet.

Fenton Hardy, a tall, distinguished-looking man, smiled broadly. "I appreciate this special reception—and a ride home, too," he added, noticing Chet's jalopy in the lot.

"Right this way, sir." Chet grinned.

Joe took his father's suitcase and everyone went to the car. As they rode along, the boys gave Mr. Hardy an account of the afternoon's exciting events.

The detective listened intently. In conclusion, Frank said, "Dad, does your new case have anything to do with the counterfeiting ring?"

Mr. Hardy did not answer for a moment. His mind seemed to be focused on another matter. Finally he said, "No. But I'll be glad to help you boys track down any clues to these counterfeiters. I have a feeling you'll be on the lookout for them!"

"We sure will!" Joe said emphatically.

As they turned into the Hardy driveway, Frank said, "Maybe more leads will show up around here."

Fenton Hardy agreed. "That's a strong possibility."

They were met at the door by Aunt Gertrude, Mr. Hardy's unmarried sister. She was a tall, angular woman, somewhat peppery in manner, but extremely kindhearted. Miss Hardy had arrived recently for one of her frequent long visits with the family. In her forthright manner she was constantly making dire predictions about the dangers of sleuthing, and the terrible fate awaiting anyone who was a detective.

She greeted her brother affectionately as everyone went into the living room. With a sigh she asked, "Will you be home for a while this time, Fenton, before you have to go dashing off on another case?"

Chuckling, Mr. Hardy replied, "I'll probably be around for a while, Gertrude—especially if the boys run into any more counterfeit money."

"What! Laura, did you hear that?" Aunt Gertrude turned to a slim, attractive woman who had just entered the room.

"I did." Mrs. Hardy greeted her husband, then urged the boys to explain.

After hearing of Chet's experience, both women shook their heads in dismay. "Well, the sooner those counterfeiters are caught, the better!" Aunt Gertrude declared firmly.

"That's what we figure, Aunty," Joe spoke up. "We'll see what we can do! Right, Frank?"

"You bet."

Chet added, grinning, "With the Hardy boys on their trail, those counterfeiters won't have a chance!"

"And Laura and I will lose sleep worrying," Aunt Gertrude prophesied.

Frank and Joe exchanged winks, knowing that actually she and Mrs. Hardy were proud of the boys' sleuthing accomplishments, though sometimes fearful of the dangers they encountered.

"What delayed you today, Fenton?" Aunt Gertrude asked her brother. "Another case, I suppose."

Mr. Hardy explained, "There is a special matter I'm investigating, but I'm not at liberty to talk about it yet."

His next remark diverted the boys' attention from the counterfeiters. "Frank and Joe, will you be free tomorrow to see the surprise I have for you both?" he asked. "It'll be ready late in the afternoon."

"We sure will!" his sons exclaimed together. They knew what they hoped the surprise would be, but did not dare count on it.

The brothers tried without success to coax a hint from their family.

"All I can say," Aunt Gertrude remarked, "is that you're mighty lucky boys!" With a deep sigh she added, "But this surprise certainly won't help my peace of mind!"

"Oh, Aunty!" said Joe. "You don't really worry about us, do you?"

"Oh, no!" she exploded. "Only on weekdays, Saturdays, and Sundays!"

Before Chet left for home, he reminded Frank and Joe of his intention to apply to Elekton Controls Limited for a job.

Overhearing him, Mr. Hardy was immediately interested. "So you want to enter the scientific field, Chet?" he said. "Good for you and lots of luck!"

The detective told the boys that the company, in addition to manufacturing controls, was engaged in secret experiments with advanced electronic controls.

"Not too long ago," he concluded, "I met some of Elekton's officers."

It flashed through Chet's mind that he might ask the detective to make an appointment for him, but he decided not to. He wanted to get the job without an assist from anyone. Frank and Joe suggested that Chet come for them early the next afternoon.

"I have an idea!" Chet exclaimed. "Let's go earlier and take along a picnic lunch. We'll be right near Willow River. After I apply for a job, we can eat by the water. Then you fellows can help me collect bark and stone specimens."

"Microscope study, eh?" Frank grinned. "Okay. It's a deal."

At supper Aunt Gertrude commented wryly, "There'll be two moons in the sky when Chet Morton settles down to a job!"

The others laughed, then the conversation reverted once more to counterfeiting. Mr. Hardy backed up Chief Collig's statement that the bogus twenty-dollar bills being circulated were clever imitations. "I heard that the Secret Service is finding it a hard case to crack," he added.

Frank and Joe were wondering about their father's other case. They realized it must be extremely confidential, and refrained from questioning him.

In the middle of the night, Joe was suddenly awakened by a clattering sound. He leaped out of bed and rushed across the room to the front window. It was a dark, moonless night, and for a moment Joe could see nothing.

But suddenly he detected a movement near the front door, then saw a shadowy figure running down the walk to the street.

"Hey!" Joe called out. "Who are you? What do you want?"

At the end of the walk, the mysterious figure leaped onto a bicycle. It swerved, nearly throwing the rider, but he regained his balance and sped off into the darkness.

"What's going on?" Joe cried out.

CHAPTER V

The Bicycle Clue

JOE ran downstairs to the front door, flung it open, and dashed outside. He reached the end of the walk and peered in the direction the mysterious cyclist had taken. The person was not in sight.

Puzzled, Joe walked back slowly to the house. Had the stranger come there by mistake? "If not, what did he want?" Joe wondered.

The rest of the Hardy family had been awakened by Joe's cries to the stranger. By this time, they were clustered at the doorway and all the lights in the house were on.

"What's the matter, Joe?" Aunt Gertrude demanded. "Who were you calling to at this unearthly hour?"

Joe was about to reply when he noticed a large white envelope protruding from the mailbox. He pulled it out, and saw that his father's name was typed on the front. "This is for you, Dad."

Joe handed the envelope to Mr. Hardy. "That fellow on the bike must have left it."

Joe was besieged with questions, and he explained what had happened.

"It's a funny way to deliver a message," Frank commented.

"Very suspicious, if you ask me!" Aunt Gertrude snapped.

Suddenly they all noticed that Mr. Hardy was frowning at the contents of the envelope—a plain piece of white paper.

"What does it say, Fenton?" Mrs. Hardy asked anxiously.

He read the typed message: " *'Drop case or else danger for you and family.'* "

There was silence for a moment, then Aunt Gertrude exclaimed, "I knew it! We can't get a decent night's sleep with three detectives in the family! I just *know* there's real trouble brewing!"

Although she spoke tartly, the others realized Miss Hardy was concerned, as always, for her brother's safety.

"Now, don't worry, Gertrude," Fenton Hardy said reassuringly. "The boys and I will be on guard against any danger. This note probably is the work of a harmless crank."

Aunt Gertrude tossed her head as though she did not believe this for a moment.

"Let's all look around for clues to the person on the bike," Frank suggested.

Flashlights were procured, and the entire family searched the grounds thoroughly on both sides of the stoop and the walk. As Frank and his aunt neared the end of the front walk, Miss Hardy cried out, "There's something—next to that bush."

Frank picked up the object. "A bicycle pedal!" he exclaimed. "Aunty, this is a terrific clue! I think we have *four* detectives in the family!"

His aunt forced a rather embarrassed smile.

"The pedal must've fallen off the bike Joe saw," Frank said. "That's why it swerved."

Back in the house, the family gathered in the kitchen. They were too excited to go back to bed immediately, and the boys were eager to question their father. They all had cookies and lemonade.

"What case did the warning refer to?" Joe asked Mr. Hardy.

"I can't be sure," the detective replied slowly.

Again the boys wondered about Mr. Hardy's secret case, and longed to know what it involved. "Maybe the threat is connected with that one," Frank thought. Before the boys went to sleep, they decided to track down the pedal clue early the next morning.

Right after breakfast, Chet telephoned. He told Frank, who took the call, that his sister Iola and her friend Callie Shaw had offered to pack lunch if they could go along on the picnic.

"Swell," Frank said enthusiastically. Callie was his favorite date. "In the meantime, how'd you like to do some sleuthing with us?"

"Sure! What's up?"

Frank quickly told Chet about the excitement of the previous night. "Meet us here as soon as you can."

When Frank and Joe informed Mr. Hardy of their plan to trace the pedal, he nodded approval. "I must go out of town for a short while," he said. "But first, I'd like to examine the warning note in the lab."

The boys went with him to their fully equipped laboratory over the garage. Mr. Hardy dusted the note carefully, but when he blew the powder away, there was no sign of a fingerprint.

Holding the note up to the light, Mr. Hardy said, "There's no watermark. Of course, this is not a full sheet of paper."

"Dead end, so far." Joe frowned. "If we could only locate the typewriter this message was written on—"

Shortly after Mr. Hardy had driven off in his sedan, Chet arrived. "Where to, fellows?" he asked as they set off in the Queen.

"Center of town," Joe replied.

On the way, the brothers briefed Chet on their plan, which was to make inquiries at all the bicycle supply stores. In the first four they visited,

Frank showed the pedal and asked if there had been any requests for a replacement that morning. All the answers were negative. Finally, at the largest supply store in Bayport, they obtained some helpful information.

"This particular pedal comes from a bike made in Belgium," the proprietor said. "There isn't a store in town that carries parts for it."

The boys were disappointed. As Frank put the pedal back in his pocket he asked the proprietor where parts for the Belgian bicycle could be purchased.

"It might be worth your while to check over in Bridgeport," the man said. "I think you'll find Traylor's handles them."

"It's an odd coincidence," Frank remarked, when the boys were back in the car. "We've come across two Belgian bikes in two days."

When they reached the Traylor store in Bridgeport, the young detectives learned they had just missed a customer who had purchased a pedal for a Belgian bike.

"Who was he?" Frank inquired.

"I don't know."

"What did he look like?" Joe asked.

The proprietor's brow wrinkled. "Sorry. I was too busy to pay much attention, so I can't tell you much. As far as I can remember, he was a tall boy, maybe about fourteen."

The three friends knew this vague description

was almost useless. There probably were hundreds of boys living in the surrounding area who fitted that description.

As the boys reached the street, Joe said determinedly, "We're not giving up!"

"Hey!" Chet reminded his friends. "It's almost time to pick up the girls."

Within an hour the five young people were turning off the highway onto a side road paralleling Elekton's east fence. A little farther on Chet made a right turn and followed the dirt road that led to the rear entrance of the plant.

"Any luck sleuthing?" Pretty, brown-eyed Callie Shaw asked the Hardys.

"What makes you think we were sleuthing?"

"Oh, I can tell!" Callie said, her eyes twinkling. "You two always have that detective gleam in your eyes when you're mixed up in a mystery!"

"They certainly have!" Iola agreed, laughing.

When they reached a grove bordering Willow River, which was to their left, Chet pulled over. "I'll park here."

The girls had decided they would like to see the changes which had been made in the old mill. As the group approached Elekton's gatehouse, they were amazed at the transformation.

No longer did the mill look shabby and neglected. The three-story structure had been completely repainted and the weeds and overgrowth of years cleared away. The grounds and shrubbery of the whole area were neatly trimmed.

"Look!" said Frank. "There's the mill wheel!"

As the Hardys and their friends watched the huge wheel turning, they felt for a moment that they were living in olden days. Water which poured from a pond over a high stone dam on the south side and through an elevated millrace caused the wheel to revolve.

"Oh!" Callie exclaimed admiringly as she spotted a little bridge over the stream from the falls. "It looks just like a painting!"

About three hundred yards from the north side of the mill was the closed rear gate to Elekton's ultramodern plant.

"Some contrast between the old and the new!" Joe remarked as they left the dirt road and walked up the front path to the gatehouse.

Suddenly the door opened and a dark-haired, muscular man in uniform came out to meet them. "What can I do for you?" he asked. "I'm the gate guard here."

"I'd like to apply for a summer job at Elekton," Chet told him.

"Have you an appointment?"

"No," replied Chet. "I guess I should have phoned first."

The guard agreed. "You would've saved yourself time and trouble," he said. "I'm sure there aren't any openings, especially for temporary help."

"Well, couldn't I go in and leave an application with the personnel manager?" Chet asked.

The guard shrugged. "Tell you what—I'll phone the personnel office instead," he offered, and went back into the mill.

While they waited, the five looked around. At the south side of the mill grounds, a slender, graying man who wore overalls was clipping the low hedges.

"Look, Callie," said Iola, pointing toward a spot near the hedges. "Isn't that quaint? An old flour barrel with ivy growing out of it!"

"Charming." Callie smiled.

The girls and boys started over toward the mill for a closer inspection. At that same moment the guard came to the door. "Just as I told you," he called out to Chet. "No openings! Sorry!"

"Too bad, Chet," Joe said sympathetically. "Well, at least you can keep on relaxing."

Despite his disappointment, Chet grinned. "Right now I'm starved. "Let's go down to the river and have our picnic."

He thanked the guard, and the young people started to walk away. Suddenly Frank stopped and looked back at the mill. Propped against the south wall was a bicycle. Quickly he ran over to examine it. "This looks like a Belgian model," Frank thought. "Sure is," he told himself. "The same type Ken Blake has."

On impulse Frank pulled the pedal from his

pocket and compared it to those on the bike. They matched exactly. Frank noticed that one of the pedals looked much less worn than the other. "As if it had been replaced recently," he reflected, wondering excitedly if someone had used this bicycle to deliver the warning note.

"And could this bike be Ken's?" the young detective asked himself.

He inspected the front-wheel spokes. None was twisted, but several had slight dents. "They could've been straightened out easily," Frank reasoned, "and the paint scratches on the fender touched up."

He felt his heart beat faster as he waved his companions to join him. When Frank pointed out the clues to his brother, Joe agreed immediately.

"It could be the bicycle which was used to deliver the message—"

Joe was interrupted by a strange voice behind them. "Pardon me, but why are you so interested in that bike?"

Frank quickly slipped the pedal into his pocket as the group swung around to face the speaker. He was the man who had been clipping the hedges.

"Because just yesterday we met a boy, Ken Blake, who was riding a bike of the same model. We don't often see this Belgian make around."

For a moment the man looked surprised, then smiled. "Of course! Ken works here—does odd jobs for us around the mill. You must be the boys he met yesterday when he was delivering some copy to the printer."

"Yes," Frank replied. "When we asked Ken about his job he was very secretive."

"Well," the maintenance man said, "he has to be! This plant is doing top-secret work. All of us have been impressed with the necessity of not talking about Elekton at all."

"Is Ken around?" Joe asked nonchalantly. "We'd like to say hello."

"I'm afraid not," was the reply. "We sent him by bus this afternoon to do an errand. He won't be back until later." The man excused himself and resumed his clipping.

"We'd better eat." Iola giggled. "My poor brother is suffering."

"I sure am!" Chet rolled his eyes. Laughing, the picnickers started away.

Joe, who was in the rear, happened to glance up at the front of the mill. He was startled to catch a glimpse of a face at one of the second-story windows. He stopped in his tracks.

"Ken Blake!" Joe said to himself.

As the young sleuth stared, mystified, the face disappeared from the window.

CHAPTER VI

A Mysterious Tunnel

PUZZLED, Joe continued looking up at the window of the old mill.

"What's the matter?" Iola asked him. "Did you see a ghost?"

In a low whisper Joe explained about the face which had disappeared. "I'm sure it was Ken Blake I saw at that window!"

The others followed his gaze. "No one's there now," Iola said. "Of course the glass in all the windows is old and wavy. The sunlight on them could cause an illusion."

Chet agreed. "How could Ken be here if he was sent on an errand?"

Joe stood for a minute, deep in thought. "I can't figure it out, but I'm sure that it was no illusion. Come on, Frank. Let's go check."

While the others walked down the hill, the

Hardys strode up to the maintenance man, who was still trimming hedges.

"Are you sure Ken went into town?" Joe asked. "Just now I thought I saw him looking out a second-floor window."

"You couldn't have. You must have been dreaming." The man gave a jovial laugh.

Joe was still not convinced. Impulsively he asked, "Does Ken ever run any errands for you at night?"

"No," the man answered readily. "He leaves his bike here and walks home when we close at five-thirty."

"Does anyone else have access to the bike after that?" Frank queried.

"It's kept in an open storage area under the rear of the mill and could be taken from there easily."

Although obviously curious, the man did not ask the Hardys the reason for their questions. He looked at his watch.

"Excuse me, boys, I'm late for lunch." He turned and hurried into the mill.

As the brothers hastened to catch up with Chet and the girls, Frank said, "Another thing which makes me wonder if that bicycle is connected with the warning is the description of the boy who bought the pedal. *He* could be Ken Blake."

"I agree," Joe said. "I'd sure like to question Ken."

"We'll come back another time," Frank proposed.

The group picked up the picnic hamper from the Queen and strolled down a narrow path through the woods leading to Willow River.

"Here's a good spot." Callie pointed to a shaded level area along the bank. "We haven't been in this section before."

Soon everyone was enjoying the delicious lunch the girls had prepared: chicken sandwiches, potato salad, chocolate cake, and lemonade. While they were eating, the girls were the targets of good-natured kidding.

"Boy!" Joe exclaimed as he finished his piece of cake. "This is almost as good as my mother and Aunt Gertrude make."

"*That's* a compliment!" Chet said emphatically.

Callie's eyes twinkled. "I know it is. Joe's mother and aunt are the best cooks ever!"

Iola sniffed. "I don't know about this compliment stuff. There's something on your mind, Joe Hardy!"

Joe grinned. "How are you on apple pie and cream puffs and—?"

"Oh, stop it!" Iola commanded. "Otherwise, you won't get a second piece of cake!"

"I give up." Joe handed over his paper plate.

After lunch everyone but Chet was ready to relax in the sun. Normally he was the first one to suggest a period of rest, even a nap, but now his new project was uppermost in his mind.

"Let's start to collect the specimens for my microscope," he urged his friends.

The Hardys groaned good-naturedly at Chet's enthusiasm, but readily agreed.

"We'll need some exercise to work off that meal." Frank grinned.

The girls packed the food wrappings in the hamper. Then, single file, the group walked downstream, paying careful attention to the rocks and vegetation. Chet picked up several rocks and leaves, but discarded them as being too common.

"Are you looking for something from the Stone Age?" Joe quipped. "Maybe a prehistoric fossil?"

"Wouldn't you be surprised if I found one?" Chet retorted.

They followed a bend in the river and came to a small cove with a rocky, shelving beach. Here the willow trees did not grow so thickly. The shoreline curved gently around to the right before it came to a halt in a sandy strip along the riverbank.

"What a nice spot," said Callie. "We'll have to come here again and wear our swim suits."

"Look!" cried Iola. "What's that?"

She pointed to a dark opening beneath a rocky ledge which bordered the beach.

"A cave!" exclaimed Joe and Frank together.

Intrigued, the five hurried along the beach for

"Hey! This looks like a tunnel!"

a closer look. Eagerly the Hardys and Chet peered inside the entrance. The interior was damp, and the cave's walls were covered with green growth.

"This'll be a perfect spot to look for specimens," Chet said. "Let's go in!"

The boys entered the cave. The girls, however, decided to stay outside.

"Too spooky—and crowded!" Callie declared. "Iola and I will sun ourselves while you boys explore."

The Hardys and Chet could just about stand up in the low-ceilinged cave. Frank turned on his pocket flashlight and pointed to an unusual yellow-green fungus on the right side of the cave. "Here's a good sample of lichens, Chet."

Soon the boys were busy scraping various lichens off the rocks. Gradually they moved deeper into the cave. Frank halted in front of a pile of rocks at the rear.

"There ought to be some interesting specimens behind these stones," he said. "They look loose enough to move."

Together, the three boys rolled some of the rocks to one side. To their great surprise, the stones had concealed another dark hole.

"Hey! This looks like a tunnel!"

Excitedly Joe poked his flashlight into the opening. In its beam they could see that the hole appeared to extend into the side of the bank.

"Let's see where the tunnel goes!" Joe urged.

"Okay," Frank agreed eagerly. "We'll have to move more of these rocks before we can climb through. I wonder who put them here and why."

Rapidly the boys pushed rocks aside until the narrow tunnel entrance was completely exposed. Joe crawled in first, then Frank.

Chet tried to squeeze his bulky form through the space but quickly backed out. "It's too tight for me," he groaned. "I'll stay here and collect more specimens. Anyhow, I'll bet some animal made the tunnel and it doesn't lead anywhere."

"I'm sure no animal did this," Joe called back, aiming his flashlight at the earthen walls of the tunnel. "Look how hard-packed the sides are—as if dug out by a shovel."

Frank was of the same opinion. He pointed to rough-hewn wooden stakes placed at intervals along the sides and across the ceiling. "I wonder who put those supports here—and when."

The Hardys crawled ahead carefully. There was just room in the passageway for a normal-sized person to get through.

Presently Joe called back to his brother, "Look ahead! I can see a sharp bend to the right. Let's keep going."

Frank was about to reply when the brothers were startled by a girl's scream from outside.

"That's Callie!" Frank exclaimed. "Something's wrong!"

CHAPTER VII

Sleuthing by Microscope

FRANK and Joe scrambled through the tunnel and out of the cave. They found Chet and the girls staring at an arrow embedded in the sandy beach.

"It—it almost hit us," Iola quavered. Callie, who was white-faced with fear, nodded.

Joe was furious. "Whoever shot it shouldn't be allowed to use such a dangerous weapon!" he burst out. "That's a hunting arrow—it could have caused serious injury."

Chet gulped. "M-maybe the Indians haven't left here, after all," he said, trying to hide his nervousness.

Joe turned to dash off into the woods to search for the bowman.

"Wait!" Frank called. He had pulled the arrow from the sand. "This was done deliberately," he announced grimly, holding the arrow up for all of them to see. Attached to the shaft just below the feathers was a tiny piece of paper. It had been fastened on with adhesive tape.

Frank unrolled the paper and read the printed message aloud: " *'Danger. Hardys beware.'* "

Chet and the girls shuddered and looked around fearfully, as though they expected to see the bowman behind them.

"You boys *are* involved in a new mystery!" Callie exclaimed. "Your own or your father's?"

Frank and Joe exchanged glances. It certainly seemed as though they were involved, but they had no way of knowing *which* case. Did it involve the counterfeit money? Or was it the case their father could not divulge?

"A warning did come to Dad," Frank admitted. "This one obviously was meant for Joe and me. Whoever shot the arrow trailed us here."

Joe frowned. "I wonder if the same person sent both warnings."

"I still think Ken Blake could give us a clue," Frank said. "But we must remember that anybody could have taken the bike from the storage place under the mill."

Frank pocketed the latest warning, then the five searched quickly for any lead to the bowman. They found none. When the group returned to the beach, Joe looked at the sky. "We're in for a storm—and not one of us has a raincoat."

The bright summer sun had disappeared behind towering banks of cumulus clouds. There were rumbles of heavy thunder, followed by vivid flashes of lightning. The air had become humid and oppressive.

"Let's get out of here!" Chet urged. "This isn't a picnic any more!"

The young people hastened through the woods and up the road to Chet's jalopy. As they drove off, rain began coming down in torrents. The sky grew blacker.

Callie shivered. "It seems so sinister—after that awful arrow."

Chet dropped his sister off at the Morton farm and at the same time picked up his new microscope. He begged to try out the instrument on both warning notes and the Hardys smilingly agreed, although they had an up-to-date model of their own.

By the time they had said good-by to Callie at her house, and Chet had driven the Queen into the Hardys' driveway, the storm had ended. The sun shone brightly again.

Immediately the three boys went to the laboratory over the garage. Here Frank carefully dusted the arrow and the second warning note for prints. He blew the powder away, and Joe and Chet looked over his shoulder as he peered through the magnifying glass.

"Nothing. Same as the warning to Dad. The person no doubt wore gloves."

"Now to compare this paper to the first note," Joe said.

"Right," his brother agreed. "You have the combination to the cabinet in Dad's study. Chet and I will rig up his microscope while you get the note from the file."

Frank and Chet focused and adjusted the microscope, making sure it was level on the table. They plugged in the illuminator and checked to see that it did not provide too dazzling a reflection. When Joe returned, Chet took the two pieces of paper and fitted them side by side under the clips on the base.

"Okay. Want to take a look, fellows?"

Frank, then Joe, studied both papers. "The quality and texture are definitely the same," Frank observed.

Next, he lifted the second note from under the clips and slowly moved the paper back and forth under the lenses.

"A watermark!" he exclaimed, stepping back so the others could look at the small, faint imprint.

"Sure is!" said Joe. "A five-pointed star. This could be a valuable clue! We can try to track down exactly where this paper came from."

"And also the arrow," said Chet. "I'll make the rounds of sport stores in town."

"Swell, Chet. Thanks," Frank said.

After their friend had left, the Hardys consulted the classified directory for paper manufacturers.

They made several calls without any luck. Finally they learned that the Quality Paper Company in Bridgeport manufactured paper bearing the five-pointed star watermark. The brothers wanted to go at once to get more information, but realized this errand would have to wait.

"Dad will be home soon," Frank reminded his brother. "We don't want to miss our surprise!"

"Right. And I'd like to tell him about the warning on the arrow."

When Chet returned from a round of the sports shops, he was glum. "I wasn't much help," he said. "The arrow isn't new, and all the stores I checked told me it was a standard model that could be purchased at any sports shop in the country."

"Never mind, Chet," said Frank. "At least giving your microscope a trial run helped us to spot the watermark on the second warning note. We've located a company that manufactures paper with the star watermark."

Chet's face brightened. "Let me know if you find out anything else," he said, packing up his microscope. "I guess I'll take off—and do some nature study for a change."

After he had driven off, Frank and Joe walked to the house. Their minds once more turned to the surprise Mr. Hardy had for them.

"Wouldn't it be terrific if—" Joe said to Frank excitedly. "Do you think it *is?*"

"I'm just hoping." Frank grinned.

Just then a newsboy delivered the evening newspaper. The brothers entered the house and went into the living room. Frank scanned the front page and pointed out an item about new trouble in an Indiana electronics plant.

"That's where an explosion took place a couple of months ago," Joe remarked. "Sabotage, the investigators decided."

"And before that," Frank added, "the same thing happened at a rocket research lab in California. Another unsolved case."

"Seems almost like a chain reaction," Frank remarked.

Any mystery appealed to the boys, but they did not have much chance to discuss this one. The telephone rang. Aunt Gertrude, after taking the call, burst into the living room. From the look on her face Frank and Joe could tell she was indignant, and at the same time, frightened.

"What's the matter, Aunty?" Joe asked.

"More threats—that's all!" she cried out. "This time by telephone. A man's voice—he sounded sinister—horrible!"

Mrs. Hardy came into the living room at that moment. "What did he say, Gertrude?" she asked.

Aunt Gertrude took a deep breath in an effort to calm down. " '*Hardy and his sons are playing with fire,'* the man said. *'They'll get burned if they don't lay off this case.'* " Miss Hardy sniffed. "I don't know what case he meant. What kind of danger *are* you boys mixed up in now?"

Frank and Joe smiled wryly. "Aunt Gertrude," Frank replied, "we really don't know. But please try not to worry," he begged her and his mother. "You know that Dad and the two of us will be careful."

When Mr. Hardy came home a little later, his family told him about the threatening telephone call. The boys, however, did not mention the arrow warning in the presence of their mother and Aunt Gertrude. They knew it would only add to their concern.

Mr. Hardy was as puzzled as his sons. "It's a funny thing," he said. "At this point it's impossible to tell which 'case' the person is referring to. If I knew, it might shed light on either one."

The detective grinned and changed the subject. "Right now, I want you all to come for a drive and have a look at the boys' surprise."

"Swell!" Frank and Joe exclaimed in unison.

While Aunt Gertrude and Mrs. Hardy were getting ready, Frank and Joe went out to the car with their father. Quickly the boys related their afternoon's experience, concluding with the arrow incident.

The detective looked grim. "Whoever is responsible for these warnings is certainly keeping close tabs on us."

Mr. Hardy and his sons speculated for a few minutes on the fact that the pedal found in front of the house apparently had belonged to Ken's bike.

"I think Joe and I should go back tonight to the place where we had the picnic," Frank told his father. "In the darkness we'll have a better chance to sleuth without being seen. And there might be some clue we missed this afternoon."

"I suppose you're right," agreed his father. "But be cautious."

As Aunt Gertrude and Mrs. Hardy came out of the house, conversation about the mystery ceased. Everyone climbed into the sedan and Mr. Hardy drove off. Frank and Joe, seated alongside him, were in a state of rising suspense. Was the surprise the one thing they wanted most of all?

CHAPTER VIII

The Strange Mill Wheel

A few minutes later Mr. Hardy was driving along the Bayport waterfront.

"Is the surprise here, Dad?" Joe asked excitedly.

"That's right."

Mr. Hardy drove to a boathouse at the far end of the dock area and parked. He then invited the others to follow him. He walked to the door of a boathouse and unfastened the padlock.

Frank and Joe held their breaths as Mr. Hardy swung back the door. For a moment they stared inside, speechless with delight. Finally Joe burst out, "Exactly what we had hoped for, Dad!" and put an arm affectionately around his father.

"What a beauty!" Frank exclaimed and wrung Mr. Hardy's hand.

Rocking between the piles lay a sleek, completely equipped motorboat. It nudged gently against clean white fenders as the waves from the bay worked their way under the boathouse door.

The boys' mother exclaimed in delight, and even Aunt Gertrude was duly impressed by the handsome craft.

"This is the same model we saw at the boat show," Joe said admiringly. "I never thought we'd own one."

"She even has the name we picked out," Frank observed excitedly. "The *Sleuth!*"

Shiny brass letters were fitted on the bow of the boat, with the port of registry, Bayport, underneath them.

Mr. Hardy and his wife beamed as their sons walked up and down, praising every detail of the graceful new craft. It could seat six people comfortably. The polished fore and aft decks carried gleaming anchor fittings, and the rubbing strakes were painted white. The *Sleuth* seemed to be waiting to be taken for a run!

"May we try her out now, Dad?" Joe asked.

"Of course. She's fueled up."

Aunt Gertrude shook her head. "The *Sleuth's* an attractive boat, all right. But don't you two start doing any crazy stunts in it," she cautioned her nephews. "And be back for supper."

When the adults had left, Frank and Joe climbed aboard and soon had the *Sleuth* gliding into the bay. The boys had no difficulty operating the motorboat. They had gained experience running their friend Tony Prito's boat, the *Napoli,* which had similar controls.

Taking turns at the wheel, the brothers ran the boat up and down the bay. "Terrific!" Joe shouted.

Frank grinned. "Am I glad we stuck to our agreement with Dad, and saved up to help buy this!"

For some time the boys had been putting money toward a boat of their own into a special bank account. Mr. Hardy had promised that when the account reached a certain sum, he would make up the necessary balance.

Now, as the *Sleuth* knifed through the water, Frank and Joe admired the way the stern sat down in the water when the boat gathered speed. Joe was impressed with the turning circle and the fact that no matter how sharp the twist, none of the spume sprayed into the cockpit.

"Wait until Tony and Chet see this!" Joe exclaimed, when they were pulling back toward the boathouse.

"Speaking of Tony—there he is," Frank said. Their dark-haired classmate was standing on the dock, shouting and waving to them.

Joe, who was at the wheel, brought the *Sleuth* neatly alongside. He turned off the engine as Tony rushed up.

"Don't tell me this dreamboat is yours?" he demanded in amazement.

"Nothing but," Joe said proudly.

Tony and the brothers inspected the boat carefully, comparing her various features with the *Napoli*. They lifted the battens from the *Sleuth's* cowling and admired the powerful motor underneath.

"She's neat all right," said Tony. "But I'll still promise you a stiff race in the *Napoli!*"

"We'll take you up on it after the *Sleuth's* broken in," Joe returned, laughing.

Tony became serious. "Say, fellows, something happened today in connection with my dad's business that I want to tell you about. Your mother said you were down here," he explained.

"What's up?" Frank asked.

Tony's father was a building contractor and also had a construction supply yard where Tony worked during the summer. "Today I went to the bank, just before it closed, to deposit the cash and checks we took in this week," he said. "The teller discovered that one of the bills was a counterfeit!"

"A twenty-dollar bill?" Frank guessed.

"Yes. How'd you know?"

The Hardys related Chet's experience. Tony's dark brows drew together. "I'd like to get my hands on the guy making the stuff!" he said angrily.

"So would we!" Joe stated.

The Hardys learned that the head teller had told Tony he would make a report to the Bayport police and turn the bill over to the Secret Service. "Did he explain how he could tell that the bill was a fake?" Frank asked.

"Yes," replied Tony, and from his description, the Hardys were sure that the bill had come from the same batch as the one passed to Chet.

"Think back, Tony," Frank urged. "Have you any idea who gave it to you—or your father?"

Tony looked doubtful. "Three days' trade— pretty hard to remember. Of course, we know most of the customers. I did ask Mike, our yard-man, who helps with sales. He mentioned one purchaser he didn't know."

Frank, eager for any possible lead, carefully questioned Tony. The Hardys learned that three days before, just at closing time, a faded green panel truck had driven into the Prito supply yard. "Mike remembers there were no markings on the truck—as if the name might have been painted out."

"Who was in it?" Joe prompted.

"A young boy—about fourteen—was with the driver. Mike says they bought about fifty dollars' worth of old bricks and lumber. The boy paid him in assorted bills. One was a twenty. Our other cash customers had given smaller bills."

"What did the driver look like?" Frank probed.

"Mike said he didn't notice—the fellow stayed behind the wheel. There was a last-minute rush at the yard, so the boy and Mike piled the stuff into the back of the truck. Then the driver gave the boy money to pay the bill."

Frank and Joe wondered the same thing: Had the man driving the truck passed the bogus bill deliberately? If so, was he the one who had fooled Chet? "It seems funny he'd go to so much trouble to dump one phony twenty-dollar bill," Joe said.

Frank agreed and added, "Besides, what would a person in league with counterfeiters want with a pile of old bricks and lumber?"

He turned to Tony. "Did Mike notice anything in particular about the boy?"

"He was tall and thin. Mike thinks he was wearing a striped shirt."

Frank and Joe exchanged glances. "Could be Ken Blake!" Joe declared. Briefly, the Hardys explained their first encounter with the boy.

"He might have been helping pick up the load for Elekton," Frank reasoned. "But why would a modern plant want secondhand building material? And why wouldn't they have the purchase billed to them?"

"What's more," his brother put in, "why didn't the driver get out and help with the loading? Unless, perhaps, he wanted to stay out of sight as much as possible."

"Too bad Mike didn't notice the truck's license number," Tony said. "Naturally he had no reason to at the time."

"Was there anything unusual about the truck besides the fact it wasn't marked?" Frank asked his chum.

Tony thought for a moment. "Mike did say there was a bike in the back. He had to move it out of the way."

"Ken rides one," Joe remarked.

"Well, Dad will be glad if you two pick up any clues to these counterfeiters," Tony said. "He's hopping mad at being cheated, and Mike feels sore about it."

"We'll keep our eyes open for that green truck," Frank assured him. "The whole business sounds suspicious—though the bill could have been passed accidentally."

"Let's question Ken Blake," Joe proposed.

He and his brother housed the *Sleuth,* and the three boys started homeward. On the way they continued to speculate on the counterfeiting racket.

"Let me know if I can help you detectives," Tony said as he turned into his street.

"Will do."

That evening, when it grew dark, Frank and Joe told their mother and aunt that they were going out to do some investigating. Before they left, the boys had a chance to speak to their father in private about Tony's report of the counterfeit bill and green truck and their own hunches.

Mr. Hardy agreed that the purchase of lumber and bricks seemed odd, but he felt that until more positive evidence could be obtained, it was best not to approach Elekton officials on the matter.

"I guess you're right, Dad," said Frank. "We might be way off base."

The detective wished them luck on their sleuthing mission. The boys decided to make the trip in the *Sleuth*. They rode their motorcycles down to the boathouse, parked them, then climbed aboard the new boat. Joe took the wheel and soon the sleek craft was cutting across the bay toward the mouth of Willow River.

When they entered it, Joe throttled down and carefully navigated the stream. Meanwhile, Frank shone his flashlight on the wooded banks.

"There's the cave—ahead!" he whispered.

Joe ran the boat astern a few yards and Frank dropped anchor. The brothers waded ashore, carrying their shoes and socks.

When they reached the mouth of the cave, Joe said, "Let's investigate this place first."

They went into the cave and moved forward to the tunnel. One glance told them that the tunnel had become impassable—it was filled with water.

"Must have been the cloudburst," said Frank, as they emerged from the cave. "We'll have to wait until the ground dries out. At least we can take a look through the woods and the area around the mill for clues to the bowman."

Shielding the lenses of their flashlights, so that the light beams would not be easily detected by anyone lurking in the vicinity, the boys began a thorough search of the wooded section. As they worked their way noiselessly uphill among the trees, the only sound was the eerie rattling the wind made in the leaves and branches.

Frank and Joe shone their lights beneath shrubs and rocks, and even crawled under some fallen trees. They found nothing suspicious. They were approaching the edge of the woods and could see the outline of the mill beyond. The old wheel creaked and rumbled.

Suddenly Frank whispered hoarsely, "Look! Here's something!"

Joe joined his brother, and together they examined the leather object Frank had picked up.

"An archer's finger guard," he said.

"It may be a valuable clue to the arrow warning," Joe said, as Frank pocketed the guard. "Let's go up to the mill," he proposed. "Maybe the men there have seen something suspicious."

As the boys crossed the clearing toward the gatehouse, they saw that it was in darkness.

"Probably everyone has gone to bed," Frank remarked.

For a moment the brothers stood wondering

what to do next. "Something's missing," Joe said in a puzzled voice. "I have it! The mill wheel has stopped turning."

"Maybe it was switched off for the night," Frank observed.

The boys were eager to question the occupants, but decided not to awaken them.

"Let's walk around the mill," said Frank, "and look through the woods on the other side."

The boys had just passed the north corner of the building when, with a creaking groan, the wheel started to turn again.

"There must be something wrong with the mechanism," Frank deduced. "The wheel hasn't been used for so many years that adapting it to work the generator may have put a strain on it."

"We'd better let the men know it's acting up," Joe said.

The boys retraced their steps to the mill door. As they reached it, the wheel stopped turning.

Frank and Joe stood staring off to their left where the mass of the motionless wheel was outlined against the night sky.

"Spooky, isn't it?" Joe commented.

Frank nodded, and knocked on the door. There was no response. After a short wait, he knocked again—louder this time. The sound echoed in the deep silence of the night. Still no one answered.

The Hardys waited a while longer. Finally they turned away. "Must be sound sleepers," Joe commented. "Well, maybe they'll discover what's wrong tomorrow."

Frank and Joe were about to resume their search for clues when they heard a loud crashing noise from the woods which bordered Willow River.

The boys dashed ahead to investigate. Entering the woods, they made their way stealthily forward, flashlights turned off. Silently they drew near the river.

After a few minutes they stopped, and listened intently. The sound was not repeated.

"Must have been an animal," Joe whispered.

Just then they heard a rustling sound behind them and turned to look. The next instant each received a terrific blow on the back of the head. Both boys blacked out.

CHAPTER IX

Tracing a Slugger

WHEN Frank regained consciousness, his first thought was of his brother. He turned his throbbing head and saw that Joe was lying next to him.

"Joe!" he exclaimed anxiously.

To his relief, Joe stirred and mumbled, "W-what happened?"

"Someone conked us on the head—"

Frank broke off as he became aware of a gentle rocking motion. He sat up. Was he still dizzy or were they moving? When his mind and vision cleared, he knew they were certainly moving.

"Hey!" he said. "We're on the *Sleuth!*"

Astonished, Joe raised himself and looked around. They were indeed aboard their boat—lying on the foredeck and slowly drifting down Willow River toward the bay. The anchor lay beside them.

"A fog's rolling in," Frank said uneasily, observing white swirls of mist ahead. "Let's start 'er up before visibility gets worse."

The boys wriggled into the cockpit and Joe pressed the starter. It would not catch. While Joe stayed at the controls, Frank climbed to the foredeck and lifted the cowling from the engine. He quickly checked to see if the distributor wires were in place. They were. There did not seem to be anything visibly wrong with the engine, but when he lifted the top off the carburetor, he found it empty.

A quick check of the gas tank revealed the cause of the trouble. The tank had been drained.

"Fine mess we're in," he mumbled. "What was the idea?"

"The man who hit us on the head can answer that one," Joe said bitterly. "He sure did a complete job—even took both the oars!"

"We'll have to tow her," Frank said tersely, "to make more speed and guide her."

While Joe stripped to his shorts, Frank quickly led a painter through one of the foredeck fairleads.

"Take this painter," Frank said, handing Joe the rope. "Make it fast around your shoulder and swim straight ahead. I'll unhinge one of the battens and use it as a paddle and try to keep her straight. In a few minutes I'll change places with you."

The Hardys knew that keeping a dead weight

like the *Sleuth* moving in a straight line would be a tough job. However, with Joe swimming ahead and Frank wielding the batten, they managed to make fairly steady progress.

It was slow, backbreaking work, and before they reached the bay, the boys had changed places three times. Their heads were pounding more than ever from the physical strain. Also, the fog had grown so dense that it was impossible to see very far ahead.

Frank, who was taking his turn in the water, did not know how much longer he could go on.

Suddenly Joe shouted from the boat, "There's a light! Help! Help! Ahoy! Over here!" he directed at the top of his lungs.

Gradually the light approached them. Frank clambered back into the *Sleuth* as a Harbor Police boat, making its scheduled rounds, pulled alongside.

"You're just in time!" Frank gasped to the sergeant in charge. "We're exhausted."

"I can see that. You run out of gas?" the police officer asked.

"Worse than that. Foul play," Frank replied.

"Tough luck," the sergeant said. "You can tell your story when we get to town."

The officer gave orders to his crew, and a towline was put on the *Sleuth*. The boys were given blankets to throw around themselves.

When the two crafts reached the Harbor Police

pier, the boys went inside and gave a full account of what had happened to them and asked that the report be relayed to Chief Collig.

"We'll give you some gas," said the sergeant who had rescued the boys. "Then do you think you can make it home alone?"

"Yes, thank you."

A half hour later the boys, tired and disappointed, cycled home. Their mother and aunt gasped with dismay at the sight of the weary boys in the water-sodden clothing. Joe and Frank, however, made light of the evening's experience.

"We ran out of gas," Joe explained, "and had to swim back with the *Sleuth*."

Aunt Gertrude sniffed skeptically. "Humph! It must have been some long ride to use up all that fuel!" She hustled off to make hot chocolate.

Mrs. Hardy told the boys that their father had left the house an hour before and would be away overnight working on his case. Again Frank and Joe wondered about it. And did the attack tonight have any connection with either case?

After a hot bath and a good night's sleep, Frank and Joe were eager to continue their search for clues to the bowman, the counterfeiters, and the writer of the first warning note to Mr. Hardy.

Breakfast over, Frank and Joe went to the lab and dusted the archer's finger guard. To the brothers' delight they lifted one clear print.

"We'll take this to Chief Collig on our way to

the paper company in Bridgeport," Frank decided.

Just before they left, Chet telephoned. "Guess what!" he said to Frank, who answered. "I have an appointment at Elekton to see about a job!"

"How'd you do it?" Frank asked, amazed. "You sure work fast."

Chet laughed. "I decided to telephone on my own," he explained. "The man in the personnel office told me there might be something available on a part-time basis. How about that?"

"Swell," Frank said. "The vacancy must have come up since yesterday."

"Funny thing," Chet added. "The personnel manager asked me if I'd applied before. I said No, though the guard had phoned about me yesterday. The manager said he didn't remember this, but that somebody else in the office might have taken the call."

Chet became more and more excited as he talked about the prospect of getting a job in the Elekton laboratory. "I'm going to make a lot of money and—"

"Don't get your hopes up too high," Frank cautioned his friend. "Elekton is such a top-secret outfit they might not hire anyone on a part-time basis for lab work. But you might get something else."

"We'll see," Chet replied optimistically.

"Joe and I have something special to show you," Frank told him. "After you have your interview, meet us at the north end of the Bayport waterfront."

Chet begged to know why, but Frank kept the news about the *Sleuth* a secret. "You'll see soon enough," he said.

"Okay, then. So long!"

The Hardys hopped on their motorcycles and rode to police headquarters. They talked to Chief Collig in detail about the attack on them, and left the bowman's fingerprint for him to trace.

"Good work, boys," he said. "I'll let you know what I find out."

Frank and Joe had decided not to mention to him the green truck and its possible connection with the counterfeiters until they had more proof.

The boys mounted their motorcycles and rode to Bridgeport. They easily located the Quality Paper Company, and inquired there for Mr. Evans, the sales manager, with whom they had talked the day before.

When Frank and Joe entered his office and identified themselves, Mr. Evans looked at the brothers curiously. But he was most cooperative in answering their questions.

"No," Mr. Evans said, "we don't sell our star watermark paper to retail stores in this vicinity. All our purchasers are large industrial companies. Here is a list." He handed a printed sheet across the desk to Frank.

The boys were disappointed not to have obtained any individual's name. Nevertheless, Frank and Joe read the list carefully. Several names, including Elekton Controls Limited, were familiar to them. The warning note could have come from any one of thousands of employees of any of the firms.

"I guess there's no clue here to the man we want to locate," Frank said to Mr. Evans.

The boys thanked him. As they started to leave, he called them back.

"Are you boys, by any chance, related to Mr. Fenton Hardy?" he asked.

Joe, puzzled, nodded. "He's our father. Why?"

"Quite a coincidence," Mr. Evans said. "Mr. Hardy was here a little while ago."

"He was!" Frank exclaimed in surprise. The brothers exchanged glances, wondering what mission their father had been on.

"Maybe I shouldn't have mentioned Mr. Hardy's visit," Mr. Evans said.

"That's all right," Joe assured him. "If Dad had wanted the visit kept secret, he would have told you."

When the boys were outside again, Frank said, "I hope Dad will be home. I'd like to find out what brought him here."

Frank and Joe rode directly home and were glad to see Mr. Hardy's sedan in the driveway. The boys rushed into the house.

They found the detective in his study, talking on the telephone. The boys paused next to the partly open door.

". . . the same eight-and-one pattern, I believe," their father was saying. . . . "Yes—I'll be there. . . . Good-by."

Frank knocked and the boys entered the room. Mr. Hardy greeted them warmly. He was startled when Joe told him, "We know where you've been this morning, Dad."

"Were you two shadowing me?" the detective joked.

"Not exactly." Frank grinned, and explained why they had visited the Quality Paper Company.

"Good idea," said the detective. "Did you learn anything?"

"No," Joe replied glumly, then asked suddenly, "Dad, did you go to Quality Paper in connection with the warning note on the arrow?"

Mr. Hardy admitted that he had gone there to investigate the watermark. "I believe I did find a clue to confirm a suspicion of mine. But I'm not sure yet where it will lead."

The boys sensed that their father's trip had been linked to his secret case. "If it was to help us on the counterfeiting mystery, he'd say so," Frank thought. "And he hasn't mentioned Elekton, so I guess he doesn't suspect any of that company's employees."

Mr. Hardy changed the subject. He looked at his sons quizzically. "What's this I hear from Aunt Gertrude about you boys coming home last night half dead?"

The boys explained, omitting none of the details. "We didn't want to alarm Mother and Aunt Gertrude," Frank said, "so we didn't tell them about the attack."

Mr. Hardy looked grim and warned his sons gravely to be extra cautious.

"There's one bright spot," he added. "The print you found on that finger guard. It could be a big break."

During lunch the detective was unusually preoccupied. The boys tried to draw him out by questions and deductions about the counterfeiting case. He would say very little, however, and seemed to be concentrating on a knotty problem.

A little later the boys rode their motorcycles straight to the boathouse and parked at the street end of the jetty. "Chet ought to show up soon," Joe remarked.

As the brothers walked toward the boathouse Frank commented on his father's preoccupation during luncheon.

"I have a hunch Dad's assignment is even tougher than usual," he confided. "I wish we could help him on it."

Frank seemed to be only half listening and nodded absently.

"What's the matter with you?" Joe laughed. "I'm talking to myself!"

Suddenly Frank stopped. He grasped his brother's arm firmly.

"Joe!" he said. "We may have found a clue in Bridgeport this morning, and didn't realize it!"

CHAPTER X

The Sign of the Arrow

"WHAT clue do you mean, Frank?" Joe demanded eagerly.

"Elekton's name was on that list Mr. Evans showed us this morning."

"Yes, I know. But Dad didn't seem excited over that."

"Well, I am," Frank said. "Put two and two together. Every time we've been near the Elekton area, something has happened. First, the warning on the arrow, then the attack last night."

"Of course!" Joe said. "I get you! Someone who has access to the company's paper supply could have sent the warnings, and knocked us out. But who? An employee of Elekton?"

"That's the mystery," said Frank. "Is the person trying to get at Dad through us? And which of the cases is this mysterious person connected with —the counterfeit case or Dad's secret one?"

"Then there's the bike," Joe recalled. "Someone from the company easily could have taken it from the storage area under the mill at night when the guard and maintenance man were inside the gatehouse."

"Joe," said Frank slowly, "we're theorizing on the case having a connection with Elekton. Do you think Dad is, too, even though he didn't tell us? The Elekton name may have been the clue *he* found at Quality Paper!"

Joe snapped his fingers. "My guess is that Dad is doing some detective work for Elekton! That would explain why he can't say anything. Elekton *is* doing top-secret space missile work."

"It's possible," Frank speculated, "that Elekton retained Dad because of the chain of sabotage acts in plants handling similar jobs for the government."

"Sounds logical," Joe agreed. "I guess Dad's main assignment would be to ward off sabotage at Elekton. No wonder he is so anxious to find out who sent the warnings."

Just then Chet arrived in the Queen and leaped out.

"I have a job!" he announced to Frank and Joe. Then he looked a bit sheepish. "It's—er—in the cafeteria, serving behind the food counter. The cafeteria is run on a concession basis, and the people working there aren't as carefully screened as the plant employees."

Joe grinned. "It's not very scientific, but think of the food! You'll be able to eat anything you want."

Chet sighed, and did not respond with one of his usual humorous comebacks. A worried expression spread over his face. He shifted from one foot to the other.

"What's on your mind?" Joe prodded. "Not nervous about the job, are you?"

Chet shook his head. He dug into his pocket and pulled out a piece of white paper. "I *am* nervous about this—another warning note! It was on the seat of my car when I came out after the job interview." He handed the note to Frank.

Unfolding it, Frank read aloud, " '*You and your pals watch out!*' " There was no signature on the boldly printed note, but at the bottom was the crude drawing of an arrow.

Chet gulped. "Must be that arrow shooter. He's keeping tabs on all of us!" he said.

Frank and Joe studied the note intently for a minute, then Frank asked Chet, "Where did you park?"

"Near the front entrance. The guard at the mill told me to go in that way to reach the personnel office." Chet smiled faintly. "Boy, was *he* surprised when I told him I had an appointment."

The Hardys were more convinced than ever that their unknown enemy must somehow be linked with the Elekton company. "We'll compare this note with the others," Frank said. "But first, Chet, we'll show you something to cheer you up."

The brothers led their friend into the boathouse. "Feast your eyes!" Joe grinned. "This is our surprise."

Chet gasped when he saw the *Sleuth*. "Wow! She's really yours?"

"You bet! How about a ride?"

Eagerly Chet accepted. As the Hardys refueled from the boathouse tank, they told Chet about the adventure they had had the previous night.

"You suspect there's a connection between somebody at Elekton and the counterfeiting?" Chet guessed.

"That's right," Frank replied.

He then told Chet about the Pritos having received a counterfeit bill. "We think," said Joe, "the boy in the panel truck who gave Mike the counterfeit twenty *might* have been Ken Blake."

"Ken Blake again," Chet commented. "Funny how he keeps turning up."

The Hardys agreed. As Frank steered the *Sleuth* into the bay, Joe suggested, "Let's run up Willow River to the mill. That'll give you a good chance to see how the boat rides, Chet, and also we can stop to question the guard and maintenance man, and Ken Blake. They might have seen some suspicious people in the area."

"I should've known this would turn into a

"Something's wrong!" Joe shouted.
"I can't slow her down."

sleuthing trip." Chet sighed. "Oh, well, I'm with you if we can learn anything about the counterfeiters."

When Frank had the *Sleuth* well away from shore and out of the path of other craft on the bay, he pushed the throttle for more speed and steered the boat toward the mouth of the river.

The *Sleuth* responded like a thoroughbred. The stern sat back in the water and in a second it was planing wide open across the bay.

"How do you like this?" Frank called from the cockpit.

"Terrific!" Chet yelled back enthusiastically.

Frank now swung the wheel back and forth to show his friend how stable the boat was. Then he said, "Joe, take the wheel and show Chet your stuff!"

The brothers changed places and Joe made a wide circle to port, with the *Sleuth* heeling beautifully. Then he headed for the river's narrow mouth.

"Better slow down!" Frank warned him.

Obediently Joe began to ease the throttle. The *Sleuth* did not respond! And there was no lessening of the roar of the engine.

Quickly Joe turned the throttle all the way back. Still there was no decrease in speed.

"Something's wrong!" he shouted. "I can't slow her down!"

CHAPTER XI

Sinister Tactics

"WHAT do you mean you can't slow down?" Chet yelled. "Turn off the engine!"

"Joe can't," Frank said grimly. "He has the throttle to *off* position and we're still traveling at full speed."

There was no choice for Joe but to swing the *Sleuth* into another wide, sweeping turn. It would have been foolhardy to enter the river at such speed, and Joe knew that under the circumstances he needed lots of room to maneuver. The motorboat zoomed back into the middle of the bay. It seemed to the boys that suddenly there was far more traffic on the bay than there had been before.

"Look out!" Chet yelled. Joe just missed a high-speed runabout.

He turned and twisted to avoid the small pleasure boats. The young pilot was more worried about endangering these people than he was about colliding with the larger vessels, which were commercial craft.

"Keep her as straight as you can!" Frank shouted to Joe. "I'll take a look at the engine and see what I can do with it."

Frank stood up and leaned forward to open the cowling in front of the dashboard, as the boat leaped across the waves in the bay.

"Watch out!" Chet yelled, as Frank almost lost his balance.

Joe had made a sharp turn to avoid cutting in front of a rowboat containing a man and several children. Joe realized that the wash of the speeding *Sleuth* might upset it.

"If those people are thrown overboard," he thought, "we'll have to rescue them. But how?" Fortunately, the boat did not overturn.

Frank quickly lifted the cowling from the engine and stepped into the pit. He knew he could open the fuel intake and siphon off the gas into the bay, but this would take too long.

"I'll have to stop the boat—right now!" he decided.

Frank reached down beside the roaring engine and pulled three wires away from the distributor. Instantly the engine died, and Frank stood up just as Joe made another sharp turn to miss hitting a small outboard motorboat that had wandered across their path.

"Good night!" Chet cried out. "That was a close one!"

Even with the *Sleuth's* reduction in speed, the other boat rocked violently back and forth as it was caught in the wash. Frank grasped the gunwale, ready to leap over the side and rescue the man if his boat overturned.

But the smaller craft had been pulled around to face the wash. Though it bounced almost out of the water, the boat quickly resumed an even keel.

The lone man in it kept coming toward the *Sleuth.* As he drew alongside, he began to wave his arms and shout at the boys.

"What's the matter with you young fools?" he yelled. "You shouldn't be allowed to operate a boat until you learn how to run one."

"We couldn't—" Joe started to say when the man interrupted.

"You should have more respect for other people's safety!"

Frank finally managed to explain. "It was an accident. The throttle was jammed open. I had to pull the wires out of the distributor to stop her."

By this time the outboard was close enough for its pilot to look over the *Sleuth's* side and into the engine housing where Frank was pointing at the distributor.

The man quickly calmed down. "Sorry, boys," he said. "There are so many fools running around in high-powered boats these days, without knowing anything about the rules of navigation, I just got good and mad at your performance."

"I don't blame you, sir," said Joe. Then he asked, "Do you think you could tow us into the municipal dock so that we can have repairs made?"

"Glad to," said the man.

At the dock, the Hardys and Chet watched while the serviceman checked the *Sleuth* to find out the cause of the trouble. Presently he looked up at the boys with an odd expression.

"What's the trouble?" Frank asked. "Serious?"

The mechanic's reply startled them. "This is a new motorboat and no doubt was in tiptop shape. But somebody tampered with the throttle!"

"What!" Joe demanded. "Let's see!"

The serviceman pointed out where a cotter pin had been removed from the throttle group. And the tension spring which opened and closed the valve had been replaced with a bar to hold the throttle wide open, once it was pushed there.

The Hardys and Chet exchanged glances which meant: "The unknown enemy again?"

The boys, however, did not mention their suspicions to the mechanic. Frank merely requested him to make the necessary repairs on the *Sleuth*. Then the trio walked back to the Hardys' boathouse.

Several fishermen were standing at a nearby

wharf. Frank and Joe asked them if they had seen anyone near the boathouse.

"No," each one said.

The three boys inspected the boathouse. Frank scrutinized the hasp on the door. "The *Sleuth* must have been tampered with while it was inside. Unless it was done last night while we were unconscious."

There was no sign of the lock having been forced open, but near the edge of the loose hasp there were faint scratches.

"Look!" Joe pointed. "Somebody tore the whole hasp off the door and then carefully put it back on."

Frank looked grim. "I'm sure this was done by the same person who attacked us last night, and sent us the warnings."

"You're right," said Joe. "This is what Dad would call sinister tactics."

Again both brothers wondered with which case their enemy was connected. There seemed to be no answer to this tantalizing question which kept coming up again and again.

Chet drove the Queen back to the Hardys', and the brothers rode their motorcycles. When they reached the house they went at once to the lab with the note Chet had found in his car.

They dusted it for fingerprints but were disappointed again. There was not one trace of a print. The boys found, however, that the paper was the same as that used for the previous warnings.

"Well," said Joe, "I vote we go on out to the mill."

The boys went in the Queen. Chet had just brought his car to a stop on the dirt road when Joe called out, "There's Ken Blake trimming the grass over by the millrace. Now's our chance to talk to him."

The three jumped out. Ken looked up, stared for a second, then threw his clippers to the ground. To the boys' surprise, he turned and ran away from them, along the stream.

"Wait!" Frank yelled.

Ken looked over his shoulder, but kept on running. Suddenly he tripped and stumbled. For a moment the boy teetered on the bank of the rushing stream. The next instant he lost his balance and fell headlong into the water!

At once the Hardys and Chet dashed to the water's edge. Horrified, they saw that the force of the water was carrying the boy, obviously a poor swimmer, straight toward the plunging falls!

CHAPTER XII

An Interrupted Chase

FRANK, quick as lightning, dashed to the mill-stream and plunged in after Ken Blake. The boy was being pulled relentlessly toward the waterfall. In another moment he would be swept over the brink of the dam!

With strong strokes, Frank swam toward the struggling boy. Reaching out desperately, he managed to grasp Ken's shirt.

Joe jumped in to assist Frank. The two boys were buffeted by the rushing water but between them they managed to drag Ken back from the falls.

"Easy," Frank cautioned the frightened youth. "Relax. We'll have you out in a jiffy."

Despite the weight of their clothes, the Hardys, both proficient at lifesaving techniques, soon worked Ken close to the bank. Chet leaned over and helped haul him out of the water. Then Frank and Joe climbed out.

To their relief, Ken, though white-faced and panting from exhaustion, seemed to be all right. The Hardys flopped to the ground to catch their breath.

"That was a whale of a rescue!" Chet praised them.

"You bet!" Ken gasped weakly. "Thanks, fellows! You've saved my life!"

"In a way it was our fault," Joe replied ruefully. "You wouldn't have fallen in if we hadn't come here. But why *did* you run away when you saw us?"

Ken hesitated before answering. "Mr. Markel —the guard at the gatehouse—said you wanted to talk to me. He warned me about talking to outsiders, because of the strict security at Elekton."

Joe nodded. "We understand, Ken. But," he added, "we have something important to ask you, and I don't think you will be going against company rules if you answer. Did anybody use your bike the night before last to deliver a message to our house?"

"Your house?" Ken sounded surprised. "No. At least, not that I know of."

Joe went on, "Did you buy a pedal in Bridgeport to replace the one missing from your bike?"

Ken again looked surprised. "Yes. It was gone yesterday morning when I came to work. I suspected someone must have used my bike and lost the pedal. When I couldn't find it around here, Mr. Markel sent me to Bridgeport to buy a new one."

It was on the tip of Frank's tongue to ask the boy if he had seen any person in the area of the mill carrying a bow and arrow. But suddenly Mr. Markel and the maintenance man came dashing from the mill.

"What's going on here?" the guard demanded, staring at the Hardys and Ken, who were still dripping wet.

Briefly, Frank told the men what had happened. They thanked the brothers warmly for the rescue, and the maintenance man hustled Ken into the mill for dry clothes. He did not invite the Hardys inside.

Frank and Joe turned to Mr. Markel, intending to question him. But before they could, a horn sounded and a shabby green panel truck approached the plant gate.

The guard hurried over to admit the truck and it entered without stopping. Suddenly Joe grabbed Frank's arm. "Hey! That truck's unmarked—it looks like the one Tony described."

The brothers peered after the vehicle, but by this time it was far into the grounds, and had turned out of sight behind one of the buildings.

"I wonder," Joe said excitedly, "if the driver is the man who gave the Pritos the counterfeit bill!"

The boys had noticed only that the driver wore a cap pulled low and sat slouched over the wheel.

"If this truck's the same one, it may be connected with Elekton," Frank said tersely.

Both Hardys, though uncomfortably wet, decided to stay and see what they could find out. They hailed Mr. Markel as he walked back from the Elekton gate.

"Does that truck belong to Elekton?" Frank asked him.

"No, it doesn't," the guard answered.

"Do you know who does own it?" asked Joe.

Mr. Markel shook his head regretfully. "Sorry, boys. I'm afraid I'm not allowed to give out such information. Excuse me, I have work to do." He turned and went back into the gatehouse.

"Come on, fellows," Chet urged. "You'd better not hang around in those wet clothes."

The Hardys, however, were determined to stay long enough to question Ken Blake further, if possible.

"He'll probably be coming outside soon," said Joe. "Frank and I can dry out on the beach by the cave. It won't take long in this hot sun."

Chet sighed. "Okay. And I know what I'm supposed to do—wait here and watch for Ken."

Frank chuckled. "You're a mind reader."

Chet took his post at the edge of the woods, and the Hardys hurried down to the river's edge.

They spread their slacks and shirts on the sun-warmed rocks. In a short while the clothing was dry enough to put on.

"Say, maybe we'll have time to investigate that tunnel before Chet calls us," Joe suggested eagerly.

He and Frank started for the cave, but a second later Chet came running through the woods toward them.

"Ken came out, but he's gone on an errand," he reported, and explained that the boy had rushed from the mill dressed in oversize dungarees and a red shirt. "He was riding off on his bike when I caught up to him. I told Ken you wanted to see him, but he said he had to make a fast trip downtown and deliver an envelope to the Parker Building."

"We'll catch him there," Frank decided.

The three boys ran up the wooded slope and jumped into the Queen. They kept on the main road to Bayport, hoping to overtake Ken, but they did not pass him.

"He must have taken another route," Joe said.

At the Parker Building there were no parking spaces available, so Chet stopped his jalopy long enough to drop off Frank and Joe.

"I'll keep circling the block until you come out," Chet called as he drove away.

There was no sign of Ken's bicycle outside the building. The Hardys rushed into the lobby and immediately were met by a five-o'clock crowd of office workers streaming from the elevators. Frank and Joe made their way through the throng, but saw no sign of Ken.

Joe had an idea. "Maybe he was making the delivery to Mr. Peters, the name I saw on the Manila envelope I picked up the other day. Let's see if Ken's still in his office."

The boys ran their eyes down the building directory, but Mr. Peters was not listed. The brothers questioned the elevator starter, who replied that so far as he knew, no one by the name of Peters had an office in the building.

Joe asked the starter, "Did you notice a boy wearing dungarees and a bright-red shirt in the lobby a few minutes ago?"

"Sure," was the prompt reply. "Just before the five-o'clock rush started. I saw the boy come in and give an envelope to a man waiting in the corner over there. The man took the envelope and they both left right away."

"I guess he must be Mr. Peters," Frank said.

"Could be," the starter agreed. "I didn't recognize him."

As the Hardys hurried outside, Joe said, "Well, we got crossed up on that one. Let's get back to the mill. Ken will have to drop off the bike."

The brothers waited at the curb for Chet. In a few minutes the Queen pulled up. "All aboard!" Chet sang out. "Any luck?"

"No."

When Frank told Chet they were returning to the mill, their good-natured friend nodded. "It's fortunate I bought these sandwiches," he said, indicating a paper bag on the seat beside him. "I had a feeling we'd be late to supper."

Joe snapped his fingers. "That reminds me. I'll stop and phone our families so they won't wait supper for us."

After Joe had made the calls and they were on their way again, he told Frank and Chet that Mr. Hardy had left a message saying he would not be home until after ten o'clock.

As the Queen went down the side road past the Elekton buildings, Frank thought, "If Dad *is* working for Elekton, he might be somewhere in the plant right this minute."

The same possibility was running through Joe's mind. "Wonder if Dad is expecting a break in his secret case."

As Chet neared the turn into the mill road, a green truck zoomed out directly in front of the Queen. Chet jammed on his brake, narrowly avoiding a collision. The truck swung around the jalopy at full speed and roared off toward the highway.

"The green truck we saw before!" Joe exclaimed. "This time I got the license number, but couldn't see the driver's face."

"Let's follow him!" Frank urged.

Chet started back in pursuit. "That guy ought

to be arrested for reckless driving!" he declared indignantly.

The Hardys peered ahead as they turned right onto the main road, trying to keep the truck in sight. Suddenly the boys heard a tremendous *bo-o-om* and felt the car shake.

"An explosion!" Joe cried out, turning his head. "Look!"

Against the sky a brilliant flash and billows of smoke came from the direction of Elekton. Another explosion followed.

"The plant's blowing up!" Joe gasped.

CHAPTER XIII

Sudden Suspicion

THE roar of the explosion and the sight of smoke and flames stunned the three boys for a moment. Chet stepped on the brake so fast that his passengers hit the dashboard.

"Take it easy!" urged Frank, although he was as excited as Chet.

All thoughts of chasing the mysterious green truck were erased from the Hardys' minds.

"Let's get as close as possible," Frank said tersely, as Chet headed the car back toward the plant. "I'd like to know what—"

Frank broke off as a series of explosions occurred. The brothers sat forward tensely.

As the Queen drew near the main entrance, the boys could see that the flames and smoke were pouring from a single building at the northeast corner.

"It's one of the labs, I think," said Frank.

Quickly Chet pulled over and parked, and the boys hopped out of the jalopy. The series of explosive sounds had died away, but the damage appeared to be extensive. Most of the windows in the steel-and-concrete building had been blown out by the force of the blast.

Smoke and flames were pouring out of the blackened spaces where the windows had been. As the boys ran toward the front, the roof of the west wing caved in. The rush of oxygen provided fuel for a new surge of flames that reached toward the sky.

"Lucky this happened after closing time," Chet murmured, staring wide-eyed at the fire. "There might have been a lot of injuries."

"I hope no one was inside." Joe exchanged worried glances with his brother. Both shared the same concern. It was for their father.

"I wish we could find out whether or not Dad's at Elekton," Frank whispered to Joe.

At this point, the boys heard the scream of sirens. Soon fire trucks and police cars from Bayport pulled up at the front gate. The Hardys saw Chief Collig in the first police car. They rushed up to him and he asked how they happened to be there.

"Sleuthing," Frank answered simply. Without going into detail, he added, "Joe and I aren't sure, but we have a hunch Dad may have been—

or still is—here at Elekton. All right if we go into the grounds and look around?" he asked eagerly. "And take Chet?"

The officer agreed.

By this time the guard had opened the wide gate, and the fire apparatus rushed in. Some of the police officers followed, while others took positions along the road and directed traffic so it would not block the path of emergency vehicles.

As the boys rode inside with the chief, Joe asked him, "Any idea what caused the explosion?"

"Not yet. Hard to tell until the firemen can get inside the building."

When they reached the burning structure, Chief Collig began directing police operations, and checking with the firemen. As soon as they seemed to have the flames under control, the firemen entered the laboratory building to look for any possible victims of the explosions.

The Hardys and Chet, meanwhile, had searched the outdoors area for Mr. Hardy, but did not see the detective.

"Maybe we were wrong about Dad's coming here," Joe said to his brother, more hopeful than before. "Dad probably wouldn't have been in the lab."

The brothers went back to Chief Collig, who told them he had not seen Fenton Hardy. Just then the fire chief came up to the group.

"I'll bet this fire was no accident," he reported

grimly to Collig. "The same thing happened in Indiana about two months ago—and that was sabotage!"

Frank and Joe stared at each other. "Sabotage!" Joe whispered.

A startling thought flashed into Frank's mind, and, drawing his brother aside, he exclaimed, "Remember what we overheard Dad say on the phone? 'The same eight-and-one pattern. I'll be there.' "

"And two months equal about eight weeks," Joe added excitedly. "That might have been the saboteurs' time schedule Dad was referring to! So maybe the explosion at Elekton was set for today!"

Frank's apprehension about his father returned full force. "Joe," he said tensely, "Dad might have been inside the lab building trying to stop the saboteurs!"

Deeply disturbed, the Hardys pleaded with Chief Collig for permission to enter the building and search for their father.

"I can tell you're worried, boys," the officer said sympathetically. "But it's still too risky for me to let you go inside. It'll be some time before we're sure there's no danger of further explosions."

"I know," Frank agreed. "But what if Dad *is* in there and badly hurt?"

The police chief did his best to reassure the brothers. "Your father would never forgive me if I let you risk your lives," he added. "I suggest that you go on home and cheer up your mother in case she has the same fears you do. I promise if I see your dad I'll call you, or ask him to."

The boys realized that their old friend was right, and slowly walked away. Frank and Joe looked back once at the blackened building, outlined against the twilight sky. Wisps of smoke still curled from the torn-out windows. It was a gloomy, silent trio that drove to the Hardy home in the Queen.

Frank and Joe decided not to tell their mother or aunt of their fear, or to give any hint of their suspicions. When the boys entered the living room, both women gave sighs of relief. They had heard the explosions and the subsequent news flashes about it.

Aunt Gertrude looked at the boys sharply. "By the way, where have you three been all this time? I was afraid that you might have been near Elekton's."

Frank, Joe, and Chet admitted that they had been. "You know we couldn't miss a chance to find out what the excitement was about," Joe said teasingly, then added with an assurance he was far from feeling, "Don't worry. The fire was pretty much under control when we left."

To change the subject, Frank said cheerfully, "I sure am hungry. Let's dig into those sandwiches you bought, Chet!"

"Good idea!" Joe agreed.

"Are you sure you don't want me to fix you something hot to eat?" Mrs. Hardy asked.

"Thanks, Mother, but we'll have enough." Frank smiled.

Chet called his family to let them know where he was, then the three boys sat down in the kitchen and halfheartedly munched the sandwiches. Aunt Gertrude bustled in and served them generous portions of deep-dish apple pie.

"This is more super than usual," Chet declared, trying hard to be cheerful.

The boys finished their pie, but without appetite. When they refused second helpings, however, Aunt Gertrude demanded suspiciously, "Are you ill—or what?"

"Oh, no, Aunty," Joe replied hastily. "Just—er—too much detecting."

"I can believe that!" Miss Hardy said tartly.

The evening dragged on, tension mounting every minute. The boys tried to read or talk, but their concern for the detective's safety made it impossible to concentrate on anything else.

Eleven o'clock! Where *was* their father? Frank and Joe wondered.

"Aren't you boys going to bed soon?" Mrs. Hardy asked, as she and Aunt Gertrude started upstairs.

"Pretty soon," Frank answered.

The three boys sat glumly around the living

room for a few minutes until the women were out of earshot.

"Fellows," said Chet, "I caught on that you're sure your dad is working on an important case for Elekton, and it's a top-secret one—that's why you couldn't say anything about it."

"You're right," Frank told him.

Chet went on to mention that his father had heard of various problems at Elekton—production stoppages caused by power breaks, and, before the buildings were completed, there were reports of tools and equipment being missing.

"This ties in with our hunch about the secrecy of Dad's case," Frank said. "The company must have suspected that major sabotage was being planned, and retained Dad to try and stop it."

Talking over their speculations helped to relieve some of the tension the boys felt and made the time pass a little faster as they waited for news of Fenton Hardy.

"I wonder how the saboteurs got into the plant?" Joe said, thinking aloud. "Both the gates are locked and well guarded. It seems almost impossible for anyone to have sneaked in the necessary amount of explosives—without inside help."

A sudden thought flashed into Frank's mind. He leaped to his feet. "The green truck!" he exclaimed. "It was unmarked, remember? It could have been carrying dynamite—camouflaged under ordinary supplies!"

"That could be, Frank!" Joe jumped up. "If so, no wonder it was in such a rush! I'll phone the chief right now and give him the truck's license number."

Frank went with Joe to the hall telephone. As they approached the phone, it rang. The bell, shattering the tense atmosphere, seemed louder than usual.

"It must be Dad!" exclaimed the brothers together, and Chet hurried into the hall.

Frank eagerly lifted the receiver. "Hello!" he said expectantly.

The next moment Frank looked dejected. He replaced the receiver and said glumly, "Wrong number."

The Hardys exchanged bleak looks. What *had* happened to their father?

CHAPTER XIV

Prisoners!

THE HARDYS' disappointment in discovering that the telephone call was not from their father was intense. Nevertheless, Joe picked up the receiver and dialed police headquarters to report the truck's license number.

"Line's busy," he said.

Joe tried several more times without success. Suddenly he burst out, "I can't stand it another minute to think of Dad perhaps lying out there hurt. Let's go back to Elekton and see if we can learn something."

"All right," Frank agreed, also eager for action, and the three rushed to the front door.

Just as they opened it, the boys saw the headlights of a car turning into the driveway.

"*It's Dad!*" Joe barely refrained from shouting so as not to awaken Mrs. Hardy and Aunt Gertrude.

The detective's sedan headed for the garage at the back of the house. Heaving sighs of thankful relief, the boys quietly hurried through the house into the kitchen to meet him.

"Are we glad to see you, Dad!" Frank exclaimed as he came into the house.

His father looked pale and disheveled. There was a large purple bruise on his left temple. He slumped wearily into a chair.

"I guess I'm lucky to be here." Mr. Hardy managed a rueful smile. "Well, I owe you boys an explanation, and now is the time."

"Dad," Joe spoke up, "you *are* working on the sabotage case for Elekton, aren't you?"

"And you were in the lab building during the explosions?" Frank put in.

"You're both right," the detective replied. "Of course I know I can depend on all of you to keep the matter strictly confidential. The case is far from solved."

Mr. Hardy was relieved that Frank and Joe had kept their fears for his safety from his wife and sister. He now revealed to the boys that for the past several hours he had been closeted with Elekton's officials. Suspecting that the saboteurs had inside help, the detective had screened the records of all employees. He and the officials had found nothing suspicious.

"I'll submit a full report to the FBI tomorrow morning, and continue a search on my own."

When Joe asked if the eight-and-one pattern referred to the saboteurs' schedule, his father nodded. "In the other plants, the sabotage took place eight weeks plus one day apart.

"In each of those plants," the detective went on, "the damage occurred right after closing time. Figuring the schedule would be exactly right for an attempt on Elekton in a couple of days, I started a systematic check of the various buildings. I planned to check daily, until the saboteurs had been caught here or elsewhere. At my request, one company security guard was assigned to assist me. I felt that the fewer people who knew what I was doing, the better. That's how I ruined the saboteurs' plan in Detroit.

"Nothing suspicious occurred here until today when I took up a post in the section of the building where the experimental work is being conducted. After all the employees had left, and the dim night-lights were on, I went toward the east lab wing to investigate."

Mr. Hardy paused, took a deep breath, and continued, "Just as I reached the lab, I happened to glance back into the hall. Things started to happen—fast."

"What did you see, Dad?" asked Joe, and all the boys leaned forward expectantly.

The detective went on, "Hurrying down the

hall from the west lab were two men in work clothes, one carrying a leather bag. I knew there weren't supposed to be any workmen in the building. I stepped out to question them, but the pair broke into a run and dashed past me down the stairs."

"Did you see what either of them looked like?" Frank asked.

"I did catch a glimpse of one before they broke away. He had heavy features and thick eyebrows. But just as I was about to take off after them, I smelled something burning in the east lab and went to investigate. The first thing I saw was a long fuse sputtering toward a box of dynamite, set against the wall.

"I didn't know if it was the kind of fuse that would burn internally or not, so I took my penknife and cut it close to the dynamite. Professional saboteurs don't usually rely on just one explosive, so I started for the west wing to check the lab there."

Mr. Hardy leaned back in his chair and rubbed the bruise on his temple. In a low voice he said, "But I didn't make it. I was running toward the hall when there was a roar and a burst of flame. The explosion lifted me off my feet and threw me against the wall. Though I was stunned, I managed to get back to the east wing. I reached for the phone, then blacked out.

"I must have been unconscious for some time because when the firemen found me and helped me out of the building, the fire had been put out."

"You're all right now?" asked Frank.

"Yes. It was a temporary blackout from shock. What bothers me is that I had the saboteurs' pattern figured out—only they must have become panicky, and moved up their nefarious scheme two days."

Joe looked grim. "I wish we'd been there to help you capture those rats!"

Chet asked Mr. Hardy if he would like a fruit drink. "I'll make some lemonade," he offered.

"Sounds good." Mr. Hardy smiled.

As they sipped the lemonade, Frank and Joe questioned their father about his theories.

"I'm still convinced," said Mr. Hardy, "that one of those men works in the plant. How else would he have known when the watchman makes his rounds and how to disconnect the electronic alarms? But I *can't* figure how the outside accomplice got in—those gates are carefully guarded."

At this point, Frank told his father about the green truck. "We suspected at first it might be connected with the counterfeiters. Now we have a hunch the saboteurs may have used it."

Fenton Hardy seemed greatly encouraged by this possible lead. Joe gave him the license number, which Mr. Hardy said he would report to Chief Collig at once.

When Mr. Hardy returned from the telephone, he told the boys the chief would check the license number with the Motor Vehicle Bureau in the morning and by then he also would have some information about the print on the archer's finger guard.

The next morning after breakfast Frank said he wanted to take another look at the warning notes.

"Why?" Joe asked curiously as they went to the file.

Frank held up the "arrow" warning, and the one received by Chet. "I've been thinking about the printing on these two—seems familiar. I have it!" he burst out.

"Have what?" Joe asked.

"This printing"—Frank pointed to the papers —"is the same as the printing on Ken's envelope addressed to Victor Peters. I'm positive."

Excitedly the brothers speculated on the possible meaning of this clue. "I'd sure like to find out," said Joe, "who addresses the envelopes Ken delivers, and if they're always sent to Mr. Peters in the Parker Building. And why—if he doesn't have an office there. And who *is* Victor Peters?"

"If the person who addresses the envelopes and the sender of the warnings are the same," Frank declared, "it looks as though he's sending something to a confederate, under pretense of having work done for Elekton. I wonder what that something could be?"

"At any rate," Joe added, "this could be a link either to the counterfeiters or to the saboteurs. Which one?"

The boys decided to go out to the mill again, in hopes of quizzing Ken Blake. Just then their father came downstairs. Frank and Joe were glad to see that he looked rested and cheerful.

Mr. Hardy phoned Chief Collig. When the detective hung up, he told his sons that the license number belonged to stolen plates and the fingerprint to a confidence man nicknamed The Arrow.

"He's called this because for several years he worked at exclusive summer resorts, teaching archery to wealthy vacationers, then fleecing as many of them as he could. After each swindle, The Arrow disappeared. Unfortunately, there's no picture of him on file. All the police have is a general description of him."

Frank and Joe learned that the swindler had a pleasant speaking voice, was of medium height, with dark hair and brown eyes.

"Not much to go on," Joe remarked glumly.

"No, but if he *is* working for Elekton, he must be pretty shrewd to have passed their screening."

Mr. Hardy agreed, and phoned Elekton, requesting the personnel department to check if anybody answering The Arrow's description was employed there.

The brothers then informed their father about the similar lettering on the warnings and Ken's Manila envelope.

"A valuable clue," he remarked. "I wish I could go with you to question Ken." The detective explained that right now he had to make his report of the explosion to the nearby FBI office.

When he had left, Frank and Joe rode off to the mill on their motorcycles.

At the gatehouse the guard had unexpected news. "Ken Blake isn't working here any more," Mr. Markel said. "We had to discharge him."

"Why?" asked Joe in surprise.

The guard replied that most of the necessary jobs had been done around the mill grounds. "Mr. Docker—my coworker—and I felt we could handle everything from now on," he explained.

"I see," said Frank. "Can you tell us where Ken is staying?"

Markel said he was not sure, but he thought Ken might have been boarding in an old farmhouse about a mile up the highway.

When the brothers reached the highway, they stopped. "Which way do we go? Mr. Markel didn't tell us," Joe said in chagrin.

"Instead of going back to find out, let's ask at that gas station across the way," Frank suggested. "Someone there may know."

"An old farmhouse?" the attendant repeated in answer to Frank's query. "There's one about a mile from here going toward Bayport. That might be the place your friend is staying. What does he look like?"

Frank described Ken carefully. The attendant nodded. "Yep. I've seen him ride by here on his bike. A couple of times when I was going past the farm I noticed him turn in the dirt road to it."

"Thanks a lot!" The Hardys cycled off quickly.

Soon they were heading up the narrow, dusty lane, which led to a ramshackle, weather-beaten house. The brothers parked their motorcycles among the high weeds in front of it and dismounted.

"This place seems deserted!" Joe muttered.

Frank agreed and looked around, perplexed. "Odd that Ken would be boarding in such a run-down house."

Frank and Joe walked onto the creaky porch and knocked at the sagging door. There was no answer. They knocked again and called. Still no response.

"Some peculiar boardinghouse!" Joe said. "I wouldn't want a room here!"

Frank frowned. "This must be the wrong place. Look—it's all locked up and there's hardly any furniture."

"I'll bet nobody lives in this house!" Joe burst out.

"But the attendant said he has seen Ken riding in here," Frank declared. "Why?"

"Let's have a look," Joe urged.

Mystified, Frank and Joe circled the house. Since they were now certain it had been abandoned, they glanced in various windows. When Joe came to the kitchen he grabbed Frank's arm excitedly.

"Somebody *is* staying here! Could it be Ken?"

Through the dusty glass the boys could see on a rickety table several open cans of food, a carton of milk, and a bowl.

"Must be a tramp," Frank guessed. "I'm sure Ken wouldn't live here."

In turning away, the young detectives noticed a small stone structure about ten yards behind the house. It was the size of a one-car garage. Instead of windows, it had slits high in the walls.

"It probably was used to store farm equipment," Frank said. "We might as well check."

They unbolted the old-fashioned, stout, wooden double doors. These swung outward, and the boys were surprised that the doors opened so silently. "As if they'd been oiled," Frank said.

"No wonder!" Joe cried out. "Look!"

Inside was a shabby green panel truck! "The same one we saw yesterday!" Joe exclaimed. "What's it doing here?"

The boys noticed immediately that the vehicle

"We're prisoners!" Frank exclaimed

had no license plates. "They probably were taken off," Frank surmised, "and disposed of."

Frank checked the glove compartment while Joe looked on the seat and under the cushion for any clue to the driver or owner of the vehicle. Suddenly he called out, "Hey! What's going on?"

Joe jumped from the truck and saw with astonishment that the garage doors were swinging shut. Together, the boys rushed forward but not in time. They heard the outside bolt being rammed into place.

"We're prisoners!" Frank exclaimed.

Again and again the Hardys threw their weight against the doors. This proved futile. Panting, Frank and Joe looked for a means of escape.

"Those slits in the wall are too high and too narrow, anyway," Frank said, chiding himself for not having been on guard.

Finally he reached into the glove compartment and drew out an empty cigarette package he had noticed before. He pulled off the foil. Joe understood immediately what his brother had in mind. Frank lifted the truck's hood and jammed the foil between the starting wires near the fuse box. "Worth a try," he said. "Ignition key's gone. If we can start the engine—we'll smash our way out!"

Joe took his place at the wheel and Frank climbed in beside him. To their delight, Joe gunned the engine into life.

"Here goes!" he muttered grimly. "Brace yourself!"

"Ready!"

Joe eased the truck as far back as he could, then accelerated swiftly forward. The truck's wheels spun on the dirt floor and then with a roar it headed for the heavy doors.

CHAPTER XV

Lead to a Counterfeiter

C-R-A-S-H! The green truck smashed through the heavy garage doors. The Hardys felt a terrific jolt and heard the wood splinter and rip as they shot forward into the farmyard.

"Wow!" Joe gasped as he braked to a halt. "We're free—but not saying in what shape!"

Frank gave a wry laugh. "Probably better than the front of this truck!"

The boys hopped to the ground and looked around the overgrown yard. No one was in sight. The whole area seemed just as deserted as it had been when they arrived.

"Let's check the house," Joe urged. "Someone *could* be hiding in there."

The brothers ran to the run-down dwelling. They found all the doors and windows locked. Again they peered through the dirty panes, but did not see anyone.

"I figure that whoever locked us in the garage would decide that getting away from here in a hurry was his safest bet."

"He must have gone on foot," Joe remarked. "I didn't hear an engine start up."

The Hardys decided to separate, each searching the highway for a mile in opposite directions.

"We'll meet back at the service station we stopped at," Frank called as the boys kicked their motors into life and took off toward the highway.

Fifteen minutes later they parked near the station. Neither boy had spotted any suspicious pedestrians.

"Did you see anybody come down this road in a hurry during the past twenty minutes?" Joe asked the attendant.

"I didn't notice, fellows," came the answer. "I've been busy working under a car. Find your friend?"

"No. That farmhouse is apparently deserted except for signs of a tramp living there," Joe told him.

The Hardys quickly asked the attendant if he knew of any boardinghouse nearby. After a moment's thought, he replied:

"I believe a Mrs. Smith, who lives a little ways beyond the old place, takes boarders."

"We'll try there. Thanks again," Frank said as he and Joe went back to their motorcycles.

Before Frank threw his weight back on the starter, he said, "Well, let's hope Ken Blake can give us a lead."

"If we ever find him," Joe responded.

They located Mrs. Smith's boardinghouse with no trouble. She was a pleasant, middle-aged woman and quickly confirmed that Ken was staying there for the summer. She was an old friend of his parents. Mrs. Smith invited the Hardys to sit down in the living room.

"Ken's upstairs now," she said. "I'll call him."

When Ken came down, the Hardys noticed that he looked dejected. Frank felt certain it was because of losing his job and asked him what had happened.

"I don't know," Ken replied. "Mr. Markel just told me I wouldn't be needed any longer. I hope I'll be able to find another job this summer," he added. "My folks sent me here for a vacation. But I was going to surprise them—" His voice trailed off sadly.

"Ken," Frank said kindly, "you may be able to help us in a very important way. Now that you're not working at the Elekton gatehouse, we hope you can answer some questions—to help solve a mystery."

Frank explained that he and Joe often worked on mysteries and assisted their detective father.

Ken's face brightened. "I'll do my best, fellows," he assured them eagerly.

"Last week," Joe began, "a shabby green panel truck went to Pritos' Supply Yard and picked up old bricks and lumber. Our friend Tony Prito said there was a boy in the truck who helped the yardman with the loading. Were you the boy?"

"Yes," Ken replied readily.

"Who was the driver?" Frank asked him.

"Mr. Docker, the maintenance man at the mill. He said he'd hurt his arm and asked me to help load the stuff." Ken looked puzzled. "Is that part of the mystery?"

"We think it could be," Frank said. "Now, Ken —we've learned since then that one of the bills you gave the yardman is a counterfeit twenty."

Ken's eyes opened wide in astonishment. "A— a counterfeit!" he echoed. "Honest, I didn't know it was, Frank and Joe!"

"Oh, we're sure you didn't," Joe assured him. "Have you any idea who gave Docker the cash?"

Ken told the Hardys he did not know. Then Frank asked:

"What were the old bricks and lumber used for, Ken?"

"Mr. Docker told me they were for repair work around the plant. After we got back to the mill, Mr. Markel and I stored the load in the basement."

"Is it still there?" asked Frank.

"I guess so," Ken answered. "Up to the time I left, it hadn't been taken out."

The Hardys determined to question Markel and Docker at the first opportunity. Then Frank changed the subject and asked about the day of the picnic when Joe thought he had seen Ken at the window.

"I remember," the younger boy said. "I *did* see you all outside. I never knew you were looking for me."

"When we told Mr. Docker," Frank went on, "he said Joe must have been mistaken."

Ken remarked slowly, "He probably was worrying about the plant's security policy. He and Mr. Markel were always reminding me not to talk to anybody."

"During the time you were working at the Elekton gatehouse, did you see any strange or suspicious person near either the plant or the mill grounds?" Frank asked.

"No," said Ken in surprise. Curiosity overcoming him, he burst out, "You mean there's some crook loose around here?"

Frank and Joe nodded vigorously. "We're afraid so," Frank told him. "But who, or what he's up to, is what we're trying to find out. When we do, we'll explain everything."

Joe then asked Ken if he had seen anyone in the area of the mill with a bow and arrow.

"A bow and arrow?" Ken repeated. "No, I never did. I sure would've remembered that!"

Frank nodded and switched to another line of

questioning. "When you delivered envelopes, Ken, did you always take them to Mr. Victor Peters?"

"Yes," Ken answered.

The Hardys learned further that Ken's delivery trips always had been to Bayport—sometimes to the Parker Building, and sometimes to other office buildings in the business section.

"Did Mr. Peters meet you in the lobby every time?" Frank queried.

"That's right."

"What was in the envelopes?" was Joe's next question.

"Mr. Markel said they were bulletins and forms to be printed for Elekton."

"Were the envelopes always marked confidential?" Joe asked.

"Yes."

"Probably everything is that Elekton sends out," Frank said.

"Sounds like a complicated delivery arrangement to me," Joe declared.

Ken admitted that he had not thought much about it at the time, except that he had assumed Mr. Peters relayed the material to the printing company.

Frank and Joe glanced at each other. Both remembered Frank's surmise that the bulky Manila envelopes had not contained bona fide Elekton papers at all!

"What does Mr. Peters look like?" asked Joe, a note of intense excitement in his voice.

"Average height and stocky, with a sharp nose. Sometimes he'd be wearing sunglasses."

"Stocky and a sharp nose," Frank repeated. "Sunglasses." Meaningfully he asked Joe, "Whom does that description fit?"

Joe jumped to his feet. "The man who gave Chet the counterfeit twenty at the railroad station!"

The Hardys had no doubt now that the mysterious Victor Peters must be a passer for the counterfeit ring!

CHAPTER XVI

A Night Assignment

GREATLY excited at this valuable clue to the counterfeiters, Frank asked, "Ken, who gave Mr. Markel the envelopes for Victor Peters?"

"I'm sorry, fellows, I don't know."

The Hardys speculated on where Peters was living. Was it somewhere near Bayport?

Joe's eyes narrowed. "Ken," he said, "this morning we found out that sometimes you'd ride up that dirt road to the deserted farmhouse. Was it for any particular reason?"

"Yes," Ken replied. "Mr. Markel told me a poor old man was staying in the house, and a couple of times a week I was sent there to leave a box of food on the front porch."

"Did you ever see the 'poor old man'?" Frank asked. "Or the green panel truck?"

The Hardys were not surprised when the answer to both questions was No. They suspected the "poor old man" was Peters hiding out there and that he had made sure the truck was out of sight whenever Ken was expected.

The brothers were silent, each puzzling over the significance of what they had just learned. If the truck was used by the counterfeiters, how did this tie in with its being used for the sabotage at Elekton?

"Was The Arrow in league with the saboteurs? Did he also have something to do with the envelopes sent to Victor Peters?" Joe asked himself.

Frank wondered, "Is The Arrow—or a confederate of his working at Elekton—the person responsible for the warnings, the attack on us, and the tampering with the *Sleuth?*"

"Ken," Frank said aloud, "I think you'd better come and stay with us for a while, until we break this case. Maybe you can help us."

He did not want to mention it to Ken, but the possibility had occurred to him that the boy might be in danger if the counterfeiters suspected that he had given the Hardys any information about Victor Peters.

Ken was delighted with the idea, and Mrs. Smith, who knew of Fenton Hardy and his sons, gave permission for her young charge to go.

As a precaution, Frank requested the kindly woman to tell any stranger asking for Ken Blake that he was "visiting friends."

"I'll do that," she agreed.

Ken rode the back seat of Joe's motorcycle on the trip to High Street. He was warmly welcomed by Mrs. Hardy and Aunt Gertrude.

"I hope you enjoy your stay here," said Mrs. Hardy, who knew that Frank and Joe had a good reason for inviting Ken. But neither woman asked questions in his presence.

"Your father probably will be out all day," Mrs. Hardy told her sons. "He'll phone later."

While lunch was being prepared, Frank called police headquarters to give Chief Collig a report on what had happened at the deserted farmhouse.

"I'll notify the FBI," the chief said. "I'm sure they'll want to send men out there to examine that truck and take fingerprints. Elekton," the chief added, "had no record of any employee answering The Arrow's description."

"We're working on a couple of theories," Frank confided. "But nothing definite so far."

After lunch the Hardys decided their next move was to try to find out more about the contents of the envelopes Ken had delivered to Peters.

"We could ask Elekton officials straight out," Joe suggested.

His brother did not agree. "Without tangible evidence to back us up, we'd have to give too many reasons for wanting to know."

Finally Frank hit on an idea. He telephoned Elekton, asked for the accounting department, and inquired where the company had its printing done. The accounting clerk apparently thought he was a salesman, and gave him the information.

Frank hung up. "What did they say?" Joe asked impatiently.

"All Elekton's printing is done on the premises!"

"That proves it!" Joe burst out. "The setup with Ken delivering envelopes to Peters isn't a legitimate one, and has nothing to do with Elekton business."

Meanwhile Ken, greatly mystified, had been listening intently. Now he spoke up. "Jeepers, Frank and Joe, have I been doing something wrong?"

In their excitement the Hardys had almost forgotten their guest. Frank turned to him apologetically. "Not you, Ken. We're trying to figure out who has."

Just then the Hardys heard the familiar chug of the Queen pulling up outside. The brothers went out to the porch with Ken. Chet leaped from his jalopy and bounded up to them. His chubby face was split with a wide grin.

"Get a load of this!" He showed them a badge with his picture on it. "I'll have to wear it when I start work. Everybody has to wear one before he can get into the plant," he added. "Even the president of Elekton!"

Suddenly Chet became aware of Ken Blake. "Hello!" the plump boy greeted him in surprise. Ken smiled, and the Hardys told their friend of the morning's adventure.

"Boy!" Chet exclaimed. "Things are starting to pop! So you found that green truck!"

At these words a strange look crossed Frank's face.

"Chet," he said excitedly, "did you say *everybody* must show identification to enter Elekton's grounds?"

"Yes—everybody," Chet answered positively.

"What are you getting at, Frank?" his brother asked quickly.

"Before yesterday's explosion, when we saw the gate guard admit the green truck, the driver didn't stop—didn't show any identification at all!"

"That's true!" Joe exclaimed. "Mr. Markel doesn't seem to be the careless type, though."

"I know," Frank went on. "If the green truck was sneaking in explosives—what better way than to let the driver zip right through."

Joe stared at his brother. "You mean Markel deliberately let the truck go by? That he's in league with the saboteurs, or the counterfeiters, or both?"

As the others listened in astonishment, Frank replied, "I have more than a hunch he is—and Docker, too. It would explain a lot."

Joe nodded in growing comprehension. "It sure would!"

"How?" demanded Chet.

Joe took up the line of deduction. "Markel himself told Ken the envelopes were for the printer. Why did Docker say Ken wasn't at the mill the day I saw him? And what was the real reason for his being discharged?"

"I'm getting it," Chet interjected. "Those men were trying to keep you from questioning Ken. Why?"

"Perhaps because of what Ken could tell us, if we happened to ask him about the envelopes he delivered," Joe replied. Then he asked Ken if Markel and Docker knew that Joe had picked up the envelope the day of the near accident.

"I didn't say anything about that," Ken replied. The boy's face wore a perplexed, worried look. "You mean Mr. Docker and Mr. Markel might be—crooks! They didn't act that way."

"I agree," Frank said. "And we still have no proof. We'll see if we can find some—one way or another."

The Hardys reflected on the other mysterious happenings. "The green truck," Frank said, "could belong to the gatehouse men, since it seems to be used for whatever their scheme is, and *they* are hiding it at the deserted farmhouse."

"Also," Joe put in, "if Victor Peters is the 'old man,' he's probably an accomplice."

"And," Frank continued, "don't forget that the bike Ken used was available to both Docker and Markel to deliver the warning note. The arrow shooting occurred near the mill; the attack on us in the woods that night was near the mill. The warning note found in Chet's car was put there after Markel told him to go to the front gate. The guard probably lied to Chet the first day we went to the mill—he never did phone the personnel department."

"Another thing," Joe pointed out. "Both men are more free to come and go than someone working in the plant."

There was silence while the Hardys concentrated on what their next move should be.

"No doubt about it," Frank said finally. "Everything seems to point toward the mill as the place to find the answers."

"And the only way to be sure," Joe added, "is to go and find out ourselves. How about tonight?"

Frank and Chet agreed, and the boys decided to wait until it was fairly dark. "I'll call Tony and see if he can go with us," Frank said. "We'll need his help."

Tony was eager to accompany the trio. "Sounds as if you're hitting pay dirt in the mystery," he remarked when Frank had brought him up to date.

"We hope so."

Later, Joe outlined a plan whereby they might

ascertain if Peters *was* an accomplice of Docker and Markel, and at the same time make it possible for them to get into the mill.

"Swell idea," Frank said approvingly. "Better brush up on your voice-disguising technique!"

Joe grinned. "I'll practice."

Just before supper Mr. Hardy phoned to say he would not be home until later that night.

"Making progress, Dad?" asked Frank, who had taken the call.

"Could be, son," the detective replied. "That's why I'll be delayed. Tell your mother and Gertrude not to worry."

"Okay. And, Dad—Joe and I will be doing some sleuthing tonight to try out a few new ideas *we* have."

"Fine. But watch your step!"

About eight-thirty that evening Chet and Tony pulled up to the Hardy home in the Queen.

Ken Blake went with the brothers to the door. "See you later, Ken," Frank said, and Joe added, "I know you'd like to come along, but we don't want you taking any unnecessary risks."

The younger boy looked wistful. "I wish I could do something to help you fellows."

"There *is* a way you can help," Frank told him.

At that moment Mrs. Hardy and Aunt Gertrude came into the hall. Quickly Frank drew Ken aside and whispered something to him.

CHAPTER XVII

Secret Signal

WITH rising excitement, Frank, Joe, Chet, and Tony drove off through the dusk toward the old mill.

Chet came to a stop about one hundred yards from the beginning of the dirt road leading to the gatehouse. He and Tony jumped out. They waved to the Hardys, then disappeared into the woods.

Joe took the wheel of the jalopy. "Now, part two of our plan. I hope it works."

The brothers quickly rode to the service station where they had been that morning. Joe parked and hurried to the outdoor telephone booth nearby. From his pocket he took a slip of paper on which Ken had jotted down the night telephone number of the Elekton gatehouse.

Joe dialed the number, then covered the

mouthpiece with his handkerchief to muffle his voice.

A familiar voice answered, "Gatehouse. Markel speaking."

Joe said tersely, "Peters speaking. Something has gone wrong. Both of you meet me outside the Parker Building. Make it snappy!" Then he hung up.

When Joe returned to the Queen, Frank had turned it around and they were ready to go. They sped back toward the mill and in about ten minutes had the jalopy parked out of sight in the shadows of the trees where the dirt road joined the paved one.

The brothers, keeping out of sight among the trees, ran to join Chet and Tony who were waiting behind a large oak near the edge of the gatehouse grounds.

"It worked!" Tony reported excitedly. "About fifteen minutes ago the lights in the mill went out, and Markel and Docker left in a hurry."

"On foot?" Joe asked.

"Yes."

"Good. If they have to take a bus or cab to town, it'll give us more time," Frank said.

Tony and Chet were given instructions about keeping watch outside while the Hardys inspected the mill. The brothers explained where the Queen was parked, in case trouble should arise and their friends had to go for help.

Frank and Joe approached the mill cautiously. It was dark now, but they did not use flashlights. Though confident that the gatehouse was deserted, they did not wish to take any chances. As they neared the building the Hardys could see that the shutters were tightly closed. Over the sound of the wind in the trees came the rumble of the turning mill wheel.

The Hardys headed for the door. They had just mounted the steps when the rumbling sound of the wheel ceased.

In the silence both boys looked around, perplexed. "I thought it had been fixed," Joe whispered. "Seemed okay the other day."

"Yes. But last time we were here at night the wheel stopped when we were about this distance away from it," Frank observed.

Thoughtfully the boys stepped back from the mill entrance to a point where they could see the wheel. They stood peering at it through the darkness. Suddenly, with a dull rumble, it started to turn again!

Mystified, the Hardys advanced toward the gatehouse and stopped at the entrance. In a short while the wheel stopped.

"Hm!" Joe murmured. "Just like one of those electric-eye doors."

"Exactly!" Frank exclaimed, snapping his fingers. "I'll bet the wheel's *not* broken—it's been rigged up as a warning signal to be used at night!

When someone approaches the mill, the path of the invisible beam is broken and the wheel stops. The lack of noise is enough for anyone inside to notice, and also, the lights would go out because the generator is powered by the wheel."

The Hardys went on a quick search for the origin of the light beam. Frank was first to discover that it was camouflaged in the flour-barrel ivy planter. Beneath a thin covering of earth, and barely concealed, were the heavy batteries, wired in parallel, which produced the current necessary to operate the light source for the electric eye.

The stopping and starting of the wheel was further explained when Frank found, screened by a bushy shrub, a small post with a tiny glass mirror fastened on its side.

"That's the complete secret of the signal!" he exclaimed. "This is one of the mirrors a photoelectric cell system would use. With several of these hidden mirrors, they've made a light-ring around the mill so an intruder from any side would break the beam. The barrel that contains the battery power also contains the eye that completes the circuit."

"I'll bet Markel and Docker rigged this up," Joe said excitedly. "Which means there must be something in the mill they want very badly to keep secret! We must find a way inside!"

The Hardys did not pull the wires off the battery connection, since they might have need of the warning system. Quietly and quickly the brothers made a circuit of the mill, trying doors and first-floor windows, in hopes of finding one unlocked. But none was.

"We can't break in," Joe muttered.

Both boys were aware that time was precious— the men might return shortly. The young sleuths made another circle of the mill. This time they paused to stare at the huge wheel, which was turning once more.

"Look!" Joe whispered tensely, pointing to an open window-shaped space above the wheel.

"It's our only chance to get inside," Frank stated. "We'll try climbing up."

The Hardys realized it would not be easy to reach the opening. Had there been a walkway on top of the wheel, as there was in many mills, climbing it would have been relatively simple.

The brothers came to a quick decision: to maneuver one of the paddles on the wheel until it was directly below the ledge of the open space, then stop the motion. During the short interval which took place between the stop and start of the wheel, they hoped to climb by way of the paddles to the top and gain entrance to the mill.

Joe ran back through the beam, breaking it, while Frank clambered over a pile of rocks across the water to the wheel. It rumbled to a stop, one paddle aligned with the open space above. By the time Joe returned, Frank had started to climb up, pulling himself from paddle to paddle by means of the metal side struts. Joe followed close behind.

The boys knew they were taking a chance in their ascent up the wet, slippery, mossy wheel. They were sure there must be a timing-delay switch somewhere in the electric-eye circuit. Could they beat it, or would they be tossed off into the dark rushing water?

"I believe I can get to the top paddle and reach the opening before the timer starts the wheel turning again. But can Joe?" Frank thought. "Hurry!" he cried out to his brother.

Doggedly the two continued upward. Suddenly Joe's hand slipped on a slimy patch of moss. He almost lost his grip, but managed to cling desperately to the edge of the paddle above his head, both feet dangling in mid-air.

"Frank!" he hissed through clenched teeth.

His brother threw his weight to the right. Holding tight with his left hand to a strut, he reached down and grasped Joe's wrist. With an aerialist's grip, Joe locked his fingers on Frank's wrist, and let go with his other hand.

Frank swung him out away from the wheel. As Joe swung himself back, he managed to regain his footing and get a firm hold on the paddle supports.

"Whew!" said Joe. "Thanks!"

The boys resumed the climb, spurred by the thought that the sluice gate would reopen any second and start the wheel revolving.

Frank finally reached the top paddle. Stretching his arms upward, he barely reached the sill of the opening. The old wood was rough and splintering, but felt strong enough to hold his weight.

"Here goes!" he thought, and sprang away from the paddle.

At the same moment, with a creaking rumble, the wheel started to move!

CHAPTER XVIII

The Hidden Room

While Frank clung grimly to the sill, Joe, below him, knew he must act fast to avoid missing the chance to get off, and perhaps being crushed beneath the turning wheel. He leaped upward with all his might.

Joe's fingers barely grasped the ledge, but he managed to hang onto the rough surface beside his brother. Then together they pulled themselves up and over the sill through the open space.

In another moment they were standing inside the second floor of the building. Rickety boards creaked under their weight. Still not wishing to risk the use of flashlights, the Hardys peered around in the darkness.

"I think we're in the original grinding room," Frank whispered as he discerned the outlines of two huge stone cylinders in the middle of the room.

"You're right," said Joe. "There's the old grain hopper." He pointed to a chute leading down to the grinding stones.

Though many years had passed since the mill had been used to produce flour, the harsh, dry odor of grain still lingered in the air. In two of the corners were cots and a set of crude shelves for clothes. Suddenly the boys' hearts jumped. A loud clattering noise came from directly below. Then, through a wide crack in the floor, shone a yellow shaft of light!

"Someone else must be here!" Joe whispered.

The Hardys stood motionless, hardly daring to breathe, waiting for another sound. Who *was* in the suddenly lighted room?

The suspense was unbearable. Finally the brothers tiptoed over and peered through the wide crack. Straightening up, Frank observed, "Can't see anyone. We'd better go investigate."

Fearful of stumbling in the inky darkness, the boys now turned on their flashlights, but shielded them with their hands. Cautiously they found their way to a door. It opened into a short passageway which led down a narrow flight of steps.

Soon Frank and Joe were in another small hall. Ahead was a partially opened door, with light streaming from it.

Every nerve taut, the young sleuths advanced. Frank edged up to the door and looked in.

"Well?" Joe hissed. To his utter astonishment Frank gave a low chuckle, and motioned him forward.

"For Pete's sake!" Joe grinned.

Inside, perched on a chipped grindstone, was a huge, white cat. Its tail twitched indignantly. An overturned lamp lay on a table.

The Hardys laughed in relief. "Our noisemaker and lamplighter!" Frank said as the boys entered the room. "The cat must have knocked over the lamp and clicked the switch."

Although the room contained the gear mechanism and the shaft connected to the mill wheel, it was being used as a living area by the present tenants. There were two overstuffed chairs, a table, and a chest of drawers. On the floor, as if dropped in haste, lay a scattered newspaper.

"Let's search the rest of the mill before Markel and Docker get back," Joe suggested. "Nothing suspicious here."

The Hardys started with the top story of the old building. There they found what was once the grain storage room. Now it was filled with odds and ends of discarded furniture.

"I'm sure nothing's hidden here," Frank said.

The other floors yielded no clues to what Docker and Markel's secret might be.

Frank was inclined to be discouraged. "Maybe our big hunch is all wet," he muttered.

Joe refused to give up. "Let's investigate the cellar. Come on!"

The brothers went into the kitchen toward the basement stairway. Suddenly Joe gave a stifled yell. Something had brushed across his trouser legs. Frank swung his light around. The beam caught two round golden eyes staring up at them.

"The white cat!" Joe said sheepishly.

Chuckling, the Hardys continued down into the damp, cool cellar. It was long and narrow, with only two small windows.

Three walls were of natural stone and mortar. The fourth wall was lined with wooden shelves. Frank and Joe played their flashlights into every corner.

"Hm." There was a note of disappointment in Joe's voice. "Wheelbarrow, shovels, picks—just ordinary equipment."

Frank nodded. "Seems to be all, but where are the old bricks and lumber that Ken said were stored here?"

"I'm sure the stuff was never intended for Elekton," Joe declared. "More likely the mill. But where? In a floor? We haven't seen any signs."

Thoughtfully the boys walked over to inspect the shelves, which held an assortment of implements. Frank reached out to pick up a hammer.

To his amazement, he could not lift it. A further quick examination revealed that all the tools were glued to the shelves.

"Joe!" he exclaimed. "There's a special reason for this—and I think it's camouflage!"

"You mean these shelves are movable, and the tools are fastened so they won't fall off?"

"Yes. Also, I have a feeling this whole section is made of the old lumber from Pritos' yard."

"And the bricks?" Joe asked, puzzled.

His brother's answer was terse. "Remember, this mill was used by settlers. In those days many places had hidden rooms in case of Indian attacks—"

"I get you!" Joe broke in. "Those bricks are in a secret room! The best place to build one in this mill would have been the cellar."

"Right," agreed Frank. "And the only thing unusual here is this shelf setup. I'll bet it's actually the entrance to the secret room."

"All we have to do is find the opening mechanism," Joe declared.

Using their flashlights, the boys went over every inch of the shelves. These were nailed to a backing of boards. The Hardys pulled and pushed, but nothing happened. Finally, on the bottom shelf near the wall, Frank discovered a knot in the wood. In desperation, he pressed his thumb hard against the knot.

There was the hum of a motor, and, as smoothly

"The door to the secret room!" Frank exulted

as though it were moving on greased rails, the middle section of shelves swung inward.

"The door to the secret room!" Frank exulted.

Quickly the boys slipped inside the room and shone their flashlights around. The first thing they noticed was the flooring—recently laid bricks. Frank snapped on a light switch beside the entrance.

The boys blinked in the sudden glare of two high-watt bulbs suspended from the low ceiling. The next instant both spotted a small, hand-printing press.

"The counterfeiters' workshop!" they cried out.

On a wooden table at the rear of the room were a camera, etching tools, zinc plates, and a large pan with little compartments containing various colors of ink. At the edge of the table was a portable typewriter.

Frank picked up a piece of paper, rolled it into the machine, and typed a few lines. Pulling it out, he showed the paper to Joe.

"The machine used to type the warning note Dad got!" Joe exclaimed excitedly. "The counterfeiters must have thought he was on their trail."

"And look here!" exclaimed Frank, his voice tense. A small pile of twenty-dollar bills lay among the equipment. "They're fakes," he added, scrutinizing the bills. "They're the same as Chet's and Tony's."

Joe made another startling discovery. In one corner stood a bow, with the string loosened and carefully wound around the handgrip. A quiver of three hunting arrows leaned against the wall nearby.

Excitedly Joe pulled one out. "The same type that was fired at the girls," he observed. "This must belong to The Arrow!"

"Docker matches his description," Frank pointed out. "He easily could have colored his hair gray."

The Hardys were thrilled at the irrefutable evidence all around them. "Now we know why Markel and Docker rigged the mill wheel—to give a warning signal when they're working in this room!"

"Also, we have a good idea what was being sent to Peters in the envelopes—phony twenty-dollar bills!"

"Let's get Dad and Chief Collig here!" Joe urged, stuffing several of the counterfeits into a pocket.

As the boys turned to leave, the lights in the secret room went out. Frank and Joe froze. They realized the mill wheel had stopped turning.

"The signal!" Joe said grimly. "Someone is coming!"

CHAPTER XIX

Underground Chase

THE HARDYS knew this was the signal for them to get out of the secret room—and fast! As they hurried into the cellar, the lights came on again. With hearts beating faster, they started for the stairway. But before the boys reached it, they heard the mill door being unlocked, then heavy footsteps pounded overhead.

"Docker!" a man's voice called. "Markel! Where are you!"

The Hardys listened tensely, hoping for a chance to escape unseen. When they heard the man cross the ground floor and go upstairs, Joe whispered, "Let's make a break for it!"

The boys dashed to the steps. They could see a crack of light beneath the closed door to the kitchen. Suddenly the light vanished, and the rumble of the mill wheel ceased.

The Hardys stopped in their tracks. "Somebody else is coming!" Frank muttered. "Probably Docker and Markel. We're trapped!"

Again the brothers heard the mill door open. Two men were talking loudly and angrily. Then came the sound of footsteps clattering down the stairs to the first floor.

"Peters!" The boys recognized Docker's voice. "Where in blazes were you?"

Frank and Joe nudged each other. Victor Peters *was* in league with the gatehouse men!

"What do you mean? I told you I'd meet you here at eleven," snarled Peters.

"You must be nuts!" retorted Markel. "You called here an hour ago and said there was trouble and to meet *you* at the Parker Building."

Peters' tone grew menacing. "Something's fishy. I didn't phone. You know I'd use the two-way radio. What's the matter with you guys, anyway?"

"Listen!" Markel snapped. *"Somebody* called here and said he was you. The voice did sound sort of fuzzy, but I didn't have a chance to ask questions—he hung up on me. I thought maybe your radio had conked out."

The Hardys, crouched on the cellar stairs, could feel the increasing tension in the room above. Docker growled, "Something funny *is* going on. Whoever phoned must be on to us, or suspect enough to want to get in here and snoop around."

"The Feds! We'll have to scram!" said Markel, with more than a trace of fear in his voice. "Come on! Let's get moving!"

"Not so fast, Markel!" Docker barked. "We're not ditching the stuff we've made. We'll have a look around first—starting with the cellar."

The men strode into the kitchen. Below, Frank grabbed Joe. "No choice now. Into the secret room!"

Quickly the brothers ran back into the workshop. Frank pulled the door behind him and slid the heavy bolt into place.

Tensely the brothers pressed against the door as the three men came downstairs into the basement. Frank and Joe could hear them moving around, searching for signs of an intruder.

"I'd better check the rest of the mill," Docker said brusquely. "You two get the plates and the greenbacks. Go out through the tunnel, and I'll meet you at the other end. We'll wait there for Blum to pay us off, then vamoose."

"We're in a fix, all right," Joe said under his breath. "What tunnel are they talking about?"

"And who's Blum?" Frank wondered.

The boys heard the hum of the motor that opened the secret door. But the bolt held it shut.

"The mechanism won't work!" Markel rasped.

"Maybe it's just stuck," said Peters.

The men began pounding on the wood.

"What's going on?" Docker demanded as he returned.

"We can't budge this tricky door you dreamed up," Peters complained.

"There's nothing wrong with the door, you blockheads!" Docker shouted. "Somebody's in the room! Break down the door!"

In half a minute his order was followed by several sharp blows.

"Oh, great!" Joe groaned. "They're using axes!"

"We won't have long to figure a way out," Frank said wryly.

"Way out!" Joe scoffed. "There isn't any!"

Frank's mind raced. "Hey! They said something about leaving through a tunnel! It must be in here."

Frantically the Hardys searched for another exit from the secret room. They crawled on the floor, and pried up one brick after another looking for a ring that might open a trap door.

"Nothing!" Joe said desperately.

All the while the men in the cellar kept battering away at the door. "Good thing that old lumber is such hard wood," Frank thought. "But they'll break through any minute."

"Look!" Joe pointed. "Under the bench!"

Frank noticed a shovel lying beneath the worktable. The boys pushed it aside, and saw that the wall behind the table was partially covered with loose dirt. On a hunch Frank grabbed the shovel and dug into the dirt.

"This dirt might have been put here to hide the entrance to the tunnel!" he gasped.

"It better be!" His brother clawed frantically at the dirt.

At the same moment there was a loud splintering noise. The Hardys looked around. A large crack had appeared in the bolted door.

One of the men outside yelled, "A couple more blows and we'll be in."

Frank dug furiously. Suddenly his shovel opened up a small hole in the crumbly dirt. Joe scooped away with his hands. Finally there was a space big enough for the boys to squeeze through. Without hesitation, Frank wriggled in, then Joe.

From behind them came a tremendous crash and the sound of ripping wood. Markel's voice shouted, "Into the tunnel! After 'em!"

The Hardys heard no more as they pushed ahead on hands and knees into the damp darkness of an earthen passageway.

Joe was about to call out to his brother when he became aware that someone was crawling behind him. "No room here for a knockdown fight," he thought, wondering if the pursuer were armed.

The young detective scrambled on as fast as he could in the narrow, twisting tunnel. He managed to catch up to Frank, and with a push warned him to go at top speed.

"Somebody's after us!" Joe hissed. "If only we can outdistance him!"

The underground route was a tortuous, harrowing one. The Hardys frequently scraped knees and shoulders against sharp stones in the tunnel floor and walls. They had held onto their flashlights, but did not dare turn them on.

"This passageway is endless!" Frank thought. The close, clammy atmosphere made it increasingly difficult for him and his brother to breathe.

Joe thought uneasily, "What if we hit a blind alley and are stuck in here?"

The boys longed to stop and catch their breath, but they could hear the sounds of pursuit growing nearer, and forced themselves onward faster than ever.

Frank wondered if Chet and Tony had seen the men enter the mill and had gone for help.

"We'll need it," he thought grimly.

Suddenly the brothers came to another turn and the ground began to slope sharply upward.

"Maybe we're getting close to the end," Frank conjectured hopefully.

Spurred by possible freedom, he put on a burst of speed. Joe did the same. A moment later Frank stopped unexpectedly and Joe bumped into him.

"What's the matter?" he barely whispered.

"Dead end," reported his brother.

Squeezing up beside Frank, Joe reached out and touched a pile of stones blocking their path. The boys now could hear the heavy breathing of their pursuer.

"Let's move these stones," Frank urged.

Both Hardys worked with desperate haste to pull the barrier down. They heaved thankful sighs when a draft of fresh air struck their faces.

"The exit!" Joe whispered in relief.

The brothers wriggled through the opening they had made and found themselves in a rock-walled space.

"It's the cave by the river, Joe!" Frank cried out. "Someone put back the rocks we removed!"

The boys clicked on their flashlights and started toward the entrance of the cave.

"We beat 'em to it!" Joe exclaimed.

"That's what you think!" came a harsh voice from the entrance.

The glare from two flashlights almost blinded the Hardys. Docker and Markel, with drawn revolvers, had stepped into the cave.

CHAPTER XX

Solid Evidence

FOR a second the two armed men stared in disbelief at Frank and Joe. "The Hardy boys!" Docker snarled. "So you're the snoopers we've trapped!"

There was a scuffling in the tunnel behind the boys. A stocky man, huffing and puffing, emerged from the tunnel. The Hardys recognized him instantly: the counterfeit passer, Victor Peters.

The newcomer gaped at the Hardys. "What are *they* doing here?"

"A good question!" Markel snapped at his accomplice. "You told us on the two-way radio you'd locked 'em up with the truck."

Peters whined, "I *did*. They must've broken out."

"Obviously." Docker gave him a withering look.

Frank and Joe realized that Peters had not returned to the old farmhouse.

Docker whirled on them. "How *did* you escape?"

The boys looked at him coldly. "That's for you to find out," Joe retorted.

"It's a good thing Markel and I decided to head 'em off at the cave," Docker added angrily. "Otherwise, they would have escaped again."

The Hardys could see that the men were nervous and edgy. "I'm not the only one who made a mistake," Peters growled. "I told you a couple of days ago to get rid of that kid Ken when these pests started asking about him, and then found the tunnel. We could have thrown 'em off the scent!"

While the men argued, the Hardys kept on the alert for a chance to break away. Markel's eye caught the movement, and he leveled his revolver. "Don't be smart!" he ordered. "You're covered."

Peters continued the tirade against his confederates. "Docker, you should've finished these Hardys off when you put 'em in the boat that night! And you"—Peters turned on Markel—"*you* could have planted a dynamite charge in their boat instead of just monkeying with the throttle."

The Hardys, meanwhile, were thankful for the precious minutes gained by the men's dissension.

"Tony and Chet might come back in time with help," Joe thought.

Simultaneously, Frank hoped that Ken Blake had carried out his whispered instructions.

Docker glanced nervously at his watch. "Blum ought to be here," he fumed.

"Who's Blum?" Frank asked suddenly. "One of your counterfeiting pals?"

Docker, Markel, and Peters laughed scornfully. "No," said Markel. "We're the only ones in our exclusive society. Paul Blum doesn't know anything about our—er—mill operation, but it was through him we got the jobs at the gatehouse. The whole deal really paid off double."

Docker interrupted him with a warning. "Don't blab so much!"

Markel sneered. "Why not? What I say won't do these smart alecks any good."

Joe looked at the guard calmly. "Who paid you to let the green panel truck into Elekton?"

All three men started visibly. "How'd you know that?" Markel demanded.

"Just had a hunch," Joe replied.

The former guard regained his composure. "We'll get our money for that little job tonight."

Frank and Joe felt elated. Paul Blum, whom these men expected, must be the sabotage ringleader! "So that's what Markel meant by the deal paying off double," Frank thought. "He and Docker working the counterfeit racket on their own—and being in cahoots with the saboteurs."

Frank addressed Markel in an icy tone. "You call blowing up a building a 'little job'?"

The counterfeiters' reactions astonished the Hardys. *"What!"* bellowed Markel, as Docker and Peters went ashen.

Joe snorted. "You expect us to believe you didn't *know* explosives were in that truck?"

Victor Peters was beside himself with rage. *"Fools!"* he shrilled at Docker and Markel. "You let yourselves be used by saboteurs? This whole state will be crawling with police and federal agents."

The gatehouse men, though shaken, kept their revolvers trained on the Hardys. "Never mind," Docker muttered. "Soon as Blum shows up we'll get out of here and lie low for a while."

Frank and Joe learned also that Docker and Markel actually were brothers, but the two refused to give their real names.

"You, Docker, are known as The Arrow, aren't you?" Frank accused him.

"Yeah. Next time I'll use *you* boys for targets!" the man retorted threateningly.

The Hardys kept egging the men on to further admissions. Docker and Markel had been approached several months before by Blum who tipped them off to good-paying jobs at the Elekton gatehouse. Docker had cleverly forged references and identification for Markel and himself.

As soon as he and Markel had obtained the jobs, Blum had instructed them to buy the truck secondhand in another state, and told them only that Markel was to lend Blum the truck on a certain day when notified, let him through the gate, then out again soon after closing time. The guard would be handsomely paid to do this.

When Markel and Docker had become settled in the mill, the two had discovered the secret room and tunnel, which once had been a settlers' escape route. The men had wasted no time in setting it up for their counterfeiting racket, and often used the nondescript green truck to sneak in the required equipment.

"Who rigged up the electric-eye signal?" Frank queried.

"My work," Docker replied proudly.

As the boys had surmised, Peters, an old acquaintance of theirs, was "the old man" at the deserted farmhouse. When the boys had left the mill that morning Docker had radioed Peters, telling him if the Hardys showed up at the farm, he was to trap them.

"No doubt you planned to finish us off when you came back," Joe said.

Peters nodded.

Frank said to Docker, "I must admit, those

twenties are pretty good forgeries. The police think so, too."

The counterfeiter smiled in contempt. "Your fat friend sure was fooled."

He explained that his skill at engraving, which he had learned years ago, had enabled him to make the plates from which the bills were printed.

"Which one of you rode Ken's bike and left the typed warning for our father?" Frank asked.

"I did," Markel replied promptly.

"Why? He wasn't involved with the counterfeiting case."

We thought he was when we overheard a company bigwig say Fenton Hardy was 'taking the case.' "

"Yeah," Docker said. "I wasn't kidding when I sent the warnings—on paper and by phone."

He had acquired some sheets of bond paper from Elekton on a pretext; also the Manila envelopes used to deliver the bogus money to Peters. Docker admitted he had "unloaded" the counterfeit twenty at Pritos' yard by mistake.

Peters broke in abruptly. "We'd better get rid of these kids right now!"

The three men held a whispered conference, but Docker and Markel did not take their eyes from the Hardys. Suddenly the boys' keen ears detected the put-put of an approaching motorboat.

One thought flashed across their minds—Chet and Tony were bringing help. But in a few minutes their hopes were dashed! A heavy-set, dark-haired man peered into the mouth of the cave.

"Blum!" Markel said.

"Who are these kids?" Blum asked, squinting at Frank and Joe.

"Their name is Hardy—" Docker began, but Blum cut him short.

"Hardy!" he said sharply. "Listen—I just gave Fenton Hardy the slip at the Bayport dock. He was on a police launch."

"We've got to move fast!" Markel urged. "Docker and I caught these sons of his snooping. Pay us what you promised and we'll scram."

Blum looked disgusted. "Stupid amateurs! You let kids make it so hot you have to get out of town?" The heavy-set man pulled out his wallet. "Here's your cut for letting me into the plant," he continued scornfully. "I'm glad to get rid of such bunglers."

"It's not just these kids that made it hot for us!" Docker stormed. "If we'd known you were going to blow up that lab, we never would've gotten mixed up with you."

The Hardys noticed that Paul Blum appeared startled at Docker's words.

Frank spoke up boldly. "Sure. We all know you're back of the sabotage. Who pays *you* for doing it? And who's *your* inside man at Elekton?"

Blum glared, then in a sinister tone replied, "You'll never live to sing to the cops, so I'll tell you. Several countries that want to stop United States progress in missiles are paying me. My friend in the plant is a fellow named Jordan."

The saboteur revealed that his accomplice had first carried out smaller acts of sabotage, the ones which Chet had heard about from his father. It had been Blum himself who had driven the truck into the grounds and placed the dynamite in the laboratory. "Jordan and I gave your father the slip, then, too!"

"You guys can stand here and talk!" snapped Peters. "I'm going. You'd better take care of these Hardys." He backed out of the cave and raced off.

The counterfeiters discussed heatedly whether "to get rid" of Frank and Joe immediately, or take "these kids" and dispose of them later.

"That's your worry!" Blum said. *"I'm* taking off!"

"Oh, no, you're not. You can't leave us in the lurch." Markel waved his gun meaningfully.

At that instant there was a crashing noise outside the cave. The three men swung around.

This was all the Hardys needed. They hurled themselves at their captors, forcing them backward onto the rocky beach. From the woods they heard Chet yell, "Here we come, fellows!"

Frank had tackled Blum, and Joe was wrestling with Docker on the beach.

Tony Prito yelled, "Got you!" as he took a flying leap at Markel and brought him to the ground.

The older men, though strong, were no match for the agile Hardys and the furious onslaught of Chet and Tony. Finally the struggle ended.

The saboteur and counterfeiters were disarmed and lined up before the cave, their arms pinioned behind them by Joe, Chet, and Tony. Frank took charge of the revolvers.

"Good work, you two!" he said to his friends.

Chet, out of breath, grinned proudly. "I'm glad Tony and I stuck around when we saw these guys high-tailing it through the woods."

Now Frank turned to the prisoners. "Okay. March!" he ordered.

But before anyone could move, footsteps were heard approaching through the woods. A moment later Chief Collig and another officer appeared. With them, in handcuffs, was Victor Peters.

"Chief! Are we glad to see you!" Joe exclaimed.

The chief stared in amazement at the boys and their captives. "I got your message from Ken Blake," he told Frank. "Looks as if you have your hands full!"

"Oh, we have!" Joe grinned, then, puzzled, he asked his brother, "What message?"

"Just before I left the house I told Ken to call

Chief Collig if we weren't back by eleven, and tell him where we had gone."

While Blum and the counterfeiters stood in sullen silence, the four boys learned that Ken had called the chief just minutes after Fenton Hardy had left in the police launch in pursuit of Paul Blum.

"When we reached the mill we met this crook running out of the woods." Chief Collig gestured toward the handcuffed Peters. "I recognized him from Chet's description. When we found phony money on him, he told me where you were, hoping to get off with a lighter sentence."

"You rat!" Docker's face contorted with rage.

At that moment the group became aware of a police launch churning toward them, the beam from its searchlight sweeping the water. In the excitement, no one had heard the sound of its engine.

"Dad!" cried the Hardys, spotting the detective's erect figure standing in the bow. Soon the launch was beached, and Mr. Hardy, with several officers, leaped ashore.

"Well," Mr. Hardy said sternly when he saw Blum, "you won't be escaping again."

The captured lawbreakers were handcuffed and put aboard the launch. Mr. Hardy looked at his sons and their friends proudly. "You've done a yeoman's job—on both cases, yours and mine," he said.

After the police cruiser had departed, Frank and Joe led their father and the others into the mill cellar and showed them the secret room.

"This is all the evidence you need against the counterfeiters, Chief," said Mr. Hardy. "I can see there are plenty of fingerprints on this equipment. We know some will match the one on the finger guard. Besides your evidence, boys, Ken's testimony should be more than enough to convict them."

"What about Jordan, Blum's confederate at Elekton?" Frank asked.

Mr. Hardy smiled. "He was my big prize and I'm glad to say he is in jail!" The detective explained that further sleuthing had led to Jordan —and through him, Paul Blum. Mr. Hardy's first break had come when he learned that one Elekton employee had seen Jordan going toward the laboratory building at closing time on the day of the explosion.

A police guard was assigned to watch the counterfeiters' workshop and its contents. Then the four boys, Mr. Hardy, and the chief left the mill. Outside, they paused and looked back at the turning wheel.

Frank laughed. "Its signaling days are over."

"Sure hope so," Chet declared firmly. "No more mysteries for a while, please!"

Tony chuckled. "With Frank and Joe around, I wouldn't count on it."

His words proved to be true. Sooner than even the Hardy boys expected, they were called upon to solve the mystery of **THE MISSING CHUMS.**

Now Joe turned to their plump friend. "Good thing you bought that microscope, Chet. We started to look for nature specimens and dug up the old mill's secret!"

The Hardy Boys Mystery Stories®

THE HAUNTED
FORT

BY

FRANKLIN W. DIXON

GROSSET & DUNLAP
Publishers • New York
A member of The Putnam & Grosset Group

CONTENTS

CHAPTER I

Scalp Warning

"CHET MORTON inviting us to a mystery—I don't believe it!" Blond seventeen-year-old Joe Hardy smiled as he and his brother bounded off the back steps toward the garage.

Frank Hardy, dark-haired and a year older than Joe, eagerly keyed the car motor to life. Soon they were headed out of Bayport for the Morton farm. Dusk was falling.

"Chet seemed too excited to say much on the phone," Frank explained. "But he did mention there might be a vacation in it for us—and a haunted fort."

"A haunted fort!"

When the brothers pulled into the gravel driveway of the rambling, brown-and-white farmhouse, pretty Iola Morton, Chet's sister, danced off the porch to greet them.

"Frank and Joe! What a surprise! You're just in time for our homemade hootenanny!"

"And I can play two chords!" Callie Shaw waved from the front doorway, a large guitar hanging from her neck. Callie, a slim blonde, was Frank's special friend, while vivacious Iola often dated Joe.

"It sounds great," Frank began, "but Chet called us over to—" He glanced suspiciously at Joe. "Say, do you think these two got Chet to lure us over here about a mystery?"

"Of course not, sillies," dark-haired Iola protested, her eyes snapping. "Besides, who wants to talk about murky old mysteries? Wait until you hear Callie's new ballad records."

As the four entered the house, a round face beneath a coonskin cap peered from the kitchen. Then the stocky figure of Chet Morton made an entrance.

"Hi, Hardys! Anybody for a haunted vacation?"

"Chet! Then there really is a mystery?" Joe's face brightened as Chet nodded and motioned the brothers upstairs to his room. But not before the girls frowned disdainfully.

"Meanies!" Callie said. "Don't be forever!"

As the Hardys took seats, Chet reclined on his bed and began, "My uncle Jim phoned late this afternoon from Crown Lake in New England. You know, he's chief painting instructor at a summer art school there."

Chet explained that the place, named Millwood, was sponsored by a millionaire for the benefit of talented teen-agers.

"Sounds like a swell arrangement for aspiring artists," Frank remarked.

"Uncle Jim loves his job," Chet continued, "or at least he did before the painting thefts started."

"You mean thefts of students' paintings?" Joe interrupted, puzzled.

"No. Something much more valuable. Uncle Jim didn't go into details, but he did mention somebody called the Prisoner-Painter. Two of his pictures have disappeared."

"What about the local police?" Frank asked.

"They've already tried to solve the case. No luck. That's why Uncle Jim wants us to live at the school for a while."

"How'd he know about us?" Joe put in.

"I mentioned you fellows in letters. 'Course, I didn't tell him any of the *bad* things about you— only that you were a couple of great detectives."

Frank grinned and arced a slow-motion swing toward his teasing pal, but in a flash Chet was on his feet, twirling his coonskin cap. "I'm half-packed already." He brightened, a hopeful look in his eye. "Will you fellows come along?"

"Try and keep us away!" Joe exclaimed. He was as excited as Frank at the prospect of adventure.

Both boys, sons of Bayport's famous detective, Fenton Hardy, had already tackled and solved many mysteries. From the baffling secret of *The*

Tower Treasure to their most recent case, *The Mystery of the Aztec Warrior,* the boys welcomed each new challenge. Chet, their loyal and close friend, though sometimes reluctant to sleuth with them, often proved to be of great help.

"Chet," Frank added, "didn't you mention a haunted fort on the phone?"

"Oh that!" Chet groaned. "Yes, I did. Uncle Jim said something about an old French fort nearby, but maybe it's not important. Gee, fellows, haunted places don't agree with me!"

"I don't know," Frank mused, winking at Joe. "I hear some ghosts are pretty well-fed. Think we could introduce Chet to one or two up at Crown Lake?"

Chet could not repress a smile as the brothers chuckled, then patted him on the back. Suddenly they heard a scream from the front porch.

"That's Callie!" Joe cried out.

The three boys rushed downstairs. Iola stood trembling in the doorway. Callie, pale with fright, pointed to a hairy object on the lawn.

"What happened?" Frank asked in alarm.

Callie said that a speeding black car had slowed in front of the house and somebody had tossed out the object.

"It looks like—like a scalp!" Iola shuddered.

The Hardys rushed out to the lawn and Frank knelt over the strange thing.

"It's a scalp!" Frank exclaimed

"It's a scalp all right—made of papier-mâché! Looks pretty real with all this red paint."

Joe picked it up. "There's a note attached!" He removed a small piece of paper from the underside. Frowning, he read the typewritten words aloud:

" *'Use your heads, stay away from*
Crown Lake.' "

"Did you get a look at the driver?" Frank asked, as Iola and Callie joined the boys.

"No, but I think it was an out-of-state license plate," Callie replied. "I thought he was just a litterbug until I saw—*that.*"

The gruesome-looking object was made from black bristles of the sort used in paintbrushes. Frank turned to Chet and Joe. "What do you fellows make of it?"

Joe shrugged. "Who would want to stop us from going to Crown Lake—and why?"

"Also," Chet added, "how did anybody even know we had been invited up to Crown Lake by my uncle?"

The young people discussed the strange warning as the Hardys returned to their car, where Frank deposited the fake scalp.

"This grisly clue indicates one thing," Frank concluded. "Somebody wants us to stay away from Millwood Art School! If that's where our 'scalper' is from, it might explain how he learned of Mr. Kenyon's invitation."

"Speaking of invitations," Joe said, "what time do you want to leave tomorrow, Chet?"

"Leave!" Iola and Callie exclaimed.

"Sure." Frank grinned. "I've always been interested in Indian haircuts—that is, unless Chet wants to back out."

"Me—back out?" Chet swallowed, then resolutely replaced the coonskin cap on his round head—backward. "Fur Nose Morton will pick you up tomorrow morning at ten sharp. Don't forget to pack some warm duds!"

The girls protested in vain. After making the boys promise not to be away for the whole summer, they wished them a safe and pleasant trip. As Frank drove the car down the drive, Joe leaned out the window.

"We'll take a rain check on that hootenanny, girls. See you in the morning, Chet!"

Full of anticipation about their new mystery, the Hardys drove directly to their tree-shaded house at the corner of High and Elm streets. After securing permission from their parents for the trip to Crown Lake, the excited boys spent the rest of the evening packing three large suitcases. Before retiring, they quickly perused several school-books on the history of the Crown Lake region. It had been an area of conflict during the French and Indian War.

"Here's a fort!" Joe remarked. "Senandaga! That may be the place Chet's uncle mentioned.

According to this, Senandaga was an impressive stronghold, though it didn't play a large role in the campaigns."

"If a fort's haunted, we can't expect it to be historical too," Frank said, grinning.

"Wait a minute!" Joe looked up. "There's a small painting of this fort right in the Bayport Museum!"

"The same one?"

"Yes. What say we have a look at it tomorrow before Chet gets here?"

After a sound night's sleep the boys awoke a half-hour earlier than usual the following morning and quickly arranged their luggage on the front porch. Leaving word that they would be back by ten, they drove in their convertible to the Bayport Museum.

A small, pug-faced man carrying a large sketch pad was just leaving the building as they reached the top of the marble steps. After bumping into Frank, he bowed nervously, then hastened down the steps and up the street.

"He's sure an early-bird artist," Joe remarked.

They passed into the cool, echoing foyer and were just about to enter the American Collection Room when they heard running footsteps and a cry for help. A distraught, bespectacled man waved to them and pointed ahead.

"That man—stop him—he's stolen our fort painting!"

CHAPTER II

Highway Chase

"FORT painting!" The words set Frank and Joe racing after the thief. They darted outside and down the marble steps three at a time! Frank went in one direction, Joe the other. But there was no sign of the fugitive.

After the Hardys had checked several side streets, they headed back and met at the museum.

"No luck," Frank said.

"He must have had a car," Joe declared.

"Another thing," Frank said, "I'll bet he hid the painting in that big sketch pad of his."

In the foyer of the museum, the brothers were questioned by two policemen. After Frank and Joe had given their statements to the officers, they spoke with the museum director, the man who had alerted them to the theft. As Frank suspected, the thief had apparently concealed the small painting in his sketch pad.

"I don't know why he chose the picture of Fort Senandaga," the director lamented, "but I'm sorry he did. So far as I know, ours was the only work of the Prisoner-Painter in this area."

The Hardys started in surprise. This was the same artist whose pictures had been disappearing from Millwood Art School!

After the director had thanked them for their efforts, they returned to their car, each with the same thought: Had the morning's theft any connection with the art school mystery?

When they reached home, Chet was sitting disconsolately on the porch steps fanning himself with a blue beret.

"Leaping lizards! What a morning you fellows pick for going to a museum," he moaned. "I could have had a second breakfast while I've been waiting for you."

"We're sorry, Chet," Frank apologized, "but it turned out to be a four-lap, dead-end workout."

While the Hardys loaded their bags into Chet's freshly polished yellow jalopy, the Queen, they told him of the museum theft. Chet whistled.

"Do you think the thief's the one who threw that scalp on our lawn?"

"It's likely," Frank replied.

When the jalopy had been loaded up to the back windows, Mrs. Hardy came out and embraced the boys warmly. "Do take care of yourselves." She smiled. "Dad will be home in a few days. I'll tell him about your case, but I feel sure you can solve it by yourselves."

Amid good-bys, Chet backed the car down the driveway, and soon the jalopy was headed north out of Bayport. After following the county road for half an hour, Chet guided the car onto the wide-laned state thruway extending like a white ribbon beneath a light-blue sky.

The boys conversed excitedly about their destination and the mystery to be solved there.

"You really did some tune-up job on the Queen, Chet," Joe commented from the back seat. "One of these days she may be a threat to approaching the speed limit."

Chet smiled good-naturedly at the gibe, then frowned, tugging at his beret to keep it from being blown off by the brisk wind. Finally he gave up. "Alas, what we artists must bear." He sighed and stuffed the cap into the glove compartment.

Frank grinned. "What happened to that coonskin job you had yesterday?"

"Oh," Chet said airily, "I thought I'd get into the artistic spirit."

As they drove by a gasoline-and-restaurant service area, a black sedan pulled out onto the thruway from the service area exit. When Chet moved to the middle lane to pass, Joe glanced at the sedan and sat up sharply.

"Frank! The driver of that car—it's the picture thief!"

Immediately Chet slackened speed. Looking over, Frank too recognized the pug-faced man at the wheel an instant before the thief saw the Hardys. Clearly alarmed, the man gunned the engine. The black car shot ahead, but Frank glimpsed in its back seat a large sketch pad!

"Stay with him!" Joe urged, as the gap widened between the two cars. Futilely, Chet floored the Queen's old gas pedal, then noticed a large sign to the right: PAY TOLL—½ MILE.

"Quick a quarter!"

Ahead, they could see the black car slow down at the exact-change booth to the right. Chet closed the space quickly before the other car moved ahead, less swiftly this time. Beyond the toll, a parked State Police car was visible.

"Now's our chance to catch him!" Frank exclaimed. Chet pulled up to the same booth and hastily flipped the coin into the collection basket. Without waiting the second for the light to turn green, he gunned the Queen in hot pursuit of the black car.

Ahead, a blast of exhaust smoke told the pursuers that the thief was tromping on the gas. As Chet strained over the wheel trying to gain speed he heard a siren behind him, and the trooper waved the jalopy to the roadside.

"What happened?" Joe asked anxiously as Chet stopped.

The trooper pulled ahead, got out, and ambled

over. "It's customary to drop a quarter in the toll basket, young fellow."

"I did."

The trooper looked annoyed. "The light still says red, and besides, the alarm bell rang."

"But—but—" Chet spluttered in surprise.

"Let's see your license."

"Officer," Frank spoke up, "we're in a hurry. We're chasing a thief!"

The trooper smiled in spite of himself. "Well, I've never heard that one before."

"But we are!" Joe insisted. "A painting was stolen in Bayport."

"You can check with Chief Collig there," said Frank.

The trooper eyed the trio suspiciously. "Okay. But if this is a hoax, I'll arrest all three of you." He strode to his car and spoke into the radio. Three minutes later he trotted back. "Accept my apologies, boys. You were right. Can you describe that car?"

As Joe gave the information, including the license number which he had memorized, Chet hurried to the toll basket. He returned waving a cloth in his hand. "That's a clever crook!" he shouted. "He dropped this rag in the basket so my quarter wouldn't register."

"He won't get away from us," the trooper said. He ran to his car, radioed to police ahead, then sped off at ninety miles an hour.

"Now we've got action," Frank said as Chet urged the Queen along the thruway.

Three exits later, they saw the trooper parked alongside the road. Chet pulled up behind him.

"Sorry, boys!" the officer called out. "The thief gave us the shake. But we'll track him down!"

After a brief stop at a snack bar the trio continued on toward Crown Lake, with Frank at the wheel.

The flat countryside gave way to ranges of dark and light green hills, several of them arching spectacularly up on either side of the broad road, curving toward the blue sky.

An hour later they left the state thruway and proceeded through several small towns before sighting the bluish-gray water of Crown Lake. It appeared, partially screened by a ridge of trees, then came into full view at a rise just beyond where there was a dirt road and a sign: MILLWOOD ART SCHOOL 500 YARDS AHEAD TO THE RIGHT. Frank swung into the road and in a few minutes the sloping green lawns of the estate came into view. Frank pulled the car into a parking area facing the edge of the slope and stopped next to a large oak.

Chet led the way vigorously down a graveled path which wound across the grounds. "Uncle Jim's teaching his class now," he called back to the Hardys.

Ahead, on a level stretch of lawn, the trio saw a

group of young people standing in front of easels. Near one student stood a tall, husky, blond-haired man in a painting smock. When he saw the boys, he beamed and hurried over.

"Chet! Good to see you again!"

"Hello, Uncle Jim!" Chet promptly introduced Frank and Joe to Mr. Kenyon, who shook hands warmly.

"Welcome to Millwood." He smiled. "Fortunately, my last class today is finishing, and I can help you with your luggage."

The painting instructor accompanied the boys back across the lawn toward the uphill path. Suddenly one of the students cried out:

"Look out! That car—it's rolling!"

A shudder passed through the boys as they saw the yellow Queen starting down the slope from the parking area. Directly in its path two girls stood rooted in terror at their easels.

Chet's jalopy gathered speed. It hurtled faster and faster toward the girls!

"We've got to stop it!" shouted Joe, on the run.

CHAPTER III

Inquisitive Student

JOE sprinted across the slope and dived for the car. Hanging on, he reached through the window and wrenched at the wheel. The Queen swerved, missed the girls by inches, crushed the easels, and came to rest in a tangle of thick underbrush.

Then Joe ran up to the frightened students. "Are you all right?" he asked with concern.

Both girls nodded, trembling with relief. One said, "We owe you our lives!"

"And our paintings too," said her companion.

Their two half-finished canvases had been knocked off the easels and lay intact, face up on the ground.

By now Frank, Chet, and Mr. Kenyon had rushed over. "Are you all right, Joe?"

"I'm fine, but I'd rather tackle a whole football team than a runaway car!"

The praises of the onlookers for his bravery

embarrassed Joe. "Let's find out what happened to the Queen," he said.

The boys found the car undamaged. "Hey!" Chet cried out. "The emergency's off! I know you set it, Frank."

The jalopy was driven back to the parking area. This time it was left well away from the rim of the incline. Frank looked around.

"The car didn't just happen to roll. Somebody deliberately released the emergency brake."

Mr. Kenyon frowned. "What a terrible prank!"

"I don't believe it was a practical joke," Frank said. "What the motive was, though, I can't guess yet."

The boys took their luggage from the car, and then Mr. Kenyon led them toward a small, newly painted building. "I'm sorry you had to be welcomed to Millbrook in this manner," he said. "But we'll try to make up for it."

He took the visitors through a side door into a large, cluttered room, piled with dusty easels, rolls of canvas, and cardboard boxes filled with paint tubes. "This is our storage house," explained the art instructor.

The boys followed him down a narrow stairway into a small basement studio. The stone room smelled of oil paints. Several unframed modern paintings lay along one wall. Mr. Kenyon reached up with a pole to open the single window near the ceiling.

"This is my little garret—subterranean style," he explained. "Make yourselves comfortable. Since the thefts, I've been rooming upstairs where I have a better view of our art gallery across the way."

The boys set down their bags on three sturdy cots. Joe grinned. "I'm beginning to feel like an artist."

"So am I," Frank said. "This room is fine, Mr. Kenyon."

"Just call me Uncle Jim. How about supper? You must be hungry."

Chet beamed. "I could eat an easel!"

First, however, he eagerly recounted the scalp incident to his uncle, then the Hardys told of their experiences at the Bayport Museum and on the thruway. Mr. Kenyon agreed there likely was a connection with the Millwood thefts.

"But the man you describe doesn't ring any bells with me," he continued. "Our summer session had been going along well until five days ago when I discovered a painting missing from our small gallery. The day before yesterday, a second was stolen during the night—both works of the Prisoner-Painter." He sighed. "We have to keep the building under lock and key now, even from our students."

"So tomorrow we'll start our sleuthing," said Joe.

"Right. Perhaps by mingling with the students you can pick up some clue," replied Uncle Jim. "Though I'd hate to suspect any of them."

"Can you tell us about this Prisoner-Painter?" Frank asked.

"I could," Mr. Kenyon said, smiling, "but I think Mr. Jefferson Davenport would rather tell you himself, since the artist is his ancestor."

"The wealthy man who started Millwood?" Joe put in.

"Yes. He looks forward to meeting you detectives, but he won't be receiving visitors today, because of the anniversary of a battle."

"A battle?" Frank echoed in surprise.

The instructor chuckled. "You'll find Mr. Davenport is quite a buff on the science of military fortification, in addition to his interest in painting. You'll see when you meet him tomorrow."

"What about this haunted fort?" Joe asked eagerly.

"Senandaga?" Uncle Jim's eyes twinkled. "There are apparently some weird goings-on there. But Mr. Davenport will fill you in on that, too."

Uncle Jim then took the Hardys and Chet to the Davenport lakeside mansion, an old gabled house staffed only by a woman cook and a part-time chauffeur-gardener.

"Mr. Davenport has invited us to have meals in

the kitchen during your stay here," the instructor said.

After a hearty supper Mr. Kenyon took the boys on a tour. He explained that the Millwood grounds were tended by the students themselves, who rented rooms in the nearby village of Cedartown. Art materials, all instruction, and part of rent costs were financed by the millionaire patron. Several townspeople also painted on weekends at the school.

Uncle Jim showed his visitors the studios, the gallery building from the outside, and finally, a boathouse near the mansion. Several canoes were tied up to a dock. These, Mr. Kenyon said, were for the students' use.

As he accompanied the boys back to their quarters the instructor said with a grin, "Don't expect Mr. Davenport to be too—er—ordinary." He did not explain further, and bade them good night, saying the art patron expected them to call at nine A.M. the next day.

Early the next morning Joe awoke to see an unfamiliar face peering down into their room through the single, high window. The boy, who appeared to be about nineteen, scowled at Joe, then disappeared.

At that moment Frank awakened.

"What's the matter?" he asked his brother, who was sitting up in bed staring at the window.

"Some fellow was looking in here. He didn't seem the cheerful type."

Frank laughed. "One of the students, probably. Maybe he's envious of our artist's garret. Let's wake up Chet and get some vittles."

After breakfast the three boys strolled around the grounds, already dotted with students setting up easels or heading for studio classes. Joe started as he noticed one student, carrying a small easel, approaching them.

"He's the one I saw at the window this morning!"

Like many of the other students, the boy wore a gray smock. His face, long and with pudgy lips, had a faintly insolent expression. He came up to the Bayporters.

"You new here?" he asked, his eyes narrowing.

"Yes," Frank answered. "We plan to pick up some painting tips as guests of Mr. Kenyon." He introduced himself and the others.

The student stared at them speculatively. "Oh, is that so? Well, my name's Ronnie Rush." He went on sullenly, "Kenyon would have to lock up the whole gallery just because two measly paintings are gone. I could be doing some research." With a shrug Ronnie added, "Guess I got nothing against you fellows, though. See you around."

Before the Hardys or Chet could retort, the student shuffled off.

"He's got some nerve," Chet said indignantly, "criticizing Uncle Jim! And why was he looking in our window, anyway?"

"I don't know," Frank said, "but he certainly seems curious about us."

At that moment Uncle Jim, wearing a fresh white smock, came over and greeted the boys cheerfully. He immediately led them in the direction of the Davenport mansion.

"I'm heading for my watercolor class," he explained, "but you sleuths can have a private conference about our mystery with Mr. Davenport."

The instructor led them onto the porch, through the open front door, and pointed down the wood-paneled hallway to a large double door at the end.

"That's Mr. Davenport's study, where he's expecting you. We'll get together later!"

After Chet's uncle had left, they walked quietly down the hall to the study. Frank knocked. A few seconds later a voice from within said, "Come along."

The boys entered, closed the doors, and found themselves in a high-ceilinged room with heavily draped windows. Bookshelves lined one wall behind a cluttered mahogany desk. The adjacent wall contained a blackboard.

As their eyes became accustomed to the gloom, Joe gave Frank a nudge. "Look there!" he whispered.

Standing on a hassock was a small, gray-haired man in a white summer suit. He held a long pointer in one hand and was looking down at a fort structure of toy logs set up on the floor.

"Never! Never!" exclaimed the man as he collapsed the fort with a swish of the stick.

The trio watched, mouths agape. The man looked up quickly and said, "Hello, boys."

"Mr. Davenport?" Chet said, nonplused.

"I am. And you are James Kenyon's nephew Chester, I believe, and the two Hardy boys! Much honored!" The man jumped down and shook each boy's hand, bowing slightly. He spoke in a pleasant Southern drawl, but his twinkling blue eyes revealed a lively personality.

"Have a seat," Mr. Davenport said.

"We appreciate your invitation to Millwood," Frank said as they settled in comfortable chairs.

"Poor strategy," the art patron muttered. He threw open the draperies and paced the room.

"Pardon, sir?" Joe hesitated.

"Vicksburg, of course," Mr. Davenport answered, frowning at the scattered toy logs. "Yesterday was my annual Vicksburg Day."

"Have you many military—er—holidays in the year, Mr. Davenport?" asked Chet.

"Fifty-seven, not a one more!" he replied. "Used to have fifty-six till I admitted Bunker Hill this year. Sad days, many of 'em, but—"

Mr. Davenport paused. Suddenly he rushed

over to the toy logs, reshuffled them into a fort, then stretched out on the floor, sighting along his pointer. Chet watched in bewilderment while the Hardys exchanged smiles. Indeed, Mr. Davenport was no ordinary person!

Seconds later, the millionaire leaped up. "Terrible defense. It would never hold! Never!" Crouching, he squinted at the logs with his face almost to the floor. Holding the pointer like a cue, he again toppled the logs.

Seating himself in a rocker, the art patron sighed heavily, thumbed his woolen vest pockets, and peered earnestly at his callers. "Now, what were you saying?"

Frank hastily told him about the scalp warning and the escaped museum thief. Upon hearing of the stolen Senandaga painting, the elderly man became upset and again paced the room.

"Could you tell us something about the Prisoner-Painter, Mr. Davenport?" Joe asked. "And the fort, too?" At that instant Frank heard a faint sound and saw the double door of the study open a fraction of an inch!

"An eavesdropper!" he thought. Frank rushed across the room, but already footsteps were racing down the hallway. Grabbing the knobs, he flung the doors wide open.

CHAPTER IV

A Crimson Clue

STUMBLING footsteps sounded at the bottom of the high porch, but by the time Frank dashed outside, the eavesdropper had vanished.

Disappointed, he returned to the others in the study. "Whoever he was, he didn't drop any clues," Frank reported.

"You're alert, boys," Mr. Davenport commented. "I like that. What's more, you're not afraid, like that custodian who guarded my fort."

"*Your* fort?" Joe asked in surprise.

"Yes, young man, Senandaga belongs to me."

"What happened to the custodian?" asked Frank.

"He left. Quit. Said he couldn't stand all that haunting—queer noises and so forth. To hear him talk, there's a whole regiment of ghosts manning the parapets." Mr. Davenport looked thoughtful. "Of course, he claims he had some close calls."

"Such as?" Frank queried.

"Said chunks of masonry nearly fell on him a couple of times. But"—the art patron looked skeptical—"I don't put much stock in that."

"Now nobody takes care of the fort?" Joe asked.

"Nobody. And there aren't any pesky visitors, either," Davenport said with satisfaction. "Anyhow, we have enough to do tracking down the art thieves without worrying about the fort."

Then the boys asked Mr. Davenport about his ancestor, the Prisoner-Painter.

"Jason Davenport was a great soldier," he began. "When hostilities broke out between the North and the South, he rose quickly to brigadier general. Then, in one rally near the Potomac, he broke the Union line but penetrated too far without logistical support and was captured. He was held prisoner for the duration at my fort."

"A brave man," Joe said. "An ancestor to be proud of."

"The fort is south of here on Crown Lake, isn't it?" Frank asked.

Mr. Davenport nodded, motioning toward the large window. "If it weren't for the promontory nearby, you could see Senandaga." He reflected. "Jason Davenport died shortly after the war ended. But had he not been a prisoner there, there wouldn't be the seventeen canvases of Fort Senandaga, three of which," he added in a rueful tone, "have been stolen."

Mr. Davenport explained that the general had taken up painting to while away the days. He was a popular hero, well liked by his captors, and received many special favors, including the art materials necessary for his new interest.

"He showed a real genius in imagining different views of the fort from the surrounding countryside."

"And that's why his paintings are valuable enough to tempt a thief?" Joe asked, impressed.

"I'd like to think so," Mr. Davenport answered, "but I fear that's not the real reason. You see, there were rumors later that Jason had discovered an old French treasure in the fort—and that he had left a clue to its hiding place. My father and uncle didn't believe it, but *I* did. So I bought the fort two years ago from a private party."

"The general left this clue in a painting?" Chet guessed.

"Yes. Either in the picture itself, or the frame." The art patron went on to explain that his forebear had fashioned a very unusual frame, which he used for all his paintings. "The frames themselves are valuable," he said. "Unfortunately, some of the originals have been lost over the years, so a few of the fort pictures in our gallery are conventionally framed."

Joe asked how many of the general's works were in the school's possession.

"Fourteen."

"Who has the others?"

Mr. Davenport's face turned an angry red. "One, I'm sorry to say, belongs to a person who doesn't deserve it." Suddenly, however, he chortled. "But I'll get back at him."

The boys were mystified, but before they could question him, the elderly man added, "Another fort picture belongs to a hermit fellow, an Englishman. He bought the painting years ago at an auction. Lives out on Turtle Island."

"And nobody has found a trace of any clue so far?" Frank asked.

"Not a one. I've been trying to find the fort treasure ever since I came here."

"What is it?" Frank asked. "Jewels?"

"Oh, no. A boom chain, such as those used with logs for blocking ships in the French and Indian War, when Senandaga was built." The man picked up two of the toy logs and seemed lost in thought for a moment. "Marvelous, marvelous idea, those log-and-chain defenses!"

"Could even a historical chain be tremendously valuable?" Joe inquired, to lead Mr. Davenport back to the main subject of discussion.

"This one is!" the man returned emphatically. "It's called *chaîne d'or*—a chain of solid gold."

"Gold!" The three sleuths sounded like a chorus.

Their host explained that in 1762 the proud Marquis Louis de Chambord, builder and commander of Senandaga, had ordered the chain to be forged, not to be used of course, but as a symbol of his fort's strength. There was a disagreement, however, among historians over whether the *chaîne d'or* actually had been made.

"I'm of the firm opinion that it was," he concluded, "which is why I had James invite you boys up here—to track down the art thief and uncover the gold treasure. So you boys feel free to come and go as you please in my home."

"Could one of Millwood's students be the thief?" Frank asked hesitantly.

The art patron wagged his head sadly. "Can't believe it. They're all fine young people! Which reminds me—young people get hungry. How about lunch?"

On a lakeside terrace the Bayporters were served club sandwiches and iced tea. As they ate, Frank questioned their host about his cook and chauffeur.

"I trust them implicitly. Both came with excellent references."

The meal over, Frank, Joe, and Chet thanked Mr. Davenport and walked back to the school. There, Frank pointed to a long, skylighted building in a grove of birches.

"What say we look for clues right where the paintings disappeared—the gallery?"

"Good idea," Joe agreed. They crossed a wide lawn and eagerly headed for the old stone structure. Reaching it, Frank used the key given him by Mr. Kenyon and opened the large padlock. The boys filed inside and closed the door.

The interior was dim and cool, but sunlight came through the panes of a skylight to brighten the three windowless walls, on which were hung some fifty paintings. The wall at the far end of the room contained General Davenport's, each of which showed a different view of Fort Senandaga.

The boys now noticed the distinctive frames mentioned by the art patron. Their corners jutted out in a diamondlike shape.

"Look!" Joe pointed to a large yellowed diagram, half of which was torn off. It hung near the fort pictures. "That must be Senandaga."

The Hardys and Chet went over to examine the ancient parchment. Beneath was a label explaining the remnant was from one of the original drawing plans for the fort. Despite the missing part, they could see enough to tell that its layout resembled the form of a star.

"The Prisoner-Painter made his frames roughly in the same shape," Joe observed.

Frank nodded, then said, "I'm sure the police searched here, but anyway, let's take a look around ourselves for a clue to the thief."

Chet took the end wall, Frank and Joe the sides. On their knees, the boys combed the stone floor, then studied the walls for possible telltale marks.

After an hour, their efforts had proved fruitless. "There's still the wall around the entrance," Joe said with a sigh. "Let's inspect every stone."

While Frank examined an empty desk, Chet and Joe pored carefully over the wall. No luck there.

"Say, fellows," Joe suddenly exclaimed, "what about the fort paintings themselves? If the thief was undecided about which one to take, he may have touched some."

"You're right!" Frank agreed. They rushed across to the row of aged canvases. Removing the paintings from the wall, they began inspecting the backs and edges of the frames.

"Look! I found something!" Chet called out.

Across the paper backing was a sticky smear of red oil paint! "This was made recently," Joe observed. "It still has a strong paint odor."

"There's no fingerprint on the smear," remarked Frank, looking at it closely, before rubbing some of the paint onto a small piece of paper.

"I wonder if the thief is an artist himself," Chet said.

The three left the gallery, and locked the door behind them. The next step, they agreed, would be to identify the paint, then track down the person who used it.

"Except for Uncle Jim and Mr. Davenport," Frank cautioned, "we'll keep this clue to ourselves."

Millwood students were now strolling from their classes, and Ronnie Rush emerged from a knot of chatting young artists.

"Pick up many painting tips today?" he asked, setting down his easel. "I see you rated getting into the gallery."

"We've just been sort of on a tour," Frank answered, deftly concealing the paint sample in the palm of his hand. "How about you?"

"Oh, I've been working on a couple of oils," Ronnie said importantly. "Want to see 'em?"

"Not right now," Joe replied. "We're busy. Thanks anyway."

Ronnie looked annoyed and eyed the three boys sullenly as they hurried to their quarters. There they found Jim Kenyon in the storage room shifting art equipment about. He was keenly interested in the paint sample, and congratulated them on finding the clue. He immediately identified the paint.

"It's called alizarin crimson," he said. "Many of our students use it."

"Pretty hard to pinpoint the culprit," Frank observed. "But we won't give up."

After washing his hands in turpentine and soap, the husky instructor accompanied the boys to supper. A tasty meal awaited them in the Davenport kitchen.

After supper the boys went to the lakeside for a look at the boathouse. They peered up at the promontory behind which Fort Senandaga lay.

"Let's go over to the fort tomorrow," Frank suggested. "Right now, we might do some boning up on art. It might sharpen our eyes to finding that treasure clue."

In their basement room, Chet and the Hardys spent the evening mulling over books on painting borrowed from Mr. Kenyon. Later, they went upstairs for a conference with Chet's uncle. Using paints and a canvas, the instructor illustrated various art techniques.

"Want to try your hand, Chet?" Mr. Kenyon offered, holding out the brush to his nephew. He winked at Frank and Joe. "I think he has the makings of a painter, don't you?"

But before either Hardy could answer, the building shook with a deafening roar that reverberated up the stairwell!

Frank jumped to his feet. "That came from downstairs!" The smell of burnt powder reached them as they all charged down the narrow steps. When they entered their room, Chet gasped.

The wall near which their luggage lay was splattered with red dots!

"A shotgun!" Joe exclaimed, picking up a used

cartridge under the window. He grimaced and held out the shell. "Look." Everyone gasped. It was covered with red.

"Bl-blood?" Chet quavered.

His uncle examined the cartridge. "No. Red paint—alizarin crimson!"

On the floor lay a small paintbrush. Wrapped around it was a piece of paper. Frank unfolded the sheet to disclose a typewritten message:

A mural for the Hardy Boys. Leave Millwood or my next painting will be a coffin—yours.

CHAPTER V

Danger Alley

CHET looked nervous. "Another threat!" he exclaimed. "I guess that scalp warning wasn't any joke."

Uncle Jim's face showed concern. "Whoever stuck a gun barrel through that window wants to scare you boys off—that's plain."

Joe said wryly, "Lucky we weren't on hand for the barrage."

Frank compared the note with that found earlier on the scalp. "Both were done on the same typewriter—and this red paint looks like that 'blood' on the papier-mâché."

With flashlights the instructor and the three boys searched the ground outside the shattered window, but no clues were found.

While the boys swept up the broken glass and fallen plaster, they speculated on the identity of their mysterious enemy. The Hardys felt he might very well be the same person who had thrown the scalp and stolen the fort painting in Bayport.

Chet gulped. "You mean—that thief trailed us here?" Then he asked, "Do you think that snoopy Ronnie Rush could have had something to do with this?" He told his uncle of their encounters with the boy.

"Well," said Mr. Kenyon, "Ronnie's sometimes a little hard to work with, but I don't think he'd do something like this. Our annual outdoor exhibit is to be held on Senandaga Day—next Saturday. I'll be pretty busy getting ready for it, so I won't have much time to help you detectives."

Jim explained that Senandaga Day was celebrated every year. The town decreed that the fort be opened at this time to the public. "By having our art exhibit then, we attract more visitors."

The Hardys decided to track down if possible the source of the empty cartridge. Frank obtained from Uncle Jim the name of a Cedartown hunting equipment shop, the only one in the area.

"It's run by Myles Warren," the painter added. "He's one of our weekend painters, by the way."

Before retiring, the Hardys fastened some slats across the window. The rest of the night passed uneventfully. After breakfast the next morning, the three attended the quaint little church in town and located the shop of Myles Warren.

"We'll come here first thing tomorrow," Frank said.

Back at the school, the boys had midday dinner, then strolled across the lawn toward several students at work on their paintings.

Frank said in a low tone, "Let's see who has been using the alizarin red." The trio split up. Each boy had a paper bearing a smear of the paint. They began browsing near easels set up not only on the main lawn, but also in various nooks on the outskirts of the estate.

"Wow!" Chet exclaimed to himself, coming upon a dazzling creation being worked on by a thin, red-haired boy in dungarees. The plump boy tried to make some order out of the reddish-brown swirls and zigzag silver streaks. "Looks like a vegetable cart that's been hit by lightning."

The student paused and greeted Chet. "Like it?" He smiled. "It's a meadow in wintertime."

"Oh—er—very unusual." Chet walked on, muttering, "Guess I'll have to get the hang of this stuff."

He stopped at several other easels, some of which bore landscape scenes, and others, views of the Millwood buildings or of the surrounding lakes.

"Hi!" A round-faced jovial girl peeked out at Chet from behind an easel. "Are you a new student at Millwood?" she asked, wiping some red paint from her hands onto a rag. Chet explained that he was trying to pick up some pointers.

"You'll have to see our exhibit," she said

brightly. "I'm just touching up my portrait. One of the other students modeled for it."

"Is that alizarin crimson?"

"Oh, you! You're an old pro to recognize it," the girl said.

Chet gulped. "She's so nice, she couldn't be the thief," he thought, then peered wide-eyed at the bizarre maze of green and yellow triangles, wavy black lines, blobs of thick red shading, and one eye.

"You say another student modeled for you? Is he all right now?"

The girl giggled. "Quit teasing. You know well enough this is an *abstract!*"

"Oh, yes, of course." Chet smiled and moved on to inspect several other student canvases before meeting the Hardys near the gallery. "Hope you fellows had more luck than I did," he said.

Frank shook his head. "Everybody is using alizarin crimson. We can't narrow down this clue."

The next morning they walked up the shady lake road to the quaint village of Cedartown. Picturesque shops, a small church, and a barnlike playhouse graced the narrow main street. Frank pointed out the Cedar Sport Store on the other side.

"If the shotgun shell was bought any place in the area, there's a good chance it was here," he said. They crossed and entered the dimly lighted shop.

A long, cluttered counter extended along a dusty wall hung with assorted hunting and fishing equipment. Frank rang the counter bell, and a slender hawk-nosed man with a full black beard emerged from a back room.

"Mr. Warren?" Frank inquired.

"Right. What can I do for you?" he asked, smiling. He spread his hands on the counter and looked with interest at the boys.

"Can you tell us whether this was sold here?" Joe asked, handing him the paint-marked cartridge.

The owner pulled a pair of glasses out of his shirt pocket, put them on, and looked closely at the shell. He shook his head and handed it back.

"If it was used in this area, it's probably my stock," Warren affirmed. "But I sell hundreds of this brand to hunters. Although without the red paint," he added, chuckling.

"Then you have no way of pinpointing the customer?" Frank asked.

"I'm afraid not." The man then asked, "You all up here for the fishing? It's great at the north end of the lake."

Frank shook his head. "Just visiting."

After thanking the dealer, the three left the shop. The next moment they heard a cry of anguish from an antique shop across the street. Its owner stood in the doorway gesturing frantically. "Help! Thief! Help!"

The boys rushed to the sidewalk. "Over there!" Joe yelled.

Directly opposite, a small man was running into a cobblestone alley. He carried a picture frame under his arm. The boys sprinted across the street and up the alley. They were closing the gap when the man stopped at a parked black sedan. The Hardys gasped.

It was the man who had stolen the fort painting from the Bayport Museum!

"He's got an old fort frame!" Frank cried out, recognizing the odd shape.

The boys put on more speed as the thief hopped into the car and started the motor.

The sedan roared down the alley directly toward the boys! "Quick, this way!" Joe yelled.

They darted to the right and flattened themselves against a building. The speeding vehicle almost brushed them. In a moment it had screeched around the corner and disappeared up the main street.

A curious crowd had gathered, but were quickly dispersed by a policeman. The Hardys and Chet then went with the officer to the antique shop. The owner explained that the pug-faced man, whom he had never seen before, had offered to purchase the frame. Upon hearing the price, the man said that it was too high, and he started toward the door.

"So I went into my workshop in back," the dealer continued, "and returned just in time to see that scoundrel making off with the frame." He groaned. "An irreplaceable loss."

Next, the boys were taken to police headquarters, where they told their story to the chief. He said a state alarm would be issued for the fugitive. Since the earlier alert, sent out right after the boys' chase on the thruway, the police had discovered through the license number that the sedan was stolen.

"We know the fellow's in this area now," the chief said. "We'll keep you boys informed."

Walking back to Millwood, the three discussed the stolen frame.

"Probably," Frank remarked, "the thief didn't have any luck finding a treasure clue in the paintings."

Joe looked thoughtful, "You think this guy stole the gallery pictures, too?"

Frank stared at his brother. "Say! He could be in league with someone else!"

Back at Millwood, Chet and the Hardys told Mr. Kenyon of the Cedartown incident. "Pretty bold move," he commented, "risking a theft in broad daylight."

"Well," Joe said glumly, "let's hope the treasure clue isn't in *that* frame."

After some further discussion of the new development in the mystery, Uncle Jim said, "How would you like to get your first look at Fort Senandaga?"

"You bet!"

"Good. Mr. Davenport has asked us to go."

The boys and the instructor went to the mansion, where they were introduced to Alex, the millionaire's chauffeur-gardener, dressed in blue uniform and cap. Tall, with a clipped black mustache, he bowed stiffly to the boys, then moved around to the rear door of a polished limousine.

"Boy, we're going to ride in real style!" Chet exclaimed. "Old Queen will get jealous."

Mr. Davenport came out, greeted them cordially, and all took seats in back. Soon the limousine was heading south along the pretty, winding lake road. Past the end of the lake, the car turned up a gentle hill and paused at a PRIVATE PROPERTY sign. Alex got out and unlocked a wire gate. The entire south end of the fort promontory was enclosed by fencing marked with NO TRESPASSING signs.

As they drove ahead through overgrown woods, the elderly Southerner spoke proudly of Fort Senandaga's history. He explained that little was known of the one battle fought there between the British and French.

"There's dispute till this day about its outcome," he went on, "and which side was the last to leave the fort. That's probably why some folks believe Senandaga is haunted—ghosts of soldiers from both forces still fighting, no doubt." He added, "Someday I aim to have that fort fully restored."

Chet asked if the public often visited the site at other times besides Senandaga Day. Davenport's face turned livid and his eyes blazed. "The—the public!" he sputtered, sitting up and thumping his cane on the floor. Chet sat petrified until his uncle put a warning finger to his lips and smoothly changed the subject.

Alex parked in a small clearing and everyone got out. The chauffeur stayed to guard the car. Mr. Davenport, his composure restored, led the others to a grass bluff. "There she is!"

The entire lake could be seen, dotted in the distance with islands like scrubby green battle-ships. To the boys' left, up a gentle slope, rose the stone fort, an expansive star-shaped ruin surrounded by a shallow ditch, overgrown with brush. Although much of the masonry was crumbling, all the walls were at least partially intact.

As they walked toward the ramparts, Chet's uncle pulled the boys aside and accounted for his employer's sudden outburst.

"I guess I should have warned you," he said, chuckling. "There are two things you should never mention in Mr. Davenport's presence. One is admitting the public to his fort—he has a great fear that someone will get careless wandering around the ruins and be injured. The other is Chauncey Gilman."

"Chauncey Gilman? Who is he?" Joe asked.

Before Uncle Jim could answer, Mr. Davenport summoned them all down the steep counterscarp, or exterior slope of the ditch. As they proceeded, the elderly man talked excitedly.

"Good walls, these," he pointed out, his voice echoing upward. "The man who drew up the plans for Senandaga followed the star-shaped design made famous by Marshall Sebastian de Vauban, military engineer for Louis XIV. Genius—sheer genius!" he added as they came to a wide-angled turn in the towering wall. "A century later my ancestor was imprisoned here."

Frank and Joe marveled at the imposing defense the fort must have provided. "How could any army capture a place like Senandaga?" Joe asked.

"Not without much bloodshed," the millionaire acknowledged. "A man like Vauban could have succeeded, though. Long before Chambord built Senandaga, Vauban devised a parallel trench system for assaulting forts." He explained how attacking armies in Europe had got nearer and nearer to fort walls by digging one parallel trench, then zigzagging ahead to dig another, and so on.

"Boy, what terrific strategy!" Frank said.

"Brilliant—brilliant," Mr. Davenport agreed. "The Marquis de Chambord, by the way, was a great admirer of Vauban's achievements."

Chet glanced out at the peaceful lake, which once was the scene of warring canoes or attacking fleets. "It doesn't *seem* haunted," he whispered to the Hardys.

Frank was about to answer when a rumbling sound came from above. Looking up, he cried out:

"Watch out! The wall!"

A huge section of crumbling gray masonry collapsed in a cloud of dust and came toppling downward!

CHAPTER VI

Chet vs. Impasto

THE crumbling wall broke into a spreading, plunging landslide.

"Quick!" Frank shouted.

Instantly he pulled Mr. Davenport to safety while the others leaped from the path of the rocky avalanche.

When the danger was past, Frank saw that Mr. Davenport was holding his hand to his chest and breathing hard. "Are you all right, sir?"

The art patron shook his head but said nothing. His face was pale and he hung onto the boy for support. Frank turned to the others. "I think we'd better get him to a doctor!"

They quickly returned to the car. Alex drove them immediately to Mr. Davenport's physician in Cedartown. To everyone's relief, an examination showed that there was nothing seriously wrong.

"Just see that you get plenty of rest," the young

doctor directed, "and stay away from dangerous ruins!"

As the limousine headed back to Millwood, the millionaire, looking somewhat better, pursed his lips and grumbled. "No sooner get to visit my own fort than it has to fall down on me. I can't understand it—Senandaga rock's not likely to give way like that."

Joe and Frank shared a frightening thought: Had the masonry been *pushed* down?

"You take care of yourself, Mr. Davenport." Joe smiled. "Frank, Chet, and I are up here to earn our keep as detectives. We'll investigate the fort and keep you posted."

All three boys were eager for a second crack at Senandaga. Was a gold chain made by order of the Marquis de Chambord hidden somewhere beneath its ruins? If so, would they be able to beat the thief, or thieves, in finding the Prisoner-Painter's clue?

During a late lunch the boys asked Uncle Jim about Chauncey Gilman, the man for whom Mr. Davenport apparently had a violent dislike.

"Gilman lives across the lake," he replied. "He's wealthy—inherited a lot—and is an art critic. Writes a column for the local paper."

Uncle Jim also explained that Gilman had bought a fort painting years ago from the Millwood philanthropist. "Mr. Davenport has regretted it ever since."

He explained that the critic, a failure as an artist himself, had grown extremely harsh in his published statements about the school. "He's not a very pleasant fellow," Jim added. "You'll probably run into him here on Senandaga Day."

When they had finished eating, the Hardys called the local police and learned that the stolen sedan used by the antique-shop thief had been found abandoned off a highway outside Cedartown. "Maybe he's gone into hiding nearby," Frank conjectured. "We'll have to keep a sharp lookout."

The boys went to tell Mr. Davenport about the theft. He was disturbed to learn of the stolen frame. "If I'd known it was at the shop, I would've bought it," he fumed.

The art patron then opened a small safe and took out a photostat. It was a copy of an old, detailed map of Fort Senandaga, labeled in script, which Mr. Davenport said the boys could borrow.

"This should be a big help when we begin combing the ruins for some clue to the treasure," said Frank, pocketing the map.

At Chet's urging, the Hardys agreed to attend a studio oil-painting class that afternoon. "You sleuths can still keep your eyes open," said the plump youth.

Joe eyed him suspiciously. "Chet Morton, I sense you've got an ulterior motive."

Chet grinned widely, but said nothing.

Uncle Jim welcomed the three boys to the cool, stone-walled room in which the class was held. Here, long, high windows let in ample daylight.

"I'll just watch," said Frank.

"Me too." Joe grinned. "We'll leave the brushwork to Chet."

The stout boy obtained an easel and the necessary art material, and chose a spot at the back of the room.

Ronnie Rush stood at an easel in front of Chet. He turned around and smirked. "You have talent?"

"I'll soon find out," Chet replied as the Hardys strolled over.

On impulse Joe asked, "Say, Ronnie, you use much of that alizarin crimson?"

Ronnie looked surprised. "Sure. Everybody does."

"In painting, that is?" Joe asked pointedly.

Ronnie stared in bewilderment. "Of course. Why?"

"Oh, just curious."

Jim Kenyon now came over to show his nephew about blending colors and brush techniques.

When he had moved away, Frank murmured to his brother, "Ronnie didn't act like he had anything to do with that cartridge shell."

Joe nodded. "I'd still like to find out why he's so resentful."

The brothers looked at Chet. Their stout pal,

completely engrossed, was wielding his brush with vigorous strokes. Joe chuckled. "Chet's really got the painting bug."

A little later the Hardys decided to take a closer look at the fort paintings and headed for the gallery. As they approached the building, footsteps came up behind them. The boys turned to face Ronnie Rush. "I'd like to see those fort pictures," he said petulantly.

The Hardys were nonplused. Finally Frank said, "Mr. Kenyon told us no students were allowed in the gallery now."

Joe added, "Do you have a special interest in forts? Senandaga, for instance?"

"Oh, just the painting techniques," Ronnie said hastily. "And why are *you* two so interested?"

"We're doing some research on the fort's history," Frank replied.

"Oh. History." Ronnie squinted. He did not seem inclined to leave, so the brothers gave up their plan for the moment and returned to the studio where Chet was still working at his easel.

"Can we see your masterpiece?" Joe asked, grinning.

"Oh, no, fellows," Chet replied earnestly, waving them off. "Not yet."

After supper Frank said, "We ought to try another tack. I vote we pay a visit to Mr. Davenport's enemy."

Chet's eyes widened. "Chauncey Gilman?"

"Yes. After all, he owns a fort painting."

Joe was enthusiastic. "Maybe Gilman himself has information about the gold chain."

Taking Chet's jalopy, the three were soon heading north along the west shore of the lake, an area lined with tourist homes. Farther on, imposing lakeside mansions came into view, and in another twenty minutes they pulled into a sloping gravel driveway. A chain-hung sign along the side read: CHAUNCEY GILMAN, ESQ. Atop the rise stood a handsome Tudor-style house overlooking the lake.

"What a setup!" Chet whistled as he parked.

From a shrubbed terrace at the rear, a plump, wavy-haired man arose from a lounge chair. He stared in disapproval at the vehicle and its smoking exhaust, then at the boys as they got out.

The Bayporters had never seen a man quite so elegantly attired. He wore a green velvet jacket, striped trousers, and white cravat.

"Are you sure you're at the right address?" he droned nasally, removing his glasses.

"Mr. Gilman?" Frank inquired.

"The same."

Frank introduced himself and the others, explaining they were vacationing at Crown Lake and hoped to see his fort painting.

"Are you one of those *Millwood* students?" the critic asked disdainfully.

"Not exactly," Joe replied.

"Very well." Gilman shrugged and ushered the boys across the terrace toward a back door.

"Real friendly type," Joe whispered to the others.

Inside, the critic led them through elaborately furnished rooms, then up winding stairs into a large hall. To one side was an arched doorway.

"My own lake-view dining room," he announced, leading them past a suit of armor and around a long table on which lay a large dictionary. On the far wall he gestured toward a painting.

The canvas, not in the original frame, showed a distant twilight view of Fort Senandaga, with a thorn apple tree in the foreground. The boys noticed that the scene had a three-dimensional effect.

"A rather good effort," Gilman intoned grudgingly. "Acquired from a most misguided man, I might add. Fine impasto, don't you think?"

"Er—exquisite," Chet replied, receiving amazed looks from both Hardys. He bit off a smile and wondered what "impasto" meant. "Sounds like a salad," he thought.

The critic turned to Frank and Joe. "No doubt," he went on condescendingly, "you'll want to see the general's other paintings at that so-called art school." He sniggered with relish. "I'll be paying my annual visit there to the students' exhibition, and pass judgment on the—er—works of those amateur juveniles—a most amusing task!"

Chet had edged over to the large dictionary. He would get one up on the Hardys, and at the same time not feel so stupid about "impasto."

Frank observed their stout friend from the corner of his eye, but made no move to give him away. Chet picked up the book and leafed through it, backing toward the window for better light.

Joe, meanwhile, could not resist asking Gilman, "Do *you* paint?"

The plump man looked out the window, his hands behind his back. "I am, first and foremost, a critic," he declared haughtily, "and widely known by the elite of the artistic world. I—"

Crash!

The Hardys and Gilman jumped and wheeled about. On the floor lay the suit of armor. Standing over it was Chet, his face flaming red. "S-sorry," he stammered. "I backed right into it." Quickly he put the dictionary on the table.

"Studying too hard?" Frank grinned as he helped right the knight figure. "No damage, sir."

The critic raised his eyes to the ceiling. "My nerves!"

Chet sheepishly placed the dictionary on the table and joined the brothers as they studied the fort painting. *"Impasto,"* muttered the plump boy, "is the thick application of pigment to a canvas or panel, for your information."

"Okay, professor." Joe chuckled.

They peered closely at the picture's surface, trying to detect some kind of telltale marks in the composition. From several strategic questions, the Hardys gathered that Gilman knew nothing of any clue to the *chaîne d'or*.

Finally, the critic coughed meaningfully. "If you don't mind," he said, "I *must* be getting to work on an important critique."

The boys, disappointed in the outcome of their mission, thanked the man and left.

"So that's Chauncey Gilman!" Joe said scornfully as they headed south on the lake road. "What a swellhead! And he sure has it in for Millwood. No wonder Mr. Davenport doesn't like him."

"You said it!" Chet agreed, "Uncle Jim and his students must resent a character like that."

Frank appeared lost in thought. "I wish we could do more in getting to the bottom of this mystery. If only we knew what kind of clue to look for!"

"Do you think Gilman has any interest in the gold chain?" Chet asked.

Frank shrugged. "He didn't act like it—but you never know."

Joe's lip curled. "He's too busy dreaming up acid criticisms."

The suit of armor crashed to the floor

A mist hung over the lake now, the water below them seeming almost colorless through the trees. Up ahead at a bend in the road, Chet noticed an observation area offering a commanding view of the lake. The boys decided to pull over for a look.

"Maybe we can see the fort from here," Joe said. Chet parked on the wide shoulder and they got out.

A strong wind coursed up the slopes from the lake. Several homes were scattered along the opposite shore. The boys looked out to their right. Barely visible in the dusk was the jutting outline of one of Senandaga's walls. The Hardys again speculated on the collapse of the fort section that morning.

Suddenly Joe leaned forward and asked curiously, "What kind of craft is that?"

The others looked down and saw a small white barge, coupled to a green tugboat. They could dimly make out two metal strands coming from the front of the barge.

"Oh, that must be the cable ferry Uncle Jim mentioned," Chet recalled. "It takes cars and passengers across the lake." He glanced at his watch. "Let's go back," he said. "Supper was a long time ago!" The famished boy grinned and the brothers laughed.

They started for the car. Joe, who was last,

abruptly stopped in his tracks. His ears strained to catch a distant sound.

"Fellows, wait! Hear that?"

They listened intently. Echoing down the lake from the ramparts came the ominous thump, thump, thump of a drum!

CHAPTER VII

An Angry Sculptor

"LISTEN!" Joe urged, as Frank and Chet joined him apprehensively at the lookout.

"What is it?" Chet asked.

Joe held up his hand for silence and they listened intently. Frank leaned far out in the direction of the mist-shrouded fort. The only sound was that of the wind through the trees.

Joe explained as they got back in the car. "I'm positive it was drumbeats!" he said emphatically. "It was coming from—the fort!"

A cold chill raced up Chet's spine. He shuddered. "Y-you think Senandaga really is h-haunted?"

"It could have been the wind playing tricks," Frank speculated. "Personally, I think it was your stomach rumbling, Chet. Why didn't you tell us you were so hungry?"

The three broke into laughter, and drove back to Millwood, where they persuaded the kind-hearted cook to provide them with a snack.

The Hardys suggested they check the grounds before going to bed. The place seemed to be deserted. Joe happened to glance over toward the moonlit gallery and noticed something move in the shadows. A man was crouched at the locked door!

"Somebody's trying to get into the gallery!"

The boys broke into a run across the lawn, but the man jumped up and tore into the woods.

"Fan out!" Frank yelled to Joe and Chet.

Separating, they crashed through the brush in pursuit. In the darkness ahead, they could hear pounding footsteps.

"This way!" Joe yelled, heading left toward the sound of a breaking twig.

"Where? I can't see a thing!" Chet stumbled into a fallen tree and groaned before following a shadow to his left. "F-Frank—is that you?"

"Yes. Come on! Over here!"

Darting quickly from one tree trunk to the next, Frank plunged forward through bushes, then paused. Hearing a branch snap, he rushed ahead to the left.

"He must have headed to the right!" Joe's voice rang out.

Squinting for a glimpse of the prowler, Frank

jumped over some rocks and darted through a clearing. As he sprinted into an adjoining wooded patch, he collided with someone and went sprawling on the ground.

"Joe—it's you!"

"Frank!"

Presently they saw Chet's chunky shadow approach. "Where did he go?" Chet panted, exhausted.

Kneeling and breathing heavily, they listened for a sign of the fugitive. But there was only silence throughout the woods.

"That guy's a phantom," said Chet, mopping his forehead.

"One thing is certain," Frank remarked. "He knows the area well. Probably somebody local."

"Wonder who he was," Joe said as they hurried toward the gallery. "He was tall—definitely not the thief we've already seen."

The boys found that the gallery padlock had been tampered with, and hastily summoned Chet's uncle.

"We didn't get a good look at the man," Frank reported, "but this is definite proof there's more than one person after the fort treasure."

He phoned headquarters, and soon an officer arrived on the scene. He dusted the door for prints, and made a search of the grounds near the gallery.

"No footprints," he reported. "Check with us in the morning."

Afterward, the young sleuths and Uncle Jim got tools and worked by lantern light to reinforce the lock.

Frank and Joe also inserted a high-watt bulb into the unused socket over the door, then switched on the light. It was past midnight when they gathered up the tools.

Mr. Kenyon wiped his brow. "This bright light may discourage intruders. This gallery wasn't designed to hold off thieves!"

Joe grinned. "I hope *we* are."

The next morning Chet was snoring contentedly when the Hardys finished dressing. Strong tugs at his legs awakened him.

"Come on," Joe urged. "Up and at 'em! You're four hours behind the birds!"

The heavy youth grumbled and burrowed deeper into his covers.

"Breakfast is ready!" Joe shouted.

Covers flew up and Chet landed squarely on the floor with two feet.

After eating, the trio went directly to the gallery. This time no one interfered. They found the remaining fort paintings were as varied in style as they were in views of the impressive fortress.

Several were painted as if from the middle of Crown Lake; others as if from a nearby mountain.

Some were night scenes, others broad daylight. Green and brown colors stood out boldly, and lighting effects were worked with fine brush strokes upon the fort's stone ledges.

All the paintings were signed with an interlaced J and D.

"As I see it," Frank observed, "there's a choice of ways in which a painter could leave a clue on canvas."

"Or in the frame," Chet added.

Frank nodded. "But I think the paintings themselves are the best bet. The clue could be a tiny word in a corner or even a symbol. Or"—he pointed to one picture—"it might be where a figure is standing—this Union soldier for instance."

"Also," Joe interposed, "we should keep our eyes open for any unusual color or brush stroke."

By noon they had found nothing definite, but all three had kept notes of possible clues. Back in their room, the boys placed tracing paper over the photostat of the Senandaga map and marked the places they wanted to check. Joe then locked the map in his suitcase and put the tracing paper in his pocket. After lunch the Hardys were impatient to begin exploring the fort, but Chet had a suggestion.

"Uncle Jim told me there's a new instructor in sculpture. He's French, and has definite views on

Fort Senandaga. Maybe we should see this René Follette."

The Hardys agreed, although they strongly suspected their chum was trying to postpone another visit to the old fort. First, Frank phoned headquarters. No trace of the thief or of last evening's prowler had turned up. The fingerprints had proved inconclusive.

The Bayporters headed for the sculpture studio. On the way, they passed Ronnie at his easel. Chet twirled his beret and sang out, "Getting ready for the exhibit?"

The student sneered. "I'm all set to take first prize. Half the kids here can't paint a barn door."

Chet glanced at the garish orange and purple circles on Ronnie's canvas. "Rush" was signed at the bottom in large flourishing letters.

"You wouldn't understand it." Ronnie guffawed, then said slyly, "I saw you three coming out of the gallery. Did you give up painting lessons?"

"Not me," Chet declared cheerfully.

"Ha! I suppose you're going to enter the exhibit."

Chet's face grew red. The Hardys winked at each other but said nothing. The young detectives moved on.

As they entered the sculpture workshop, the fresh smell of clay reached their nostrils. Colorful pottery and ceramic figures stood on high tables, as well as several in bronze. A stocky, red-faced man with snapping black eyes was darting among his students. About fifteen boys and girls were standing before long tables, working on both clay and metal sculptures.

When he saw Chet and the Hardys the instructor beamed. "Come in, come in!" He made a sweeping gesture of welcome. "You are new, *n'est ce pas?* I am René Follette."

The boys explained that they were visiting Millwood as guests. "We're especially interested in Fort Senandaga," said Frank. "Could—"

"Ah! *Magnifique!*" the Frenchman broke in dramatically. "I shall tell you the story." The boys settled down at an empty table by a narrow open window. Follette removed a denim apron and joined them.

His first words were startling. "Senandaga! *Bah!* Fort du Lac is the real name!" He struck his chest. "It was built by a Frenchman—le Marquis de Chambord."

Intrigued by the peppery sculptor, the Hardys asked him about the battle said to have taken place during the French-Indian conflict. "Is it true the British conquered the fort?" Frank asked.

"*Jamais!* Never!" was the violent protest. Waving his hands, the Frenchman told how the British, under the command of Lord Craig, coming by boat down Crown Lake, had attacked the bastion. They had forced the French to flee, but apparently had not held the fort long, since Chambord's men had returned to drive out their foe.

"Chambord was a great man!" Follette exulted. "His men were the last seen on the ramparts of Fort du Lac—*not* the Englanders!" He pounded the table fiercely.

At that moment Joe glimpsed a flash of gray moving away from the window. He could not be sure, but assumed it was someone in an artist's smock. Had the person been listening, or just passing by?

Frank was asking René Follette about the gold boom chain ordered by Chambord.

"I believe it *was* made," the sculptor replied. His voice lowered. "I also believe it was stolen— by the Britishers. It is my intention," he added, "to find the truth. In my own way."

With that, the excitable Frenchman arose and resumed his instruction.

Outside, the boys looked at one another. Chet grinned. "Mr. Follette is ready to fight that battle all over again," he said. "Think it's true about the French being the last holders of Senandaga?"

Frank chuckled. "Mr. Davenport may know. Why don't we drop over and see him?"

"Let's take the map along," Joe said. "I'll go back for it and meet you outside the mansion." He headed across the grounds to the storage building.

At the top of the stairwell inside, he heard a scrambling noise from below. Somebody was in their room!

Tensely, Joe swung down the winding metal steps and burst inside the open door. Too late he heard a sound behind him. A crashing blow descended on his head. The room reeling, Joe sank to the floor.

CHAPTER VIII

Treacherous Detour

REGAINING his senses, Joe found himself on his cot, looking up at the anxious faces of Frank and Chet. He sat up groggily, wincing as he touched his throbbing head.

"Ooo, who—scalped me?"

"The same person who stole our map of the fort," Frank said, handing his brother a cool gauze compress.

"The map!" Joe exclaimed. "Stolen!" He remembered hearing the rummaging noise before he was struck unconscious.

Frank pointed to their scattered clothing. "Somebody pried open our suitcases. Anyhow, the photostat's gone. Too bad we didn't come back sooner to find out why you didn't show up."

Joe insisted he felt well enough to accompany Frank and Chet to inform Mr. Davenport.

"I hope this theft won't upset him too much," Chet said worriedly.

"If it wasn't the picture thief or whoever we saw at the gallery last night, I've got another guess," Joe proposed. "Ronnie Rush."

"Possibly." Frank's brow creased. "It would help to find out if he's only being nosy, or if he has a special interest in the gallery besides 're-search.'"

They picked up Jim Kenyon at his studio and walked together to the mansion.

"Too bad," he said upon hearing the boys' story. "As far as I know, Ronnie's background is okay. But I'll try to keep a closer watch on him."

They trudged up the drive and came upon Alex, now in overalls, weeding a flower border. Even in work clothes, the man had a formal manner. He nodded slightly to the boys as they passed.

Inside, the Hardys and their companions found the elderly Southerner in his study, moodily poking his cane at the toy fort. He brightened at the entrance of his visitors.

"I declare, I'm delighted to see you all. My fort problem's sort of getting me down. Any progress on the treasure?"

Frank took a deep breath. "I'm afraid we have another theft to report."

Mr. Davenport was greatly agitated after hearing of Joe's experience. "Bad business," he muttered. "Don't like any of you boys getting hurt."

Joe grinningly assured him, "We're rugged. I'm sorry about the map, though."

"Have one other copy tucked away." Mr. Davenport extracted a photostat from his safe and handed it to Frank.

"We'd like to visit the fort again," Frank said.

"Go right ahead. I don't mind *you* boys being there, so long as the confounded pub—"

Joe broke in hastily to query him about the strange drumbeats. Mr. Davenport was intrigued, but had never heard the sounds.

Frank then asked about the sculptor's claim that French soldiers had been the last to leave the fort in the disputed battle.

The elderly man gave a little smile. "My feeling is, boys, that there's truth on both sides. Trouble is, both Lord Craig and Chambord lost their lives at a battle just after Senandaga. There are questions no one may ever be able to answer."

Chet spoke up. "We've studied the pictures some more. We even visited Chauncey Gilman—oh!"

The forbidden name was out of Chet's mouth before he realized it! Mr. Davenport began thumping his cane on a tea table, jarring the china.

"Gilman!" his voice rose. "Gilman! That long-nosed, uppity Yankee! If that stuffed-shirt critic's trying to carpetbag more of my fort paintings—or the treasure— Why, I'll—"

Chet's uncle quickly eased the breathless art patron into a chair while Frank said soothingly, "Mr. Davenport, we understand how you feel. But as detectives we have to investigate every lead. Mr. Gilman isn't very likable, but I don't think he's a thief."

The old man gradually calmed down, and wiping his brow, apologized for his outburst. He gave Joe a key to the fort gate and a short while later the boys departed.

Outside, Joe said eagerly, "I'm for a trip to the fort, pronto."

Chet looked unhappy. "You go, fellows. I—er—have some work to do."

"Work!" Joe echoed teasingly.

Uncle Jim grinned. "Chet has promised to help spruce up the grounds for our exhibit. My students are devoting all their time to finishing their entries."

Joe grinned. "We'll pitch in and give you a hand if you'll drive us to Senandaga. Is it a bargain, Chet?"

"Okay, okay!"

While Jim went off to a class, the Bayporters set to work. Chet and Joe teamed up to wash windows. Frank mowed the grass, starting with the area around the gallery.

Still wondering about the stolen fort map, he

kept his eyes open for Ronnie. But the youth was nowhere to be seen.

Later, at the sculptor's studio, as the students were leaving, Frank found Joe washing the outside panes.

"This is one way to earn our keep." Frank grinned. "Say, where's Chet?"

"Don't know," Joe replied. "He and Uncle Jim went to the oil-painting studio about an hour ago. Let's check."

Joe put down his bucket and rags and the brothers walked over to the studio. Chet was perched atop a high, three-rung stool before an easel. He moved the brush slowly over his large canvas.

"Well," Joe said, laughing, "from window washer to artist. I should've known—from those fine rag strokes on certain windows."

Chet looked up. "I'm sorry, Joe," Chet said. "I'll do my share. But I just got so interested in—er—my painting. Besides, Uncle Jim thinks it's not bad."

"You know, Chet," Frank said, "I have a wild hunch your painting will turn up at the exhibit."

Somewhat embarrassed, Chet admitted this was his secret plan. The Hardys watched as their pal continued to work. When not biting the end of his paintbrush with indecision, he would hunch forward, dip the brush in a thick purple blob on his palette, and absorbedly make a squiggle on the canvas.

"What's it going to be?" Joe asked at last.

"You'll see," was all Chet said.

After a while the boys returned to their chores, and it was not until after supper that everything was finished.

The Hardys and Chet went down to the lake for a cooling dip before starting out for Senandaga. The afterglow of sunset cast the opposite shore in a pale-rose light. Dusk shrouded the wide lake. Frank was swimming some distance from shore when he heard a sound that made his spine tingle.

Like a distant heartthrob behind the promontory came the single beat of a drum, then silence, then the beat again!

"Fellows! Listen!" he shouted and swam over to Joe and Chet. They strained their ears.

"The drum!" Joe hissed.

The boys dashed out of the water. They found Uncle Jim and Mr. Davenport talking near the mansion. Upon hearing the boys' report, both men agreed the young sleuths should investigate the fort at once, but cautioned them to be on guard.

"Not that I believe in any haunts, of course," added Mr. Davenport. "But there could be some kind of danger lurking there."

The boys hurriedly dressed and drove off in the jalopy. Darkness was falling as they headed south. Chet switched on the high beams and guided the

Queen around a series of curves until they reached the end of the lake. There were few houses, and only rarely a light in one. Chet slowed down.

The trees grew dense and overhung the road. From deep in the woods came the hoot of an owl, mournfully echoing over the constant whisper of cicadas. Like brittle witch fingers, branches clawed the side of the car.

"Willikers, it's spooky!" Chet said, rolling up his window. He turned right up a winding dirt road, then left.

Suddenly Chet screeched to a halt. The road was blocked by two wooden sawhorses! By the light of a flashing red lantern, the boys saw an arrowed white sign: DETOUR—LEFT—ROCKSLIDE.

"Guess we haven't much choice," Joe said. Chet turned the car and started down what proved to be an extremely narrow, steep lane.

The lake was visible below. Suddenly a tree loomed directly in their path. Hastily Chet yanked the wheel, but the car scraped against high rocks. As the Queen bounced over a yawning hole, Frank cried out:

"This isn't any detour! It's a trap!"

Panicky, Chet hit the brakes. But the left front tire had already pitched steeply down. Desperately he tried to swerve the rolling car.

"I can't stop!"

Faster and faster they skidded downward. Like

bulky phantoms, trees grazed the fenders as Chet steered frantically between them. Jolted, his hands lost control of the wheel.

"We're going into the lake!" Joe yelled.

The front of the car seemed to lurch into the air. Their heads banged the roof an instant before the Queen struck water. She stopped almost instantly.

Frank shouldered his door open and sloshed through the shallow depths to pull Chet out. Joe crawled from the back window and the three waded to shore.

"Everybody all right?" Frank asked breathlessly.

"Yes—but the Queen!" Chet exclaimed in dismay. The jalopy stood fender-deep in water.

Joe scrambled above to get help. Frank and Chet, grabbing a rope out of the trunk, moored the car to two trees to keep it from rolling out any deeper. There were dents and a smashed headlight, but the boys were worried there might be serious mechanical damage.

Chet heaved a sigh. "My poor Queen!"

Shivering in wet clothing, the two boys waited in the darkness for what seemed hours. Then they heard vehicles stopping and excited voices. Soon Joe appeared, accompanied by two policemen.

"I finally flagged down a car," he panted. The driver had notified the police, who in turn summoned a tow truck.

Joe had already given a report to the officers. "A nasty trick—that fake detour," one said. "We'll step up our patrol along there."

The boys wanted to stay until Chet's car was pulled to safety, but the policemen insisted on driving them back to Millwood.

Huddled under blankets, the three sleuths speculated among themselves on the return trip. Who could have set the dangerous trap? And why?

"I'll bet someone rigged it to keep us from Fort Senandaga!" Joe exclaimed.

"How'd he know we were going?"

"Could've overheard us talking about it," said Frank. "Maybe those drumbeats were to lure us there."

At the Millwood entrance they thanked the officers and headed quickly toward their quarters. "Wait until Uncle Jim hears about this!" Chet's teeth chattered.

As they cut across the wide lawn, Joe glanced over at the grove in which the gallery stood. It was in total blackness.

"Funny," he murmured. "What happened to the light we put over the—?"

Instinctively sensing trouble, the Hardys streaked across the lawn. Chet followed. They found the front door unlocked and cautiously pushed it open.

A flashlight beam struck them squarely in the eyes! A shadowy figure approached. The boys dashed in, ready for a fight. The next moment they stopped short.

"Uncle Jim!" Chet gasped. "What—?"

The instructor's face was ashen. Wordlessly he flicked on the light switch and pointed toward the far wall of the room. *The twelve fort paintings were gone!*

CHAPTER IX

The Hermit's Story

"ALL the Senandaga paintings—stolen!" Jim Kenyon's words echoed dismally across the stone gallery as the boys rushed over. The wall showed twelve empty picture hooks.

Uncle Jim told them he had returned from Cedartown a short while ago. He had gone to check the gallery, found that the bulb had been smashed, and a moment later, discovered the theft. "I was about to phone the police, then break the news to Mr. Davenport."

"But how did the thief get in?" Joe asked.

The instructor pointed upward. "The skylight."

The boys noticed a large section of panes was missing where the glassed roof met a wall.

"The thief must have had a lookout," Frank surmised, "while he was cutting the panes."

The police were called and arrived shortly to

examine the gallery. They found the missing glass panes, but there were no fingerprints. Nothing of significance was discovered. When the officers had left, Jim and the boys went to the mansion.

It took them a long while to persuade Mr. Davenport that the twelve paintings actually had been stolen. The art patron kept shaking his head, as if in a daze.

"What are we to do?" he lamented. "The thieves are still at large and growing bolder— Jason's paintings in their possession, and likely, the clue to Chambord's gold chain."

Suddenly he and Uncle Jim became aware of the boys' disheveled appearance. "What on earth happened to you?" asked the instructor.

In the excitement, the Hardys and Chet had temporarily forgotten their own experiences. Quickly they described the ill-fated drive.

The two men listened in great astonishment and concern. Mr. Davenport snapped out of his gloom. "Desperadoes!" he stormed. "Why, you boys could've been hurt something dreadful!"

"They're desperate all right," said Frank. "Which means they may tip their hand soon and give themselves away. The trouble is," he added, "somebody in the area seems to know every move we make, or are going to make."

"Do you think," asked Uncle Jim, "those drumbeats and your accident are related to the painting thefts?"

"Yes," replied Frank. "Whoever the mastermind is, he doesn't want us at Fort Senandaga to look for the gold chain."

Joe set his jaw. "We'll get there yet and do some hunting."

The weary boys slept late the next morning. After breakfast Chet phoned the Cedartown police. His jalopy had been salvaged, but it would take at least a week for repairs.

Chet groaned. "How will the Queen live without me?"

"Cheer up!" Joe grinned. "You're going to be pretty busy painting from now on. We're expecting big things from you at the exhibit!"

Chet slapped his forehead. "You're right! I've only got a little more than two days!" He pulled his beret from a pocket and pulled it on. "This calls for short-order genius!"

"In the meantime," Joe said seriously, "we're stymied for transportation."

"Not quite," Frank replied. "We'll use one of the canoes."

"Great!" said Joe. "What's the first stop?"

"Turtle Island." Frank proposed that they visit the English hermit and have a look at his fort painting.

Chet wanted to go with his friends, but finally decided to work on his painting. The trio were about to separate when they saw Ronnie Rush setting up his easel near the main path.

At once the Bayporters hurried over. Joe asked bluntly, "Ronnie, we're missing a photostat of an old map. Have you seen it around?"

The student bit his lip. "Map? Why ask me? If I had, it'd be my business anyway."

"This one happens to be our business," Joe retorted. "You seem to be pretty good at spying. Maybe you saw the person who knocked me out, broke into our luggage, and stole the map."

Ronnie's face reddened, but he merely blustered, "I—I didn't see anybody. What's so special about an old map?"

"It's of Fort Senandaga," Joe said.

Ronnie gave a perceptible start, but at once took up his palette and brush. "Stop bothering me. I've got to finish my picture."

"Your prize-winning one?" Chet asked airily.

"A lot you know about art, fatso!" Ronnie muttered.

The three boys turned away. "I'll show him," Chet vowed.

Joe grinned. "The brush is mightier than the sword!"

"Anyhow," Frank said, "we got a rise out of Ronnie about the map, though we still can't be sure he took it."

"Yes," Joe said, "but he sure didn't like our questions."

The Hardys got directions to Turtle Island from Uncle Jim, and permission to use his own canoe, then hurried to the boathouse. They lifted the handsome red wooden craft from its berth into the water. Joe settled himself in the bow, and Frank in the stern, then they paddled off.

Bright white sails were visible downlake as they glided across the sun-speckled water. Here and there a motorboat sped along. The canoe traced a shimmering line over the surface as Frank steered toward a group of small islands a mile out.

"There's Turtle Island," Joe said presently, spotting a wooded hump of land straight ahead where a cabin of stone and log was partially visible.

Coasting between two large, jutting rocks, Frank steered the canoe onto a sandy strip. Nearby lay a weatherbeaten rowboat. Joe jumped out and pulled in their craft. Suddenly they heard a ferocious barking, then a flurry in the bushes, and a huge German shepherd dog appeared.

"Look out!" Frank cried.

The dog bared his teeth threateningly. Growling, he crouched as if to spring. The Hardys darted backward.

"Basker!" shouted a deep voice. "Hold, boy!"

The dog subsided instantly as a tall, sunburned man in a brown tweed suit emerged from the brush. Frank and Joe relaxed as he stroked the panting animal. The tall man peered at them beneath bushy eyebrows and greeted them in a British accent.

"Hello there!" he said cordially. "Terribly sorry about Basker—he's not used to seeing many people out here." He extended his hand. "Lloyd Everett's my name."

The boys introduced themselves, thinking Everett unusually well-dressed for a hermit. They told him why they had come. He agreed to let the Hardys inspect his Prisoner-Painter picture and led them toward the cabin.

"Dare say you chaps have had wind of that French gold-chain legend," he remarked. "I don't take any stock in it myself—it's false, like most of the past French claims about Fort Royal."

"Fort Royal?" Joe repeated.

Everett nodded. "Senandaga is its Indian name, but it's properly called Fort Royal, named by its last holder during the French-English campaigns, the great Lord Craig, my ancestor."

Remembering the French sculptor's account of the fort, Frank glanced at Joe.

In the simply furnished but comfortable living room, Everett lifted down the painting from its place over the fireplace. Frank took out a pocket magnifying glass and studied it closely. The view was painted as if from below the ramparts at Crown Lake's edge.

"A fine rendition," the Englishman remarked. "I don't generally collect art, but since I'm interested in the historical aspects of Fort Royal, I persuaded Mr. Davenport to sell it to me a few years back."

While Joe scrutinized the picture, Frank asked if it were true that French soldiers had been the last on the fort's ramparts.

"Nonsense! Sheer nonsense! Who told you that?" Everett demanded.

When Frank mentioned the Millwood sculptor, the hermit clutched his hair.

"Blast it! A Frenchman! What else?" Striding angrily over to a small cork board, he plucked out seven darts. In rapid order he pitched them at the board.

"This Follette told you a pack of lies about Chambord, no doubt," Everett growled. He did not pause for a response and proceeded to relate how Lord Craig had taken Senandaga. The French had apparently mismanaged their cannon defense and fled before Craig's forces.

When Joe mentioned the story of the English having stolen the *chaîne d'or,* Everett angrily plucked the darts from the board.

"As a descendant of Lord Craig, I shall not tolerate such lies. Here!" He handed the boys a small book. Its title was *The True Story of Fort Royal.* "Read this—you may keep it," he said. "I wrote the book myself when I first moved here to my island retreat."

The Hardys thanked him, intrigued by his

differing account of the battle. The boys studied the Senandaga painting again. Suddenly Frank noticed a slight irregularity in a corner brush stroke.

"Joe, let me have the magnifier!"

Excited, he held the glass over the area. But he looked up in disappointment. "It's just a scratch."

Nothing else unusual was detected in the painting. The brothers made a note of the location of two soldiers standing below the ramparts. They thanked the Englishman as he walked back with them to the canoe.

"Wish you boys luck, of course," said Everett. "Take my advice—the so-called *chaîne d'or* doesn't exist. Just another of many French exaggerations." He added that he rarely crossed to the mainland except to buy provisions. He had not left the island in a month.

The Hardys waved as they pushed off. "Cheerio!" called Everett. "Be sure to read my book!"

Joe was dejected. "That painting was another lost hope. I guess all we can do now is search the fort itself for the chain. If there is one!"

"We also have the job of tracking down the thieves and stolen pictures," Frank said. "By the way, Everett told us he hadn't been off the island for a month. But his rowboat was wet and muddy—and it hasn't rained for days!"

Joe remembered seeing oars in the boat also. Was the recluse lying? Did he know anything about the Millwood thefts?

"Well," Joe quipped, "we could always take a new case: Who *were* the last holders of Fort Senandaga—I mean, Fort Royal!"

"Or Fort du Lac!" Frank smiled, shifting his paddle to the right.

Smoothly, the brothers stroked forward. They were halfway to shore when Joe first noticed water around his feet.

"Frank! We're taking in water!"

Ceasing to paddle, Joe slid back carefully to locate the leak. "I can't find it!" he cried out.

Frank quickly pulled in his paddle and crept forward. But he had no sooner taken a step than he heard a cracking noise.

"Joe—this wood—"

With a splintering noise, the section of flooring beneath Frank's left foot gave way, entrapping his leg. Water poured in as the sinking canoe capsized.

The lake surface closed over the Hardys!

CHAPTER X

Mysterious Flag

COLD stinging water coursed through Joe's mouth and nose as he sank beneath the surface. He could see the shadow of the capsized canoe above.

Shooting up for air, he immediately plunged beneath again.

With a mighty yank he freed Frank's leg from the hull, and both boys were soon hugging the splintered boat.

"Are—are you all right?" Joe gasped.

Frank coughed for several moments before answering. "Yes, except my leg's a bit sore. I don't get it, Joe. This canoe is practically new."

As the Hardys signaled an approaching motorboat, Joe noticed something on the canoe's hull. "Frank, look!"

Joe pointed to a wide crusted hole where Frank's leg had gone through, then noticed several smaller holes edged with a painted paste.

"This canoe was sabotaged!" he panted, treading water. "Somebody must have cut these holes, then used a sealer and paint! Whoever did it knew that it would just be a matter of time before water—or we—went through."

The motorboat, manned by a man and his wife, pulled abreast of the stranded sleuths and helped them aboard. With the canoe in tow, they were soon on their way back to Millwood. Frank pulled a wet book from the pocket of his slacks.

The True Story of Fort Royal was soaked but safe!

At the school dock the Hardys thanked their rescuers and hurried across the grass. Several students eyed the water-soaked boys curiously. Chet and his uncle spotted them and came rushing up. The two were mystified and worried upon hearing of the boat incident.

"Somebody must have been hoping you'd use my canoe," the instructor said grimly.

"You mean the trap was intended for Frank and Joe," Chet finished. "And maybe me too. No place is safe around here!"

As the Hardys changed into dry clothes they told of their visit to Lloyd Everett. Uncle Jim grinned. "He takes that battle as seriously as René Follette and Mr. Davenport."

"And how!" Frank looked thoughtful. "He's friendly enough—doesn't look or act much like a hermit."

During a late lunch the three boys and Uncle Jim discussed possible suspects in the canoe episode. Ronnie Rush? The short thief? The gallery prowler?

Joe noticed that Chet was staring into space and said, "You decided what your picture's about?"

Chet grinned good-naturedly. "Okay, mind reader, I have. But you'll have to wait and see."

"Is your entry a still life, Chet?" Frank asked.

"Yes. A moving still life!"

The others groaned at the pun.

They were just leaving the kitchen when the art patron stormed out of his study, swinging his cane. A magazine was clutched in his hand.

"Confound him! That fogbound, silky-voiced, boiled shirt! That honey-dewed melonhead—"

"Now what?" murmured Chet.

Mr. Davenport was finally persuaded to calm down and explain. "Just look at this!" he directed, opening the magazine and pointing to a paragraph which read:

"In the coming days, it will be my consummate pleasure to review the Millwood Art Exhibit, the annual artistic joke of the region. The public would better spend its time at nearby Fort Senandaga than risk dying of laughter at the 'wood' painted at the Davenport 'mill.' "

Frank looked up in disgust. "This was written by Chauncey Gilman."

Mr. Davenport said that the critic himself had mailed him the magazine. As soon as possible the Hardys changed the subject. The boys told the patron of their unsuccessful study of Everett's fort painting, then of the canoe incident.

The Southerner, who had been tapping his cane rapidly on the floor, suddenly stopped. To the others' amazement, he announced, "There's one more painting. It's in my attic."

"What?" cried Joe.

"I declare, it slipped my mind," said the art patron. "Guess because it's the one work by Jason I never did like. Style's different from all the others, so I just plumb hid it."

"May we see it?" Frank asked quickly.

"Might as well." Mr. Davenport led the excited group to the third floor and into a dim alcove. There he removed a dust-covered canvas from a closet and set it on an antique table. The boys studied it closely with the magnifier.

"This is a contrast to the other fort paintings," Frank remarked. "It's all done in blacks, grays, and pale yellows. The storm clouds over the fort are ghostlike."

"Indeed they are," said Mr. Davenport. "I don't know what got into Jason."

Frank examined the back of the picture. He pointed to one corner, where a faded date was scrawled in a wavering hand: April 1, 1865.

"That was just before the Civil War ended," said Uncle Jim.

Again the boys scrutinized the gloomy scene. The artist's initials were as usual in the lower corner, but were fainter than in the other paintings. Frank's mind was racing. Why had the Prisoner-Painter changed to such a somber style?

Just then Mr. Davenport looked at his watch. "I'm afraid you'll have to excuse me," he said. "Expecting the carpenter any minute. He's working on a project for me." A mischievous twinkle came into the man's eyes, and as they went downstairs, he chuckled softly. His visitors were curious, but he offered no explanation.

"Let's try the fort again," urged Joe. "Right now."

The Millwood owner insisted they borrow his limousine. "Alex isn't here today, so I won't need it." He handed them the car keys.

Outside, Uncle Jim excused himself to return to his students. Chet decided to stick with his painting. "I'll keep an eye on Ronnie Rush," he promised.

The fort map in Joe's pocket, the brothers headed for the mansion garage. On the way, they passed a tall, bearded man at an easel set up on a knoll. The Hardys recognized Myles Warren, who ran the Cedar Sport Shop.

"Hi," said Joe. "You must be one of the weekend painters, only this is Wednesday."

"Yes," the man said pleasantly. "I'm pushing to finish my picture for the exhibit."

The Hardys glanced at the canvas—a landscape in vivid greens, reds, and yellow. Warren kept his brush moving. "Tried that fishing at the north end yet?"

"No." Frank smiled. "We'll keep it in mind."

In the garage Frank slid behind the wheel of the luxurious limousine and pulled out into the road above Millwood.

It was late afternoon by the time they reached the fort. There had been no trace of the phony detour sign. Frank parked, and they unlocked the gate, then climbed the hill toward the ramparts. Pausing on the glacis, the boys looked at the map, then at the tracing showing the locations of figures in the pictures.

The actual shape of Senandaga was that of a square with diamond-shaped bastions at the corners of its four ramparts.

Frank pointed to a high, wedge-shaped defensive stonework which stood in front of the ditch. "That must be the demilune—the south one. There's another to the west."

They decided to begin their hunt by checking outside the fort walls and ditch. First, the Hardys walked north along the zigzagging ditch, then to the spot where the wall had fallen. They stopped to examine the rubble.

"Hey!" Joe yelled, pushing aside a rock. Underneath lay a round black object. "An old cannon ball!"

The Hardys wondered: Had it been hurled against the ancient wall to cause the collapse? They surveyed the crenelated walls of blocked stone. Although its soldiers and cannon were long gone, a forbidding, ominous silence seemed to make itself felt around the bastion.

As Frank's eyes passed over the crumbled roofs visible above the walls, he stopped suddenly. "Joe, look!"

Waving atop a flagpole on the southeast rampart was a white and gold flag!

"It's the flag used by the French before their revolution!" Frank exclaimed, recognizing the pattern of three white lilies. "But it wasn't here the first time we came."

"One thing is sure—it's no relic," Joe said. "Mr. Davenport didn't mention anything about a flag."

They stared at the mysterious banner, recalling the drumbeats they had heard earlier. Who had placed the old French colors over the fort?

Hastily the Hardys continued along the ditch to an area which they had marked on their tracing sheet. They hoped to find some kind of marking or rock formation at the same spots the figures stood in the paintings.

"Over here, a little more to the right," Joe said,

comparing the map and sheet. Frank noticed that freshly churned-up soil surrounded their feet.

"Joe! Somebody's been digging!"

"You're right!" Joe reached down and felt the earth.

"If the treasure was here," Frank reasoned, "we're out of luck."

They walked toward the west demilune. But halfway, Joe noticed a pillar of black smoke in the sky. It came from beyond a shadowed promontory to the north of the lake.

"Frank, that looks like a fire!"

"It is. I wonder— Joe! It's coming from Millwood!"

CHAPTER XI

The Lake Monster

"WE'VE got to get back!" Frank urged.

The brothers raced down the slope to the parked car and soon were streaking around the lake road leading to Millwood. The column of black smoke swirled higher and they heard sirens.

Reaching the school, Frank wheeled the limousine to the parking area and they jumped out.

"It's the boathouse!" Joe exclaimed.

Waves of intense heat rolled out from the flaming structure. The Hardys ran toward the lakeside, where a crowd watched the firemen fighting the holocaust.

The dock was already lost, and what had been canoes were smoking shells on the bank. Voices echoed as spumes of water played against the blazing boathouse. Suddenly Frank detected a strong oily smell in the air.

"Kerosene!" he said. "This fire must have been set!"

The Hardys spotted Uncle Jim and Chet among the spectators back of a cordoned area near a police car. Chet was glad to see his pals.

"Was anybody hurt?" Frank asked, worried.

"Fortunately, no," Mr. Kenyon replied. "But our boat area is a complete ruin."

In an hour the fire had been extinguished. According to a student, the conflagration had apparently broken out suddenly—on the lake itself.

"Which means somebody poured a kerosene slick on the water and ignited it," Frank said.

Chet nodded solemnly. "With the wind and floating pieces of burning wood, we're lucky it didn't spread along the whole shore front."

By now, most of the onlookers had dispersed and the fire trucks and police car were leaving.

The Bayporters surveyed the grim, charred skeleton of the boathouse, wondering who the arsonist could have been, and what his motive was. Another attempt to discourage the Hardys from investigating Fort Senandaga?

"It wasn't Ronnie Rush who set it, anyway," Chet declared. "He was too busy making fun of my painting."

The three boys searched the burned wreckage for evidence. They found nothing but a fat, charred cork, smelling of kerosene, bobbing on the waterfront.

"A pretty slim clue," Joe muttered, stuffing the

cork into his pocket. After supper they stopped in with Uncle Jim to see Mr. Davenport. He seemed inconsolable. The school's exhibit was only two days away, and the blackened ruins would detract greatly from the estate's appearance. Joe had an idea.

"We'll begin clearing away the debris first thing tomorrow, and have the lake front in good shape by Senandaga Day."

Mr. Davenport brightened, and Uncle Jim said, "That would be a big help. At least the lake residents will be able to beach their boats."

"There's one person I suspect," the art patron burst out angrily, "who would want to spoil our exhibit. A certain party down the lake."

The boys assumed he meant Chauncey Gilman, but somehow they could not picture the critic in the role of an arsonist.

The brothers then told the others about the mysterious French flag they had seen at the fort. Mr. Davenport expressed complete bewilderment.

"A flag over Senandaga!" he exclaimed incredulously. "It must be the work of some blamed tourist! A trespasser!"

Frank doubted this, saying that even a practical joker might not go to the trouble of climbing the fence.

"Don't tell me a ghost put up that flag," Chet gulped.

Mr. Davenport shook his head. "You can get to the fort by boat, too."

The Hardys left him, wondering if the strange incident was part of the puzzle they were trying to solve.

Directly after breakfast the boys plunged into the task of cleaning up the dock site. With axes and wheelbarrows, charred wood was cut up and carted away, as well as burned shrubbery. Up to their waists in water, Frank and Joe hewed down the remaining boathouse supports and dock stakes.

"Whew!" Chet exclaimed as noontime approached. "I feel as though I'd been building a fort."

Ronnie Rush came up just then and looked on smugly. "Want to help?" Joe asked him.

"My time is too valuable," Ronnie said, and sauntered off.

"He may not have burned the docks, but he sure burns me up!" Chet muttered.

At last the boys finished their project, having set up bright buoys offshore. After lunch they were summoned to Cedartown Police Headquarters, where the chief handed them a photograph. "Recognize him?"

"The picture and frame thief!" Joe exclaimed.

"His name's Adrian Copler," the chief informed them, adding that the man had a long criminal record as a thief, especially of art objects.

There was no indication of his being an arsonist.

"I wonder if he's the brains behind the thefts at Millwood," Frank said, "or if he's working for a higher-up."

The chief shrugged. "Copler seems to be as elusive as he is clever. But I'll keep men on the lookout."

Back at the school, the boys discussed their future trips to the fort. "The Queen's still laid up and we can't keep borrowing the limousine," said Frank. "A canoe would be fine—but the fire took care of that."

"Guess we'll have to rent a boat," Joe said.

When Mr. Davenport heard of the boys' quandary, he called them into his study.

"We can't have you detectives grounded," he said. "How would you like to use a Colonial bateau?"

"A what?" Chet asked.

He smiled. "A bateau was a boat used during the French and Indian campaigns." Mr. Davenport explained that the wooden craft, resembling a modern dory, had been used by the English as well as the French for carrying supplies and for scouting. The original bateaux were up to forty-five feet long; later, they varied in length.

"Sounds great!" Joe broke in. "But where can *we* get a bateau?"

"My carpenter, George Ashbach, has a keen interest in historical boats. Out of curiosity, he put together a bateau last year. Doesn't use it much, but I understand it's navigable. I'm sure he'd be glad to let you boys borrow it."

"Super!" Chet exclaimed.

The elderly Southerner beamed. "Mr. Ashbach will be finishing up—my—er—job today. I'll talk to him."

"Are you building something?" Joe asked.

A devilish gleam sparkled in the patron's eyes. He smiled, but gave no answer.

That evening, as dusk fell, the boys sat on the bank, wondering whether they would hear the eerie drumbeats again.

"I'd like to know if that French flag was lowered at sundown," Joe commented.

"By the same ghost, maybe," Frank said, grinning.

Chet was not amused. "Aw, fellows!" He shivered. "Can't we talk about something—er—cheerful?"

The only sound was lapping water, ruffled by a chilly breeze. Chet glanced out over the lake to the grayish islands, huddled like waiting phantom ships. Dim lights were visible across the water, but to the south, where the fort lay, all was black.

Suddenly Chet stiffened. Out on the water, about fifty yards from where the boys sat, something broke the surface, then disappeared!

Rooted to his place, Chet blinked and looked again, his eyes as big as half dollars.

"What's the matter?" Joe asked. "Do you—?"

He broke off with a gasp as all three stared in disbelief.

A speck of white showed on the dark water. Then an immense, curved black shadow loomed larger and larger, gliding, waving toward them.

Chet stuttered with fear as the shadow drew near. It had a long neck and a huge glistening head, gaping jaws and long sharp teeth!

CHAPTER XII

A Strange Tomahawk

JUMPING up, Chet screamed. "A sea monster!"

In a burst of foam, the phantasmal creature sank beneath the surface and again emerged, its white eyes gleaming above moving jaws.

Frank and Joe dashed along the bank until they were abreast of the weird figure. It seemed at least thirty feet in length!

"It's a serpent!" Joe cried out.

They watched for the monster to surface. Then a subdued, drawling laugh broke the silence. Chet, terrified, had caught up to the brothers. The three stopped short as two figures emerged from the nearby woods.

"Mr. Davenport!" Joe burst out, recognizing one of them.

"Frank! Joe! Chester!" The art patron grinned. "I reckon I must ask your forgiveness for being victimized by my Crown Lake monster!"

He introduced the tall, lean man with him as Mr. Ashbach, the Cedartown carpenter.

"You mean that thing we just saw was *artificial?*" Joe asked.

The carpenter chuckled. "Joe," he said, "we had to test it on somebody, and we figured you young detectives were as tough a test as anybody."

Mr. Davenport nodded. "Now you know what my building project is!"

Still mystified, the boys noticed wires in the men's hands trailing off into the water. They began reeling in and soon the "serpent" broke the surface. A minute later it lay on the shore. The boys walked around the huge object.

Shaped like a brontosaurus with gills, it had been built over a wood-and-wire frame. The "skin" was of inflated rubber, touched in spots with luminous paint. Both the neck and jaws were hinged, and the snouted head had been fitted with two light-bulb eyes and jagged rubber "teeth."

"It's ingenious!" Frank laughed.

"Thank you." The millionaire smiled, patting the wet rubber proudly.

Chet kicked a pebble, embarrassed. "Jiminy, do I feel like a goof! But what are you going to do with this—er—serpent, sir?"

"You boys will see, soon!"

The curious sleuths could learn no more about the redoubtable monster.

"A sea monster!" Chet screamed

The Hardys arranged with Mr. Ashbach to pick up the bateau at his shop the next day.

Later, walking back to their room, Chet was preoccupied with Mr. Davenport's lake serpent. "I bet he's going to give rides on it!" Chet guessed finally.

Joe grinned. "Beats me."

After breakfast the next morning the Bayporters found the school grounds a beehive of activity. Uncle Jim and the students were busy getting the pictures in final shape for Saturday's exhibit.

Hurriedly the Hardys and Chet tidied up their quarters. Frank's mind kept turning over an idea which had been growing steadily. "Maybe it's a wild one, but—" Suddenly he dashed from the room. "Come on, fellows!"

Mystified, Joe and Chet followed him across the grounds to the Davenport mansion. The door was open. Frank led the way upstairs to the musty attic alcove. Joe was excited. What inspiration had struck his brother so forcibly?

Frank lifted the fort painting carefully onto the table. Chet wore an expression of utter perplexity as Frank pointed to the date on the back of the canvas. "This was the last picture Jason Davenport did. I think that's why the style is so different—he knew he was going to die."

"I get it!" Joe exclaimed excitedly. "He must

have left the clue in this picture, knowing he'd never have a chance to get the treasure himself," Joe guessed.

"Right." Frank now indicated the specklike daubs on the canvas. "Let's study them from a distance."

Frank set the painting against an opposite wall. At first the boys noticed nothing unusual. Then they were startled to see, out of gray and yellowish dabs, a design taking shape in the corner!

It was a tomahawk, entwined by a chain!

"The treasure clue!" Chet whooped.

The image seemed to lose itself as they stepped closer, then to reappear when they stood back.

"There must be a similar marking somewhere inside the fort!" Joe exclaimed.

The boys then noticed that the tomahawk handle had small notches, and wondered what these meant.

"The main thing is to keep this a close secret," Frank cautioned.

When they showed Mr. Davenport their discovery, he congratulated the boys heartily.

"It was Frank's brainstorm," Joe said.

The art patron looked at the painting. "I should have known Jason had a special reason for using that strange style."

The millionaire, too, was puzzled by the notched tomahawk.

"Did Indians fight at Senandaga?" Frank asked.

"They were involved in the Crown Lake campaigns," Davenport replied, "but it's not known whether they played a major role at the fort itself. I've studied the battle for years, but there always seems to be a piece missing."

The boys wondered if the chain-entwined tomahawk had any relation to the mysterious fort conflict?

"We've got to get inside Senandaga," Joe declared.

The boys hurried to tell Uncle Jim the good news, and their plan to search the fort that evening. Chet then excused himself to work on his painting. The boys were about to part when the French sculptor came running over. He carried three pamphlets.

"*Bonjour!*" he cried. "I hear you will use a bateau. Wonderful! A fine boat it is, used by le Marquis de Chambord. Here, my friends, these for you!"

He handed each boy a pamphlet. The title was *The Final French Victory at Fort du Lac.*

Follette pounded his chest proudly. "This I wrote to give the true account of this battle. Read it. *Au revoir!*"

Joe chuckled. "The second 'true' story of Senandaga."

After the Hardys left for Mr. Ashbach's shop,

Chet worked feverishly on his painting, even forgetting to eat lunch. By midafternoon the chunky boy realized he was ravenous and went to the house for a snack.

As Chet came outside he heard a horn beep urgently. He looked up in astonishment. A car, with a trailer bouncing behind it, was pulling into the lot. On the trailer sat an unusual-looking gray boat, flat-bottomed and tapered at both ends.

The car stopped and Frank and Joe hopped out. As Chet hurried over, Joe grinned. "Behold the bateau!"

"You sure she's seaworthy?" Chet asked, cocking his head.

"Indeed she is," came a deep voice as the carpenter, Mr. Ashbach, got out of the car.

He and the boys hauled the old-fashioned craft down to the lake and beached it a short distance from the water. The young detectives thanked Mr. Ashbach, who wished them luck and left.

Chet now studied the bateau curiously, noting its overlapping board construction. He asked about a pair of long poles lying in the bottom beside the paddles.

"The poles are used in shallow water," Frank explained.

As soon as dusk fell, the boys eagerly launched the bateau and clambered in. Jim Kenyon came to see them off. "Be careful," he warned. "Weather doesn't look good."

Heavy dark clouds shrouded the lake and the wind was rising, but the boys were undaunted. Chet was in the middle seat while Frank stood in the rear and Joe in the bow. Plying the poles, the Hardys got the Colonial craft under way.

"Wow, this is smooth!" Chet said. "How long is she?"

"Fifteen feet," Joe answered, "and four wide."

The brothers at first had trouble but soon were poling in rhythm. They were amazed at the ease with which the bateau could be moved.

With the strong wind at their backs, they passed several islands. The darkening sky remained overcast and few private boats were out. "Hope the rain holds off for Senandaga Day tomorrow," Chet said anxiously.

Joe grinned. "You can always put an umbrella over your painting."

Reaching deeper water, the Hardys switched to paddles. Presently they approached the cable-ferry dock on the west shore.

The passenger barge was just pulling out. There was only one car aboard. The boys could barely see the cables stretching taut, reaching into the water.

The wind was now lashing the lake into a mass of whitecaps.

"It won't be any picnic returning against this gale," Joe remarked, as they paddled abreast of the chugging ferry. Its tugboat pilot waved to them from the lighted cabin.

Suddenly they saw him spin the steering wheel frantically, then race out onto the passenger barge.

"Something's wrong!" Joe exclaimed. The three boys leaped to their feet. Frank looked back at the dock and saw two metal strands lying slack on the choppy surface!

"The cables have broken!" he cried out.

The pilot had dashed to the rear of the pitching barge. Suddenly he staggered in a terrific blast of wind and toppled overboard!

Horrified, the boys watched the ferry veer wildly off course!

CHAPTER XIII

Detective Guides

THE ferry drifted aimlessly on the storm-tossed lake past the dock, while its pilot was struggling to keep afloat. Paddling strenuously, the Hardys swung about to the rescue.

Swiftly the bateau closed the gap. The ferry passengers, two women, huddled panic-stricken in their car.

"You fellows get the pilot!" Frank said, flipping his paddle to Chet. "I'm going for the boat."

In a flash he was overboard and swimming through the choppy waves. Finally he managed to grasp the end of the ferry barge and pull himself aboard. Frank ran past the car, tore into the pilot's cabin of the tug, and spun the wheel hard to the left.

He realized cutting the motor would be dangerous, since the heavy craft would only drift farther.

Determinedly, he steered against the strong current.

At first it seemed useless. Then, slowly, the ferry backed toward the cable area, where Frank swung her to the right and headed for the far dock.

Just before reaching it, Frank cut the engine. Three men quickly secured the ferry and raced into the pilot's cabin.

"Young fellow—we can't thank you enough!" one of them said to Frank. "There could have been a tragic accident."

The women, shaken and pale, added their praise, then were helped ashore.

Frank peered worriedly out over the wind-driven water. To his relief he saw the bateau, with Joe and Chet paddling and the pilot safely aboard, plowing crosscurrent. When they pulled in, all three boys were warmly congratulated.

"Your presence of mind saved us all!" the pilot said gratefully.

Trying to determine what had happened, two of the dockworkers began reeling in the cable sections attached to the pier.

"How could they have broken so suddenly?" Chet asked, as the ends of the cables came to view. To everyone's astonishment, there was no sign of fraying.

"The cables were cut!" Joe cried out.

The pilot and dockers agreed. They said that

the ferry had run for years without a cable break-down. "I'm afraid," said the pilot, "it'll be some time before we're able to repair the damage."

After local authorities had been notified, the pilot insisted on driving the boys back to Mill-

wood. He located a boat trailer on which to tow the bateau.

During the trip they discussed the accident. Who could have cut the ferry cables? Was there any connection between this, the art thefts, and the other strange occurrences?

"It'll probably cut down the turnout at our exhibit tomorrow." Chet sighed gloomily.

"It sure didn't help our treasure search," Joe murmured.

Once back in their room, and after a hot shower, the boys felt less despondent. Frank sug-

gested that he and Joe offer to act as guides at Senandaga. "It'll give us a chance to look around inside the fort," he added.

They consulted with Uncle Jim, who was shocked to learn of the ferry mishap. He readily agreed to the Hardys' proposal and was sure Mr. Davenport would concur.

The exhausted sleuths then went to bed. "At least," thought Chet in satisfaction as he dozed off, "my painting is ready."

When Joe woke the next morning he hopped to the window. "The sun's out!" he exclaimed. "Wake up, fellows!"

After breakfast the Hardys wished Chet luck as he hurried off with his painting. The entire school grounds were devoted to the display. Some students hung their watercolors and oils on a long wooden backing sheltered by a red-striped awning. Other paintings stood on easels scattered about the lawn. The sculpture entries were displayed on several long benches near the judges' table.

Meanwhile, the Hardys were ready to tackle their job at the fort. They had decided to go in the bateau. Heading for the lake, they met Mr. Davenport, dressed impeccably in a white summer suit. He was in good spirits.

"Happy Senandaga Day, boys!" he drawled. "Great idea you two being guides." Frowning slightly, he cautioned them to admit the tourists only in groups and to keep them at the ground level of the fort ruins.

"Safer that way," he said. "Also, less chance for someone to sneak off alone and look for the treasure."

"We'll do our best," Frank promised.

Soon the brothers were paddling downlake in the bateau. They passed several canoes and motorboats heading in the direction of Millwood.

"Looks as if the ferry accident may not affect attendance too much," Joe said.

Rounding the promontory, the Hardys looked up at the flagpole over the sprawling, gray fortress. They could not believe their eyes. A banner fluttered from the staff, but this one bore three crosses, two red and one white on a field of blue.

"It's the British Union Jack!" Frank exclaimed.

Quickly the boys poled into a cove at the foot of the fort and beached their craft. They scrambled up a steep path and made their way around to the moss-covered entrance passageway in the north wall.

The brothers hurried through it and found themselves on the old parade grounds. Around the sides stood the ruins of two barracks and the officers' quarters. In the center was a deep hole which, according to their map, had once been a well. As a precaution, they placed some old planks over it.

The Hardys once more stared up at the British flag.

"Well," said Frank, "if there's a ghost prowling around Senandaga, now's the time to track him down. Visitors will be arriving soon."

They walked about the massive, crumbling interior. After circling the parapets, the boys reached the south demilune by a wooden drawbridge, which Mr. Davenport had had reconstructed. After checking the west demilune, they headed back through the entrance tunnel.

"No flag-raising ghosts so far," Joe quipped as they walked inland to unlock the promontory gate.

"The ramparts seem safe enough," Frank observed, "but the west demilune, dungeons, and stores are in bad shape. They'll have to be off limits."

Soon a trickle of tourists began. Frank and Joe took turns meeting them at the gate and escorting them, careful to keep the visitors in groups. After a while the sightseers swelled in number. Several times the Hardys were asked about the ghost rumors, and also about the British flag. The brothers would grin, merely saying these were mysteries no one had yet solved.

Frank and Joe were kept so busy they had little opportunity to look for any tomahawk marking. At noon they hastily ate sandwiches they had brought, then resumed their job. Later, Jim Kenyon stopped in to see how they were faring.

"Business here is fine," Frank reported. "How is the exhibit doing—and Chet?"

"We have a good crowd. And my nephew's as happy as a lark. His painting has attracted a lot of attention." Uncle Jim left, reminding the Hardys that the judging would be at seven o'clock.

"We'll be there," Joe said.

During the afternoon the boys overheard some of the visitors commenting on the Millwood exhibit. One elderly lady said to her companion, "That still life by that Morton boy is striking!" The Hardys exchanged grins.

They found most people to be impressed by the brooding majesty of the Senandaga ruins and several spoke in favor of the fort's being restored.

Minutes before closing time, Frank led the last tour around the fort. Suddenly, from the ramp, he noticed a boy of about six make a beeline for the fort well. Frank saw with horror that the boards no longer covered it, but had been shifted to one side!

"That's dangerous—stop!" he shouted, running down the ramp.

But the child ignored the warning and leaned far over the yawning hole. A cry broke from the boy's lips as he lost his balance. Frank just managed to yank him to safety. He patted the youngster's head reassuringly as the frightened mother dashed up.

"I'm sorry," Frank said. "We had these boards over the hole. They were moved."

The woman thanked Frank and quickly led her son away.

When the last visitor had left, the Hardys went over to the well. Each wondered the same thing:

Had somebody moved the boards on purpose, hoping to cause an accident? If so, was it the work of the same enemy?

"I sure wish we could wait for sundown to see if anybody lowers that flag," said Joe.

"So do I. But we promised to be back. Chet will be disappointed if we don't show up."

It was now a little before six o'clock. They hurried down and set off in the bateau. Poling off, they looked back at Fort Senandaga. The Union Jack was still waving from the mast.

"I wonder," Frank said, "if these flags popping up have some connection with Senandaga Day— and that mysterious battle."

"Could be."

As soon as they had landed at the Millwood beach, the Hardys sought out Chet among the throng of visitors and art students.

They spotted him under a tree, and were astonished to see Chet, looking dejected, lifting his canvas from the easel.

"Why so glum, pal?" Frank greeted him. "We heard you were a big hit!"

Chet's face grew longer. "It was swell until just this minute," he mumbled. "I went to get some lemonade. While I was gone—"

Unable to finish, Chet swallowed and held up his painting. Frank and Joe gasped. What had been a still life of purple grapes in a yellow basket was smeared with blobs of dripping, green paint!

CHAPTER XIV

Lucky Watermelon

"My painting's ruined!" Chet looked sadly at the ugly blotches on the canvas.

"That's a dirty trick!" Joe said, as Frank looked around angrily for possible suspects.

"What about Ronnie Rush?" Joe asked. "I wouldn't put it past him, especially if he was jealous of the hit your painting made."

At the moment Ronnie was not in sight. Frank had an idea. "Chet! You've still got a little time before the judges arrive. Maybe you can fix up the picture."

Chet seemed doubtful, but Joe quickly joined in to raise his hopes. "Look—only the grapes in the center are ruined—the rest is okay. You could make those green paint blobs into something else!"

"Maybe you're right!" Chet acknowledged,

brightening. "I'll try it!" Carrying his canvas, he trotted excitedly toward the painting studio.

"What a blow for Chet!" Frank commented.

Joe agreed. "He was really crushed."

The Hardys met Uncle Jim. His face fell when they told him of the prank, but he was reassured on hearing of Chet's last-minute attempt. "I'll run over and try to keep up his inspiration!"

The Hardys then saw Mr. Davenport at the sheltered exhibit area, and went over. The elderly patron was walking from one canvas to the next. He spoke volubly, proudly commending his students.

"Well constructed, Bob, good attack!" he told one smiling boy, and moved on to a large, historical battle scene done by another youth.

"Excellent subject, Cliff! You've got your figures well deployed!" Twirling his cane happily, he proceeded to another entry. Next to it, looking nervous, stood a blond-haired girl. Her entry was an imaginative view of the Millwood mansion.

"Good thickness of paint there, Ellen." Mr. Davenport beamed. "Invulnerably designed!"

Joe chuckled. "He sounds as if he's talking about the construction of a fort!"

Frank laughed, but quickly became grim. He pointed to a knoll some distance away.

Ronnie Rush stood on the slope near two easels. He had a garish painting displayed on each. The Hardys hurried up to him.

"Say, what happened to your fat friend?" he asked, smirking. "He get cold feet and withdraw from the exhibit?"

"Not yet," Frank said coldly. "Do you know who messed up Chet's painting?"

The smug look on Ronnie's face turned to one of anxiety but only for a moment. He sniggered. "Fatso probably messed it up himself." He pointed to his canvases. "The judges will know *good* stuff when they see it. Say," he added abruptly, "why are you two cruising around in that weird boat, anyhow?"

"Part of our research," Joe replied tersely. By now it was almost seven o'clock, and the Hardys wondered how Chet was making out. They started for the studio and met Chet coming out, his canvas grasped carefully in both hands.

"Any luck?" Joe asked eagerly.

"I hope so." Chet held out his revised painting.

The yellow basket now contained a large, green, elliptical fruit. Below was the title—"Still Life of a Watermelon in a Basket."

Frank and Joe praised their friend's ingenuity. "It looks good enough to eat, Chet!" Frank grinned.

For the next hour four men judges viewed the paintings and sculptures, frequently jotting down notes.

The Hardys diverted Chet somewhat by telling of their experiences at the fort that day. The plump boy grew tense, however, as the judges paused at his easel. Inscrutably they eyed the still life, scribbled on their pads, and passed on to the next painting. Chet shrugged. "Guess I don't have a chance."

An air of anticipation hushed the crowd as the judges returned to their table and conferred privately. Finally they handed a sheet of paper to Jim Kenyon, who announced:

"Ladies and gentlemen, we're ready to award the prizes."

The crowd surged close, and waited silently. First, the sculpture awards were read by René Follette. Mr. Davenport stood next to the prize table and handed out a ribbon and a gift to the three winners.

Uncle Jim stepped forward to give the painting awards.

"Boy, even I've got butterflies—they're coming out of my ears!" Joe whispered.

"First prize for the best watercolor goes to 'Night Crossing' by Carol Allen."

Applause accompanied each announcement as the lucky students accepted a ribbon and a gift. A smile crossed the instructor's face.

"And finally, first prize for the most original work, in all categories, goes to 'Still Life of a Watermelon in a Basket' by Chester Morton!"

Chet was speechless with delighted surprise.

"Go ahead, pal!" the elated Hardys shouted

above the applause, slapping their friend on the back.

Proudly Chet went forward to receive handshakes from both his uncle and Mr. Davenport. Several students congratulated him warmly as he squeezed his way back to Frank and Joe.

"Look what I got—a complete oil-paint set!" He beamed, cradling a large wooden box in his arms. "Thanks a lot, fellows, for your encouragement."

Joe could not resist a pun. "We knew it'd just be a matter of time before something tickled your palette!"

The three Bayporters laughed.

"O-oh, look who's coming," Frank said as Ronnie Rush pushed through the crowd. His name had not been among the prize winners and his face showed it.

He glared resentfully at Chet. "Just plain dumb luck, fatso!" Ronnie kicked at a rock and marched angrily up the hill.

"What a poor loser!" Joe said.

"Maybe I should have thanked him," Chet said, "if he did try to make trouble for me."

"Speaking of trouble," Joe said tersely, "look at what's coming." He pointed to the lake where a cabin cruiser was anchored a little way beyond the promontory. Standing on deck was Chauncey Gilman! Then the pilot rowed him to the beach and helped Gilman step ashore.

The critic, as elegantly dressed as before, moved disdainfully through the throng. The Hardys and Chet watched as Uncle Jim greeted the newcomer guardedly. Mr. Davenport followed, clearly exerting all his will power to keep calm. "I trust, sir," he said in a formal manner, "you will be fair in your review."

"Fair?" Gilman repeated loftily. "Why, the only way I could be fair to your juveniles' exhibit would be to shut my eyes!"

With a shrill laugh, he moved away and began viewing the student paintings. Mr. Davenport, scowling, trailed behind, accompanied by Jim and the three boys. Gilman paused at the painting which had taken the first prize.

"My, my. If this is one of the best, what *must* the worst be!"

With apprehension, the boys watched Gilman proceed, audibly abusing the paintings and sculptures one after another.

"Tsk! Tsk! Who victimized *this* canvas?" He pointed at a landscape done in watercolor. The girl who had painted it seemed on the verge of tears.

When he came to Chet's still life, the reviewer burst into high-pitched laughter.

"Oh, priceless, priceless! The blue ribbon must be from a fruit market!"

Although annoyed, Chet was not greatly upset

by Gilman's remark, and Uncle Jim said, "The judges thought the exhibition today was one of the finest they had ever seen. The worst thing," he added, "is that Gilman's derogatory comments about Millwood will be printed."

Mr. Davenport had been unusually quiet. The boys noticed a peculiar expression on his face as Chauncey Gilman closed his notebook and said, "Thank you all for a most entertaining evening. Better luck next year!"

As Gilman strutted toward his rowboat, Mr. Davenport whispered to Jim Kenyon. The instructor, looking puzzled, called for everyone's attention. "Mr. Davenport wants us all to go right out to the promontory," Uncle Jim announced. "It's a surprise."

The group, sensing something unusual afoot, soon gathered at the end of the dusky headland. Gilman's rowboat could be seen approaching the lighted cruiser.

The Hardys and Chet were surprised to see Mr. Ashbach crouched beneath them on the bank, and, at some distance to the right, Mr. Davenport, also bending low. Each man held the end of a wire!

Gilman's droning laugh could be heard over the splash of the oars. Then, at a signal from the millionaire, Mr. Ashbach began pulling his wire.

The next moment a luminous serpent's head

with gleaming white teeth broke the surface just ahead of the rowboat! Writhing, it headed for the craft.

Gilman shot up out of his seat, giving a shriek of terror.

"A m-monster! It's—it's a monster! Rogers! Help! Rogers!" he blubbered. "Save me!"

CHAPTER XV

An Eerie Vigil

THE hideous serpent bumped violently into the rowboat. With howls of horror, Chauncey Gilman and his pilot were pitched overboard. They floundered wildly in the lake, and the soggy notebook sank out of sight.

As the glistening monster hove from the water toward them, Gilman and the boatman splashed furiously for the cabin cruiser.

The group gathered on the promontory rocked with laughter. Doubled up with mirth, the Hardys, Chet, and Uncle Jim saw a grinning Mr. Davenport finally relax his wire, and the carpenter did the same.

"So the 'monster' was constructed just for Chauncey Gilman!" Joe said as the millionaire climbed up to join them.

"Yes, siree. And I'll see that he reads a detailed account—*in print*," declared Mr. Davenport.

Happily, the group dispersed for the night. All the next day the Millwood grounds echoed with laughter at the successful serpent scare.

Monday morning, as Frank hung up the phone in the mansion hallway, Joe asked, "Any word on Adrian Copler?"

"Not a thing," Frank reported. "The chief says Copler's done a complete vanishing job. The police did find an unrusted hacksaw underwater near where the ferry cables were cut. They're following that clue."

Frank also had learned that a statewide check was being made on art dealers for the stolen fort paintings.

Chet, having just finished breakfast, joined the brothers. "Well," he said as they went outside, "what's for today?"

"A camp-out tonight," Joe said promptly.

"Great!" Chet responded. "Where?"

"Senandaga."

"S-Senandaga?" Chet gulped. "Of all places to pick!"

Frank grinned. "Chet, you may have a chance to paint some ghosts." He added seriously, "We've got to unearth that tomahawk clue before somebody else does."

"You're right."

The Bayporters went into Cedartown to buy food and other necessary supplies. Finding no hardware store, they went to the sport shop. Myles

Warren was not there, but a crew-cut youth waited on them. With difficulty, he finally located three folding-type spades.

"Sorry for the delay," he apologized. "Don't know the stock as well as Mr. Warren."

"Is he on vacation?" Frank asked.

"No, but several days a week he goes out to do some painting. Can I get you anything else?"

The boys picked out three high-beam flashlights, sleeping bags, and a scout knife. "Guess that's all," Joe said.

"Where are you fellows going to camp?" asked the clerk.

"Probably down at the south end of the lake," Frank replied noncommittally.

The clerk shook his head. "You wouldn't catch me in that neck of the woods. From what I hear about that fort, I'd keep as far away as I could. But—good luck."

After informing Uncle Jim and Mr. Davenport of their camping plan, the boys loaded up the bateau. Swiftly they pushed off and headed south. When the fort came into view, they glanced at the flagpole. The Union Jack was gone.

Joe stopped paddling. "That's weird," he said. "First French, then British, now none!"

"Whoever put them up," said Frank, "may come by boat. He'd have an easier time getting in than climbing the fence."

"By boat," Joe repeated.

The brothers exchanged glances. "You two have an idea," Chet said knowingly. "What is it?"

Frank reminded him of the wet rowboat on Turtle Island, which contradicted the hermit's claim that he had not left the island for a month. "He was mighty opposed to the French claims at Senandaga," Frank recalled. "And don't forget his true account of—Fort Royal. He might have raised the Union Jack."

The bateau was guided past protruding rocks, and into the cove. The boys landed and climbed up to the old fort.

"We might as well start on the outside," Frank suggested, referring to the map. "If you see anything resembling a tomahawk, let out a war whoop."

The boys split up, each taking a designated area of the stone perimeter. They moved slowly along the shallow ditch, inspecting the huge stone blocks as far up the wall as the eye could see.

The task seemed endless and tedious, but they could not afford to dismiss the possibility of finding clues lying outside the fort.

Several hours later Joe called to Chet, "Any luck?"

A fatigued voice echoed from around a bend in the wall. "No. I think I'm going to be counting stones in my sleep."

The young sleuths paused to eat a sandwich, then resumed their search. The afternoon sun grew hotter by the hour. Twice they took breaks at the lakeside, refreshing themselves from canteens.

"There must be a million square miles of stone in this fort." Chet sighed, cooling his bare feet in the water.

A little later first Joe, then Chet, came upon freshly dug and refilled holes outside the ditch.

"Someone else is still searching," Joe remarked.

Suddenly Chet glimpsed a figure watching them from the wooded shore below.

"Ronnie Rush!"

They started toward the student. He turned and disappeared into the woods.

"Snooping again," Joe said. "Maybe he dug these holes."

They decided not to waste time in pursuit—Ronnie had too much of a head start.

It was late afternoon before the boys had finished examining the wall sections still standing. No luck. There were piles of fallen masonry they had not even touched.

"It'll take us days to go through them," Frank said. "I think tomorrow we should concentrate on the inside."

"Whew! I'm bushed—and empty!" Chet declared. "Let's pitch camp and cook up some grub."

The boys decided not to build their campfire near the fort. "No use advertising our presence," Joe said.

As they started down to the bateau, Frank's foot struck something metallic.

"Look!"

Reaching down, he picked up a wooden-handled, chisel-like tool. There were traces of clay on the blade, which was only slightly rusted.

"It's a sculpture knife!" Frank said, turning it over in his hand. He detected two letters scratched on the wood—R. F.

"The owner's initials."

"René Follette, the French sculptor!" Joe burst out. "I wonder what he was doing here!"

"And he believes in Chambord's gold chain," Chet put in. "Except he thinks the British took it. Wow! I'm mixed up!"

Frank said decisively, "We're going to have a talk with Mr. Follette when we get back tomorrow."

Tired and hungry, they set off in the bateau. Reaching a point on the shore beyond the promontory, Joe spotted a small clearing inland. Quickly they tied up and soon had a fire going. The hungry boys thoroughly enjoyed a simple meal of frankfurters and beans. When the sun had dropped behind the western hills, they doused the fire and pushed off in the bateau.

A chilling wind rolled down the lake as they neared the fort, its massive, jagged hulk outlined against the night sky.

The Hardys paddled cautiously between the outjutting rocks and pulled ashore. Carrying sleeping bags and flashlights, they crept up the slope.

Some fifty yards from the western rampart, they set their gear down behind a thorn apple tree. From here they could also keep watch on the bateau.

For a long time the trio kept their eyes fixed on the fort, alert for any moving figure or signs of activity. Their ears strained for any suspicious sound, such as the clank of shovels or picks.

Only the noise of summer insects broke the silence. Chet shifted to a more comfortable position.

"Don't even hear a drumbeat," he said in a reassured tone.

The Hardys were beginning to feel discouraged when Chet whispered, "What's that?" He inched closer to his pals. "L-listen!"

The boughs above them thrashed in a gust of wind. But the Hardys could also hear a hollow, echoing, breathlike sound from the fort!

"Maybe only wind—along the moat," Frank

reasoned, listening as the wind died down. The strange sound subsided, but was still audible.

"Wind! I've never heard wind like that!" Joe whispered. "Unless it's coming through the holes and notches in the walls. It sounds like a seashell when you hold it up to your ear."

"I know what it is—a ghost breathing!" Chet muttered.

The vigil continued until the boys' eyes ached. Finally the three campers decided to sleep in turns. Past midnight, the wind became stronger and the moon broke through the clouds.

As it did, Frank tensed at a strange image on the fort wall. It looked like a skull!

But it proved to be only an area of gutted masonry with spaces resembling eye sockets and teeth.

Later, Chet took his turn on watch and propped himself against the apple tree. "So far nothing suspicious," he thought, relaxing. One second later he suddenly froze.

Thump! Thump! Drumbeats!

His breath locked tight, Chet sat up, trying to detect the direction of the sound.

Thump! Silence. *Thump!*

Frantically he shook Frank and Joe, who bolted awake. "What is it?"

Above the sighing wind, the Hardys clearly heard the drumbeats. They were not coming from the fort but from somewhere near the lake!

Leaping to their feet, they looked down the moonlit water. Frank scanned the calm expanse.

"Look—out there!"

A hooded black figure was gliding toward shore!

Joe, unable to believe what he saw, was the first to gasp.

"It's a g-ghost—walking on the water!"

CHAPTER XVI

The Deserted Cottage

THE black, billowing figure glided over the moonlit lake, its wind-blown shroud trailing a shimmering shadow.

For moments Frank, Joe, and Chet remained transfixed until Joe cried, "Come on!"

The Hardys raced down the slope. Chet, although shaking with fear, stumbled after them.

The ghost, its draped arms outstretched, was already nearing shore. The boys saw it disappear beneath overhanging trees beyond the fort promontory.

They ran back for flashlights, then hurried downhill to the area where the specter had vanished. But it was nowhere to be seen.

"I still don't believe it!" Frank said. "Maybe I was just having a nightmare."

"Not unless we all had the same one," Joe said. "We all saw that—*thing*."

"But—walking on water!" Chet exclaimed, shivering. "Nobody'll believe us."

"Listen—the drumbeats have stopped!" Frank said. They checked the bateau, found nothing disturbed, and returned to their post on the slope.

Hoping to get another glimpse of the ghost, all three remained awake for some time. But the phantom did not reappear. Near dawn the boys finally fell asleep.

They awoke several hours later, took a dip in the lake, and had breakfast. A search along the shore turned up no clues. Eager to report their experience, they returned to Millwood. Mr. Davenport and Uncle Jim were incredulous when they related their ghost story.

The art patron looked hard at the boys. "You all aren't pulling an old Confederate's leg, are you?"

"Oh, no! We saw it. Honest!" Chet said earnestly.

"Sir," said Joe, "this ghost walker wasn't another—er—lake monster, was it?"

"No. At least, not mine."

"We'll keep at our investigation," Frank assured him.

Later in the morning they told Uncle Jim about seeing Ronnie Rush near the fort. The instructor said that Ronnie had not appeared for any of his classes the day before. "Maybe he's still sore about losing out at the exhibit," said Joe. "But I wouldn't be surprised if he's after the fort treasure himself."

The boys then showed Uncle Jim the sculpting tool. "It may be Follette's," he said. "I'd like to go with you to see him, but I'm getting ready for a class."

He filled two bowls from a glass turpentine container, then placed several brushes in one. He was about to dip his paint-covered hands into the other when Joe dashed over and grabbed his wrists.

"Don't!"

"What's the matter?"

Joe pointed to the bowl containing the brushes. "Look!"

Faint smoke rose from it. They all could see the brushes disintegrating!

"That's not turpentine—it's an acid!" Frank cried out.

Mr. Kenyon sniffed the liquid. "You're right! Somebody must have put it in the turpentine bottle during the night!"

"Could it have been just a mistake?" Chet asked.

"I'm afraid not. I've never had any reason to keep acid here." He thanked Joe for his quick action, then asked the Hardys, "Do you think whoever did this caused the other accidents and left the shotgun warning?"

"Yes," Frank said. "Or else a confederate. But I doubt that any of the students are involved except maybe Ronnie Rush."

Joe looked thoughtful. "One thing is sure. It's someone who knows his way around here—night or day." The Hardys and Chet left, and went to the sculpture studio. They drew René Follette aside and showed him the initialed tool.

"Yes, yes, it is mine!" he said readily. "It has been missing—oh, maybe two days. Where did you find it?"

The sculptor gave a start when the boys mentioned the mysterious flags at Senandaga but denied any knowledge of them.

Feeling it wise not to reveal details of their visits to Senandaga, the boys left. Outside, Frank said, "Follette didn't act guilty. Perhaps someone stole his knife."

The Hardys debated their next move, eventually deciding to do some detecting on the property of both Gilman and the English hermit.

"I still think there's something fishy about Everett's wet boat."

"And Gilman," Joe added. "He might have had his own reasons for getting hold of the Davenport paintings!"

They divided forces. Joe and Chet would go in the bateau to scout Turtle Island. Frank got permission to borrow the limousine to visit Gilman's estate.

"Here are the keys, sir," said Alex, outside the mansion garage.

Frank thanked him and soon was driving north. He parked in a wooded spot, and trudged along the overgrown shore. Soon he reached the Gilman property.

The Tudor house, as well as the lake-front patio, looked deserted. Circling the grounds convinced Frank that Gilman was not at home.

His ears keen for the sound of a car on the driveway, Frank peered into first-floor windows. If Gilman were behind the gallery thefts, where might he hide the paintings?

"The attic or the cellar!" Frank thought, wishing it were possible to search these places.

He found the garage open and looked around inside. Nothing suspicious there. Next, Frank pressed his face against a cellar window but saw only garden furniture, tools, and piles of old newspapers. Feeling thwarted, Frank then walked to the lake front. Through a grove of willows to the right, he noticed a boathouse and a long dock.

"I'll check there," he decided, and followed a path through the woods. Suddenly Frank heard footsteps behind him. He was about to spin around when he was struck hard on the head.

Frank's legs turned to rubber and everything went black.

He had no idea how much time had passed when he came to with a throbbing headache.

Sensations spun through his consciousness . . . a strong, acrid smell . . . hushed voices . . . echoing . . . a feeling of being adrift.

Suddenly he felt a trickle of water on his face. Frank opened his eyes to darkness. He was encased in something made of metal.

Then he saw jagged holes of light above his head. A chill of horror jolted him!

He was trapped in a steel barrel!

Frantically, Frank tried to turn over. But the container rolled with his movement, forcing water in through the holes.

The steel drum was sinking in the lake!

CHAPTER XVII

The Accused

FRANK kicked at the bottom of the container, then gagged as water rose over his chin.

Sputtering, he pounded his heels against the steel, but it was no use!

In a last desperate effort Frank gave a mighty push upward with his head and hands. The top gave a little. He pushed again, this time loosening the lid enough to free himself. His lungs at the bursting point, Frank swam away from the sinking trap and shot to the surface.

Gasping and gulping in air, he found himself about fifty yards offshore from the limousine.

No boats were in sight as he made it to the shore and collapsed, exhausted. As soon as his strength returned, he stood up and looked about for signs of his attackers. "Maybe someone is hiding in the boathouse," he thought. Frank headed for the building, moving with caution. Finding the padlock open, he slipped inside.

Gilman's lavish craft swayed gently in its berth. Frank peered about the dim interior but saw no one lurking in the shadows. He kicked at a tarpaulin, uncovering a pile of wood molding. "Wonder what they're for," he mused, and picked up several pieces. Underneath lay a familiar-looking, ridged strip. It had a diamond-shaped corner!

"It's part of an old fort frame!" Other fragments also appeared to be from the Prisoner-Painter's originals. "Gilman!"

The evidence pointed to the critic as the thief. But Frank was puzzled. Would Gilman have gone so far as to try to drown him?

"The police should know about this immediately," he decided, covering the frames. He ran to the limousine and drove directly to the school. He called the chief, who sent officers Bilton and Turner to meet him at Gilman's. After changing clothes, Frank went back to the critic's house. To his surprise, Gilman was there.

"What is the meaning of this?" the owner demanded as Frank and the policemen approached.

"We'd like to take a look inside your boathouse," said Officer Turner. He showed a search warrant.

Gilman climbed to his feet, his face a mixture of alarm and bewilderment. "Why? What—?"

"Because this young man tells us some stolen property is in there."

"Which I discovered," Frank added, "after

someone knocked me out and tried to sink me in a steel drum."

Gilman was flabbergasted. "I'm not guilty of such a terrible thing," he protested. "I'll have you know I am a reputable citizen."

"Come along with us," Officer Turner ordered.

Inside the boathouse, Frank pointed out the diamond-shaped piece of wood. "Recognize that, Mr. Gilman?"

"Of course. It looks like an original frame for a Davenport painting."

"Yes. A stolen frame," Frank challenged. "Maybe you can tell us what it's doing in your boathouse?"

The critic threw up his hands. "I don't know how any of this wood got in here. I am innocent of these hideous accusations. My driver, who also pilots the cruiser, can testify to that. He's been with me for the last few hours."

The driver was questioned closely. He provided a perfect alibi and vehemently denied any part in the attack on Frank. He also maintained that the stack of wood had not been in the boathouse earlier that day.

After searching the premises for the stolen paintings, the officers decided to recover the drum. Frank offered to dive for it, so the three took the rowboat to the spot where he had surfaced. Stripping to his shorts, Frank plunged overboard and streaked downward. Fortunately the water was clear, and he soon spotted the drum, and the lid near it, resting on the sandy bottom at a depth of ten feet.

When Frank bobbed up bearing the evidence, he was helped aboard and the trio returned to the boathouse. The critic paled when he saw his address printed on the side of the drum. "That contained insecticide," he said. "We used up the last of it a week ago."

Gilman looked completely deflated and his chin slumped to his chest. "I didn't have anything to do with this fiendish thing," he muttered.

The officers ordered him not to leave the premises. "You'll have to stay here until we find out the truth," said Turner. He and Bilton took the container and pieces of frame as evidence. By now, Frank had dried off in the hot sun and dressed, so they drove back in the limousine.

"You're lucky to be alive," Bilton remarked.

Frank nodded. "I'm thankful that lid wasn't put on any tighter," he replied. He remembered the voices he had heard just before sinking. "There must have been two men at least."

"At any rate, this is pretty heavy evidence against Gilman," said Turner.

Chet, Joe, Uncle Jim, and Mr. Davenport were first stunned, then angered upon hearing of Frank's experience. He had told them his story in the art patron's study. The elderly Southerner kept muttering, "I know Chauncey Gilman's dead set against me—but this—incredible."

"I feel the same way," Frank said. "I don't believe he's to blame."

Joe agreed. "If Mr. Gilman was so shook up by a fake monster," he said wryly, "I can't see him having the nerve to do anything criminal."

"How about the paintings?" Jim Kenyon asked.

"Not a sign," Frank replied.

"Do you think Gilman knows anything about that ghost we saw last night?" Chet put in.

Frank shrugged. "Remember, Adrian Copler's still at large, and his partners. If we only had some leads to their identity!"

Joe reported that he and Chet had found Turtle Island deserted. Everett and his rowboat were gone. There was no trace of the stolen paintings.

"His dog was there, but chained up, lucky for us," Chet added.

Mr. Davenport declared he himself would visit Chauncey Gilman that afternoon. "I don't like him, but I won't judge him guilty till it's proved."

The boys had a late lunch, after which Frank suggested revisiting the fort. "We can give the interior a good going-over this time," he said.

Jim Kenyon offered to accompany the boys, since he had the afternoon free.

"Swell," said Joe. "We could use a hand combing the fort."

After getting some digging tools, they climbed into the bateau and set off. When they reached Senandaga, the foursome went directly through the entrance tunnel. Pausing in the middle of the parade ground, Frank took out their map.

"Let's see. We're facing south." He pointed to a long, roofless building to his right. "That must be the West Barracks—"

"Or what's left of it," Chet interrupted.

"—And the ruin behind us—here—the North Barracks. This building to our left was for officers. Other than the two demilunes outside, the four corner bastions, and the ramparts themselves, that's the setup aboveground."

"How about the dungeons?" Joe asked. "Jason Davenport must have been kept prisoner in one."

Frank turned the map around. "They were under the West Barracks." They walked over to the stone structure, which rose just above the rampart. Rubble clogged an entrance which evidently led underground.

"It'll be a job getting down there," Frank said.

"Of course General Davenport likely had the run of the fort," Mr. Kenyon reminded them. "He could have found the *chaîne d'or* anywhere."

They decided to comb the barrack ruins first, Frank taking the one to the west, Joe the old officers' building, and Chet and Uncle Jim the North Barracks.

Originally three-storied, these were now little more than shells with empty window and door frames. Two bleak chimneys remained standing.

Joe climbed through a broken wall section and began searching among the chunks of stone and mortar, most of it from the fallen upper floor.

Hours passed as the boys and Jim worked. Senandaga echoed with the sound of shovels and shifting stones. Each began to doubt the clue could ever be found. What if it were hopelessly buried?

"Look, here's an old sword blade!" Frank called out.

"Great!" Chet responded. "We just found a rusted grapeshot rack!"

Joe later uncovered a wooden canteen almost intact. But none of them saw anything resembling a tomahawk or a chain. Finally the weary searchers took a break, relaxing on the shore near the bateau.

Suddenly they were startled by men's angry shouts from inside the fort!

Frank and Joe, followed by Chet and his uncle, ran up the slope and through the tunnel, then halted in amazement.

At one side of the parade ground, two men were furiously exchanging blows!

CHAPTER XVIII

A Sudden Disappearance

"RENÉ FOLLETTE and Lloyd Everett!" cried Frank in astonishment.

The Hardys, Chet, and Jim Kenyon rushed over and separated the fighting men. Mr. Kenyon silenced them. "What's this all about, René?"

"This hermit—he insults my ancestor, the great Marquis de Chambord!"

Everett snorted. "Who was brought to heel by *my* forebear, Lord Craig!"

"Then it's *you* two who have been raising the French and British flags," Frank declared.

Reluctantly, first Everett, then Follette admitted having done so to have his country's flag flying for Senandaga Day. Each man had lowered the other's banner, but neither had been looking for the golden chain. Each had, however, come at various times to search for proof of his ancestor's victory.

René grunted. "You, Everett, struck me unconscious last Tuesday!"

"Utter nonsense! Besides—you struck *me* cold yesterday!"

"A lie!"

The Hardys exchanged glances. Who had knocked out the Englishman and the sculptor? Frank asked them if they had seen a black-robed "ghost" around the fort.

"Ghost, no!" Follette waved emphatically. "But I still feel that blow on my head!"

Jim Kenyon, with some difficulty, got the two to shake hands and declare a truce.

After the men had pushed off in their boats, the boys and Uncle Jim resumed their explorations, skirting the ramparts. Frank and Joe noticed small openings at foot level along the entire parapet, evidently rifle ports to reinforce cannon fire. But looking through one, Joe found it obstructed.

"Look!" he called to his brother. "Somebody's wedged a tin can in here! And in the next opening, too!"

Frank found the same thing true along the north rampart.

"This explains the eerie noise of the wind we heard!" he said. "These might have been stuck in to make the spooky sounds!"

Suddenly he knelt down and yanked out a rectangular can from one port. Joe sniffed at the open top. "This held kerosene!" he exclaimed. He pulled the cork from his pocket. It fit perfectly.

Frank held onto the tin. Crouching, the Hardys moved along the notched wall guarding the fort. Bend by bend, they checked for markings or loose stones.

"Let's try the demilunes," Frank urged at last.

They were just crossing the wooden planking to the southern demilune when Chet's voice rang out.

"Frank—Joe—Uncle Jim, come here!"

Rushing down to the end of the North Barracks, the others found Chet holding up a piece of black cloth. Excitedly the Hardys examined it.

"Frank—you think—?"

"It's from the ghost? Could be!"

Jim Kenyon took the torn fragment and rubbed his fingers over the cloth.

He looked at the boys. "If so, your ghost got his costume from Millwood! This is a piece of a painting smock—dyed!"

He pointed out white markings still faintly visible beneath the black dye. They spelled "Mil."

"Wow!" Chet burst out. "You think the phantom is an artist?"

"Whatever he is," Joe said, "how did he walk on water?"

Frank showed Chet and his uncle the kerosene tin, and told of the other cans he and Joe had found. "They look like fruit-juice cans," he added. "Maybe someone bought supplies in Cedartown."

"Like Adrian Copler!" Joe ventured. "Or a crony. I'll bet a cracker that thief is in hiding near Senandaga."

Although disappointed at not unearthing the treasure clue, they felt encouraged by Chet's discovery, and the Hardys planned to try tracing the piece of smock.

They had just pulled up the bateau on the Millwood beach when Alex the chauffeur came running toward them, a troubled expression on his face.

"What's the matter?" asked Uncle Jim.

"Have any of you seen Mr. Davenport?"

They shook their heads. "No, we just came from the fort," Frank answered. "Why?"

"He had me drive him to Mr. Gilman's early this afternoon," Alex reported, worriedly fingering his cap. "Mr. Davenport was to phone me to pick him up before dinnertime. It's past that now, and I haven't heard a word!"

"Do you think something has happened to him?" Joe asked.

"I just telephoned Mr. Gilman. He told me he hasn't seen Mr. Davenport." Alex added that the art patron had gotten out of the car on the road just before the critic's property.

"Could Gilman be lying?" Chet put in.

"Let's find out," Joe urged.

Hastily leaving their gear outside the mansion, the boys jumped in the limousine and drove to Gilman's home. The man appeared completely bewildered. "I don't know what's going on," he whined. "Everything is blamed on me."

A thorough search of the grounds proved futile. There was no sign of Jefferson Davenport. Next the Hardys and Chet made inquiries in town. No one there had seen the man, nor could any of the Millwood students provide the boys with a clue.

By midnight, with still no word on the millionaire, Chet's uncle telephoned headquarters. The chief said a missing-person alarm would be sent out.

Next morning the school buzzed with the news of Mr. Davenport's disappearance. The Hardys felt that there was a strong link between it and the art thefts.

"It could be a desperate move by Copler and his gang to get information about the treasure," Frank said. "I move we check the fort again. If that's their hideout, they may be questioning Mr. Davenport there."

Joe and Chet agreed, and the three hurriedly took off in the bateau.

Once inside Senandaga, they searched for the millionaire. Finding no sign of him aboveground, they decided to tackle the dungeon entrances.

There were two in the West and two in the North Barracks. "Let's try the north first," said Frank. The opening was blocked by what seemed tons of rubble. The old steps were barely visible.

"How'll we ever dig through this stuff!" Chet groaned.

The boys found many of the rocks too large to be moved with shovels. In minutes their faces were covered with perspiration.

They tried the second north entrance. Here they found decayed timber poking out of the rocks. Frank and Chet lifted out a rotting door and set it against a wall.

The diggers proceeded, making a little headway.

Suddenly they heard a splintering thud. The boys whirled to see a hatchet embedded in the old door! It had narrowly missed Frank's head!

"Who threw that?" Joe yelled angrily.

"Look!" Chet quavered, pointing.

They saw, fleeing out the main gateway, a hooded black figure!

The three boys raced in pursuit.

"You two go that way!" Frank yelled, jumping into the ditch and running off to the left. Chet and Joe sped in the opposite direction.

But they circled the fort walls without spotting the ghostly figure. Back at the digging site, Joe pulled the hatchet from the door. "It's an ordinary camping type, but I'm glad we weren't in its way!"

"Who threw that?" Joe yelled angrily

Frank studied the broad blade of the ax, then took out the photostat of the fort map and spread it on the ground.

"What's up?" Joe asked curiously.

"Look at this hatchet," Frank urged, "then at the shape of any side of the fort!"

Joe looked at the eastern rampart on the map as his brother's hand covered one of the corner bastions. "It's like a tomahawk!" he exclaimed. "It must be the clue painted by General Davenport!"

The three boys were greatly excited. "Which side of the fort is the right one, though?" Chet puzzled.

"In the painting the tomahawk was parallel to the west wall! And remember the notches on it near the end of the stock?" said Frank.

"The West Barracks!" Joe said. "The notches must refer to one of the dungeon cells! But that hatchet-throwing ghost—could *he* know about this clue?"

"I doubt it," Frank said. "He was trying to scare us out of this fort, but the joke may be on him. If we're right, he gave us a swell lead. Maybe we can find Mr. Davenport and the treasure too! Come on!"

Grabbing their shovels, the three moved over to the West Barracks, at the entrance nearest the notches shown in the picture. Spurred by renewed hope, they worked furiously.

An hour later Frank managed to wriggle through a hole they had opened in the rubble. Joe and Chet watched tensely as he lowered himself into blackness.

"It's all right!" Frank called.

The others passed the shovels down and joined Frank. Chet squeezed through with the Hardys' help. The boys switched on their flashlights and found themselves in a long, dank corridor, partially filled with debris.

A row of cells extended along the left wall. The Hardys were eager to explore and started for the nearest cell. Together, the boys inspected one dungeon after another, their rotting wood doors sagging on rusty iron hinges.

Frank and Chet were playing their lights on the floor of the fourth cell when Joe shouted behind them. "Look—on the back wall!"

His beam focused on faint scratch marks in the stone.

The boys hurried over. Now they saw the scratches formed a definite shape: a broad blade, notched handle, and an encircling chain—identical to the one in the Davenport painting!

"This must have been the Prisoner-Painter's cell!" Frank exclaimed.

They felt the wall with their fingers. Joe frowned. "Solid as steel," he commented. "How about the floor?"

Frank kicked aside the remains of what had been the prisoner's cot. As his foot touched one of the floor stones, it rattled!

"Joe—a shovel!"

Prodding with the spade, Frank levered the large slab, and the others lifted it out. Their flashlights revealed a gaping hole!

CHAPTER XIX

Dungeon Trap

"IT's not very deep." Frank crouched. "I'll go first."

The Hardys dropped down into the opening and beamed their lights around.

"It's a tunnel!" Joe hissed.

Behind them was a blank stone wall, but ahead stretched the low, dirt passageway. Chet lowered shovels and all three moved forward, ducking their heads.

"Easy—this ceiling doesn't look safe," Frank cautioned. "I don't get it. We're going west, which means the chain must be hidden outside the fort. Why?"

"Beats me," Joe replied.

There appeared to be no turns. Farther on, they were surprised to find the tunnel angling downhill, then realized this was because of the fort ditch above.

Suddenly the trio were brought up short by a wall of dirt. Joe whispered. "Do you think it's the end, or a cave-in?"

Frank probed the sloping earth with his spade. "It looks like a cave-in, and a big one."

The three debated about digging through the dirt barrier.

"We'll be risking another cave-in," Frank said. "If only we knew whether or not this tunnel continues. And if it does, where to."

"Let's chance it," Joe urged.

The Bayport sleuths set their flashlights on the floor and began shoveling with utmost care.

Beneath its hard-packed outer layer, the dirt was loose. The boys dumped spadeful after spadeful to one side. Suddenly they stopped digging, and listened, motionless.

Stealthy footsteps were approaching!

Grabbing a flashlight, Joe swung the beam back down the passage. It fell on the face of a tall, sullen-faced youth.

"Ronnie Rush!"

"Well, I finally caught up to you three. I hitched a ride in a motorboat, and trailed you here at the fort. Did you find the gold chain?"

Ronnie, striding forward defiantly, forgot to duck. His head struck the low ceiling. A thunderous sound followed as the tunnel walls gave way.

"Look out!" Frank cried.

Ronnie leaped ahead. He and the boys went

down beneath a barrage of falling earth. Choking dust filled the tunnel pocket. Joe staggered to his feet and thrust a shovel into the mass of earth. "Frank! We're cut off!"

The Hardys dug furiously, but it was no use. They were sealed in!

"There's not enough air to last the four of us even a couple of hours!" Frank warned. "So every move will have to count."

Chet glowered at Rush, who lay stunned. "If it weren't for you—"

"You really scored this time, Rush," Frank agreed. "But we can't waste air arguing about it."

"I'm—I'm sorry," Ronnie said, contrite for the first time. "I was wrong to snoop, and steal your fort map. I had overheard Mr. Davenport and Mr. Kenyon talking about this treasure, and that you fellows were coming up here and—"

"Conked me to get our map," Joe finished.

Ronnie shook his head, puzzled. "No! I took the map, but I don't know anything about knocking you out—honest!"

As the youth seemed genuinely contrite, the other boys traded glances. If he hadn't struck Joe, who had? Ronnie looked fearfully around at the enclosing walls.

"I just want to say, in case we—we don't get out of here, I—uh—well, I'm really sorry about Chet's painting and all—"

"Right now, you can be our shovel relief," Frank said tersely.

First the boys recovered their flashlights, then dug steadily. When Chet collapsed with fatigue, Rush took up his shovel. The three lights cut bright spears through the small black space. Breathing was difficult and their clothes were drenched from exertion.

"Come on! We've got to get through!" Ronnie panted.

Seconds later, Joe's shovel pierced the barrier and a cool draft hit their hot faces.

"We've made it!" Frank shouted.

The boys clawed rapidly with their tools, cutting a wider opening. Then they ducked through single file and advanced slowly; their flashlights beamed ahead. A short distance farther on was a wall with openings to the right and left.

"I'll bet these are infiltration tunnels!" Joe exclaimed.

They entered the opening to the right, and found it littered with old French weapons, including rusty muskets and three small cannon, but as Frank feared, the tunnel ended in a solid blank wall.

The searchers hastily returned to enter the left-hand opening.

"Frank, how far out from the fort wall do you think we are?" Chet asked.

"Maybe a hundred yards west, probably to the

woods. What an ingenious idea—if Chambord ever did use this for infiltration!"

He recalled Mr. Davenport's mention of the Vauban parallel trenches, once used by attacking armies to close in on fortresses. Had Chambord reversed this idea, building these tunnels for defense?

Fifty yards ahead, they reached another dirt wall.

"There's got to be a way out!" Frank reasoned. "Let's try the wall."

They spread out, and with Chet holding the lights, gently probed the dry earth. Minutes later, a section fell away under Ronnie's shovel.

"Here it is!"

Carefully widening the hole just enough, they ducked quickly through and proceeded down a tunnel heading back toward the fort.

"It's parallel to the other," Joe observed.

Presently they came to the beginning of the passageway—a wall of dirt.

"Funny," said Frank. "The other tunnel started from a stone wall."

Just then Joe flashed his light above and exclaimed, "Look!"

The beam revealed a square slab of stone. Hopefully the boys pushed it up and minutes later climbed out to find themselves in another cell. Covered with grime, the companions trudged along the dungeon corridor, and picked their way through the debris outside the entrance. They emerged on the parade ground again as dusk was falling.

Suddenly Frank spotted a uniformed man standing at the fort entrance. He ran toward them.

"Alex!" Frank cried out.

"Thank goodness you're safe!" the chauffeur exclaimed. "Mr. Davenport has been found. He's with Mr. Kenyon right now!"

"Where?" Frank asked.

"Come with me!" Alex led them across to the North Barracks, where an opening had now been cleared through a dungeon entrance—the same where the boys had started digging before the hatchet was thrown. "Mr. Kenyon found him down here—he's not well!"

Concerned, they slid below, where several lanterns illuminated a dank corridor. The boys stared in amazement at two figures at the far end. One was Jefferson Davenport, propped against the wall with his legs bound. The other was a short, pug-faced man who held a rock over Mr. Davenport's head.

"Adrian Copler!" Joe exclaimed. "Why, you—" Stepping forward, he was blocked by Alex!

"One move, my young Mr. Hardy," he said, smiling coldly, "and Davenport is done for."

As Copler swung the rock menacingly, the

chauffeur thrust Frank back. "All of you—on your stomachs on the floor!"

"Why—you're in with them!" Chet muttered incredulously.

"Shut up!" Alex barked.

The boys exchanged hopeless glances, and in order to spare Mr. Davenport, submitted to being tied hand and foot. Then Alex dragged his four prisoners roughly along and pushed them against the wall a short distance from the millionaire.

"I told you we'd get 'em!" Alex said. "Those snooping Hardys!"

"Good work!"

A hooded black figure appeared out of the shadows. Spellbound, the boys heard a soft laugh, then saw a gloved hand whisk down the hood to reveal a bearded, hawk-nosed face.

Myles Warren!

CHAPTER XX

The Final Link

THE trapped boys stared at Warren in astonishment, hardly able to believe their eyes.

"Then you, Alex, and Copler have been behind the painting thefts *and* the haunted fort!" Joe exclaimed.

"No doubt you're surprised," Warren answered with an irritating air of superiority. "Too bad you had to find out. But you may be able to tell us more than stupid Copler."

The art thief flushed. "Oh, yeah? You haven't been holed up in this miserable dungeon—all because of that worthless junk!"

He jerked a thumb over his shoulder. It was then, in the dimness, that the boys noticed a stack of paintings, some without frames, against the wall farther up the corridor. The stolen fort pictures!

"Shut up!" Warren snapped at his partner. "You talk too much!"

"Alex, it was you who kidnapped Mr. Davenport for the treasure clue," Frank prodded. "Where does Gilman fit in?"

Warren laughed. "He doesn't. After we failed to find any clues in the old frames, we removed several in order to 'frame' Gilman, so to speak." The merchant went on to admit being the ringleader, and that he and Alex had put Frank in the steel drum.

"We didn't intend to drown you," Alex put in. "That's why we didn't put the lid on tight."

The sport-store owner had quickly engineered the fake detour after Alex phoned him that the boys were heading for the fort that night. Warren also had been responsible for the canoe sabotage, as well as the dock fire. It was Alex who had learned the Hardys had been asked to come to Millwood.

"No doubt you, Alex, and Warren stole all the fort paintings from the gallery," Frank said.

Warren nodded, boasting, "Pretty clever I was to get into Millwood by playing the weekend painter bit."

He said that the red paint smear had accidentally been rubbed off from his artist's smock onto the back of the picture while he had been examining it in the gallery.

"And of course you had a swell chance to shotgun that red paint into our room," Joe said.

"Naturally." Warren's eyes glittered. "I trust you remember that message I left."

The Hardys and Chet felt a chill of fear as they recalled the ominous threat.

Ronnie spoke up. "Joe, he must be the one who hit you on the head!"

Warren glared. "And you must be the twerp who beat us to that map!"

"Did you push my car down the slope?" Chet asked. Warren pointed to the chauffeur.

"My orders, of course, though your pal was lucky enough to foul them up. Alex tells me he gave you three quite a runaround in the woods one night."

Not to be outdone, Alex boasted of cutting the ferry cables. "We had to do something to discourage tourist pests. Unfortunately that zany French-man and Everett kept nosing around the fort— they had lumps on their heads to show for it."

"By the way," Copler whined proudly, "those well boards didn't move by themselves. You Hardy pests kept me cooped up that day, but I sneaked out once."

The boys learned that the drumbeats were made by Copler who had used an Indian tom-tom to signal his partners for meetings.

"What have you done to Mr. Davenport?" Frank demanded, worried because of the elderly man's silence and drawn face.

"He hasn't been cooperative." Warren smirked. "He'll get worse treatment if you don't tell us where the gold chain is hidden!"

Even Chet now realized they must spar for time. "One thing still puzzles us," he said, "is how you walked on the lake Monday night. It was great."

"Simple," Warren bragged, holding up two black slotted objects resembling small surfboards. "Water shoes, made of urethane. Copler trimmed 'em down. By the way"—he chuckled—"Alex provided Kenyon with a little acid 'turpentine—' "

"You batted zero out there, Warren," Joe taunted. "We already uncovered that."

Warren became furious. He struck Joe across the face. "Wise guy! What's that painting clue? When you almost dug into our setup here, Copler overheard you say something about a tomahawk —what? Better still, where's that gold chain?"

"We don't know yet—we've been looking in a tunnel," Frank said.

"Tunnel? Where?" Alex demanded. "You've got a lead—out with it!"

The Hardys explained the clue, adding that Warren's hatchet had given them the lead. "The west dungeons, either entrance," Joe said. "There are loose cell stones. One tunnel leads to a cave-in. We can show you."

"No you don't!" Warren said harshly, satisfied with the information. He picked up two lanterns.

"Copler, you stay here and keep your eye on these punks. Alex, we're going for that chain!"

After Warren and the chauffeur had left, Frank racked his brain for a way to escape. Joe looked over and shrugged. Adrian Copler boasted, "You fools should have paid attention to my warning in Bayport. You'll be sorry you didn't!"

A few minutes later Copler began pacing the room nervously. Frank glanced at Mr. Davenport, who winked and signaled the boy closer.

Though bound hand and foot, Frank inched along the floor until he was two feet from the millionaire. Suddenly Davenport moaned and slumped over. In alarm Copler rushed to him.

"Davenport! What's happened? Don't die! Please. Not here!"

All the while Frank was pulling his knees up until he was poised like a spring.

Wham! His feet flew forward and caught Copler on the side of the head. The thief collapsed like an empty sack.

Instantly the millionaire opened his eyes and smiled. "Good work!" He untied Frank, who promptly released the others. As they freed Mr. Davenport's legs, he assured them he was all right. He chuckled. "Some act I put on, eh?"

Ronnie agreed to stay with him while the Hardys and Chet went after Alex and Warren. The Bayporters emerged and crossed the vacant parade ground to the West Barracks. "They could have gone in either one," Frank surmised. "Let's check the first!"

They squirmed below and crept along the silent corridor into the clue-marked cell. Frank switched off his light before dropping soundlessly into the hole at the beginning of the tunnel. Chet followed, then Joe.

They listened carefully before flashing on their beams. The lights hit the barrier of caved-in dirt sixty feet ahead. Nobody in sight.

"They must be in the other tunnel," Joe said, and turned about. "Come on!" But his attention was suddenly caught by a straight fissure in the stone wall at the start of the tunnel. On a sudden hunch Joe grasped a projecting stone edge and he tugged with both hands. Frank did the same. The stone moved slightly. Excited, the Hardys pulled with all their might. Finally a door creaked open!

"What do you know about that!" Chet exclaimed.

Cautiously they stepped inside a paved passageway.

Wondering if they would meet Warren and Alex, the three boys followed the newly found tunnel beneath the fort interior. At its end, they played their flashlights around a large chamber.

Frank spotted a glitter of metal and followed it with his ray. Link by link, a huge gold chain was revealed, hanging majestically around the vault!

"The treasure!" Joe exclaimed. "We've found it!"

"And look at this," said Frank, pointing to a dusty book and tomahawk on a table.

"I knew the Prisoner-Painter had a reason for putting the clue in that one cell!" Joe said.

The boys were curious about the book, but Frank rushed the others back into the passage. "Let's get to that other tunnel!"

They went up to the second dungeon entrance and slipped down to the cell above the tunnel. The stone had been pushed aside from the hole.

"Quiet!" Frank whispered, turning off his light. They dropped below and tensely moved forward into the darkness. After a while they saw a lantern flash ahead!

"Get down!" Joe whispered. They dropped to their stomachs, hearing first Alex's voice, then Warren's.

"But the kid said something about a cave-in down there to the right—it's a dead end."

"You're crazy—the cave-in's the other way!" Warren retorted. "There must be a link-up in this direction."

"I say left," the chauffeur persisted.

As the men's voices rose in argument, Chet and the Hardys crept closer.

"Suit yourself," Warren said finally, "I'm trying the right. Yell if you find it." Their footsteps receded. Frank signaled the others to their feet.

"They've separated—let's take Warren first!"

With Joe remaining on guard, Frank and Chet turned down to the right, moving along opposite walls. When they reached the pale glow of the leader's lantern, Frank jumped him.

Startled, Warren wrenched him off and swung his lantern. He was about to bring it down on Frank's head when Chet tackled him.

"Alex!"

Warren's cry echoed as he kicked Chet away, only to reel staggering into the wall from Frank's smashing uppercut. A second punch dropped him unconscious before Alex rushed out of the shadows.

"Why, you—" As the man lurched toward Frank, Joe caught him from behind with a stinging bang on the left ear. Enraged and thrown off balance, Alex threw a backhand blow. Joe ducked it and at the same time Frank swung a roundhouse right. It landed on the point of Alex's jutting chin. Out cold, he fell face forward on the tunnel floor.

As Frank rubbed his bruised knuckles, Chet and Joe bound the captives with belts.

"Wow! You really bombed him," Chet praised Frank. "Hey, what's that noise?"

They left the conspirators and hurried outside to the parade ground. Mr. Kenyon rushed up to them, followed by half a dozen policemen!

"Frank! Chet! Joe! You're a sight for sore eyes! Did you find Mr. Davenport?"

"Yes. He's okay." Chet grinned. "We have three prisoners, too."

Rapidly the boys related their amazing adventure, ending with outwitting the thieves.

"I knew something was fishy when you didn't get back to Millwood," Uncle Jim explained, "especially after the housekeeper said Alex had gone to look for Mr. Davenport, and never showed up again."

He expressed astonishment at Warren and Alex being in cahoots with Copler, and surmised that the chauffeur had forged his references. "But it sounds like Ronnie Rush has reformed a little," he added, smiling.

The Cedartown police chief congratulated the boys, then sent his men below for the prisoners. The Hardys, Chet, and Uncle Jim rejoined Mr. Davenport and Ronnie. Grinning, Joe asked the art patron if he could stand another shock.

The elderly Southerner straightened his shoulders. "Reckon so if I can deal with criminals."

With Ronnie meekly trailing behind, the Hardys led the way to the secret chamber beneath the center of the fort. There the group gazed in awe at the magnificence of the gleaming chain of gold.

"It's beyond words!" Mr. Davenport said

happily. "Thanks to you detectives, and Jason's clue, this priceless treasure is safe! I'll see that it's properly displayed near the paintings of my esteemed ancestor."

Chet looked slyly at Ronnie. "If I do a painting of the treasure, will you 'help' me win another prize?"

Ronnie grinned sheepishly. "Never again!"

The Hardys then explained their theory about the infiltration tunnels, and Joe pointed out the old book. Mr. Davenport leafed through it. He looked up, astonished.

"What you boys have uncovered will rewrite history!" he declared. "This is a ledger left by Chambord hours before he and his garrison evacuated Senandaga, using these tunnels to escape to another battle area. According to this account, he planned to station Iroquois Indians—*disguised as French soldiers*—on the ramparts."

"To decoy Lord Craig!" Frank guessed.

"Precisely."

"Then the men the British attacked were actually *Indians!*" Joe put in, then frowned. "But Follette said 'Frenchmen' had been seen on the ramparts after the English had left."

The boys recalled Everett's account of the "French" fleeing when they could not manage the cannon.

"The disguised Iroquois must have come

back!" Chet exclaimed. "Maybe to loot the fort."

Mr. Davenport nodded. He said that Craig, after taking the fort, must have suspected the trick, and left immediately. "Chambord's estimate here of the size of the attacking British force seems too large—Craig himself may have played a trick!"

"So the last true holders of Senandaga were the Iroquois!" Joe exclaimed. He held up the tomahawk. "Wait until René Follette and Mr. Everett hear about this!"

Frank and Joe looked at the *chaîne d'or* and wondered when another challenge as baffling as the haunted fort would come their way. Sooner than they expected, they would be called upon to solve **THE MYSTERY OF THE SPIRAL BRIDGE.**

Mr. Davenport grinned. "I'm hereby inviting you all to celebrate with a hearty Southern repast. How does that sound to you, Chet?"

The stocky boy beamed. "Super! Right now, I could use some *real* fortification!"

1	The Tower Treasure	0-448-08901-7	32	The Crisscross Shadow	0-448-08932-7
2	The House on the Cliff	0-448-08902-5	33	The Yellow Feather Mystery	0-448-08933-5
3	The Secret of the Old Mill	0-448-08903-3	34	The Hooded Hawk Mystery	0-448-08934-3
4	The Missing Chums	0-448-08904-1	35	The Clue in the Embers	0-448-08935-1
5	Hunting for Hidden Gold	0-448-08905-X	36	The Secret of Pirates' Hill	0-448-08936-X
6	The Shore Road Mystery	0-448-08906-8	37	The Ghost at Skeleton Rock	0-448-08937-8
7	The Secret of the Caves	0-448-08907-6	38	Mystery at Devil's Paw	0-448-08938-6
8	The Mystery of Cabin Island	0-448-08908-4	39	The Mystery of the Chinese Junk	0-448-08939-4
9	The Great Airport Mystery	0-448-08909-2	40	Mystery of the Desert Giant	0-448-08940-8
10	What Happened at Midnight	0-448-08910-6	41	The Clue of the Screeching Owl	0-448-08941-6
11	While the Clock Ticked	0-448-08911-4	42	The Viking Symbol Mystery	0-448-08942-4
12	Footprints Under the Window	0-448-08912-2	43	The Mystery of the Aztec Warrior	0-448-08943-2
13	The Mark on the Door	0-448-08913-0	44	The Haunted Fort	0-448-08944-0
14	The Hidden Harbor Mystery	0-448-08914-9	45	The Mystery of the Spiral Bridge	0-448-08945-9
15	The Sinister Signpost	0-448-08915-7	46	The Secret Agent on Flight 101	0-448-08946-7
16	A Figure in Hiding	0-448-08916-5	47	Mystery of the Whale Tattoo	0-448-08947-5
17	The Secret Warning	0-448-08917-3	48	The Arctic Patrol Mystery	0-448-08948-3
18	The Twisted Claw	0-448-08918-1	49	The Bombay Boomerang	0-448-08949-1
19	The Disappearing Floor	0-448-08919-X	50	Danger on Vampire Trail	0-448-08950-5
20	Mystery of the Flying Express	0-448-08920-3	51	The Masked Monkey	0-448-08951-3
21	The Clue of the Broken Blade	0-448-08921-1	52	The Shattered Helmet	0-448-08952-1
22	The Flickering Torch Mystery	0-448-08922-X	53	The Clue of the Hissing Serpent	0-448-08953-X
23	The Melted Coins	0-448-08923-8	54	The Mysterious Caravan	0-448-08954-8
24	The Short-Wave Mystery	0-448-08924-6	55	The Witchmaster's Key	0-448-08955-6
25	The Secret Panel	0-448-08925-4	56	The Jungle Pyramid	0-448-08956-4
26	The Phantom Freighter	0-448-08926-2	57	The Firebird Rocket	0-448-08957-2
27	The Secret of Skull Mountain	0-448-08927-0	58	The Sting of the Scorpion	0-448-08958-0
28	The Sign of the Crooked Arrow	0-448-08928-9			
29	The Secret of the Lost Tunnel	0-448-08929-7		*Also available*	
30	The Wailing Siren Mystery	0-448-08930-0		The Hardy Boys Detective Handbook	0-448-01990-6
31	The Secret of Wildcat Swamp	0-448-08931-9		The Bobbsey Twins of Lakeport	0-448-09071-6